THE
OTHER SIDE
OF LOVE

By Jacqueline Briskin

THE OTHER SIDE OF LOVE

THE NAKED HEART

DREAMS ARE NOT ENOUGH

TOO MUCH TOO SOON

EVERYTHING AND MORE

THE ONYX

PALOVERDE

RICH FRIENDS

AFTERLOVE

CALIFORNIA GENERATION

JACQUELINE BRISKIN

THE OTHER SIDE OF LOVE

Delacorte Press

Published by
Delacorte Press
Bantam Doubleday Dell Publishing Group, Inc.
666 Fifth Avenue
New York, New York 10103

Library of Congress Cataloging in Publication Data

Briskin, Jacqueline.
The other side of love : a novel / by Jacqueline Briskin.
p.   cm.
ISBN 0-385-29918-4
ISBN 0-385-30455-2 (large-print ed.)
I. Title
PS3552.R49084   1991
813'.54—dc20   90-22032 CIP

Manufactured in the United States of America
Published simultaneously in Canada

May 1991

10 9 8 7 6 5 4 3 2 1
BVG

THIS IS FOR BERT.

ONE

1936

Ich rufe die Jugend der Welt
(I summon the youth of the world)

—inscription on the bell
cast for the Olympic Games of Berlin

We swear that we will take part in the Olympic
Games in loyal competition, respecting the regulations which govern them and desirous of participating
in them in the true spirit of sportsmanship, for the
honor of our country and the glory of sport.

—Olympic Oath

ONE

I

That July of 1936 the weather had been exceptionally fine in Berlin; however, Saturday, August 1, dawned with a fine, chill drizzle. By afternoon the rain had stopped but raw gray clouds sagged above the festively decked city and over the immense new sports facilities nine miles to the west, threatening to drench the crowd packed within the massive granite, limestone, and basalt walls of Hitler's new Olympic Stadium.

The guest teams had entered in alphabetical order and the final group, the athletes from the Vereinigten Staaten, the United States, had marched jauntily around the oval perimeter and taken their place on the infield. A hush fell over the great bowl. Then a roar erupted as tier upon tier of spectators jumped to their feet, shouting and applauding.

Out of the entrance known as the Marathon Gate strode the German women's team.

From the upper reaches of cement benches, the young women in smart white suits and little yachting caps who marched in perfect alignment appeared identical, but from the lower stands, where the foreign dignitaries as well as the high-ranking party officials were seated, individual features could be made out. A bemedaled Luftwaffe general in his sky-blue uniform shouted over the din that the little blonde in the second row, the one with the swinging braids, she was really something special. His neighbor bawled a qualified agreement: She would be more to his taste when she grew up. The pair consulted their programs, hoping for some clue to her identity. For months now the press, newsreels, and radio, as well as a magazine devoted solely to the Olympics, had been pumping out information about each German contestant. The program showed no photograph of the girl, an omission that was puzzling. For though too finely built to be the Third Reich's ideal of womanliness, she possessed that aura of health and vitality prized by the Ministry of Propaganda, and those braids were so pale as to be almost platinum, a true Aryan color.

The Luftwaffe general gazed with yearning lubriciousness after the slim girl.

II

Her name was Käthe Kingsmith.

At seventeen, second to the youngest on the German women's team, Käthe had been a mere alternate until ten days earlier, when the much-touted German record-holder in the two-hundred-meter dash—and a hopeful in the hundred-meter —had fractured her left ankle.

Käthe's cheeks were flushed with excitement, her upper lip was raised, giving her a look of vulnerability that was increased by the tension around her green-blue eyes. Last night she had lain in her Spartan cubicle at the Friesen-Haus, where all the women's teams were quartered, staring into the darkness and visualizing alternating tableaux of herself being crowned with laurel or stumbling to the loud jeers of this compassionless mob.

The standard-bearer, reaching the reviewing stand, dipped the swastika flag until it was an exact two inches from the red cinders of the oval track. The din grew intolerable—a cannon-roar crescendo of *"Sieg Heil! Sieg Heil!"*—as the team, in practiced synchronization, swung their upper bodies to face the Führer, shooting their arms skyward in the Nazi salute. Käthe's arm went up a fraction less vehemently—had she been strolling with a friend, it might have seemed that she was pointing out the Chancellor's seat rather than paying homage.

Käthe Kingsmith was congenitally incapable of the pure patriotic exultation that apparently gripped every other German in the huge amphitheater. Her heritage cursed—or blessed—her with double vision. Her father, Alfred Kingsmith, was English. This side of her couldn't help but view the Olympic spectacle squarely for what it was: a masterful job of salesmanship. In Germany, land of her birth, her mother's country, she saw through the bright cloth waved by the Ministry of Propaganda to the bones of truth below, the Nazi repressions, the racial policies, which she actively loathed. Yet during her annual summer holidays at Quarles, the rambling old country house in Kent that belonged to her uncle and aunt, Euan and Elizabeth Kingsmith, she found herself defending everything about the Third Reich. Aubrey and Araminta, her English cousins, though her best friends, teased her endlessly about her country and its dictator.

The last row of women had passed Hitler's reviewing stand. Female arms snapped down in unison. Out of the corner of her eye Käthe glimpsed a group of foreign dignitaries nodding. She knew exactly what they were thinking: The Nazis might be a crude bunch, but what did a little bullying and strutting matter when the end result was this parade of magnificent young athletes, these orderly, polite people, these clean toilets and well-swept streets—this handsome, immaculate capital?

To gain the world's good opinion, Adolf Hitler had insisted on hosting the Olympic Games. It was his will that each German be neatly dressed and respond with warm courtesy to foreign visitors. Houses were freshly painted, window boxes filled with colorful flowers rather than vegetables, shopkeepers had traced the Olympic symbol, five interlocking circles, on their windows. Anti-Semitic signs had been removed and orders had gone out that no Jews were to be arrested this month, their persons and property were to be respected. This stadium, the largest in the world, the six lavish new gymnasiums, the tennis courts, the polo field, the swimming pools, the red-tile-roofed Olympic Village, had been built amid recently transplanted trees and hedges that appeared to have grown here for centuries.

The team had halted on their patch of green turf. The amplified orchestra struck up the "Horst Wessel Lied," and standing

German spectators roared the words as the Reich's men's team entered.

Now, with athletes assembled, the speeches began. Though the women had been instructed to keep their gaze fixed on each speaker, Käthe couldn't resist a glance toward the Americans. Her New York cousin, Wyatt Kingsmith, whom she had never met, was a member of their basketball squad. Which one was he?

Since earliest childhood Käthe's natural curiosity about her transatlantic cousin had been enhanced by the family conversations cut short when she—or any other child or outsider—came into earshot. She had often speculated with her English cousin, Araminta, about the enigmatic haze surrounding Wyatt. Araminta, redheaded and even as a small girl knowingly sophisticated, had also been unable to come up with an acceptable reason for the secrecy.

The trumpets sounded another long fanfare, distant gun batteries rumbled, and twenty thousand white doves were released, their wings susurrant as they swirled upward into the clouds. A great chorus raised their voices in the Olympic Hymn written by Richard Strauss, and as the final soprano notes soared and faded, a single runner appeared in the Olympisches Tor. The man held high a torch that spread a glow across the drab afternoon, a sacred flame kindled three thousand miles away on the ancient altar in Olympus and borne here by a relay of runners.

Eyes filling, Käthe forgot her anxieties, forgot the political machinations behind the Games, forgot her dual loyalties. She was captured by the ancient spirit of athletes assembling to perform their chosen sport to their utmost capability. She watched the runner, the mythic symbol of pure international goodwill, trot lightly up the stairway built into the Marathon Gate. Pausing at the top, he extended the torch toward the assembly, then rose on tiptoe to dip the torch into the waiting caldron. Golden tongues of fire leapt and danced.

Tears were streaming down Käthe's cheeks while she took the Olympic oath.

III

Outside the Marathon Gate the athletes milled together, a kaleidoscope of uniforms overcoming language barriers with descriptive gestures, smiles, and laughter. Käthe moved through the crush to where most of the Americans were assembled.

"May I help you, fräulein?" asked a red-faced older American, obviously a coach, in passable German.

"If you'd be so kind, I'm trying to find one of your contestants. Wyatt Kingsmith." She spoke in English so flawless that the red-faced man glanced at her uniform as if to reassure himself that she was indeed on the German team rather than the British. "That's him over there, see?" He pointed out an exceptionally tall group. "With the other basketballers. The one holding his hat."

The man moving his straw boater back and forth at his side was not only tall but also broad shouldered and strong looking with sun streaks in his thick shock of sandy-brown hair. He was gazing around with his brows drawn together, an expression of perplexity—or maybe anger.

Drawing a breath, Käthe went up to him. "You're Wyatt, aren't you?" she said. "I've been looking forward to meeting you."

He blinked at her as if he hadn't a clue who she might be. Or maybe he hadn't heard her. Her voice was soft and when she felt awkward, which she did now, she had a woeful tendency to blush and swallow her sentences.

"I'm your German cousin," she murmured.

The snapshots that Uncle Humphrey and Aunt Rossie had brought on their European tour two years earlier had not done their son justice. Large craggy features like Wyatt Kingsmith's do not photograph well, and neither could black and white capture the dazzle of white teeth against a dark tan. Except for the light hair, Käthe decided, he might have been an idealized American Indian. Finally he smiled, a smile suffused with irony that somehow made him yet more attractive.

Angry at herself for noticing his good looks, irritated at him for putting her through her paces, Käthe thought: *Americans! They didn't even dip their flag for the Chancellor, and like him or not, he's the host of the Games.*

"You must be Kathy," he said. "You made the Third Reich's track team at the last moment, didn't you."

Nodding, she said, "Käthe."

"Cater?"

"My name. It's pronounced Käthe."

"In America we say Kathy."

"But this is Germany." She managed a smile. "And we say Käthe."

"Sorry, but it's not a sound we have, so if you're a linguistic purist you'll have to avoid us Americans."

Now the grin was openly mocking, and this released her from good manners. "That sounds good to me," she said. "But we'll be seeing each other this evening." Her parents were giving a reception to introduce the London and New York Kingsmiths to their circle. Käthe and Wyatt, as the clan's Olympic athletes, were the guests of honor.

"The coach doesn't want us racing around," Wyatt said. "I've sent Uncle Alfred a note, explaining I can't make it."

"Grandpa told me he's looking forward to talking to you." Their mutual grandfather, Porteous Kingsmith, was the founder of Kingsmith's, that renowned Bond Street purveyor of rare art objects, fine china, crystal, and silver. Porteous decades ago had established Kingsmith colonies on Unter den Linden and Fifth Avenue by sending forth his two younger sons, Alfred to Berlin, Humphrey to New York. "He'll be disappointed."

Wyatt blinked. Käthe sensed that she had pierced some barricade he'd erected between himself and her. Then his lips tightened. "Tomorrow I'm heading into the center of town, so I'll be having a bite of lunch with the gang at the Hotel Adlon."

His meaning was only too obvious. He wanted no part of the German branch of the family. Obviously he was one of those foreigners who lumped anybody within the boundaries of the

Third Reich as a jack-booted supporting actor in the Nazi drama.

"Then *willkommen in Berlin,*" she said, hoping to match his acidity. To her dismay her voice cracked.

Two

I

The much-touted Olympic Village, spacious, comfortable tile-roofed cottages, had been built for the male athletes, but Dr. Goebbels, as minister of propaganda, having accurately gauged that the world press would pay little attention to the women contestants, had quartered them on the outskirts of the Reichssportfeld in Friesen-Haus, an already existing, Spartan barracks. Regulations dictated that for the entire sixteen days of competition the female contingents would remain here under the stern chaperonage of the Baroness von Wangenheim. Only because her mother was a distant connection to this dragon was Käthe allowed out this evening.

As she emerged, the immaculately kept 1924 Austrian Steyr was waiting, and Gunther, the chauffeur, snapped his arm up in a Nazi salute, giving off the aroma of his sweat-drenched uniform. "Heil Hitler. Fräulein Käthe, I never cheered so loud in my entire life as when you went marching past the Führer."

"Thank you, Gunther." Her voice was constrained.

Nobody in the family liked Gunther, but he was an Ancient Combatant, honored as one of the brown-shirted young toughs already on the Nazi party roster in January of 1933, so firing him would have brought Alfred Kingsmith, who was British born, to the less-than-welcome attention of the Gestapo.

Gunther rambled on about the true Germanic spirit of the opening ceremony. Käthe, blocking out the rise and fall of his voice, stared into the twilight. An evening wind lifted the damp bunting of the Olympic flags and the long crimson banners centered with black swastikas that alternated in colonnades along the entire nine miles of the Via Triumphalis, a brilliantly lit ceremonial boulevard comprised of the various thorough-fares that ran in a straight line from the Alexanderplatz in the heart of Berlin to the Olympic Sports Complex.

They turned, winding through the dark Grunewald, that vast wooded parkland outside the city, coming to where lights and silhouettes of immense rooftops could be glimpsed through the trees. This was the Grunewald's Villa Colony. A mere merchant like Alfred Kingsmith could not have afforded so impressive a neighborhood had he not bought here during the lunatic inflation of the early twenties. With a laughably small sum of hard currency—pounds sterling—he had purchased a lumber magnate's furnished mansion. As Gunther eased between ivy-covered gateposts the big, exuberantly gabled house burst into view, lights ablaze in various-shaped windows and on the fret-work porches. The gingerbread motif was carried out within. Every molding, doorjamb, and dado was etched with birds and animals, with wreaths, with unknown flowers. The furniture was adorned with similar fancifulness. When Käthe was small, she had often imagined herself inside a cuckoo-clock palace.

II

"Ahh, there you are, Kate," called Alfred Kingsmith in English, the language he invariably used with his only offspring. His German, though grammatically impeccable, was grotesquely accented.

He was leaning over the lavishly embellished railing that surrounded the stairwell. From here, even with his thick-lensed pince-nez, he could see only the slender white blur of his daughter's uniform. He had inherited the poor vision that af-flicted most of the Kingsmith family—a flaw that had bypassed Käthe. Her eyesight was perfect.

Alfred was tall and full-bellied. With his graying hair combed flat from a precise center part and his somewhat shiny Savile Row dinner suit he presented the stiffly dignified appearance that takes most men a lifetime to acquire. Alfred, however, had looked much the same in 1909, when at the age of twenty, a gravely deliberate young Englishman, he had first arrived in Berlin to open a Kingsmith branch on Unter den Linden.

Alfred sedately descended the stairs. "Well," he asked, patting his daughter's hand, "have you decided where to hang your gold medals?" The slight gruffness in his teasing indicated his paternal love and pride.

She kissed him, feeling the smoothness of his heavy, recently shaved jowl. "Let's wait and see how fast the others can run."

"The von Graetz family have always been top-notch sportsmen." As he said his in-laws' name, Alfred's mouth stiffened.

Clothilde Kingsmith was a direct descendant of Erhart of Graetz, who in the early thirteenth century had pledged his sword to the militantly Christian Teutonic Order, fightly valiantly to bring the True Faith to the heathen Prussians. Erhart's line had produced warriors and daughters who wed warriors. Clothilde's first marriage, to Captain Siegfried von Hohenau, scion of an equally aristocratic Junker family, had come to an untimely end when the captain was killed on peacetime maneuvers a few days after the first birthday of their son, also named Siegfried. Both the von Hohenaus and the von Graetzes had attempted to cut short the stately young widow's inclination toward Alfred Kingsmith. Not because he was an *Engländer* several years younger than she, no, not at all. What made the match impossible was the suitor's plebian birth. A shopkeeper! In 1914 there was a muted outburst of thanksgiving that Clothilde's misguided affections had been ended by the Great War. Alfred returned to his side of the Channel, where his eyesight rendered him unfit for active duty, so he served in the Foreign Office. In December of 1918, when he returned to war-ravaged Germany, Clothilde, aged thirty-four, mother of a ten-year-old son, married him immediately. The von Hohenau family kept up a limp relationship because of Siegfried, known as Sigi. The von Graetzes, however, wasted no time on the Kingsmiths. Käthe had never met her widowed grandmother or her spinster aunt. Though this rift was never mentioned and Clothilde seemed untouched, and though Alfred made it a point of duty to mention their maternal line to his daughter and stepson, Käthe was aware how much the snubbing had wounded him.

Linking her arm in his, she said, "I'll give it my all."

They fell silent as feminine footsteps echoed with heavy firmness on the stone floor of the dining room. Alfred bowed formally as his wife came into the hall.

Clothilde Kingsmith's matronly curves were rendered pillar-like by a dark green silk gown cut in the waistless style of a decade earlier. Her graying blond hair was coiled around her ears and she used no cosmetics. Utterly secure in her background, she gave no thought to self-embellishment or the vagaries of fashion. Her plumply mild, unpainted, and unwrinkled face gave no clue to her remarkable strength of will. Here, after all, stood a woman who during four long and bitter years of warfare had refused to break off her unsanctioned engagement to an enemy—a lower-class enemy at that—despite the family outrage that had increased geometrically after her two brothers had fallen.

"Good evening, Käthe," she said in German—she spoke not a word of English. Looking with disapproval at the trim white uniform, she added, "The *baronin* should have permitted you to wear a party dress to greet our guests."

"Oh, Mother." Käthe groaned. "You can't really mean we're going to stand in a receiving line?"

"Naturally."

"But now only politicians stand and shake hands all night."

A slight frown showed in Clothilde's still firm skin. "I don't understand you, Käthe. How else can one welcome guests?"

"My dear," Alfred interposed, "this is a special evening for the child. Possibly after a respectable time the young people may be excused?" His words ended on a questioning note.

Clothilde drew her lips together. Once having determined a course of action, she found change all but impossible. At a chime she glanced at the wall clock. "Eight. Where is Siegfried?"

"I'll see if he's in his room," Käthe said, darting up the overcarved staircase.

III

As she neared the corner room, she heard the radio playing a waltz. Sigi's door was ajar.

Lieutenant Siegfried von Hohenau wore trousers with the deep red stripe of the High Command of the Army, yet in no way did he present the picture of a smartly turned-out career officer. Comfortably slouched in an armchair, ashes from his pipe salting his tunic, circling a pawn back and forth above the chessboard in time to the waltz, he looked amiably content, a family man at home—which he was. Though he had left for a military gymnasium in Potsdam when he was fourteen and thereafter had slept infrequently in this large room with the twin gable peaks, he considered the Grunewald house as his true anchor-place. With much the same affable contentment he viewed his mother's English husband as his father.

Käthe's glance was drawn to the left wall, which was adorned with a tapestry so ancient that the picture had faded to scarcely differentiated browns. Once the tapestry had graced the stone castle whose original tower had been raised by Erhart von Graetz. Above the pair of dimly seen, badly fraying knights was woven the von Graetz family motto: *Liebe zum Vaterland, Treue zum Eid.* From earliest childhood Käthe had been drawn to the frayed, must-odored cloth with its inscription. Loyalty to country, fidelity to oath. . . .

Sigi, seeing his half sister at the door, gave her a smile of remarkable sweetness. Despite the gulf of over eleven years and paternal bloodlines from opposing sides of the trenches, Sigi and Käthe were close. "A day to remember," he said.

"My main worry was that I'd trip and fall." She sank to the patterned carpet near his chair, clasping her hands around her upraised knees. "Sigi, I'll get killed in the first qualifying heats."

"Stop fishing for compliments. We both know how fast you run." The waltz stopped. An announcer began his excited description of the fireworks display over the Olympic Stadium. Sigi reached to turn off the radio.

"I finally met my American cousin," Käthe said.

"Oh? He introduced himself?"

"Vice versa. Then he glowered."

"At my little sister? I'll challenge him to pistols at dawn!"

"He thinks we all have swastika-shaped hearts and pray every morning and every night to the Führer."

"Hitler!" Sigi snorted. Though not remotely military in his attitude (he had entered the army only because he was too softhearted to deny the wishes of his dying paternal grandfather) he wholeheartedly shared one tenet of the Prussian officers' creed: Lance Corporal Hitler was a jumped-up politician. "Americans aren't all for their President's New Deal. Why should they assume we're a hundred percent behind the Nazi hero?"

She shrugged, showing her own bafflement. "He's not coming tonight. He said their coach won't let them gad around. In the next breath he was telling me that tomorrow he's visiting his parents and the British side at the Adlon."

Sigi tumbled chess pieces into the box. "Is that a note of disappointment?"

"The party's to honor him."

"What's he like, this American cousin? No, don't tell me. I can see by your eyes. He's a handsome brute, a Hollywood film star."

"Oh, stop it, Sigi. You know I can't bear teasing." Car doors slammed outside. English voices.

Käthe pushed to her feet with rapid grace. "They're here! Mother sent me to get you, and she'll slaughter us both if we aren't in line when the doorbell rings."

Sigi's eyes twinkled. "Our Lady of the Clock." Clothilde's habit of moving through her days on a schedule—and attempting to get her family onto similar timetables—was a source of kindly amusement to Sigi and of massive irritation to Käthe. Pulling his shoulders back, sucking his stomach in, he clicked his heels and bent his elbow stiffly for her. *"Gnädiges fräulein."*

"Oh, Sigi, you fool!" Laughing, Käthe brushed a few stray ashes from his tunic collar and took his arm.

THREE

I

"Well, Kate, so you're up to big doings," said Porteous King-smith. Through his years of success he had taken no effort to enhance his accent, and Käthe, as always, found the faint trace of Cockney endearing.

It was after ten and the two of them were alone in what her father referred to as his study and her mother—in the German way—called the *Herrenzimmer*, a smallish, dark room with book-cases and a thick, arched door that muffled the booming of convivial conversations in the hall outside. Their plates with the remnants of the supper buffet—thin-sliced cold *Rinder-braten* and jellied chicken breast with cucumber salad—were on the massive desk.

"Me, with those champions, in front of that crowd! Grandpa, just thinking of the first heat makes sparrows flutter in my stomach."

The old man smiled, showing strong yellow teeth. "How well I know that feeling. It comes over me before I dive into any-thing that takes pluck. It's a good sign, Kate. When a chap's too full of himself—or herself—it means he won't give it a proper try."

"What if I let the team down?"

"Don't worry about the others," he said. "That's your big-gest fault, Kate. You must learn to let others take care of them-selves. If you want to get anywhere in this life, you have to look after number one. Otherwise you're a girl after my own heart.

Your pluck and determination. The way you never go back on your word." He appeared to be beaming at her through his thick spectacles.

It was a trick.

Porteous Kingsmith probed the direction of a voice with an expression so observant and so filled with interest that even those who knew him intimately forgot that he was legally blind. From birth on he had been able to make out only light and darkness. Despite this handicap he had built a large, highly esteemed business on his ability to gauge the beauty of unique objects. His sensitive fingertips and often his lips acted as proxy for sight.

Involuntarily, Käthe responded to his smile.

Porteous, as always, sat erect, his lean height apparent. At eighty, with his massive domed forehead and fine, glossy mane of brushed white hair, his starched, old-fashioned high collar and frock coat, he might have been, or so Käthe thought fondly, a British prime minister.

Because of his handicap he found crowds unnerving, and so had requested that Käthe, his favorite grandchild, share her meal with him in privacy. Before her release from the receiving line, however, she had been subjected to her American uncle and his endless variations on the theme of her cousin Wyatt's superiority. Humphrey had waved his soft, freckled hands expansively as he spun tales of Wyatt's prowess. Wyatt, according to Uncle Humphrey, was not only the star center of the United States basketball team but, if he'd tried out, could have also made the track team. Not that he was solely a muscleman. He had graduated summa cum laude from Columbia University this past June, and come autumn, when he would enter Columbia Law School, he'd assuredly rise to the top of the class. Humphrey's boastfulness made him the butt of family jokes, but he never blew his own horn; he was guilty only of praising what he held dear: his adopted country, his son, and his wife, Rossie.

Porteous inquired, "What is there for sweet?"

"We have *Apfelkuchen mit Schlagsahne.*"

"What's that in English?"

"Apple cake and whipped cream."

"Too rich for my blood, but you go ahead."

"I'm meant to eat lightly. Coach's orders."

"Stuff and nonsense, you're thin as a rail. I don't know what's come over you girls nowadays. Men like an armful—not that you're ready to think about that sort of thing."

She was ready. Thus far, though, the Swiss boys who had managed shy kisses at the weekly dancing classes at La Ramée, her finishing school in Lucerne, and the sons of her mother's staid Berlin circle who brought her small bouquets had roused not so much as a shiver in her soul.

"I suppose you heard about the opening ceremonies," she said.

"Who could avoid it? Loudspeakers blaring from every lamppost and tree in the city. That Führer of yours! A hooligan who served time in jail, a gangster urging on his blackshirt and brownshirt swine to kick defenseless old Jews! And here he is, three years after he stuffed the ballot boxes, showing off and ranting in front of the world!"

Käthe stirred uneasily in her chair. "The Chancellor said exactly one sentence to open the Games," she said.

Porteous took out his cigar case and a small gold scissors: he might have been sighted as he precisely clipped the Havana. But Käthe noted a tremor in the large, rope-veined hands. Though filled with chagrin, she could not bring herself to apologize for defending Hitler.

When the cigar was cut and lit, Porteous asked, "Now that you're not in school anymore, why don't you have a year in London? You could live at my house. Your cousin Araminta could introduce you to her friends—every young man in England falls over himself to be near her. I know Aubrey would come down from Oxford to see you to the opera and museums."

Käthe's expression showed that the offer tempted her, but she said, "Mother would never go for that idea, Grandpa."

Porteous frowned. He had sent sedate Alfred to Berlin, the easygoing Humphrey to New York, so they would fit in with the prevailing atmospheres of the two cities. The boys had never been anything alike. Yet it turned out that they shared one weakness. They both allowed their wives to rule the roost. Alfred let Clothilde make all the decisions about his only daughter, including christening the little thing with a name hunched under two German dots. Humphrey went him one better, giving Rossie a free hand not only at home but also in the Fifth Avenue branch—Porteous often thanked his lucky stars that she was a girl with a good head on her shoulders. The New York shop did tidily. Quite tidily indeed. On the other hand, Porteous's oldest son, Euan, who now occupied the glass-encased managerial office overlooking the ground floor of the Bond Street shop, was a very cool husband indeed.

Inhaling his cigar appreciatively, Porteous said, "Well, I've kept you away from the other young people long enough—" As Käthe started to protest that she preferred being with him, he raised the hand with the cigar. "Go on, Kate, do as I say."

After she left, he smoked reflectively. He didn't for a minute believe she admired the Nazis, but at the same time he understood her defense of Hitler, that nasty bit of business. His poor little Kate with her lovely bones, her skin smooth as warm Minton china, her soft, low voice, her tender dreams, was a victim of his, Porteous's, desire for aggrandizement. It was his fault. By sending Alfred to this benighted, strutting country he had cursed his granddaughter with divided loyalties.

II

The receiving line had dissolved and the hall was noisy and crowded. The *Servierfrau,* who came in to help at parties, bustled around collecting discarded plates. An aroma of camphorated mothballs drifted from the coats that older people were putting on as they stood by the front door. A group of Kingsmith employees perched on the staircase carefully balancing coffee cups and small Meissen cake plates as they gazed at the grander guests. Junior Wehrmacht officers and their wives stood in a respectful circle around Sigi's uncle, Generalmajor Baron Klaus von Hohenau. The general, who had lost his right eye at Verdun, wore a black patch that emphasized the gaunt hollows below his cheekbones. From the drawing room came the chords of stately music with a jazz idiom. *Porgy and Bess.* One of the foreign Kingsmiths must have brought along the sheet music, for the opera, concerned as it was with Negro people and composed by a Jew, had been banned in the Third Reich.

Käthe was offered good wishes and congratulations as she moved toward the music. Beneath the carved ceiling beams of the huge drawing room, the younger guests had congregated in a large group around the piano. Her cousin Aubrey, who had the Kingsmith eyes, frowned through his glasses at the notes as his long fingers swept in skillful chords through "Bess, You Is My Woman Now." *That's Aubrey in a nutshell,* Käthe thought with an affectionate smile. *Worried sick no matter how well he's doing.* Araminta sat atop the piano, swinging a slender ankle in time to her brother's playing.

Araminta was by far the more vivid of the siblings. Her exuberant curls, the shade and luster of a new-minted copper penny, set off her clear white skin. Her blue eyes sparkled flirtatiously at the younger men close by—she was nearsighted but refused to wear glasses except at the theater. Aubrey's subdued russet hair was combed back from his sensitively lean, freckled face. Nineteen, older than his sister by a scant eleven months, he was up at Oxford, at Magdalen reading Literature. Araminta, who hadn't opened a book since leaving Roedean, swam in a bubbling sea of debutante parties and boyfriends.

Käthe stood in the entry. It was an old game from those childhood Augusts in Kent, waiting for invisible nerve endings to inform the others of one's presence.

III

Aubrey saw Käthe first. Smiling, he missed a note. Araminta turned. With an animated wave she dropped gracefully to her feet, her evening dress catching on the piano top to briefly display one shapely leg nearly to the top of the silk stocking. The bias cut of Araminta's aquamarine silk gown discreetly advertised her undulant curves, the full breasts, slender waist, and rounded buttocks. Aware that every man was ogling her, she ran without any hint of self-consciousness to her German cousin.

"Darling, after that stupid receiving line faded away, I searched high and low. Low and high too. Where have you been?" The innuendo lurking in Araminta's high, pretty soprano made it sound certain that Käthe had been romping with a male guest in one of the bedrooms.

"Having supper with Grandpa in the study."

"A likely tale." Linking her arm in Käthe's, she drew her a bit away, whispering under the music, "The mystery of the Kingsmiths is solved. At long last."

Käthe couldn't help responding with laughter to the way the pointed tip of Araminta's nose wiggled. "What mystery?" she asked.

"The *American* mystery," Araminta emphasized, then fell abruptly silent.

Aunt Rossie—Wyatt's mother—had come into the drawing room and was swooping toward them. "I figured you girls'd be in here!"

With her hair swept on top of her head, her smart black dress with the two diamond clips side by side on the stylish square neckline, Rossie Wyatt Kingsmith looked exactly what she was, a clever, energetic New York career woman. Bored by her shy, bibulous English sister-in-law, Elizabeth, unable to converse with the German Clothilde, Rossie was seeking out the company of younger, livelier folk. After several minutes of spiritedly regaling her nieces with the latest in American fashion, she moved toward the piano, where Aubrey, who preferred Mozart and Haydn, was being egged on to play "Yes! We Have No Bananas."

As their aunt left, Araminta grabbed Käthe's arm. "Katy darling, I'm dying to see those marvelous new roses your father was telling me about." She yanked her toward the glass doors.

The garden was cold, but Araminta, who seemed to exist in her own thermostatically controlled weather, strolled unconcernedly in her thin silk. Knowing that her cousin would tease out the riddle for all she was worth, Käthe wrapped her arms around herself for warmth. The festive strings of Japanese lanterns were twined on the oil-black smoothness of the small lake, and chinks of light showed from the big houses on the far side. On the path that led to the rose garden, Araminta inquired, "What did you think of the other teams?"

"I met Wyatt, if that's what you're asking."

"He's a dream, isn't he?" Araminta had spent several weeks in New York three years earlier, when the English Kingsmiths had vacationed in the States, and since then had been, in her own soaringly emphasized phrase, "absolutely *nuts* for Americans in general, Wyatt in particular."

Käthe reached up to a dangling willow branch. "After we marched out of the stadium, I went over and introduced myself. He hardly seemed delighted."

"You mean his Heathcliff look? Darling, the very sign he's wonderful at *it,* don't you know. He is divinely sexy, isn't he? And don't you adore that American sense of humor?"

"He didn't waste it on me. Araminta, I'm freezing. Unravel the sphinx so we can go back inside."

Araminta slowed to mincing steps. "You know Aunt Rossie . . ." she mused. "So sensible, and from a good family—is there such a thing as a good American family?"

"Araminta!"

"Well . . ." Araminta shrugged. "It seems Wyatt arrived one month after the wedding."

Startled, Käthe hit her anklebone on the brick edging of the path. What Araminta had just said was flatly impossible. Aunt Rossie? The smartly turned-out American matron? The sensible career woman who held the reins of the Fifth Avenue Kingsmith's in her red-lacquer–tipped hands? Aunt Rossie having a passionate fling with dear, ineffectual Uncle Humphrey? Halting, Käthe stood one legged like a stork and rubbed her ankle. "Gossip," she said flatly. "Pure gossip."

"A few days ago, just before we came here, I overheard Mother talking to a dreadful old crone, they went to school together or something equally dreary. Mother was holding forth on the fast ways of American womanhood—it had to do with the darling Prince of Wales, and his penchant for American lady friends. The case that proved her point was our Aunt Rossie and how she married in the nick of time."

"I don't believe it. Uncle Humphrey never would have seduced her, he thinks the world of her. And besides, in those days people didn't go to bed before they were married."

Araminta gave a throaty chuckle. "That's why there's no such a word as *bastard.*"

" 'Minta . . . Say she *was* going to have a baby, he'd have married her right off, wouldn't he?"

"Darling, I've given you my all. The family mystery unveiled at long last only to reveal yet more tantalizing intrigues."

Käthe said nothing. Clasping her arms around herself, she was swept by inexplicable sympathy for the tall, defiantly caustic American cousin.

IV

When the two girls returned to the drawing room, Aubrey pushed up from the piano stool. Moving toward them, he asked Käthe in his diffident way, "What about a drive back to the dormitory?"

Forcing the dark garden conversation from her mind, Käthe smiled. "Wonderful."

"I'll get the keys from your man," Aubrey said.

She searched out her family to kiss them good-bye. Everyone wished her good luck, assuring her in various accents and languages that she would win both of her races.

"I'll tell Wyatt to be sure to look you up and give you some pointers," Humphrey added. "What a magnificent sprinter, that boy!"

As they started for the front door, Euan planted himself squarely in front of his son. "Aubrey, you're not to take the wheel."

"The chauffeur's turned in," Aubrey said.

"Then you'd better keep a sharp eye on yourself, you hear? I don't want you crashing your Uncle Alfred's motorcar, too." Euan's eyes were piercing and his rather high-pitched voice had taken on volume.

Aubrey helped Käthe into the car, stammering an explanation that he had dented the bonnet of his Morris Minor up at Oxford. "Since then Father's positive that I'm a menace on the road."

Euan had always demanded perfection from his only son. Just as he had felt obligated to punish Aubrey's childhood misdeeds with a caning, so now his son's occasional ineptitudes spurred him to tongue-lashings. And Aubrey on his side, despite his stammering and mildness, possessed an inner courage that would not permit him to back down from his bellicose sire. The two were forever at loggerheads.

"Parents," Käthe said sympathetically.

Aubrey drove slowly. "After the end of the Games, would it be all right if I get some tickets for the Philharmonie?"

"I'd love it, but what about Araminta?" Araminta made no bones that classical music bored her silly.

"By then she'll have any number of boyfriends begging to take her around to parties and nightclubs."

"Then do let's."

"If Aunt Clothilde doesn't object."

"Why would Mother say anything?"

"Just the two of us." Aubrey mumbled the explanation. "No chaperone."

Even though nineteenth-century decorum was bred in Clothilde's rather-too-large bones, she would never kick up a fuss about her daughter going to an evening concert with Aubrey. "That rule doesn't apply to brothers and cousins." Käthe laughed.

It was too dark for her to see Aubrey's hurt little grimace.

FOUR

I

The first round of the basketball tournament would start in ten minutes.

Wyatt hunkered on low benches with the other tall men wearing gray sweatsuits stenciled USA. The shack smelled of wood rot and fresh paint: the German Olympic Committee, who considered the sport negligible, had painted basketball markings on an old clay tennis court, converting the two sheds where the nets were stored, into locker rooms. The players, trapped in pregame tension, watched the coach diagraming a play on the blackboard. Wyatt stirred restlessly, scratching between his shoulders. Ever since he'd arrived in Deutschland his sense of being persona non grata had physically manifested itself as a skin irritation. Even here, among other Americans, he felt distinctly itchy.

What the hell am I doing in Berlin, anyway?

Wyatt never would have asked himself such a question before this July.

The coach was reprising the strategy of the play. Wyatt didn't hear the earnest voice. He was remembering a hot July night a bit over a month earlier, a muggy night on the island of Manhattan when his vision of Wyatt Kingsmith had been irrevocably shattered.

II

He had come home to the commodious apartment on Seventy-second Street and Madison at a little before ten. The corner windows were open and the hum of Madison Avenue traffic had covered the sound of the front door opening and closing. Buoyed with elation, he had paused in the foyer, smiling fondly at his parents' predictability. They had been in the brightly lit ell of the big living room, facing each other across the cabriole-legged game table. Though they worked together they seemed more than content to spend most of their evenings alone at the game table, fitting together thousand-piece jigsaw puzzles, playing honeymoon bridge or rummy.

His mother had fanned her cards on the tooled green leather. "Gin," she'd said, her tone pleased yet not triumphant. Rossie Wyatt Kingsmith was a great one for driving a hard bargain with wholesalers, yet with her spouse she was noncompetitive, nurturing, protective. She never showed him up when he struck a bad business deal or nagged him to stop his harmless boasting.

"The card shark strikes again," Wyatt said.

They both turned.

"Wyatt"—Humphrey beamed—"you're home early."

"We were just about to have ice cream," Rossie said.

"Thanks, Mom, but none for me. On the way home I grabbed a steak and some cheesecake."

This was the cook's night off, so Rossie went to the kitchen. Wyatt waited until she'd set down the crystal bowls before springing his news.

"Well, it looks as if I'll bump into you two in Berlin," he said in a casual tone.

"What?" Humphrey's spoon halted halfway to his mouth. He had worked endlessly to convince Wyatt to join in the Kingsmith reunion at the Games. "You're spending August in Newport, aren't you?"

"Well, it's like this, Dad," Wyatt said. "That was arranged before I promised to represent my country on the basketball squad."

"You'll be playing in the Olympics? How absolutely ripping!" Humphrey lapsed into the slang of his English school-days as he hugged Wyatt. "They must have heard how good you are."

"I wouldn't put it quite like that." Wyatt was grinning. His friends' big complaint was that they never satisfied their fathers, but Humphrey formed a one-man fan club. "The team all work at Universal Studio. Because of this Jewish thing in Germany, the studio refused to support them financially. Some of the guys couldn't afford passage or to take the time off. They needed players. I applied. The coach, it seems, was at the Columbia-Yale basketball game."

"So he saw for himself how good you are!" Humphrey chortled. "I can't wait to cable everybody!"

Rossie had been staring down at her ice cream, which being homemade was melting rapidly. Her hair was neat, her face perfectly made up, yet she looked vaguely disheveled. "What about your friend in Newport?" she asked.

"St. John'll understand."

"You promised to spend the month with him."

"What's come over you, Rossie?" Humphrey asked. "Wyatt's received a great honor."

"Berlin . . ." Rossie spoke softly, as if to herself, then added firmly, "You shouldn't break a commitment."

"Hey, it's great the way you're cheering me on," Wyatt snapped. He finger-combed his hair. "Sorry, Mom," he said quietly. "I'm bushed is all."

"Go on to bed, dear."

He was too keyed up to sleep. He sat at his sleek modern desk, writing to St. John, explaining why he wouldn't be able to make it this summer. He paid a couple of bills, balanced his checkbook. He showered. He was in bed reading a Dashiell Hammett mystery when a single tap sounded on the door.

"It's me," Rossie called softly.

"Come on in," he said, splaying the book.

Her tailored navy-blue silk robe was neatly tied, her brown hair smooth, yet once again Wyatt had a sense that his trim mother wasn't well groomed. Maybe it was because her fists were clenched. She sat on the foot of the bed.

He nodded toward the envelope propped on his desk. "That's to St. John. Mom, he'll get a kick out of my being on the team."

The alarm clock ticked, a horn honked on Seventy-second Street. Then Rossie opened her hand. The large gold pocket watch was misted by the heat of her palm. "This belonged to my first husband," she said.

He could feel his jaw come unhinged. "What?"

"I was married before."

"You were? That's a closely guarded secret."

"I should have told you years ago. But it never seemed fair to Humphrey. He's so proud of you."

"Are you saying Dad's not my real father?" He detested his croaking voice.

"He isn't. But he's forgotten he isn't. Wyatt, so help me God, I often think facing up to it would kill him." A straightforward businesswoman, Rossie avoided the least hyperbole. "He loves you so much."

Wyatt leaned back against the wooden headboard. Three years ago he had used part of his inheritance from his Wyatt grandparents to buy the sleek Danish-modern bookcases, the pinch-pleated linen curtains, the desk. Suddenly the familiar room seemed alien. Though he had often inwardly wondered why the nuptials hadn't taken place until a month before he made his arrival, he'd never questioned his siring. Why should he? Humphrey was forever pointing out that he, Wyatt, had the Kingsmith height, that he had inherited dark eyes and sandy hair from his long-dead Kingsmith grandmother, that he had Porteous's high IQ.

Wyatt's hand hovered above the round gold watch, but his muscles refused to grasp it. "What happened? Did he leave you in the lurch?"

"Wyatt, I said he was my husband." She paused. "I met him my first year up North at Radcliffe."

Rossie Wyatt Kingsmith came from Wyattville in Rossie County, Georgia. Prior to the War Between the States, as the Rossies and the Wyatts referred to the Civil War, the two inter-locking families had accumulated more than three thousand slaves, a cotton gin, warehouses, and a railroad spur. Now his maternal kin, attended by what they still called their "darkies," descendants of their property, nursed their superiority and talked in softly slurred voices of genealogies. Whenever he visited Wyattville he'd been filled with gratitude that his mother had been smart enough to leave—the first woman in the intertwined families to head North to college.

Rossie was watching him. "Both our families disapproved," she said.

"Because you were too young?" His mother hadn't been twenty when she'd married his father—Humphrey Kingsmith.

"Oh, you know what unreconstructed southerners my folks are. And he was a damn Yankee." She paused as a car racketed up Seventy-second Street. "His name was Myron Leventhal. He was in his second year at Harvard Medical School. His parents were beside themselves that he was going around with a Gentile girl."

"Jewish . . ." Wyatt whispered.

His spine was stiff against the headboard. Though he had no close Jewish friends and had never taken out a Jewish girl, he'd also never guffawed at casually told anti-Semitic jokes and had preferred not to go through rushing because fraternities were discriminatory. He was therefore shamed by the images of Jews tumbling through his brain. A fat woman who smelled of sweat and garlic grabbing the taxi he'd hailed. A pair of bearded, hatted men talking a guttural language. The short, belligerent commie called Goldberg arguing Marxism in poli sci class. Wyatt wore only his pajama bottoms. Looking down, he had a certifiably insane thought. The upper half was familiar and Episcopal, the lower half, hidden by his striped pima-cotton pajamas, belonged to a stranger. *Shouldn't I have been circumcised?*

Rossie tilted her head. "I realize this is all coming as a shock."

"I'm an adult." He managed a wry smile. "So you were married because I was on the way?"

"Good heavens, no. It wasn't like that at all. We just wanted to spend our lives together. We were married by a justice of the peace, and the next day we took the train to New York to see his parents. They lived not far from Columbia, in one of those big old houses. His father was a judge, humorless and stiff. When we refused to get an annulment, he said that Myron was dead to them. They would sit *shiva* for him—-that's a week-long mourning rite the Jews have. Now that I'm older, I can see how hurt they were—he was their only child. But back then I hated them for what they did to Myron." Tears lay on her cheeks.

Wyatt swallowed. He had seen his mother weep only twice, after the deaths of each of his Rossie grandparents.

"What was he like?"

"You," she said, wiping her eyes. "Exactly like you. He was such a nice boy, Wyatt. Generous, kind. Impulsive. A sense of humor. He would lose his temper and then be sorry right away. Tall, good looking, rangy. Extremely smart, but not one of those pretentious intellectual types. A wonderful athlete."

"Me? He sounds like the next evolutionary step up."

Shaking her head, she touched his cheek. "Pa came to Boston to meet Myron. He hadn't wanted me to go North in the first place. He cut off my support and made Myron feel so hangdog. Myron worked as a longshoreman on the Boston docks. He could have gotten a white-collar job, but they paid well on the docks, and we needed to save so he could go back to medical school. He'd always wanted to be a doctor." She sighed convulsively. Most of the longshoremen had despised Myron for being a Jew and educated. "We found a cold-water flat—I'd call it a tenement now. Still, we were young and hopeful, happy together."

Tears stood in Wyatt's eyes. Swallowing hard, he gripped Rossie's hand.

She went on, "We were married six months, and I was two months pregnant. That day was rainy, windy. They were unloading a Canadian freighter, the *Star of Nova Scotia,* it was called. He slipped between the boat and the wharf. I've always prayed he was killed instantly. When they fished him out his bones were all broken."

"God . . ." Wyatt blew his nose.

"Having a baby, I should have gone back South. That was the

sensible thing to do. But crawling home to my family seemed like a breach of faith with Myron. Instead I went to New York and looked for a job."

Wyatt picked up the watch, turning it over, his forefinger tracing the initials MHL as Rossie described being hired for secretarial work by the easygoing young Englishman who ran the small floundering American branch of a London concern. She had never worked, but she could type and was good at arithmetic. The activity of the shop acted therapeutically. "Humphrey was very dear, and soon I was helping him with the books. But of course he wanted to beau me around."

"He knew that you were a widow?"

"I applied for the job as Mrs. Leventhal." When he found out she was pregnant, he grew more insistent. "But you know the rest," Rossie said. "He's a wonderful father, isn't he?"

"The greatest. Mom, this'll stay between us."

"Thank you, dear. I never intended telling you. But since you're so intent on going to Berlin, I had to warn you. There's a rumor that the Nazis have spies checking every American contestant's racial background."

"Where did you hear that?"

"I pay attention to that kind of thing. Being married to Myron made me pay attention." She paused. "The marriage license was issued to Rossie Wyatt Leventhal, widow. Myron's name is on it. And you were born a month later."

"How farfetched can you get? They'd have to check the marriage licenses, the death certificates."

"I heard they're making very complete dossiers."

"Come on, Mom, this isn't like you."

"Maybe I am overreacting," Rossie said. Getting to her feet, she rested both hands on his bare shoulders, looking down at him. "So you're all right, dear?"

"Just sad that you and he had such a rotten time."

She bent down and tugged his hair the way she had when he was a kid. "You're positive?" she said.

"Nothing's changed," he lied.

She had left the watch on the blanket cover. He had sat holding it until the gold was warm. Then he had padded barefoot to the foyer, where the telephone was, and opened the Manhattan book to *L,* running a finger down the line of Leventhals. . . .

"Kingsmith." The coach was looking at him. "Is that play clear?"

Wyatt realized that everybody else was standing. "Yeah, absolutely," he responded.

"Then let's go and beat the hell out of the Eye-talians," the coach said.

III

A German guide bearing a placard emblazoned VEREINIGTEN STAATEN led the team into the chill gray morning. The Italians were already shooting and dribbling on the lumpy clay of the tennis court. Obviously the spectators shared the German Olympic Committee's disinterest in basketball. The shallow stands were nearly empty. The Kingsmith clan sat on the north edge of the court. Wyatt grinned as he marched past his waving family—no matter his turmoil since Rossie's revelation, he never considered them to be anything other than his true family.

Directly behind the American bench a section had been roped off: at all venues good seats were saved for other Olympic contestants. Four Americans and a couple of Italians sat far apart. In the second row a white German blazer and skirt shone like a beacon in the dreary morning.

It was Käthe. He was surprised to see her here after the way he had mowed her down at the opening ceremonies. He was also surprised that he was smiling and waving. This, after all, was one of Hitler's *mädchens.*

Since his conversation with his mother his vision had altered, as if he'd been fitted with corrective glasses. Before the conversation, though he and his family were "tolerant," a word he now loathed, he hadn't properly seen the anti-Semitism around him. Oh, he'd known about restricted apartment buildings, hotels, schools, the quotas in colleges, the classified job ads that said "Jews need not apply." But the knowledge had been intellectual. Now he viewed these wrongs sharply and personally. At home it was bad enough. In the Third Reich bigotry was the law of the land. He had been chilled to the bone by a newsreel of Nazi plug-uglies standing around forcing a dignified old gentleman to scrub a pavement with a tooth-brush. He had written a check to a Jewish relief fund that helped refugees. He had visited Judge and Mrs. Abraham Leventhal. Firmly he pushed the memory of that painful afternoon from his mind. There was a match to win.

The whistle shrilled. The teams were introduced.

He was playing center. As the ball was tossed, he jumped, slashing it with all his force away from the Italians, allies of the Nazis.

Every time the U.S. scored, Wyatt found himself glancing at Käthe. She was always applauding. Every time he made a basket, she was on her feet. The sky cleared in patches, the sun came out. The final score was U.S.A. 53, Italy 32.

Winners and losers shook hands.

Käthe was on her feet, smiling at him.

FIVE

I

As Wyatt returned to the bench, his uniform soaked with sweat, his chest still heaving, Käthe moved forward.

"Congratulations," she called in that soft, low English voice.

"Hey, thanks. And I hear you survived your heats in both races."

"Sheer fluke."

"In the Olympics you don't make the finals by a fluke."

"You play marvelously."

He pulled on the top of his sweats. "But you've never seen a basketball game before, right?"

"You've caught me out."

"Stick around for the Philippines versus Uruguay, and I'll teach you the game's finer points."

Across the court the family was standing, waving, gesturing. Wyatt jogged over. Rossie smoothed back his hair, Humphrey embraced him. Porteous said, "Well done, my boy, well done." Aubrey, Uncle Euan, and Aunt Elizabeth shook his hand. Araminta rose on her high-heeled sandals to kiss him, leaving two smears of lipstick on his flushed cheeks.

Then the family gathered together coats, umbrellas, handbags. Wyatt held Porteous's arm, not as if guiding his grandfather down the steps of the stand but as if it were natural for them to be so linked, as he explained that the United States would go on to the next round tomorrow. Humphrey pounded his shoulder for a final congratulation, and then they all were gone. Wyatt trotted toward the shower hut.

II

The Uruguay-Philippines game was well under way when he emerged, exuding the clean smell of soap. Käthe still sat in the second row.

The openness of her smile made him nervous. "So you stuck around," he said.

"Of course. I told you I would."

During the game he explained the plays, shifting his body, moving his arms in a modified version of throwing, leaning forward at every free throw, his eyes narrowed and intent. Neither team was any good, but he rooted ardently for the Philippines, a United States protectorate. She cheered them on too. They stayed a few points ahead. Just before the end of the first quarter, however, Uruguay managed to tie the game. As the short Filipino center's shot teetered on the rim of the basket, then swished through, Wyatt clenched his hand, triumphantly punching air in front of him. His bicep touched Käthe's. Through their layers of clothing he could feel the warmth and fragility of her arm. He turned. Her irises were very clear, the color of a good aquamarine, and the whites had a bluish cast, like a young child's. Her lashes were thick and astonishingly dark for anyone with platinum hair.

She's wearing a Nazi uniform, you ass. And you're a Jew by half. Shifting farther from her, he asked, "How come you didn't root for the Italians?"

"Why would I? You're on the American team."

"The Germans and Italians are the Axis."

She bit her lip, watching as another basket was scored. "It's a bit like hockey," she murmured. "Except for the hoop."

"Me, I think it's an extension of an ancient Mayan game," he said. "The losing side had their hearts cut out as a sacrifice to the gods. Who knows, maybe the losers were Jewish Mayans."

She was silent.

"Aren't you going to challenge me? Point out that some of your teams have Jews on them?"

"They do. Rudi Ball was on the ice hockey team in the Winter Games. Helene Mayer's going to win a medal for us in fencing. . . ." Her soft voice almost inaudible, she mumbled an excuse about returning to Friesen-Haus in time for lunch.

With her head bent, she hurried along the edge of the court to the nearest exit. *You're a prick,* he told himself. *An unthinkable prick, taking out your confusion on her.*

III

The women's two-hundred-meter final was scheduled for ten-fifty the following morning. Käthe slept very little. She kept turning the tough dormitory pillow. Why couldn't she have admitted that she despised the Nuremberg laws that humiliated Jews and cut them out of the fabric of German life? Why couldn't she have told him that she had been best friends with Anna Elzerman, who had also lived in the Grunewald Villa section? Six months ago Dr. Elzerman, banned from his mostly Aryan practice, had emigrated with his wife and daughter to Mexico. Why was it so easy to talk against the Nazi regime with Sigi? And so impossible with her non-German family—with her American cousin?

Before dawn she was slipping out of Friesen-Haus, jogging on the lit paths. She cut across the Maifield, the huge parade ground. By the time she reached the track-and-field practice area near the south gate of the Olympic Stadium, the morning mist was silver, and she could see wraithlike shadows in motion. A vaulter was examining his pole, a shot-putter limbered up with slow, loose shakings of his thick arms. A broad jumper kept charging in a series of approaches at the long, sandy pit: peering, she saw it was Jesse Owens, the black American gold medalist whose victories on the track had been studiedly ignored by the Führer.

The Olympic Committee had issued every runner a silver trowel. Käthe took hers from the back pocket of her loose warm-up jacket, gouging her starting holes into the rough, dew-wet cinders. Toes dug in, she crouched forward on her hands, rocking back and forth slightly to get her center of balance.

"Bang!" she whispered, sprinting forward. Reaching the two-hundred-meter marker, she slowed, bending over to catch her breath. She didn't need to peer at her stopwatch to know her time was rotten.

When she looked up, she saw a hazy but familiar tall silhouette at the far end of the practice lane. How could it possibly be Wyatt? There was no reason for him to be at the track-and-field practice area. He had made it abundantly clear that he disliked all Germans, and her in particular. She waited uncertainly while he trotted up to her.

"I rattled you pretty badly," he said.

"What?"

"Yesterday. At the basketball match. Either that or it's the wrong time of the month."

Her face grew hot—no male, not even her coach, certainly not Sigi or her father, had ever broached the taboo subject of menstruation.

"Hadn't you heard? I'm only on the team because Silke Ernst broke her ankle." Her anxieties had bubbled into her voice.

"I could give you a pointer or two—"

"I'm rotten," she said. "Now go and gloat about it someplace else."

Blinking at her sharpness, he studied her. "I summon the youth of the world," he said in a hollow tone, swinging his head from side to side, mimicking the clapper of the Olympic bell.

After a moment they both broke into laughter.

"I keep thinking I'm going to stumble," she confessed. "In front of the entire stadium."

"All of us have the jitters," he said sympathetically. "I lettered in track. Let me see you run, okay?"

She sprinted to the marker. Her time was considerably improved.

"Dig those starting holes again," he ordered.

"Why?"

"Just dig the damn holes."

Kneeling, she complied.

"Deeper," he commanded.

"Our coach showed us what to do. He medaled in the Paris Olympics."

"He's a man. You're a girl, a very slight girl. Hey, no kidding, deeper holes give you more traction for your breakaway."

"You don't want us to win any medals," she said. "Why're you helping me?"

He didn't answer. Taking the silver trowel from her hand, he cut away more cinders. "Like so," he said. "Your hair's a great color. I'll bet it looks terrific loose."

IV

The pole vaulting and the broad-jump preliminaries riveted the attention of the capacity crowd. Only a few people glanced at the contestants in the women's two-hundred-meter race as they entered. Käthe Kingsmith's unbraided hair flowed in silvery gold down to her waist.

She stared across the stadium to the section between the reviewing stand and the finish line, where the family had reserved a row of seats. Even at this distance she could make out Aubrey windmilling his straw boater to attract her attention. Her father, and, yes, there was her mother, who considered the Games vulgar and had not shown up for her preliminary heats. Porteous had left the Hotel Adlon, braving this mob to "see" her run. Her American and English uncles and aunts sat together, then Araminta, her hair a crimson splotch under her wide-brimmed hat. Sigi was standing, his uniform blending in with the field-gray uniforms in the row behind.

Wyatt wasn't in the group.

Käthe sat on the prickly grass, taking off her warm-up suit, carefully folding it in the basket marked K. KINGSMITH. She did her stretches. At the whistle she went to her lane markings.

Again she glanced toward the family. In the shadows of the tunnel just above them stood Wyatt. He was gesturing with his hand, a scooping motion.

She made the identical gesture before kneeling to dig deep into the red cinders behind the starting line.

He raised his clenched hands above his head, as victorious prizefighters do.

V

The gun roared near her ear.

Propelling herself forward with her hands, she launched herself. As she went into her sprint, the air surrounding her seemed exceptionally thin, as if on a mountain peak where gravity offered less resistance, yet perversely her lungs filled with abnormal quantities of rich oxygen. Her chest expanded and contracted without pain. Each muscle in her arms and her legs moved in perfect synchronization. Time itself was transformed, with the seconds stretching to accommodate her smooth motions. Through her veins pulsed a certainty that no woman born could outrun her.

Helen Stephens, the six-foot American speed demon, had drawn the lane to her left, but Käthe did not glance in that direction, nor to her right either. A mighty rhythm roared against her eardrums and she knew vaguely that it was the predominately German crowd yelling her name. *Käthe, Käthe, Käthe, Käthe, Käthe.*

She was alive as she had never been before, exulting in the expansion and contraction of leg and thigh muscles. She willed herself to move yet faster, and her knees rose.

She arched her chest.

A slight pressure touched her breasts.

She had snapped the finish tape.

Slowing, she turned toward the tunnel. In the shadowed darkness Wyatt stood, arms still upraised. She lifted her own arms over her head in the same victorious gesture.

Collapsing on the grass, she thought, *I've won.*

The thought held sadness, for it meant that she had been thrust forth from that bubble of purity, her performance.

Käthe . . . Käthe . . . Käthe . . . The roar continued, and this time when she looked up Wyatt was gone.

*   *   *

She stood on the central platform, bending her head while a general in a sky-blue uniform draped around her neck the ribbon that held the heavy gold medal, then placed a laurel wreath on her hair. He handed her a little oak tree to plant in commemoration of her victory. Three huge flags, two lower American flanking the German, rose slowly atop the stands. The band brazed out the national anthem and thousands of voices joined in singing.

"Deutschland, Deutschland über alles . . ."

VI

A polite messenger came to escort her to the reviewing stand.

Hitler clasped her hand. For other German medalists this would be the culmination of their lives. Käthe, however, found herself taking the measure of the dictator. His brown uniform fit badly across his narrow shoulders. His skin had a pasty, grayish pallor that didn't show in photographs or newsreels. The famous mustache looked like cat fur.

"On behalf of the entire *volk*," he said, "I congratulate you."

"Thank you, Herr Reichschancellor."

"It gave me the greatest pleasure," he continued in a less oratorical manner, "when you turned, dedicating your victory to me with that sign. Fräulein Kingsmith, you are a credit to the true Aryan spirit of the Games."

"Thank you," she repeated.

"With your blond hair flowing," he continued, "you were a symbol crying out the superiority of pure Nordic blood to all the lesser races."

His pale blue eyes were intent on her. People wrote and talked about the Führer's mystic, all-seeing eyes, his preternatural eyes, his hypnotic eyes, his spiritual eyes. The studiedly penetrating gaze combined with the voicing of his master-race dogma brought chilling goose bumps to Käthe's arms.

Hitler turned to an aide. "See that Fräulein Kingsmith and her family are invited to the Chancellery reception next Thursday."

Six

I

"Of course Katy will explain to them at the Chancellery that she has to send her regrets, but this Thursday evening her cousin's taking her to some dreary concert."

"Brahms's Third is her favorite."

"Aubrey, you aren't normally such a nit. Say King George invited you to Buckingham Palace, could you turn it down? This is a command. But why make it such a disaster? Just exchange the tickets."

"Every seat at the Philharmonie has been booked for months. These only came my way by a miracle."

"Well, share your miracle with somebody else. Katy will be tête-à-tête with Adolf."

They were in Araminta's small bedroom on the third floor of the Adlon. Wearing a kimono with a vivid green dragon curling up the back, she stood at the window overlooking Pariserplatz, making the best of the light as she drew tiny strokes of eyebrows.

"You're right," Aubrey said, sighing. "It's too inane to discuss. This is her moment. I'm a pig."

"You, selfish? Darling, I'm the sibling who got the trait of wanting everything. Lord, what I wouldn't give for a few of your visible eyebrows." Araminta set her cosmetic pencil on the dressing table. "You really must come with Jürgen and me tonight. Jack Hylton's over here at the Mocca Efty, but they say Teddy Stauffer at the Delphi Palast is just as good—and believe me, Jack's the tops. Shall I give Jürgen a ring to find you some lovely fräulein?" Lieutenant Jürgen von und su Gilsa was one of the young Germans showing Araminta the smartest cabarets and escorting her to the livelier parties in the nearby mansions and embassies.

"Nightclubbing's not my style, and you know it."

"What an attitude! How do you expect to be a writer if you haven't sampled life?" Araminta came over to the bed, sitting next to him. Her untied kimono pulled apart, displaying the lush curves above the lace of her silk teddy. "You do look a bit off," she said sympathetically. "Daddy's been riding you, hasn't he?"

"No worse than usual."

"The next time he carps about some stupid detail like not hailing a German taxi properly, tell him to bugger off."

"The ensuing explosion would level Berlin," Aubrey said with a rueful smile.

"There, that's better," Araminta said. "When you're not sunk into yourself, you're not half bad." She pressed a dramatic hand against the upper curves of her left breast. "Ahh, if only they'd lift this damnable bar against incest!"

He laughed.

She went on, "So now that you're out of the Slough of Despond, tell me, since your erstwhile moodiness wasn't caused by Daddy, was it brought on by fiddling about for ideas to put in your essays?"

Ibis, one of those London literary quarterlies that annually sprouted and withered like leaves, had asked Aubrey to write his impressions of Berlin and the Olympic Games. "Hardly. There's so much going on."

"Then it has to be a certain lady athlete."

His smile had faded.

"Darling, you're so awfully clever and sensitive about people, so why can't you understand how Katy feels? Listen to me. Katy adores you, of course. But like a brother. You're the same as Sigi to her. Maybe even more of a brother—after all, you're only a couple of years older. So stop wasting your time on cousins."

"I'm holding you up," he said in a flat tone. "Enjoy yourself this evening."

II

As the door closed quietly, Araminta felt minor qualms at hurting her brother, then told herself she was doing him a favor. *It's high time he faced up to the truth,* she decided. Moving to the commodious wardrobe, she strewed the bed with her three summer evening dresses. The Marina-blue silk jersey did the most for her figure, but Jürgen had seen it. The white organza was lovely, but as she spread out the skirt she saw a straggling line of pale spots. She held the pink crepe de chine to herself, smiling into the mirror inset in the wardrobe door. This was her favorite. The shade of pink made her skin glow and turned her hair into jewellike ruby. She slid the silk off the wooden hanger. *And that old sow at Harrods said redheads can't wear pink!* she thought rebelliously.

Araminta Kingsmith rebelled against the conventional wisdom invoked by the older generation with the same spirited gusto that she did everything else. In her rare moments of introspection she understood that she was being true to herself, not to others.

Fastening the small pearl buttons, she appraised herself in the pier mirror. She was not beautiful—her hair and glowing white skin, yes, those were exceptional. But she lacked eyebrows; her lashes, though long, were pale and needed mascara, otherwise her large blue eyes appeared bald. And she had inherited her father's pointed nose and squareness of jaw. She tightened the belt. Blessedly, nature had canceled out her flaws by equipping her with this exceptional body. Her verve—call it invisible magnetism—drew men. Why not use her gifts to have a lovely time? Maybe she was a bit wild and selfish, but she wasn't hurting anyone—except an occasional stray bachelor, and weren't bachelors put on this earth to have a bruise or two on their hearts?

Her thoughts turned again to Aubrey.

Hedonist that she was, Araminta wasted little time delving into the psyches of others; however, she had always accepted that her brother and she were polar opposites. She reached out for what she could lay her hands on, real things like fast motorcars, stunning clothes, jewelry. He found his pleasures in concerts and scribbling his poems or stories. She knew how to cajole their dominating, irascible sire. Aubrey didn't. Aubrey was far too diffident. Now, if she had eyes for some eligible bachelor (married or engaged men were strictly off limits in her somewhat unorthodox moral code) she would blow her own horn a bit if that were necessary. And here was Aubrey half cracked about their cousin, and what did he do about it? Either fade into the background or buy tickets to some fusty concert attended by ancient Teutons.

Turning, she raised the long skirt high on her shapely legs to ensure her stocking seams were straight.

Even the traits she and her brother shared, like courage, generosity, loyalty, were differently expressed. She had very little fear. Aubrey needed to conquer his but then he reacted magnificently. For example, it was she who had first rushed into the burning stables at Quarles, but it was Aubrey who had followed and thrown blankets over the heads of their maddened riding-horses and coaxed them through the flames. She splurged on gifts while his were not lavish but invariably suited the recipient. His loyalties were quiet and steadfast, hers intense, demonstrative, and shifting.

All in all, she decided, it was easier by half to be she.

Humming, she gave her hair a final fluff, and picked up her long white kid gloves and small brocade evening bag. She was seldom on time, and poor Jürgen had been waiting in the lounge for a half hour.

III

Jürgen von und su Gilsa was an inch or so shorter than she in her silver evening sandals, but his tall Luftwaffe cap and gleaming black boots made up for it. He was quite handsome, with dark hair, lively brown eyes, and a wide smile. He was attentive, his manners were polished without being obtrusive, he complimented her smoothly, he had an excellent command of English, a necessity for Araminta, whose German was limited to *dankeschön, bitte,* and *auf wiedersehen.* She used her vocabulary often that night as Jürgen helped her on and off with the little pink bolero jacket in various crowded nightclubs.

Around midnight she was on the broad sidewalk of the Kurfürstendamm dancing in a circle around a standard topped with the Nazis' eagle emblem. She needed Jürgen's ever-courteous assistance into his low-slung, open two-seater Mercedes-Benz.

"How I do adore this motorcar's long bonnet," she said. "What does it mean, five hundred–K?"

"That she has eight cylinders," Jürgen responded, starting the engine. "She'll go a hundred miles an hour."

"But how d'you know?"

The car started smoothly forward. "I've tested this baby." Jürgen larded his conversation with British and American slang.

"I can drive. Do let me test her too."

"Araminta, in Berlin there are laws against speeding."

"You Krauts are too law abiding."

"I've heard the same about you Limeys," he said. "Someday we'll both give her a whirl."

"Now," she said.

Jürgen, immensely proud of his new car, his twenty-first birthday gift, glanced around. It was almost midnight. Here and there along the Kurfürstendamm groups of revelers were walking, waiting for the bus or going into the S-Bahn station. Only one set of taillights showed.

"We'll take a spin out to the stadium on the Via Triumphalis, as our dearly beloved Führer has renamed our streets." Jürgen, nearly as snookered as she, showed the Junker class's routine scorn for Hitler—in the three hundred traceable years of the von und su Gilsa family prior to the Nazi ascendancy, nobody had ever done anything but bark orders at a corporal.

They sped through the open countryside beyond the Olympic grounds. The headlights bathed the fields in an emerald brilliance, and big German farmhouses whizzed by. The wind streaming above the open car swept away Araminta's pretty, high-pitched laughter.

"Oh, isn't this too divine?" Araminta cried. "Jürgen, are we doing a hundred?"

"Let me convert from kilometers. No, more like eighty-five."

"Faster, faster."

"This is nearly as good a thrill as flying," he shouted, pressing his foot all the way down.

Araminta rested her head back on the leather seat. "Does the *Hindenburg* float around up there all night?" By day the zeppelin, trailing an enormous Olympic flag, hovered above the Reichssportfeld.

"If I had my Stuka, I'd fly up and find out for you."

Laughing, she squinted up at the darkness. Even if there were stars, she couldn't have seen them, for she wore her glasses only when it was absolute necessity.

Over the rush of wind and the roar of the supercharged roadster, she heard a shrill cry that sounded nothing like Jürgen's voice. *"Gott im Himmel!"*

As he jammed on the brakes, Araminta's head snapped forward, then back. There was a sickening squeal of tires. The car swerved across the roadway. With an immense and drawn-out crashing noise and sharp clatter of breaking glass, the world turned upside down.

Araminta sank into the deep silence.

IV

Far over her head a man was muttering some sort of foreign incantation.

With a tremendous effort she opened her eyes. A hard slant of light showed Jürgen's face up close. The dark strands of hair falling across his forehead were like thin snakes. A streak of blood showed on his jaw.

"Jürgen . . ."

"Thanks are unto Gott," he said, his English frightened from him. "I vas praying for you not to be die. Dead."

"Dead . . . ?"

"You is thrown from the car. And I find you here, by the ditch. So still you vere." The way the light was falling darkened the worry lines etched between his eyes.

She half sat to reach her white arms around his neck, pulling him down with her as she fell back into the moist, matted grasses of the roadside. Although she had done considerable kissing and caressing in dark automobiles, her moral code dictated that she keep her virginity. Now, though, she was confronted by the awesome face of eternity. Jürgen must have been going through a similar emotional upheaval. With a groan he buried his face in the lush curves of her breasts.

There were no words. There were no kisses, no caresses. She shoved aside her silken garments that separated them, he rose up to unbutton his blue Luftwaffe trousers.

At the tearing pain between her thighs she gave a shrill cry.

Then there was only his hoarse, rhythmic gasping, the breath rattling between her clenched teeth until a spasm uncontrollable as hiccups shuddered within her and the living blood tingled to her earlobes and fingertips.

V

Jürgen stood, turning to button his trousers. "It was your first time?" he asked in a tight voice.

" 'Fraid so."

"*Gott.*"

"Darling, it had to happen sooner or later," she comforted.

"I will speak to your father first thing tomorrow."

"Daddy?" She got up. Her left ankle stabbed. "But whatever for?"

"To ask for your hand."

This old-fashioned turn of events took Araminta by surprise. She looked at Jürgen's tensed face and knew he was no more in love with her than she was with him. He was behaving decently.

She'd enjoyed a ripping two weeks in Berlin—but to live in Germany? She thought of the reception in Grunewald and Aunt Clothilde's friends, the women dowdy and dull, the men uniformed with thin mouths and iron crosses around their wrinkly necks. How different would the von und su Gilsa clan be? And how could she survive so far from England and her family? Besides, although her brief joining with Jürgen had sent her into involuntary spasms, she didn't love him.

"You're being very sweet, Jürgen. Honestly, though, we don't take this sort of thing so seriously."

"But I adore you," he muttered.

"And me you," she lied, saving his face. "Still, we come from two different countries, so we must be sensible."

"What if a child results?"

"We'll cross that bridge if we come to it," Araminta said.

SEVEN

I

"Tell me every detail, darling. I have it on the best authority that you and Adolf had an endless tête-à-tête, and he as good as invited you to a holiday at Berchtesgaden."

"Araminta," Aubrey interjected, "that's Uncle Humphrey's version and—"

"He's won all the gold medals in exaggeration," Käthe finished.

The three of them laughed indulgently at the predictable foibles of the older generation.

It was late afternoon, and they were sitting in a secluded corner of the Hotel Adlon's writing room. The cast encasing Araminta's left leg from above her knee to her visible, pearly toenails was propped on an ottoman. Because of her cousin's automobile accident the Baronin von Wangenheim had permitted Käthe to leave the Olympic environs before the evening of the following Sunday, August sixteenth, when the Games would come to an end.

"The Chancellery looks so cold and gray from Wilhelmstrasse," Araminta said. The Adlon was close to the government buildings with their swirl of Nazi flags. "What's it like inside?"

"The courtyard's nice, but the interior's impersonal and grandiose. Blond bodyguards all the same size were stationed along the walls like black-dressed statues. There were several hundred guests and we waited in line for an hour until the

Chancellor shook our hands—he told me I should have med-aled in the hundred-meter." Helen Stephens, the tall American, had taken the gold, and Käthe had placed a dismal fifth. "The cakes afterward were stale. You would have adored every moment."

"Having Hitler make goo-goo eyes at me would be an improvement on sitting around here all day."

"A terrible ordeal," Aubrey said, smiling at Käthe. "Why, thus far today this poor unfortunate's been visited by only five of her young men."

Jürgen, a tape across his jaw, had presented himself each afternoon, but with a fellow officer, comforting proof in case she needed any that he was not ardently in pursuit.

Araminta smiled, then frowned. "It just occurred to me that every one of them was in a uniform."

"I'd noticed," Aubrey said quietly. "It's a nation of uniforms —Thor's hammer, on the ready to be hurled."

"Darling, what a writerly thing to say. But think of how civilized everything is, how divinely clean the public loos are. The people are so friendly." Araminta shifted in the settee with an overdramatic little pout that meant they shouldn't take her continuous movements to heart. In actuality the broken bone ached and the itching under the cast was driving her mad. "I must say it's impossible to believe that anyone I've seen here would go around bashing communists and innocent Jews."

"The country's been given orders not to go in for any rough stuff during the Olympics," Käthe murmured.

Aubrey glanced around. An elderly matron sat at a table, writing, otherwise they had the room to themselves. "I assumed that," he said quietly. "But isn't it dangerous for you to be saying this?"

"Dangerous? Aubrey darling, she's talking to *us.*"

"I'm a journalist."

"Twelve people read *Ibis.* Everybody knows you're an Oxford man writing essays for a lark."

"Not everybody." Aubrey edged his chair closer to them. "Yesterday a man came up to my room. Don't ask how he found out about me. He told me I ought to take a trip to Oranienburg.

'It's less than an hour from the Olympic Stadium, you get off
the electric railroad where the line ends,' he said."

"There's a prison camp in Oranienburg," Käthe said.

"So he told me. Konzentrationslager two-oh-eight." Aubrey
paused, tapping his chest pocket. "He gave me a handwritten
report about the place. The dormitory was a brewery cooling
room, and it's always damp. Men are packed like sardines into
three-tiered wooden bunks. They're fed slops. They're
marched out before dawn every morning for hard labor—his
squad drained swampland." Aubrey took out the closely written letter, reading a description of fearsome twelve-to-four-
teen-hour workdays followed by drills on the parade ground.
Shuffling the three flimsy pages, he read a paragraph about the
meager rations. Refolding the papers carefully into the envelope, he said, "For any minor offense they're whipped or
beaten with rubber truncheons. And the punishments for more
serious offenses . . ." He shivered.

"Well, it's a prison, isn't it?" Araminta said. "They're criminals."

"Not necessarily." Käthe's whisper shook and her face and
throat were crimson with shame. "The Nazis have put in something called *schutzhaft,* protective custody. That means people
the government thinks of as enemies, some are Jewish, others
are communists or union leaders, anyone can legally be put
away without a trial." She clenched her hands. "I knew there
were camps, everybody does. But I never heard any details."

"Not many people do. The man told me that when he was
released, he was commanded never to describe what had gone
on. If he did he'd suffer far worse and—"

"Look who's come!" Araminta interrupted, beaming and
waving at the foyer. "Wyatt! In here!"

Wyatt, raising a hand and smiling, moved toward the open
glass door of the writing room. Käthe, despite the horror of
Aubrey's disclosures, felt a clearly delineated stir of pleasure.

Wyatt leaned over to kiss Araminta's vivid hair, handing her a
crimson chocolate box. "To cheer you up," he said.

Araminta thanked him prettily. Aubrey shook his hand and
complimented him on the United States gold medal in basket-

ball. Käthe, who had remained silent, added her congratulations.

"To you too," Wyatt retorted.

Remembering the wonder of that perfect race, Käthe's lips parted in a soft smile. "Your advice made all the difference in the world."

Araminta, who was untying the satin ribbon, looked up. "Advice? Wyatt, you can't have coached the opposition. How dare you help these Jerries win even more medals!" She laughed. "Have you heard? Dear little Adolf is now one of our Katy's close friends."

Käthe flushed. "We were invited to a reception at the Chancellery. He told me he was disappointed in my hundred-meter performance."

Wyatt's face was expressionless as he pulled a straight chair close to Araminta. "Now give your old cousin the straight dope, 'Minta. Dad's been spreading the word that you were out with some Habsburg prince who races at Le Mans."

Araminta laughed. "Jürgen's a pilot, and his father's a baronet—that's what *Freiherr* means, isn't it, Katy? The true story is . . ." She launched into a vivacious, bowdlerized report on the midnight prank—or as much of it as she cared to disclose.

Käthe and Aubrey, who'd heard the story before, couldn't control their laughter, and when she reached the part about driving home in a horse-drawn Bolle milk wagon Wyatt laughed so loudly that the woman at the writing table ostentatiously gathered together her postcards and departed. When Wyatt spoke to Käthe, he was cordial but removed, and she could hear a stilted note in her responses. Araminta kept a lively shuttlecock of conversation going during the tea and cream cakes.

Käthe glanced at her watch. "Nearly five-thirty. I have to dash."

Aubrey jumped to his feet. "Let me get a taxi and take you back to Friesen-Haus."

"A shuttle bus is stopping by for me."

"I promised the guys to be back at the Olympic Village for a victory celebration," Wyatt said. "Okay if I grab a ride with you?"

Käthe gave him a startled glance before she nodded.

After they had disappeared in the bustling foyer, Aubrey continued to stare at the glass doors.

II

It was a beautiful late afternoon, warm, with a soft bronze haze of sunshine. Traffic was flowing in heavy streams between the great columns of the Brandenburg Gate and into the vast green vistas of the Tiergarten. The only way Käthe could keep herself from gazing at Wyatt was by focusing her attention on the Victory Quadriga, the bronze statue that topped the Gate.

"What if you miss that bus?" Wyatt asked.

"Impossible. The baroness—"

"We'll have a short stroll in the park, I'll take you back to the dorm in a cab, and your guardian jailer will never know the difference."

"But—"

"Why not try something new and different. Just do something without an argument, okay?" He took her arm, leading her across the Pariserplatz toward the Brandenburg Gate.

III

She hadn't walked in the Tiergarten since the afternoon two years ago when she had come here with Anna Elzerman. That was the first time she'd seen the signs that forbade Jewish people to sit on benches. Trapped in shame, she had gripped her friend's trembling hand and made an inner vow to forgo the park and its pleasures, including the zoo. Kingsmith's was nearby, on Unter den Linden, and her father sometimes invited her for an ice cream at one of the park's open-air cafés: she always suggested they go to Bauer's or the Victoria-Café instead. Not enjoying the park was a protest known only to her, a meaningless protest. Yet strolling at Wyatt's side in the shade of the tall trees along the newly broadened Charlottenburger Chaussee toward the distant golden Siegessäule, the statue of winged Victory, she couldn't help staring guiltily at the benches with their paler rectangles. The signs had been removed before the Games.

Wyatt said, "Maybe the chaperone will hear you played hookey. You're not exactly incognito in that outfit."

Preoccupied, she hadn't realized that the cyclists and strolling pedestrians, the people passing in automobiles, were eyeing her trim white uniform.

"There's a pretty pond that way," she said, raising her left hand.

"Sounds good to me."

The meandering little lake had retained its enchantment. A graceful willow wept into the green lily pads, a pair of gliding swans carved V-shaped ripples beneath the humpbacked stone bridge.

Wyatt slowed. "Nice," he said, then looked at her. "I've been pretty rough on you. And the thing is, I don't usually go around like Jack the Ripper."

"The Games, competition, everybody watching us. We've all been under tremendous stress—"

"Ye gods," he said with a mock sigh. "Can't I apologize without a battle?"

"I'm not arguing."

"What, then? You've pulled your head back, your eyes are narrowed. You're one goddamn irritating, sensational-looking female."

"Is that a compliment?"

"Mixed." The smile faded and he stared at the swans with a curiously hurt expression. "What a laugh. Me! Making time with a big pal of Hitler's."

"The Nazis make me cringe."

"Hey. Aren't you the girl who leaps to defend that group of thugs like they walk on water?"

"If I attacked Roosevelt, how would you react?"

"I'm surprised. Why aren't you putting that nasty twerp on a far higher level than the President?"

Sudden tears filled her eyes. It was like the basketball match, but this time there was no escape. She fished in her purse for a handkerchief.

"Hey, I was trying to say I'm sorry." He touched her arm gently. "You shouldn't take me so seriously. I'm famed far and wide for my short fuse."

"It's an insect in my eye. . . ."

"Shhh," he whispered, and put both arms around her, holding her loosely. She had the same feeling that had come to her during the race, that she had stepped out of normal time and into a bubble of perfection. Tears still oozing between her closed eyelids, she let her cheek rest on his jacket, hearing and feeling the strong beat of his heart.

"Käthe," he whispered hoarsely, pronouncing her name perfectly. "Käthe . . . what's happening to me?"

A pair of stout matrons were curving into sight on the path. Wyatt moved away. Käthe loathed the fat hausfrauen.

"Let's go over there," he said, and they crossed the little bridge. Halting by the marble statue of a nymph, he said in a low voice, "You feel the old chemistry, too, don't you?"

"It's crazy," Käthe murmured. "You're my cousin."

"No."

"What?"

"We're not related at all," he said.

EIGHT

I

Her mind swirling with Araminta's disclosure of Humphrey and Rossie's unlikely premarital fall, she looked at him and said nothing.

"This isn't coming out of the blue, is it?" he said. In the shadowy twilight his face seemed heavier, older.

"I just found out that your parents didn't get married until right before you were born." She moved the toe of her pump carefully along the marks left by a recent raking. "It didn't seem possible. Aunt Rossie is, well, too sensible. And Uncle Humphrey's not like that either."

"Exactly. But until last month I took Dad for granted. You know how it goes, he was my father, so of course he loved me. Frankly, sometimes it got embarrassing—he might as well have been wearing a badge, *Wyatt Kingsmith's my son and I'm proud of him!* So when—"

"*Sondermeldung!*"

One of the loudspeakers that reported on the Olympic events had been planted on the bridge. From the quadruple megaphones poured an announcement of another victory for the Reich.

"Christ, there goes the perfect background noise for this particular conversation." Wyatt began to stride rapidly along the curving path. Käthe hurried to keep up. The voice faded into the rustle of leaves and he slowed. Thrusting his hands in the pockets of his gray flannel slacks, he asked, "Has the German press mentioned the makeup of our basketball team?"

At this abrupt retrenchment to the impersonal, Käthe moved a bit apart. "No, but basketball's not considered a real sport here."

"Tell me about it!" he said. He explained that this was originally a movie-studio team but some of the players had been forced by financial considerations to stay home in Hollywood. "I was scheduled to spend August with a buddy, but suddenly I was hot to show these Nazi bullies what it was like to be up against the great Kingsmith. I made the team. When I told my folks I was coming to Berlin, Mom went crazy."

"Aunt Rossie? That's hard to imagine."

Wyatt walked a few steps. "Let's face it," he said. "You're not the only one who wondered why they waited so long to make it legal. After Dad was asleep, Mom came to my room. It seems she'd been married before. The guy's name was Myron Leventhal. Jewish, in case you're wondering."

Käthe felt the blood drain from her face as the pieces tumbled into place. Wyatt's outbursts against Germany, his impulsive anger at her, the baiting remarks about those Jewish Mayans.

A muscle jumped in his jaw. "So tell me, Brünnehilde in the white suit, why the stunned expression? Have I sprouted horns?"

"Please stop doing this to me," she whispered.

"Forget I said that," he said repentantly, and began telling her of the Wyatts' displeasure and the Leventhals' chopping Myron from the family tree. His voice grew low and he swallowed when he came to the end of the lovers' brief marriage. He picked a lime leaf and tore it apart before he continued with Rossie's refusal to go back South. "It must have been a truly rotten time for Mom. Widowed. Pregnant. Nineteen. She'd never worked before, but she landed a job at Kingsmith's. Dad fell for her immediately. After he found out I was on the way, he insisted on a wedding. When Mom finished I told her that was in the past, and I didn't feel any different. In other words, lied. Because everything was goddamn different. If I wasn't a

Kingsmith, who was I? I consulted the Manhattan telephone book for Leventhals."

"Were there any?"

"You sure don't know New York." The fading light glinted on his smile. "Damn near a pageful. Fortunately, Mom had mentioned Myron had lived near Columbia. There was a Judge and Mrs. Leventhal on West 102nd Street. I fought against going, but after a sleepless night there I was. I stood outside so long, I could diagram the ironwork grill. Finally I rang the bell —my hand shook. An ancient family retainer answered. He hobbled away and returned to say that they would see me, his tone indicating that I had been granted an audience with the Lord God of Hosts."

"They must have been so happy."

"Are you kidding? It was obvious they'd kept track of Mother and knew exactly who I was. Mrs. Leventhal—she's thin, with a long, bony face—left it all to the judge. He asked what it was I wanted. He had a slight German accent and spoke deliberately, as if handing down a verdict. Mom had given me Myron's watch. I put it down. 'This belongs to you,' I said. They both sat very still for a few seconds, then Mrs. Leventhal rang for coffee. Neither of them referred to the watch. The judge asked me a couple of questions, did I go to college, what was I studying, that kind of thing. After that he talked about them. In a way it was like the Rossies and the Wyatts. Ancestral net worths. Except the Leventhals could trace their families back farther, to fifteenth-century Spain. When the Inquisition expelled the Jews, they moved on to Germany. The judge obviously thought it swell that both his and his wife's parents had come from Germany, which struck me as wild. Why would a Jew be proud of being German? A cousin of his owns a place called Leventhal's."

"The department store?"

"From the way he spoke I should be impressed."

"Since 1933 it's been called the Berliner."

"Hey, on Leipzigerstrasse? Acres and acres of shop with a glass-covered central court?"

"That's it."

Wyatt whistled, then squinted up at the rays cast by the setting sun. "We had seconds on coffee, then the judge picked up the watch. 'Young man, we have no connection to this.' "

"Rotten," she said. "Rotten."

"Sad's more like it. Here they knew I was their grandson, their only descendant, yet even after all these years they couldn't back down. I still can see them sitting on those stiff chairs, two old people, lonely, so lonely." Wyatt sighed. "At the time, though, there was no measured compassion in me whatsoever. I was ready to howl at the moon. Here was rejection on the most basic level. Because their son had married a gentile he was dead to them. They had mourned him. I didn't exist."

Käthe touched his arm consolingly. He gripped her hand, then released it.

"I'd been considering visiting the local Leventhals to see if they needed anything. On the Q.T., of course—it'd be a shot through the heart to Dad if he knew. Hearing they're in the Rothschild league takes a load off my mind."

Käthe thought of the letter delivered to Aubrey's hotel room. She thought of Anna Elzerman emigrating because her father's fashionable practice had been ruined, she thought of the signs stripped down for the Games, she thought of the crude, hate-drenched anti-Semitic cartoons in the chauffeur's newspaper. Yet in a sense Wyatt was right. The German Jews were not subjected to the same beatings and indignities as the emigrant *Ost-Juden,* which was what the press called Eastern European Jewry.

"Wyatt, if there's ever anything you want me to do . . ."

"Keep Myron between us, that's all."

"I won't ever tell anyone."

"Is that right hand of yours on a Bible?"

"I never break my promises."

"This isn't just about hurting Dad. It's me. I like being a Kingsmith. Oh, God, Käthe, Käthe. I'm so damn confused."

She put her arms around him, and for a few seconds they clung together.

II

That Sunday of the closing ceremonies the entire family gathered at the Grunewald house for a midmorning meal of cold meats and rolls. The gold medalists were toasted with raised steins of weiss beer, the light, fizzy beer unique to Berlin. Everyone trooped outside onto the sun-splashed terrace. Porteous sat on an ornate armchair brought from the drawing room; Araminta reclined on a deck chair with a leg rest for her cast; the others stood.

Halfway down the lawn that sloped gently to the small lake stood a carriage house that had been converted to a garage and chauffeur's quarters. Here, where a stone retaining wall divided the garden, Herr Ley, the gardener, had dug two holes. Käthe and Wyatt, laughing yet self-conscious in their Olympic uniforms, walked down to the small excavations. She planted her oak sapling. As she knelt to press the soil around the roots a light breeze came up, blowing pale gold strands across her forehead.

Above them Aubrey shouted, "Three cheers for Käthe." Ragged cries of "Hip, hip, hooray" echoed in the sabbath quiet.

Wyatt planted his tree, and three more cheers went up.

"So you'll let me know how my oak's doing?" Wyatt asked as they returned to the terrace.

"I'll write to you often."

"Good," he said. "Great."

III

The stadium was jammed. Twenty thousand more than the official hundred-thousand capacity had crowded inside. The reddening sun slipped behind the Olympic flame atop the Marathon Gate, distant cannon boomed, and high atop the Glockenturm the Olympic bell began its steady tolling. Trumpeters sounded a stately fanfare, and the flag bearers of each nation entered, followed by the teams. When all the athletes stood assembled on the infield, the Olympic banner was ceremoniously hauled down. Eight men were needed to carry it outspread to the *bürgermeister* of Berlin.

The orchestra sounded and a vast white-clad chorus broke into the farewell hymn. Here and there groups of German spectators crossed their arms, clasping the hand of the person next to them. The linking spread through the amphitheater to the athletes, and all were joined, swaying to the voices.

Slowly the lights in the great stadium went out. The flame of the Olympic torch drew all eyes. From the loudspeaker system a clear voice called: "I summon the youth of the world to Tokyo four years hence."

As though a mighty hand were descending on the sacred fire, the Olympic flame that had blazed steadily for the past sixteen days was deliberately snuffed out.

Thus far the closing ceremony had gone as planned. Now that the Games had officially ended, the spectators were intended to move toward the well-lit exits. But something spontaneous occurred. The majority remained, standing to raise their right arms and sing first "Deutschland Über Alles," then the "Horst Wessel Lied." After the strident march beat had faded into the night, the German fencer next to Käthe muttered, "Why don't they shine the spotlight on the Führer? This is his Olympics."

There were similar mutterings all through the darkened stands. A group of masculine voices on the floor of the stadium shouted, *"Sieg Heil! Unser Führer Adolf Hitler! Sieg Heil!"*

Others joined in, and the shout spread outward and upward. The stone amphitheater reverberated with the cadenced screams.

Sieg Heil.

TWO
1936–1938

While the rest of the world went about the business of making a living, rearing families, dancing "The Lambeth Walk," and enjoying *Snow White and the Seven Dwarfs,* Germany was bathed in the fiery glow of a thousand torchlight rallies.

—from *A Brief History of Europe Between the Wars,* Sir Aubrey Kingsmith

NINE

I

"Not another word. You're going back up to Oxford," Euan Kingsmith said in a low voice whose dangerous fury reached across the dinner table to his son. "I won't hear any more Frognall idiocy!" By "Frognall idiocy" Euan meant any step that to his mind could remotely lead to a financial decline akin to that suffered by his wife's family.

"Why can't you let me finish, Father?"

"There's nothing further to say. Tonight you'll pack your bags and first thing tomorrow morning you'll get in your motorcar. It's Oxford for you and that's that! If I'd only had your chances." (Euan's often-voiced plaints about his lack of educational opportunities ignored the facts: true, his formal schooling had ceased at fifteen, but that had been his choice. Itching to enter the business, he'd seen extraneous knowledge as a waste of his time and his father's money.)

"I'm appreciative, but reading Literature seems trivial compared with what's going on in the world."

"A fat lot you know about the world! At nineteen—"

"Twenty," Aubrey interjected.

"So long as you're under my roof," Euan shouted, "you will do as you're told!"

Elizabeth Frognall Kingsmith's terrified gaze focused down the length of the long oval table at her husband. She had sat at this Sheraton table in this dining room—called the Blue Room because of blue Wedgwood ovals set above the doors—since childhood. In those days there were no scenes of this type. Sometimes she wondered if Quarles had ever heard violence like the hisses and roars that erupted from Euan in all the years since 1707, when Thomas Frognall had raised the rambling cream-painted brick walls. The Frognalls were reticent, bookish people who hugged their emotions to themselves, and the same blessed if bottled-up calm would have prevailed now if her two brothers hadn't been killed in the War, leaving her the inheritor. Both she and Euan, however, considered Quarles his house. Indeed, as he'd just hissed at Aubrey, the roof *was* his. He had paid for the new slate and reglazed the stained-glass dome that sent multicolored light into the stairwell. He had also hired a firm of landscape gardeners to replant the flower beds and prune the fine old trees that shaded the fifteen acres, wired the house for electricity, added central heat, transformed the three small bedrooms into bathrooms—he had, in his own words, restored Quarles to a fit home for a gentleman.

This remark invariably drew smiles from the neighboring squirearchy. Among themselves they referred to Euan as poor Elizabeth Frognall's little husband, for although he was stout and almost six feet tall, he was in trade, which entitled them to feel larger than he.

"That's what I've been trying to tell you," Aubrey said. "I'm moving up to London."

"The flat is mine too."

"Grandpa's offered me a room."

Euan knew his own father's quiet intractability. His neck turned a dangerous maroon and he altered his attack. "For the sake of argument let's say you do finish scribbling this book of yours. Who d'you think'll be interested in what a young pup like you has to say?"

Aubrey, who had inquired the same of himself, took a tiny nibble of blancmange.

Seeing he had scored a point, Euan sat back, his hard mouth curving into a smile of triumph. "Well, my budding literary genius? Who'll buy the book?"

"That doesn't matter. I'm going to write it."

"Here we go round and round, ooha, ooha," Araminta sang, paraphrasing the words of a popular song.

"Don't be cheeky, miss." Euan's grumpiness was put on. Araminta, his spirited pet, rarely invoked his ire.

"Why must you always have an audience for these boring father-son rows?" Araminta asked.

"Yes, Euan," quavered Elizabeth Kingsmith to her husband. "It would be better if Araminta and I both—"

One glare from her husband silenced her.

Araminta shrugged. "You'll have to finish minus little me. My poor leg feels beastly." Blowing kisses at her pale brother, cowering mother, and protesting, sputtering father, she moved toward the door to the hall. The cast was off and it was obvious from her jaunty step that nothing hurt.

II

"Darling, you went at it all wrong."

"With Father there's no way for me to go at anything right."

Aubrey and Araminta sat in the easy chairs in front of the library fireplace, she lounging back gracefully, he hunched forward clasping his hands, which were still shaking although his father had stamped upstairs almost an hour earlier.

"He never lets on how proud he is of those essays of yours, but at business he keeps copies of *Ibis* on his desk."

"I've never seen one there."

"He pushes them in a drawer when you come to the shop. Poor darling, that's how he is." Araminta yawned. "I'm dead. It must be this fresh air. Aubrey, tap on my door no matter how early tomorrow morning you steal away."

After she left, Aubrey looked around. A dozen or so of the small diamond-shaped panes of glass that covered the bookcases were cracked, and the oak pillars that separated the cases were inexpertly repaired. Euan, who had little respect for the moldering leather-bound volumes, hadn't restored the room, and in part this was why his son, who had been born with the Frognall love of books and shabby, inherited objects, considered the library the true heart of Quarles. Resting his elbows on his knees, he stared gloomily into the fire. As always after

these scenes his confidence was at a low ebb. His father, who
dealt in tangibles, was right, he was giving up everything for a
book that probably would never be published.

But the closely written German on flimsy paper had shot cold
mercury through Aubrey's veins. He had described the concentration camp in his longest essay. The *Ibis* editor, a languid
young man who worshiped beauty rather than truth, had refused it as "too brutal." Aubrey had considered expanding the
piece into a slim volume, broaching the idea to his friend Rupert Keiffer. Rupert had introduced Aubrey to his father, head
of Keiffer Press. Keiffer senior had read the essay himself, and
said: *You're barking up the wrong tree, young Kingsmith. Essays don't
sell. No profit in 'em at all. But this concentration camp of yours has the
gore that novel readers gobble up. If this were fiction I might, just might,
consider a contract.* Hardly a promise. Yet even with the knowledge that his attempt might well end in his own desk drawer,
Aubrey could not flee from the task of bringing the horrors to
light.

Thinking of what he had seen in Germany, thinking of Käthe,
thinking of his banishment from Quarles, Aubrey watched the
embers turn white. Slowly he replaced the brass fire screen and
climbed the staircase, his fingers searching out the familiar
bulges and depressions in the oaken banister. Passing his
mother's room, he heard sobbing.

Bottle tears, he thought.

Elizabeth's secret drinking had been a scab across his boy-
hood, for he believed—erroneously—that the outbursts between him and his father triggered her binges. His hand lifted
to tap on the door; then, aware that her desolate sobs would
continue as she begged him to obey his father, he moved on,
hearing Euan's muffled snores in the adjoining room.

III

Euan Kingsmith had been Elizabeth Frognall's first and only
young man. It wasn't that she'd been ugly. Her face had been a
bit too long, true, but the features had been regular and her
silky hair the same nice shade of russet as the family collies.
Though she had been tall for a woman, her bosom was ample,

her waist trim. Being shy, she had made the worst of her assets, disguising her figure with heavy, unstylish tweed suits and clumping about in thick, laced shoes as she'd performed her numerous tasks.

Her mother was dead. Colonel Frognall couldn't afford a housekeeper. It was up to Elizabeth to run Quarles. She hired girls from the nearby hamlet of Marwych, she cosseted the ancient grump of a gardener, she pleaded with the tradespeople from Faversham and Canterbury not to press for payment. Though not yet twenty-three she was well resigned to spinsterhood that spring of 1914 when Mr. Euan Kingsmith had come down to buy the Matthew Boulton silver and take a look at the ivory and jade bric-a-brac. Euan was ten years her senior, taller than she, with a hard mouth that she found dizzying. She didn't dare dream that he might notice her. Yet that same weekend his wonderful mouth was pressed against hers. In hindsight Euan put a practical slant on his choice of a wife, informing himself that he had picked Elizabeth because of this handsome if badly run-down house, her accent, the dogs, the Frognall crest on the family silver. At the time, however, the shy woman with the golden-red hair had beglamoured him utterly. When he asked for her hand, there was a pause during which Colonel Frognall's thoughts, *It's the gel's only chance—but dammit, the chap's so common!* were all but audible and Euan shook with fear.

On their wedding night he took his bride urgently. She was ignorant of the conjugal relationship—innocent it was called in those days. She muffled her scream, but afterward she wept. The stifled sobs cut Euan as unendurably as her father's near rejection. So she, too, looked down on him, did she? He battered at her again.

During the Great War, Euan was sensible enough not to enlist. His two less pragmatic brothers-in-law were killed within minutes of each other at the First Battle of the Marne. Later, when conscription came in, his poor vision served him well. By the end of 1916, when Aubrey was born, the Euan Kingsmiths' marriage had solidified into its ultimate pattern, hurt rage on his part, frightened submission on hers, responses that showed in their rawest form in her canopied bed. Marital rape. Burying his sense of inferiority in the conjugal act never ceased to excite Euan. Beautiful, titled, and possibly complaisant ladies shopped at Kingsmith's, yet Euan never strayed. Why should he? He already owned a lady.

From her birth on Euan favored his daughter: he saw himself replicated in her. His son he considered like Elizabeth. He misjudged both offspring. Araminta, though thoughtless and at times foxy, was far less selfish than he. And while Aubrey possessed what Euan called the Frognall idiocy, that is, a tendency to act against his own best interests, he had also inherited a full measure of the Frognalls' quiet, unassuming courage.

IV

Porteous was at the breakfast table when his grandson arrived at the tall, narrow house on the Bayswater Road not far from Marble Arch.

"Good to see you, my boy," he welcomed, beaming as if he could indeed see the young man. "Mrs. Plum's airing out the front room, so you'll have a view of the Park."

"You're being topping, Grandpa."

"Bosh. You're obliging me by being here. No, don't argue, what this house needs is the sound of young laughter. Now, pull up a chair. The girl"—Mary, the Irish parlormaid, had been with him for forty years—"will bring you porridge, a nice egg, a rasher or two of gammon."

Aubrey, leaving Quarles before six-thirty, hadn't wanted to wake the cook, and due to the fight he had scarcely touched his dinner. Normally he wasn't much of a breakfast eater. This morning he put away a large meal. Sated, he leaned back in his chair.

Porteous heard the creak. "You mustn't think any the less of your father for chucking you out. He's a hard man, Euan, but a fair one. To his mind he's bringing you to your senses."

"Has Father always believed that he has the lock on universal truth?"

Porteous chuckled. "You've hit on the secret of his getting ahead. Maybe you need to let a bit of that certainty rub off on you. You're too modest, too much the gentleman." The old man's smile grew pensive. "Sometimes I think life would be simpler for all of us if my boys had married in their own class. Before my father opened his secondhand shop in Shoreditch, the family trade was rags and bones. And your grandmother, God bless her, was in service. Mark you, I'm proud of what I've accomplished with Kingsmith's, but I know where I come from. And my sons, well, for whatever reason, they all married above themselves."

"The Frognalls were plain country people."

"Gentlemen. And Euan's angry because he can't evolve into one." Porteous took out a cigar and started his ritual of lighting it. "What do you think of that little cousin of yours, Kate?"

His grandfather was blind, but Aubrey kept his features noncommittal. "I'm not following you, Grandpa."

"D'you think she's happy there in Germany?"

"It's her country."

"She said the same thing. All the same, she's as much English as German. Being split down the middle is hard on a dreamy girl like her."

"Dreamy? Käthe's got a lot of spirit."

"Those Nazis are such swine. You were at the closing ceremony, you heard them. Chilled my blood it did, thinking two of my grandchildren were down there in the arena. Wyatt's a strong chap, but my Kate, she's only a slip of a girl." Porteous sniffed at his cigar again. "I asked her to come to London, but she turned me down. Maybe I should suggest she go to university in the States."

"No," Aubrey said, his voice low and hard. "America would be a mistake."

"Funny, you sounded a bit like Euan just then. I never heard it before." Porteous took another puff. "Probably you're right. She'd end up marrying some American chap. But why shouldn't I give her a holiday there? Yes. She and Araminta. Rossie's got her head screwed on right, she'll keep them in tow. Wyatt can introduce them around to a few nice young chaps. Maybe once my Kate sees a bit more of the world she won't be

so stuck on Germany." The hall clock chimed. As Porteous
hoisted himself to his feet, he said, "I'm late for business."

Although nominally retired, he continued to spend six hours
each weekday in the fishbowl offices that overlooked the spacious ground floor of the Bond Street premises.

"Grandpa, I can't thank you enough for letting me stay here,
it's a lifesaver."

"Then show your gratitude by not talking about it. Write
your book, Aubrey, buckle down and write your book."

V

"You must believe me when I tell you that I have found it
impossible to carry the heavy burden of responsibility and to
discharge my duties as king without the help and support of the
woman I love. . . ." The high-pitched voice, metallic yet emotional, came from the radio.

Porteous, who seldom sat in the drawing room, had selected
the formality to hear Edward VIII's abdication speech, which
marked an end to the crisis brought about by his announced
intention to make an American divorcée his queen.

Aubrey stared at the fountain pen he still held in his ink-
smudged fingers. Araminta, who had arrived only moments
earlier, had not yet taken off her coat: her hair showed flamboy-
antly against the black Persian-lamb collar.

The speech ended. Porteous sighed deeply. "Poor Queen
Mary, first her husband dies, now this." Shoulders bowed as if
the scandal were resounding in his own family, the normally
erect old man paced slowly from the room.

Araminta rushed after him. "Don't go to pieces, Grandpa.
We'll have a new king and queen and two lovely little prin-
cesses." She kissed his nose.

"You girls today wear too much scent," he grumbled fondly.

With another kiss Araminta watched the old man climb the
stairs. Returning to Aubrey, she said, "There went the voice of
the Victorian age." She rolled her eyes at the drawing room,
which embodied the same era. Massed bric-a-brac, tall urns
filled with pampas grass or peacock feathers, flocked maroon
wall covering, heavy-legged furniture. Araminta, after all a

Kingsmith, knew the collection of silver birds in the bowlegged cabinet was exceptionally fine. Yet her droll expression said the entire roomful of furnishings should be chucked out. "Are you working beastly hard?"

"Well, this Clive, the main character, has rather taken over, and I scribble away to keep up with him."

"Mmm," she said with a smile. "Aubrey, you'll never guess who I bumped into having a curry lunch at Veeraswamy's. Your old friend, the Honorable."

"Peter Shawcross-Mortimer?" Aubrey and the Honorable Peter Shawcross-Mortimer had become firm friends at Oxford.

"Yes, Peter. He's far too young for me, of course—"

"A year older."

"As I said, far too young. But now that his spots are gone he's quite terribly handsome. He asked about you, and I told him the long, sad tale. He said his father doubtless would have behaved with the same stodginess—the only difference being that his father's a belted earl." Araminta pulled a face as if to say that nobody cared about this sort of nonsense anymore; however, in truth she relished a friendship with an Honorable. "Aubrey, you are coming down for Christmas, aren't you?"

"I haven't been invited."

"Mother's petrified to ring you up without Daddy's permission. And he, poor darling, well, you know it's impossible for him to make the first move."

"What makes you think I can?"

Araminta's face grew serious, and the pointed nose and squarish jaw were suddenly evident. "You're better than he is," she said quietly. "You always have been a better man."

VI

That Christmas of 1936 Aubrey took out his Morris Minor and drove with his grandfather through the lightly falling snow to Kent. The spirit of the season prevailed. By the time the enormous Christmas pudding burst into blue brandy flames, Aubrey and Euan were bickering quite amicably about the Spanish civil war.

* * *

"Didn't you adore your present?" Araminta asked. "The one from Daddy?"

"It was pretty decent of him."

"Decent. Darling, this is me, Araminta. When you opened that box and saw the portable typewriter, you practically bawled."

It was late in the afternoon and the two were taking a drive, she at the wheel of Euan's pride, a stately Daimler.

Araminta went on, "Now, my favorite gift, barring the tickets to *Intermezzo*"—from Aubrey, who could afford no more than first-run tickets to the Swedish film—"was from Grandpa. A trip to America! Glorious, glorious America! How I hope that Aunt Clothilde lets Katy come. What a time we'll have without parents. I'm positive Wyatt will take us around."

Aubrey peered silently at the thin coating of snow that lay on the fields.

"Ah, Wyatt . . . That Yank sense of humor, the way he's always suntanned, the half smile—he's absolutely thrilling. The problem is he's too damn decent to respond to a cousinly offer of my pure white body."

Aubrey's gloomy expression altered to a smile. "Buck up," he said. "America's not filled with moral paragons. Your maidenhood will be in jeopardy every moment."

It was Araminta's turn to stare silently at the wintry countryside.

TEN

I

Käthe was crowded next to Araminta at the rail of the HMS *Duchess of York*. Other passengers jostled around them, shouting to attract the attention of friends or family on the Cunard dock below. Horns honked, porters bawled, gulls cawed. To complete the pandemonium the ship's band was blaring "Sidewalks of New York." Käthe searched the upturned faces. Had Wyatt come to meet her? His spasmodic correspondence had been filled with farcical tidbits about his law professors, the newest dance crazes, and films like Charlie Chaplin's *Modern Times*. She'd lived for the days the postman had delivered a letter, afterward fretting that he'd written not a word that couldn't be read aloud to her parents. Of course she wrote to him in the same vein.

The gangplanks were adjusted and people on the wharf shoved their way aboard.

"D'you see Uncle Humphrey and Aunt Rossie?" Araminta cried in her ear.

"Not yet. But . . ." Käthe's hand went to the rapid pulse at her throat. There he was. Taller than the other men, he was shading his tanned forehead to search the passengers massed at the rails as he thrust up the gangway immediately below them. "But there's Wyatt."

Araminta squinted nearsightedly. "Where?"

Käthe was already pushing her way through the crowd.

She met Wyatt in the shade of a lifeboat, halting. The couple of feet of decking between them seemed as wide as the Atlantic Ocean.

"Hi," he said.

Her heart was beating in her throat and she couldn't speak.

"Welcome to the New World."

She nodded.

He was staring at her. She wondered if Araminta was right, she should have done something more elaborate with her hair and put on mascara. "Mom and Dad are tied up," he said.

She nodded again.

"They said they're sorry."

Another nod.

"What's wrong?" he asked.

"I missed you so much," she blurted.

He reached forward to touch her hair. "Pretty," he said, and put his arms around her.

A woman nearby was shrilling about baggage. Käthe and Wyatt pressed closer together, his eyelashes fluttering against her cheek. "Brought you a present," he said in her ear. "It's poetry, so put it in your purse."

And then Araminta was there.

II

New York did not revere age like London or Berlin, New York was an energy-charged city where youth held the ascendancy. New Yorkers hurried as if racing the breezes that fluttered through their granite canyons, they chattered in a babel of accents and languages. The wealthy women were unassailably chic as they stepped in and out of their long, glittering automobiles; the working girls looked equally smart in their Seventh Avenue knockoffs and Woolworth pearls. By night the lights of Broadway twinkled merrily and the smoke-hazed Cotton Club in Harlem tapped and bounced. The precisely timed legs of the Rockettes pistoned in synchronization with the city's rapid pulse. New York was, in Araminta Kingsmith's opinion, "too divine for words." She drew Käthe—who seemed dazed by it all —into the whirl.

* * *

"It's good on you." Araminta tilted her head appraisingly at Käthe. "As a matter of fact, it's quite marvelous."

It was three days after they had landed and they were in a large dressing room with a dozen or so other women in various stages of dishabille—a strong smell of perfume and sweat pervaded the hot air. Araminta had taken it upon herself to exchange the first-class tickets that Porteous had purchased for third-class accommodations, pocketing the considerable difference so she and Käthe could splurge on American clothes. Rossie had sent them here to Klein's, where there was no service but the prices were far cheaper than at the big shops on Fifth Avenue. Their initial selections from the racks outside hung on the rods protruding from the mirrored walls.

"But black?" Käthe asked.

"How can you ask? Look at yourself. With that hair black's your color." Araminta, shamelessly voluptuous in her stockings, panties, and brassiere, was stepping into a white jersey dinner dress. "Katy, you simply have to take my word for it, German clothes are a disaster, and English aren't much better. Only Americans know how to make smart things at low prices, so we both absolutely must stock up whilst we can." Moving in front of the stout matron next to her, she craned her neck to look at her rear. "Tell me honestly. Does this sag ever so slightly over my bottom?"

After three and a half hours of trying on and discarding, they carried armloads of their final selections to the long counter where gum-chewing clerks expertly jangled cash registers. The cousins silently translated dollar amounts into Reichsmarks and pounds sterling.

Then Araminta led the way along Thirty-fourth Street and up a staircase into a cut-rate beauty salon. After their shampoo-sets they took off the smocks and put on new dresses. As they were cocking new little hats over their eyebrows, Araminta broached the subject that disturbed her: Käthe's refusal to join in the fun of New York's nightlife.

"This evening you're coming with Charlie and me." Charlie, heir to a Chicago meat-packing fortune, had seen to it that Araminta and her quieter, lovely German cousin spent all the waking hours of their transatlantic crossing in the purlieus of first-class passengers. "He has a friend who went to university with him."

"I can't tonight. Wyatt's taking me on a ferry that goes to Staten Island."

"You can't mean you're going to let that marvelous hairstyle be blown to bits by sea wind?"

"There's a poem by Edna St. Vincent Millay about riding this ferry." Käthe turned away from the mirror, her cheeks very pink. It was in the book that Wyatt had slipped to her on the *Duchess of York.*

"Well and good for the two of you to practice running around Central Park early in the morning. But can't you see? He's obligated to show us the town." She paused. "Charlie tells me his friend looks rather a bit like Robert Taylor, and rumbas like an Argentinean."

Käthe said nothing.

"That's your stubborn Kingsmith look, darling," Araminta said. "Katy, do be sensible. Wyatt's divine, but he's our cousin. And he has his own girlfriends. Explain to him that you'll do the ferry some afternoon. Say that we're going to the Colony for dinner—I'm positive I can wheedle the boys into taking us."

There was a loud knocking on the changing-room door.

"People are waiting," Käthe said.

Outside on Lexington Avenue the heat hit them like a blast from a hair dryer.

"I can't carry all these things another step," Araminta said, waving a hatbox at a yellow cab. She gave the address of Kingsmith's in the Dejong Plaza.

III

Two days earlier, when Käthe had first seen the Fifth Avenue Kingsmith's, she had been astounded. Though she had known the New York branch was highly profitable, she had assumed it would be the American version of the branch on Unter den Linden. Instead, it was far larger and more posh than the main Bond Street shop, almost a department store.

A series of curved alcoves formed bays for customers to tranquilly browse over shelves of silver, china, crystal. A deep inset held three bridal-registry tables presided over by handsomely dressed *Social Register* matrons forced by the Depression into the genteel job market. Beyond the pair of small elevators, which carried customers upstairs to buy less formal dinnerware, linens, and stationery, a half-dozen steps led down into a subtly lit area that resembled a drawing room. Here reproductions of Georgian breakfronts held antique silver, ivory, and jade. The finest pieces, however, were kept in Humphrey's luxurious office, giving buyers the sense that they were purchasing a unique item from Mr. Kingsmith's personal collection.

Rossie's office was seen only by the staff and manufacturers' representatives. Tearsheets of recent advertisements were taped to the walls, the battered desk was piled with catalogs and ledgers. The pair of sagging armchairs had been discarded from the flat.

Wyatt was lounging in one. As Araminta and Käthe came in, he rose with an approving whistle. "Wow!"

Rossie was also enthusiastic. "You girls have a real eye."

"It's all Araminta," Käthe said. The doorman was bearing in the rest of their packages. "Wait until you see the gorgeous bargains she fished from the racks."

"Later." Rossie glanced at her wristwatch. "I have to get out on the floor. Mrs. Van Vliet is here from the Coast. A very good customer. Her secretary telephoned ahead to make an appointment."

She hurried away and Humphrey appeared. "You girls have to take a closer look at the bridal registry," he said. "There's nothing like it in the world."

"Wyatt," Araminta said, taking Wyatt's arm, holding him back, "I need a word with you."

When the two of them caught up with Humphrey and Käthe in the bridal registry, Wyatt cocked an eyebrow, moving his head in the direction of the traffic on Fifth Avenue. "Käthe, want to take in the view from the top of the Empire State Building? It's really something when the sun's setting."

Araminta darted him an angry look.

IV

"Why was 'Minta upset?" Käthe asked.

"She says I'm toying with you." He put his arm around her waist. "In that dress, with your hair done up on top of your head, you look terrifyingly spectacular. Mind if I toy just a little bit?"

The Fifth Avenue sidewalk glittered beneath Käthe's new black patent sandals, and the crowd moved in a haze of sunlit motes. The only uniforms in sight were worn by doormen, children were merrily disorderly, nobody darted nervous glances, and Wyatt seemed to have completely forgotten that she came from Germany. His fingers were playing a little tune above and below her waist. She leaned closer, wishing they were alone and could kiss.

"Oh, Christ," he muttered. His hand fell, and he moved away from her.

"What's wrong?"

"It's them."

"Them?"

"The Leventhals."

The elderly couple coming toward them must have witnessed the byplay. Their faces were long with disapproval before recognition dawned. Then the thin woman stumbled a little and the straight-backed, gray-haired gentleman gripped her elbow.

The four of them made an island in the thronging crowd of pedestrians.

"Good afternoon, Mr. Kingsmith." Judge Leventhal raised his hat. "So we meet again."

"Always swell to bump into you, Judge." Wyatt spoke with a trace of sarcasm. "Mrs. Leventhal, allow me to present my cousin, Miss Kingsmith."

"It's a pleasure to meet you," Käthe said automatically.

"You are from England, Miss Kingsmith?" asked the judge.

"Our grandfather is." She flushed. *Our?* This elderly man looking down his narrow nose at her was Wyatt's grandfather. "But I was born in Berlin."

"Berlin?" The judge's expression showed a fraction more cordiality.

"My father is in business there. My mother comes from near Potsdam."

"I know the Potsdam area quite well. What was her maiden name?"

"Von Graetz."

"Are you by any chance connected to the late Graf Walther von Graetz?"

"He was my grandfather."

"Is that so! I had the honor of his acquaintance. Yes, you do resemble him."

The oval silver frame on Clothilde's bureau showed the grandfather whom Käthe had never met to have been a bald old man with a white Kaiser Wilhelm mustache that extended over his pendulous jowls.

There was an awkward pause. Tipping his homburg, Judge Leventhal bowed and repeated his pleasure at seeing Wyatt, meeting Käthe. As the elderly couple moved on, Mrs. Leventhal said something inaudible to her husband, he put his hand under her arm again, and they moved at a slow, labored pace in the direction of Central Park. Wyatt watched them disappear into the crowd. His mouth was twisted into the acid, unhappy smile that Käthe had seen so often during the Games.

V

The first two weeks of their holiday melted away. As far as Araminta was concerned, Käthe's continued turn-down of dates with Charlie's friends was the only flaw amid Manhattan's shops, nightclubs, and theater.

Finally, after one refusal too many, Araminta said, "It's high time you face the facts."

" 'Minta, I don't want to go to the '21'."

"You're evading the point. Wyatt's having a bit of a summer

romance with you." Araminta formed an odd, gritted little smile. While it was only too clear to her that Wyatt, a ladies' man, had no idea of the havoc he was wreaking on their highly sheltered cousin's impressionable heart, at the same time she was honest enough to accept that a strong hint of jealousy was mixed in with her concern. "Americans do love to lead a girl on."

Käthe looked down at the rose-patterned carpet of the guest room. "I know he's not any more serious than you are with Charlie."

"As I said, a summer romance. Well, at least I've warned you."

After that Araminta refused to let anything deter her pleasure.

Humphrey and Rossie owned a roomy, ugly gray clapboard house on Cape Cod and there they spent every August. This year, though, they had decided to forgo their quiet relaxation and treat their nieces to a tour of the Eastern Seaboard in the big Packard. Wyatt had volunteered to drive.

VI

At nine on the last morning before their trip, Käthe and Wyatt, having run in Central Park, were showered, dressed, and drinking orange juice. Araminta, who seldom got home from dancing before three, would be asleep for hours; Rossie and Humphrey had already left for the shop. Martha, the cheerful colored cook, set the morning mail on the table.

Wyatt sharply slit open a pale-gray envelope, reading it, then silently handing Käthe the deckled stationery.

> Dear Mr. Kingsmith,
>   Would you and Fräulein Kingsmith give us the pleasure of your company for tea this afternoon, July the thirty-first, at half after four?
>
> Eleanor Leventhal

"We aren't busy," Käthe said.

"Are you nuts?" He snatched the note from her fingers, ripping the heavy paper in half, then quarters. "You saw how clear they made it that I'm nothing to them. Well, as far as I'm concerned they can go drown in their damn tea!"

ELEVEN

I

The brown velvet curtains in the Leventhals' high-ceilinged living room had been partially drawn against the brassy heat, thrusting deep shadows into the corners. The looming Italianate furniture was set formally apart and Käthe, unable to reach any of the tables, balanced her half-empty cup and the plate with the remnants of a small, pink-iced petit-four on her lap. Wyatt, who had refused refreshments, sat in a stiff-looking sofa with his long legs thrust out. His face was expressionless except for the slight sardonic grin that Käthe knew by now hid his pain.

Mrs. Leventhal, behind an antique Dresden coffee service, appeared yet frailer and older. On Fifth Avenue her hat had hidden the sparseness of her neatly drawn-back white hair and her coat had disguised her spinal osteoporosis as well as how flat her chest was. The mournfully webbed wrinkles around her mouth looked like crumpled tissue paper.

The judge was winding up his opinions on the improved conditions in Germany. "The Ruhr is producing at full blast." His earnestly somber voice, although cadenced like a German's, had no accent. "Employment is at an all-time high. The currency is stable—quite a dramatic change for the better since I was last there in 1929. Though one can never be certain of the future, I personally find myself optimistic. There is every reason to believe that the . . . repressions . . . are at an end." He looked at Käthe for verification.

"The Nazi party's in power," she said faintly. Not breaking into the judge's optimistic monologue had made her feel uncomfortably as if she were agreeing with him. Yet she knew had he spoken against the Reich, she would have felt equally awkward. "Very much in power."

Since the letter had arrived this morning she had been keyed up for some kind of rapprochement on the Leventhals' part. She had decided that they had included her in the invitation to act as a buffer and make Wyatt less volatile, more amenable to the grandparental advances. How naively hopeful she had been. The old couple continued to call Wyatt Mr. Kingsmith, a form of address that Käthe, after all a European and therefore accustomed to mandatory use of surnames, found grating and sad—this was America and he, even though unacknowledged, their grandson. After the initial greetings, Mrs. Leventhal had used her whispery voice only to inquire what they desired from the tea cart. Judge Leventhal had dominated the conversation with his magisterial certitude about German politics. Wyatt hadn't argued, but one glance at his set face and the unpleasant little smile would have told anyone that he couldn't have disagreed more.

"Precisely why the earlier toughness is no longer necessary," the judge responded. "The country's unified behind the government."

"The opposition's been stamped out," Käthe mumbled. "Nobody says what they think anymore. They're afraid."

"In any event, our newspapers haven't reported any new . . . outbreaks."

"And last summer, during the Games," murmured Mrs. Leventhal, "one read of politeness and order in Germany."

"Politeness toward *everyone,* " the judge emphasized.

"That's Dr. Goebbels for you." Wyatt balled his fists in the pockets of his flannel slacks. "The Ministry of Propaganda decreed every German be friendly, honest, kind, and good, especially to the Jews."

Before this nobody had voiced the word *Jew.*

Mrs. Leventhal stared down at her hands. In this gloomy light the long, bony fingers appeared an odd purple.

The judge asked, "Did you see that in print?"

"Sure thing. Billboards on every corner. 'This Is Be Kind to Jews Month.' "

The judge frowned. "I beg your indulgence, but perhaps it would be easier if Fräulein Kingsmith and I discuss the matter in our own language." He turned to Käthe, saying in German, "You must believe me when I say it's important that you tell me the truth. Have you any knowledge of the concentration camps?"

"Not much. A little." Käthe shivered. She, too, spoke in German. "Our cousin Aubrey is English. He was commissioned to do a series of essays on the Olympic Games by a magazine that had a very small circulation and was quite new. Before then he'd been published only in school papers and at Oxford. Still, an ex-prisoner tracked him down at the Hotel Adlon to give him a report. It was a tremendous risk for the man—anyone who talks can be put back inside. The conditions are unbelievable. The cruelty, the privation."

"Then you read this, uh, report?"

"No," she admitted. "Aubrey read a few sentences out loud and summarized the rest. But it shocked him so much that he left Oxford to write a book. In February, when he came over to do research, he couldn't get any more information." Through a German friend Aubrey had been put in touch with several released prisoners. None would talk about the time spent behind barbed wire. The last interview was with a violinist who had been in the new camp in the village of Dachau near Munich. The musician, too, had refused to elaborate, but Aubrey had said the man's hands told the story. *They were all twisted. He'd been concertmaster with a symphony orchestra and he couldn't bend any of his fingers.*

"So as far as we know, then, the report given to your cousin might well have been exaggerated?" The judge's tone held an impersonal contempt for hearsay evidence.

"I don't believe so." Käthe's hands were shaking, and she got to her feet to replace the delicate Dresden chinaware on the tea cart. "Judge Leventhal, have you heard about the racial laws?"

"The Nuremberg laws, yes. A terrible step backward for German jurisprudence." He swallowed twice, then pulled at his lapels as if to readjust his robes. "Believe me, I'd never be questioning you like this, but a few days ago I was visited by an emigrant from Germany. He came here to tell me that my cousin is in one of these places. My cousin was head of Leventhal's—the Berliner, it's been called since he stepped down. Perhaps you know of it?"

"Of course. Everybody shops there."

Wyatt was watching them with a blank look, but he understood the entire conversation: this past year he had taken courses in German, and although he spoke with only fair fluency, his comprehension was remarkable.

"So then you realize how impossible the story is to believe. We're talking about a man whose family for generations has been active in the cultural and philanthropic circles of Berlin, a man with a fine military record—he was wounded in the War and awarded the Iron Cross, First Class, for bravery—detained in a prison camp? Yet according to this, er, refugee, he has been held since May. Over two months." Though the judge's jaw trembled, his magisterial tone did not falter. "What kind of charges could have been brought against Heinrich—my cousin?"

"We now have something called preventive custody." She sighed. "I'm so ashamed of what's happening. The police can take in a person who *might* commit a crime, which means they can take in anybody."

The judge drew a breath as if steeling himself. "Fräulein Kingsmith, you are excellently connected, you are an Olympic champion—"

"Leave Käthe out of this!" In one swift, elastic movement Wyatt was on his feet. The slightly doltish laxness had been replaced with taut anger.

Both Leventhals turned to him in surprise.

"You speak German," the judge reproached. "You've been less than candid with us."

"Candid?" Wyatt's fists were clenching and unclenching at his sides. "That's a laugh! *You* were using a language you figured I didn't understand! *You* pried around to learn about Käthe! Me, of course, you already know about—no matter how much you pretend not to!"

"Our conversation was intended to be private." The judge's erect spine seemed as brittle and friable as the antique Dresden cups.

"Please believe me, my husband had no intentions of insulting you, or of using Miss Kingsmith." The papery wrinkles on either side of Mrs. Leventhal's mouth trembled as she leaned toward Wyatt. "He and I are concerned about our cousin. We are old, and probably our ways seem peculiar to you. But that doesn't mean . . ." Her voice wavered into inaudibility.

"Eleanor," the judge said, "you mustn't agitate yourself."

"We care very much for . . ." Mrs. Leventhal lifted her thin arm, extending the palm placatingly toward Wyatt. "For all of our family."

"Wyatt," Käthe murmured, "maybe I can find out—"

"No. You will not put yourself on the line. If anyone steps in here, I do."

"Mr. Kingsmith, stop making so much of my request. There is no reason either of you should be involved—"

"Yes, let's cut involvement out of our lives," Wyatt said. "This German refugee guy who came to see you was obviously lying, and so was the man who risked his life to see Aubrey last summer. Let's face it, the Nazis are right. The Jews are the snakes in the Teutonic Garden of Eden, inventing all these ugly lies about having their rights taken away and being beaten up by brownshirts."

"Please," Mrs. Leventhal whispered. She had gone yet more pale. "Wyatt, please . . . don't be angry." She raised a hand to her flat chest.

The judge rose to his feet with jerky, arthritic haste. "My wife has a heart condition. I must give her the medication. If you will forgive us."

"I'll see what I can discover—" Käthe started.

But Wyatt had yanked her from the drawing room.

II

He propelled her past the handsome old houses, across Riverside Drive and down the sloping yellow grass of the parkway that ran along the Hudson River, plunking her down on the first free bench. That caustic half smile was gone, and he hunched forward, his face bleakly miserable. Käthe longed to comfort him. But he sat apart from her, fair warning that he wanted no consoling touch or words. Following his example, she stared across the heat-shimmery reddish surface of the Hudson River to the Palisades. There were no trees to shade their bench, and she could feel the slow trickle of sweat between her breasts.

"So how about that?" Wyatt said with a shrug. "She'd literally rather die than admit that I'm connected to her."

"They looked so old, so defenseless."

"You think I didn't notice?" He bent his head, burying his fingers in his thick tawny hair. "Käthe, I'd convinced myself it didn't matter whether or not they owned up to being my grandparents—"

"Mrs. Leventhal was trying to say they care about you."

"Oh, Christ. Käthe, maybe I'm crazy, but do you know what I'd give to hear one of them say, 'You're our Myron's son'?"

"You told me it was a religious thing for them. They can't go back on it."

"Yes, it's a religious thing. But that doesn't alter the fact that rejection hurts—hurts like hell." He shrugged. "Okay, so I tell myself I'm meant to be a logical law student—another big laugh, me going into the same profession as him. Logically the Leventhals have it right. I didn't even know they existed until last summer. And as far as they're concerned, I'm a biological accident committed by their late son *after* they'd officially declared him dead."

"Uncle Humphrey's your father."

"Not the way we're talking about." A sound came from Wyatt's throat. "So where do I belong?"

"Wyatt—"

"I'm a half Jew, which is fine as far as I'm concerned. But if they say I'm not, where does that leave me?" Wyatt was clenching and unclenching his hands the way he had in the Leventhals' drawing room. "How can they make me feel like such garbage? And why was I all hot to jump into the fray for them?"

"I wanted to help them too."

He gripped her wrist. "You are not to search out this Leventhal joker, Käthe."

"But—"

"You're going to mind your own business."

"Maybe I could—"

"No ferreting around the concentration camps. Is that clear?" After a couple of moments he released her. The marks of his grip faded. "I didn't mean to blow my stack at you. I'm just so damn confused." He turned, letting her see the tears in his eyes.

"I care for you, Wyatt."

"Yes?"

"So very, very much."

He touched her cheek. At the light caress the air seemed yet stiller and her breath caught. She shifted closer to him. He put his arm around her shoulder, drawing her to his damp side. He rested his forehead against hers, then kissed her nose.

A nasal Bronx accent intruded. "Can you beat that, necking on a day like this?" Two sweating women were shoving perambulators uphill along the parkway.

"Is there someplace we could be alone?" Käthe murmured.

"Alone?"

"Just us. . . ." Her eyelashes fluttered and she couldn't look at him.

"Am I getting the message right?" His voice was stretched out of shape.

"A room somewhere. . . ."

He was silent so long that she felt as if the sun were focusing its entire heat upon her. "Yes, there are rooms available," he said finally.

They climbed the slope to Riverside Drive; he hailed a cab. As they lurched forward, he pulled her into a tight embrace. Reaching under her skirt, he urgently caressed the smooth flesh of her thighs above her stockings. Until now, despite their long, tremulous kisses, he hadn't gone in for what Araminta described as "the favorite masculine sport," maneuvers in which the man attempts to fondle the girl under her clothes— or to remove them—and the girl, while appearing equally ardent, gracefully fends him off. Käthe, shaking, opened her legs to Wyatt's touch, and kissed him. Their kiss involved teeth and tongue, lasting endlessly. The cab stopped, started, horns honked. She had no idea of how long the journey took. When the motor was cut, Wyatt pulled away, digging the fare from his pocket. Flushed and dizzy, she stepped onto the sidewalk.

They were on East Thirtieth Street.

A few mean-looking bars and shops were interspersed beneath tenements festooned with drying clothes. Old women sat fanning themselves on a rusty fire escape. The half-dozen men in undershirts drinking beer on a nearby stoop shouted arguments about Roosevelt into the stagnant air. Boys torpidly played stickball in the street.

Across the blackened bricks directly in front of them was painted: CARSON HOTEL. As the cab pulled away, the front door opened. A floridly made-up woman in a tight orange dress teetered down the steps, clinging to a short sailor. The couple's drunken laughter joined the other racket trapped in the mugginess.

Wyatt reached for her hand. "Let's get away from here."

"The place isn't important."

"To me it is. Well, this time it is. Besides, you're sorry for me."

"That's not the reason—"

"No?"

"I love you," she said in a low, clear voice.

He continued to stare at her.

"I've loved you from that first time I saw you," she said.

A ball came hurtling at them, and he reached up, catching it, tossing it back to the boys. "There's a subway entrance very close." He tucked her hand under his arm. "Come on, buy you a drink at the Plaza."

They walked along the mean street and descended the steps. Wyatt dropped nickels into the turnstile.

On the platform he thrust his hands in his pockets. "Ever thought of coming to college in New York?" he asked.

"My parents would never let me."

"So you have given the idea consideration."

"It's impossible."

"I could get a part-time job in a law office," he said. "You could learn to eat less."

She gaped at him in bewilderment.

"Marry me." He dropped to his knees on the tiles, one hand over his heart in a parody of a suitor. "Marry me."

"Wyatt, stop it. Get up, please get up. Everybody's watching."

"So what? It's an honorable proposal." He raised his voice. "Come on, say yes, please say yes."

A subway attendant shouted, "Say it, blondie. Put the poor slob out of his misery."

Käthe couldn't help laughing.

"Good," Wyatt said. "That's settled."

The train was roaring through its tube. Jumping to his feet, he said close to her ear, *"Ich liebe dich, Käthe."*

She forgot the spectators, forgot the shadowy image of an old man bent over a thin, tallow-white old woman, forgot her jealousy of the girls he'd taken inside the battered door of the Carson Hotel, forgot the mountains of time piled up behind her in Germany. "I'll love you always," she said into the roar of the train. "Always and forever."

III

They sat at one of the small wicker tables in the Palm Court at the Plaza Hotel, slowly sipping cold Tom Collinses while a string trio played "Smoke Gets in Your Eyes." Neither of them said much, their words trailing away as they gazed at each other. The yearning desire between them was so palpable that she imagined a halo had formed around them, an aura of sensuality that was surely visible to the people relaxing amid the cool palms and slow, romantic music.

After the waiter brought their check, Wyatt took her hand, caressing the ring finger. "Käthe, there's one thing you should know. Two, actually. First, I've been intending to ask you to marry me for over a week now. And second, forget the insult. When I get hot under the collar, I hit out."

"Insult?"

"Hey, come on." He held her hand against his cheek. "You're hardly the sort of girl I'd take to that fleapit."

"But I asked."

"Don't look so worried, love. Getting you in the hay is high on my agenda too. But since we have the rest of our lives, I vote we have the ceremony first."

They walked languidly home through the twilit heat, halting several times to embrace.

IV

The foyer and the big living room were dark. The corridor lights were off.

"It's all this *sturm und drang*. I forgot," Wyatt said. "Mom mentioned that they'd be working late, cleaning up their desks. And Martha's already taken off. So we scrounge in the icebox. No, I've a better idea. We'll head over to the Oyster Bar at Grand Central."

"Wyatt . . . Katy . . . ?" Araminta's voice came down the bedroom corridor.

"Hi," Wyatt called back, switching on the lights. "Are you primping up to paint the town red with Charlie—" He stopped abruptly.

Araminta had padded shoeless into the foyer. The skirt of her two-piece linen dress was awry, a wet strand of hair snaked down her cheek, her eyes and the pointed tip of her nose were red. Obviously she had been crying for some time.

"Have a fight with Charlie?" Wyatt asked sympathetically.

Araminta held out a wad of yellow paper.

Wyatt uncrumpled the cable. " 'Father suffered massive heart attack,' " he read. " 'Stop. Imperative you come home. Love Aubrey.' "

"Oh, poor Uncle Euan," Käthe whispered.

Araminta drew a shuddering breath to compose herself. "How do I get home? Oh, God, what do I do?"

Wyatt patted her shoulder consolingly. "Let me call around," he said. "Find out what's sailing. If there's anything available tonight, shall I go ahead and book?"

Nodding, Araminta began to weep again.

Käthe put her arms around her cousin. "Two passages," she said over the disheveled red hair, silently pleading for Wyatt's understanding.

His features seemed to become more prominent, his mouth tensed, and he nodded. "Two passages coming up," he said.

V

A festive midnight crowd thronged through the brilliantly lit *Manhattan*—the same liner that had carried Wyatt and other athletes to Germany for the Olympics. The ship had been booked solid, but an outside second-class cabin had been canceled at the last minute.

Humphrey and Rossie had rushed home from Kingsmith's. Rossie had packed the old and new clothes in the steamer trunks while Humphrey—shaken at this felling of his powerful oldest brother—had leaned against the telephone alcove nodding as Wyatt made the arrangements. Now they were both in the small cabin consoling Araminta, who kept bursting into tears of frustrated anxiety that she was still nearly a week away from Euan's sickbed.

Käthe and Wyatt stood outside in the companionway, his hands pressed flat against the bulkhead so that his arms sheltered her as laughing, champagne-odored voyagers and their guests shoved by.

"I'll be over as soon as humanly possible," he said.

"Law school starts on the first of September."

"The American judicial system won't crumble if I start a week or so late."

"You can't miss your classes."

"All it takes is a bit of cramming to catch up. The important thing is my talk with Uncle Alfred."

"What about your parents?"

"We have here a situation too important and too tricky not to follow protocol. My folks second. Uncle Alfred first. There'll be a bit of a muck because we're cousins."

"Will you explain—"

"Never," Wyatt interrupted. "Hey, aren't you the gal who promised you wouldn't say anything to anyone?" He waited until she nodded. "But watch me mow down all such objections. You won't even have to change your name."

"Married . . ."

"Us," he said in the same bemused tone.

A tinkling rang close to their ears. A steward was maneuvering down the passageway with a little bell as he called, "All ashore that's going ashore."

Araminta was too distraught to go topside to bid her American kin farewell. Käthe stood at the rail, waving at the brightly lit pier as hooting tugs towed the *Manhattan* farther and farther from land. The other passengers drifted off and finally she was alone. The salt breeze had chilled her bare arms. Shivering, she went below.

TWELVE

I

Aubrey met them at Southampton. As they came down the gangplank, he shouted through megaphoned hands, "Father's on the mend!"

The chauffeur drove them up to London through bright August sunshine and Araminta bubbled over with droll stories of New York and Charlie, "my American conquest." To look at her now, it was impossible to guess the tensions of the passage. Either she had been fretting about the liner's slow movement across the calm blue Atlantic or visiting the purser's desk to make certain there were no dire undelivered cables. She had needled Käthe, who missed Wyatt to the point that everything rubbed her raw. In the hot little cabin quarrels between the cousins erupted, followed by copious tears and reconciliations.

When the Daimler pulled to a halt on Harley Street, Araminta wrenched open the car door, and before the chauffeur could come around, she was darting up the shallow marble steps of the small private hospital.

"You certainly were a long time driving up from Southampton," Euan said to his daughter after their greetings, hers emotional, his gruff with pleasure. "I've been expecting you for hours."

"It took simply eons to get through customs."

"You should have let Aubrey handle it."

She had. Aubrey, though, lacked his father's bullying panache with officialdom of the lower order. "They were baffled by all our new American clothes—did you know Katy came home early with me."

"A good thing too. I don't even like to think what the pair of you laid out for fripperies, but it must have been a pretty penny."

"Not at all, Daddy. You would have been proud of me." Araminta told bright tales of her shopping forays at New York discount houses, mimicking accents, blowing out her cheeks to describe the fat customers in the Klein's dressing room. Her vivacity overlaid fear. The sight of her father's tough grayish face beaming at her from the pillow chilled her. "Daddy darling, how could you have let such a thing happen to you?"

"My ticker's been acting up a bit, that's all," Euan said. "It's the limit the way these doctors build up every minor ache. I s'pose they must justify their fat fees. They've terrified your mother. She sits and frets over me until I have to comfort her." Euan's idea of comforting Elizabeth was to bark at her to go shopping, go to the theater or cinema, go anywhere, but get out of his room. "Believe you me, the real problem's at the business. How the staff must be enjoying themselves!"

"Aubrey said Grandpa's taken charge."

"A blind man over eighty! And as for your brother, I've been trying to talk some sense into him. High time he stopped cadging and gave up this book-scribbling nonsense."

"You're worrying over nothing, Daddy. As far as I can see, you'll be back in harness next week—September at the latest. Anyway, you've always complained how slow business is in the summer. Why not pretend you're in the South of France, lounging about."

Euan formed a grim little smile at the thought of himself lounging about. "The young men nowadays, no sense of duty," he grumbled, tightening his grip on his daughter's hand.

The feeble fluttering of his fingers reached a place inside Araminta, and her own heart felt weak.

II

The late-August dusk was falling when Araminta stuck her head out the door and told the others to go on home, she would keep Euan company at supper.

Euan had a London pied-à-terre just off South Audley Street. Set amid aristocratic old Mayfair mansions, the large apartment block—new and ultramodern, with curves of white marble along the street and above the ground floor—reminded Käthe of the ocean liner from which she'd disembarked this morning. Aubrey had left his grandfather's house on the Bayswater Road and was staying here with his mother. As the three of them were borne upward in the mirrored elevator, Elizabeth said she would have a bite of cold chicken in her room. Aubrey sighed, knowing that this meant she intended to spend the evening with the bottle; yet at the same time an unfilial shiver of delight ran through him. He would have Käthe to himself at the round, pale ash dining table.

He sat opposite her. "I can't tell you how grateful I am that you cut short your holiday," he said.

"Araminta was mad with worry."

"She adores a good time, but she's not shallow, not by a long shot." After he poured the Spanish wine, he looked across the table at Käthe. The candles that threw a silvery light on her hair also shadowed her eyes. "What is it, Käthe? Since you stepped off the boat you've been in a brown study."

Just then the maid came in with the cutlets.

Waiting until the door had swung shut behind the woman, Käthe blurted out, "In February when you were doing your research on the concentration camps, who put you in touch with that violinist from Munich?"

"That's private, Käthe."

"There's . . . somebody . . . I need to find out about." Käthe flushed. During the tension-wracked voyage she'd had time for reflection about the Leventhals' cousin. Fortunately she had given Wyatt no promises, for as they neared Europe it had become obvious to her that, insane as she was about him, obeying his order to stay clear would be impossible. How could she live with herself if she didn't do her best to trace Herr Leventhal and, if he were in need of help, do all in her power for him? "It would be difficult on my own."

Aubrey used his knife on the cutlet. "Mine's a little tough. How's yours?"

"Please?" she said. "It's important."

"Käthe, no. I won't have you barging in where you shouldn't."

"Often the only possible choice *is* to barge in, the way things are at home." She voiced this disloyalty a bit too loudly, then gazed across the table at him. "You of all people know that."

The admiration in her luminous blue-green eyes excited him and he sipped some wine, attempting to compose himself. "Here in England I've become quite friendly with several refugees who were in prison camps. None of them will discuss what happened to them. Then I met a chap on a bus, and we started to talk. He agreed to let me interview him. Käthe, believe me, that letter didn't tell the worst, not by a long shot. This chap saw another prisoner kicked to death by the guards. Everybody was lined up on the parade ground before roll call, and there seemed no rhyme or reason to the way they chose their victim; two of them just yanked him forward and threw him into the dirt. Probably they'd had a few too many beers. They laughed as they kicked him. When he was absolutely still, the largest guard jumped hard on his stomach a few times, and the men in the front row could hear the bones break. The guards were still laughing."

Käthe shuddered. "In New York I was asked about a man stuck in one of those monstrous places."

"A Jewish prisoner?"

"Yes. I'm going to see what I can find out."

"Weren't you listening? Didn't you hear? Even after people leave Germany, they're still afraid."

"Then won't it be best for me to contact your friend? He'll know how to go about it more safely than I would."

"I refuse to help you land yourself in hot water!" The lights of the chandelier flashed on Aubrey's glasses as he abruptly looked down. Embarrassed by his atypical outburst, he sawed at his cutlet.

They were on the raspberries and double cream before either of them spoke again. "That man you're worried about," Aubrey said. "What's he called? Let me see what I can find out."

The maid was rattling dishes in the kitchen. A car passed on the street below them. Telling Aubrey anything more would constitute an active betrayal of Wyatt—or, more properly, the well-kept secret of his dual paternity. She could no more say "Leventhal" than if her tongue had been cut out. "You'd be in hotter water than I would. It's not likely that anything will happen to an Olympic gold medal winner who's been applauded by the Führer."

"Nobody's immune."

"Oh, you and Araminta! Everybody. Always making me feel so rotten being German!" Käthe cried. Weariness rolled over her. "I didn't mean to sound so childish. It's been a long day."

She was in bed when there was a quiet tap on the guest-room door.

Aubrey's ears were crimson as he dropped a slip of paper on the counterpane. "Against my better judgment," he said. "Memorize it, then tear it up."

"Thank you, Aubrey, thank you. You're absolutely topping."

"In small pieces," he said, stumbling on the rug as he hurried from her bedroom.

She looked down at the card.

Christian Schultze
Telephone E2 11 21

III

Käthe love,

You've been gone twelve hours and already the country seems decimated. That's the good news. The bad news is I've been on the phone all morning and it seems the world's flocking to and from Europe. The only available August passage arrives at Bremen on the twenty-first, and the only available passage home leaves Bremen on the nineteenth. As you can see, a minor problem in logistics. So I've arranged to come over during the Christmas break.

Here the handwriting switched to pencil and grew more uneven.

My pen just ran out of ink.

Käthe, I think about all the times we've had together here in New York, but the memory that comes to my mind most often is of you running the two-hundred-meter race. Everything about you seemed right, the long platinum hair streaming out behind you, those fine legs pumping in a long stride, the other parts looking great too. When you crossed the finish line, you looked up at me. The stadium was jam packed and screaming, yet somehow I felt we were the only two people alive on the planet.

I need to get this letter in the mail right away or it won't catch you on the day you're in London, so I'm not going to read any of this junk to see if it makes sense.

He had forgotten to sign his name.

THIRTEEN

I

The German border was all efficiency. Visas and passports were collected and returned to the first-class compartment while the customs inspector selected and opened one suitcase from each passenger—how different from the welter of dirty and clean clothes that had spilled from their luggage in the customs shed at Southampton. Käthe's homecoming pleasure lasted until the train started again and they chugged past a bench adorned with a JUDEN VERBOTEN sign.

As the sunlit farmland rushed by, doubts jumped in her mind. Wyatt had told—no, commanded—her to steer clear of the Leventhals' affairs. Aubrey had overflowed with dire warnings. *And let's say I do find out Herr Leventhal's in a camp, then what?* Sigi was the only person she knew with top-notch connections. Would Sigi, dear, sloppy Sigi, help her? SS Reichsführer Himmler held sway over the malignancy that was the concentration-camp system and Sigi, who admitted goodnaturedly that the warrior qualities of his Prussian forebears had skipped him entirely, had made it a point to avoid tangling with the black-clad SS. Even if he were willing, how could she ask her beloved half brother to stick his pudgy neck out for a complete stranger?

The side of her clenched hand was thumping involuntarily against the starched white antimacassar on the armrest. What was the point of attempting to be logical? She could no more ignore the judge's evasive and formal cry for help than she could soar like a bird above this train.

At the Anhalter terminal her parents and Sigi pushed their way through the dense crowd, Alfred and her brother bearing the requisite bouquets.

Driving out to Grunewald, Sigi and Käthe sat on the jump seats leaning toward Clothilde and Alfred, the four of them talking in quiet tones. Even so, and though the glass was shut between them and Gunther, the conversation remained guarded, centering on Euan's condition. *Willkommen in Berlin*, Käthe thought. Beautiful, neat, and orderly city where respected merchants and general-staff officers whisper their innocuous questions in front of a chauffeur who's a Party member.

"How did you find New York?" Clothilde asked.

"Uncle Humphrey and Aunt Rossie were wonderful to me. And the Fifth Avenue branch took my breath away—but I wrote that."

"And you didn't miss a sight," Sigi said.

"If Wyatt doesn't become a lawyer, he'll make a wonderful tourist guide." Käthe attempted to sound casual. "He showed me every nook and cranny of New York."

"You?" Alfred asked. "Where was that flapper cousin of yours?"

"Oh, Father! Nobody says flapper anymore. Lucky Araminta. She snagged herself a young man. Charlie Eberhardt, we met him on the *Duchess of York* going over."

"That's not a proper introduction, and I'm surprised that your aunt and uncle permitted him to call," Clothilde said. "Käthe, we're grateful that you behaved like a lady. It was the proper thing for your cousin to take you around."

Käthe turned to look out the window. Young men in earth-brown Labor Service uniforms swung along in unison, singing. The sunlight caught on spades shouldered like guns.

II

The next morning Käthe walked her bicycle to the Grunewald station, which was designed like a peak-roofed cottage to fit in with the wooded, rustic surroundings. Using the public telephone, she asked the operator for the number that Aubrey had so reluctantly given to her, then held her breath until the ringing ceased.

"Schultze here." The masculine voice with a coarse Berlin accent sounded angry.

"This is Käthe Kingsmith. You don't know me, but my cousin Aubrey asked me to look you up."

"So, Aubrey Kingsmith. How is our *Engländer?*"

"Fit as a fiddle. I saw him two days ago, on the way home from New York. He thought you might be able to tell me about a friend of a friend. Herr Heinrich Leventhal."

"Like the old department store?"

"Exactly."

"What is this, a joke? Aubrey knows I don't move in such exalted circles. But that cousin of yours is a lunatic. Tell me, is he still cracked about ancient Egypt? The last time I saw him he never stopped raving about our Tel el Amarna exhibit here in Berlin, you know, on the first floor of the New Museum."

"We've been there often together," she lied.

"In the afternoon, I'll bet. He was forever blathering how rotten the light was in the morning. He said he could see best around three. Can you beat that? Your crazy cousin even has a favorite time to look at that old junk."

III

By two-thirty, thick gray clouds had gathered threateningly, and Käthe carried an umbrella as she trotted across the statue-adorned Schloss Bridge to the island in the Spree River known as Museum Island because of its forest of museums. At the New Museum she paid her admission and bought a catalog. She was far too early. Climbing the broad staircase, she pretended to examine the grandiose murals, dawdling at the glass cabinets filled with papyrus. Her destination, the Tel el Amarna gallery, was almost empty. A somnolent guard leaned his chair back against the entry. Retreating from him, she studied limestone sculptures with the ferocity of a devout Egyptologist. She was poring over a small ebony head of the Pharaoh Akhenaton's mother when slow masculine footsteps came down the gallery, halting at her side. Her mouth went dry.

"Interesting old girl, isn't she? Can't accuse the artist of flattering her, can you?" The amused voice spoke in the patrician tones of the *Offizierkorps*.

Turning, she saw a tall, lean man in his late forties. The way his smile fit into the humor lines carved into his face was naggingly familiar, yet she was certain she had never met him. His cheeks were sunken, as if he were convalescing from a debilitating ailment, and his suit, too, seemed overlarge, yet despite this he had a youthfully raffish air. Without knowing why, she liked him.

"May I be so bold," he said. "Aren't you Käthe Kingsmith, our Olympic running champion?"

She nodded.

"I thought so," he said. "I'm Heinrich Leventhal."

The catalog slipped from her hands. She'd had no idea who would contact her, but it hadn't crossed her mind that it might be Heinrich Leventhal, whom she had pictured as the stiff, elderly German equivalent of the judge. She glanced swiftly around. Halfway between them and the distant guard a female tourist consulted her Baedeker.

"You seem startled?"

"I wasn't expecting you'd be here yourself."

Leventhal returned her catalog. "This seemed the safest place for us to meet. Akhenaton was the one pharaoh who permitted realism in art, doubtless why Berliners don't flock to this particular gallery nowadays."

"Herr Leventhal, I was wondering how I could help . . . uh, find out about your father?" She spoke rapidly and awkwardly. What could be more ridiculous than for her, a girl not long out of the *Lyzeum*, to offer aid to this urbane, confident man?

"Have you a connection in that other, better world, Fräulein Kingsmith?" He was smiling again. Now she knew why he had seemed familiar. Wyatt had this same wry grin. "My father died in 1928."

"*You*'re the head of Leventhal's—the Berliner?"

"Not since it was Aryanized. You expected somebody longer in the tooth, is that it?"

"Yes, I'd heard you won the Iron Cross."

"At twenty a man has those berserk moments. But who told you all this?"

"In New York I met Judge Leventhal—actually it was less than a fortnight ago. He'd heard a rumor that you were in a camp?" Her voice rose questioningly.

"It's more than a rumor. I spent three delightful months in Esterwegen, and the holiday only cost me ten thousand marks."

The sum was more than the price of a home. "You had to give *them* money?"

"Privileges of that sort are expensive. Tell me, has the judge had his surgery?"

"Surgery?"

"The last I heard was he had been considering whether to remove the poker and replace it with a spine."

She laughed.

"There, that's better. We're still allowed to laugh. I shouldn't make fun of the judge—after all, obviously the old boy was worried about me. But frankly we're nothing alike. The Leventhal family has lived here in Berlin for generations, so I looked down on him for moving to New York. Also I found him pompous and old fashioned. Obviously my opinion was dead off the mark. No fossil, the judge. He was avant garde. Nowadays every Jew in Berlin is struggling to follow him to America." Heinrich Leventhal shrugged. "When I went to New York as a very young man, I palled around with the son. Myron. What a sense of humor he had, poor fellow. He was killed, some sort of accident."

Staring at the ancient ebony sculpture, Käthe felt dishonest at not saying the unsayable, that her aunt had been Mrs. Myron Leventhal for six months.

"Fräulein Kingsmith"—his voice had lowered—"I take it

that you and your British cousin are of the same mind about our regime?"

"I'm ashamed of being a German," she murmured.

"Let's move on to Nefertiti," he said. They crossed the gallery to the exquisite painted limestone head. "Some papers have to be delivered to Herr Schultze in Neukölln," he said. "The person who should have taken them is ill, and it's best if I don't show up there too often."

"The Neukölln station's on my way home, almost."

"You won't be in any danger," he said, then paused. "Well, several degrees less danger than talking to a Jew in a museum from which Jews are barred. He's an Aryan."

"What's the address?"

"I took the liberty of giving you my catalog. It's in there with the papers. Please be careful, don't drop anything."

"I'll put it in my purse." She added awkwardly, "Herr Leventhal, isn't it possible for you and your family to leave the country?"

"My wife's dead. We had no children." He grimaced wryly. "Besides, I'm a Berliner. Does that sound strange to you? I'm no longer considered a citizen, yet in my own heart I remain quite the German. Besides, there's a lot of work to be done here. We're helping young people emigrate. I still have money, so I fork over the departure tax."

"How generous."

"Not at all. Better the kids should have a chance than for Herr Hitler to feather his nest. But we're talking too much, the guard's coming this way." Leventhal bowed with a grin that ridiculed his formality. *"Gnädiges fräulein,* I thank you in advance for going to Neukölln."

IV

Before 1933 Neukölln, a working-class quarter, had been home to a large number of labor-union supporters, but now the labor slogans painted on walls were gone. The leaders of the unions had been killed or were in concentration camps and the erstwhile membership, gone underground, were known to each other as beefsteak Nazis—brown shirted on the outside, red inside.

The S-Bahn passengers, most of them factory workers, jolted along in weary silence. The rain had started and the crowded car smelled of wet synthetic wool, perspiration, and cheap cigarettes. Käthe got off at the Neukölln station, following the conductor's directions along winding, shabby cobbled streets. Herr Schultze's building was typical of Berlin in that each courtyard led to another. At the third courtyard Käthe went inside, climbing stairs that smelled of boiling potatoes, sauerkraut, and rancid bratwurst, peering her way along the unlit corridor to 2D.

Her knock was answered by a deeply wrinkled man. Short with thick, rounded shoulders and a grumpy expression, wearing a cardigan and carpet slippers, he was anything but a heroic figure. Yet Käthe knew he was risking his freedom, if not his life, with his anti-Nazi activities.

"Herr Schultze?" Käthe asked.

"Well?" he barked. "What idiotic cause are *you* collecting for?"

She took the catalog from her purse. "I believe you lost this."

"Come on in," he said in a tone only slightly less cantankerous. "And don't drip that umbrella across the floor, leave it out there." In the windowless hall he flipped with nicotine-stained fingers through the pages of the catalog, deftly extracting two stamped visa forms, pocketing them.

As he opened the door on a tiny sitting room crowded with furniture, there was a rustling sound. A little girl with black pigtails slipped into a bedroom. Not commenting on the child, he turned on the radio. A Schubert sonata overrode their conversation.

"You came by the bus?" he asked.

"The S-Bahn."

"Good, good. On your way back you'll walk the kid to a house on the Reuterplatz. I was planning to take her myself, but this is better."

"Is she—"

He held up his hands. "Listen, the less you know the better off we all are." He went to the curtained corner with a tiny stove top, pouring two mugs of coffee.

"You can count on me," Käthe said.

"It's good to know that all Germans haven't turned into Nazi weasels."

"You won't tell Aubrey, will you?"

"Fräulein, didn't I just make it clear that this is no Kaffee-klatsch? I don't talk, you don't talk, none of us talks. Jabbering's dangerous." He lit a fresh cigarette from the butt. "So. You'll run an occasional errand?"

"Anytime."

"Go in and help the kid to change."

A few minutes later a young woman holding an umbrella over herself and a dark-haired little girl in a Jungmädel uniform passed the windows of the *kneipe*, the corner bar. None of the beer drinkers paid any attention.

After dinner Käthe wrote a long letter to Wyatt, her heart pounding as she filled the pages. She could not mention what lay foremost in her mind—the familiar mordant smile on Heinrich Leventhal's thin face, the gruff, chain-smoking old man, the dark-haired child's small hand trembling in hers. Each word she wrote, therefore, seemed a lie.

THREE
1938

Guns not butter.
— Nazi slogan

SPONTANEOUS UPRISINGS CONTINUE
TO PUNISH JEWS FOR BRUTAL
SLAYING OF VOM RATH

Headline in *Völkischer Beobachter*, November 10, 1938

FOURTEEN

I

In September the doctors released Euan. An ambulance drove him to the Mayfair flat, and a heavy-hipped Scottish nurse helped him into his own bed, Elizabeth hovering in attendance. After a few days of having his wife flutter over his bed, he sent her packing back to Quarles. Araminta stayed on in London, lunching and shopping with friends, returning to change and kiss her father's balding head before she went dancing with her young men.

Aubrey felt obligated to remain in the flat to keep an eye on the convalescent. He finished his novel, now entitled *The Thousand Years,* corrected the typos—he found a great many—and packed the pages in a box, carrying it on foot all the way to Hampstead, where Keiffer Press was located.

He passed the next week looking over the carbon copy. Every page seemed a betrayal of the truths he had attempted to pin down, the emotions he had experienced in the writing. He turned hot and red-faced as he imagined the editors at Keiffer Press laughing over certain passages.

Then, on a windy October day when Aubrey was having a cup of tea alone in the lounge hall, the doorbell rang. It was the second afternoon-mail delivery, and there was a letter for him on Keiffer Press stationery. Aubrey carried it to his room, standing at his window while a Rolls-Royce pulled up to the mansion opposite. The two chauffeurs bowed as a stately fur-coated woman was admitted by a liveried footman. Aubrey wasn't watching the Mayfair street scene. He was staring down at the envelope. Drawing a breath to steel himself, he pulled at the flap.

> Dear Mr. Kingsmith,
>
> Mr. Keiffer has requested that I pass on his admiration for your work. The entire house is enthusiastic about *The Thousand Years.* It is a finely wrought novel, a serious novel. Exposing as it does the cancer of our times, we will endeavor to ensure that it reaches a broad readership.
>
> Publishing this, your first book, is a source of honorable pride to us, and needless to say, we look forward to a long and fruitful relationship. We at Keiffer Press are firmly convinced that the finest in British literature and the name Aubrey Kingsmith will become synonymous.

Aubrey straightened his shoulders. First grinning, then laughing, he raised his hand, lifting an imaginary hat in a victorious gesture.

All at once his face drained of pleasure. He dropped on his bed, staring up at the ceiling.

He was realizing that the name Kingsmith couldn't be joined with the finest in British literature, at least not in a novel depicting the dark side of the Third Reich.

Hadn't he met enough refugees who refused to speak of any ill treatment for fear of endangering relatives still in Germany? What fatal blind spot had prevented him from seeing that he couldn't publish the novel under his own name? The answer was only too obvious. He had longed to dazzle his family—to dazzle Käthe.

Still lying on the bed, Aubrey reached to his bedside table for the notepad and pencil. Lifting a knee, he rested the pad and began to draft a letter that would express his gratitude at Keiffer Press's belief in his novel. The second paragraph, by far the longer, he devoted to the urgent need for pseudonymous authorship and a change in title. If this were not agreeable, the manuscript would be withdrawn—

The phone rang outside in the hall. He lifted his head, listening. He heard the murmur of the maid. Heavy, lagging footsteps, then his father bullying some hapless Kingsmith employee.

Aubrey set his notepad on his concave stomach, pressing his hands over his eyes. Here was a decision that—unlike the one he had just reached regarding anonymity—he had been brooding over since he'd first seen Euan lying pale and comatose in the Harley Street hospital.

To be at Kingsmith's or not to be. . . .

You know the answer already, he told himself. *Go ahead, leap onto the pyre of duty. But don't expect the least praise ever, ever will be directed your way by that raging, pitiful voice.*

II

Later that same afternoon he told his father the novel had been rejected.

"Didn't I tell you all along that your scribbling would be a dead loss?" Euan, home from his slow promenade with his nurse to South Audley Street and back, sprawled on the lounge-hall sofa with a triumphant smile. "You had your way and now you need a job, is that it?"

"Yes, Father."

"What about Oxford?"

"It seems a waste of time."

"Well, there's nothing for it, then, but to give you a try in the business."

"Thank you."

"No more lolling about, Aubrey. I'm only taking you on with the clear understanding that you'll put your shoulder to the wheel."

"I expect to work."

"You'll learn the business from the bottom up, the way I did, or out you go." Euan, attempting to hide his delight, sounded gruffer than he intended.

Aubrey had known his father's inevitable response would smart. But he was taken by surprise that the hard, pale face propped up by sofa cushions could cause this choking tenderness in his throat.

"And don't try to run circles around me with your grandfather. He and I're in complete agreement. You'll be treated identically to every other apprentice."

". . . There's a seventeenth-century *Jungfrauenbecher,* and a matched pair of *Ananaspokal*—extremely rare, it says, but I don't have to tell you that, Grandfather. And a *Reisenpokal,* described as an unusually excellent example of Wenzel Jamnitzer's work." Aubrey was reading the inventory of German drinking vessels to Porteous. The pair were lunching in the wainscoted grill of the Connaught. It was December, and Aubrey had been at Kingsmith's for two months. "Uncle Alfred's written a note at the bottom. 'Each of the pieces is exceptionally fine, but we're already overloaded on high-priced items, and quite a few of our customers have their own sources.' " Aubrey looked up. "I suppose that's the most tactful way of saying that high-ranking Nazis are taking over Jewish collections."

"Filthy thieves."

"I'd like to take a look."

"You? Didn't you read that Alfred has to decide in a few days? And this is the heart of the Christmas rush."

"I'll take an airplane. I won't be gone more than three days, including Sunday. Grandpa, I have an American customer, a brewer, filthy rich, coming in. He's keen on early tankards and that sort of thing."

"Mr. Kingsmith, sir." The skeletal old waiter set down their plates of mutton—Porteous's was discreetly sliced in small pieces.

After the waiter had hobbled away, the sightless yet penetrating eyes rested on Aubrey. "Euan will pretend to be furious that I'm letting you gad about during our busiest time." Though Euan hadn't yet returned to work, he kept close tabs. "But if you handle your American brewer chap right, he'll be very proud—not that he'll tell you. Go ahead, my boy. Safe journey."

III

Lines of rain dashed across the small round windows as the plane descended at Tempelhof airport. Aubrey, who had vomited twice during the long, bumpy flight from Croydon, again felt queasy, but he forced himself to take in the scene rushing toward him. There were far more hangars than at the London airport and raincoated soldiers patrolled everywhere. He knew by now that German airports were built with military use in mind, and that the pilots and navigators of commercial flights were Luftwaffe officers who knew the aerial views of the capitals of Europe as well as the lines in their own palms.

As they bounced onto the runway, the pleasant young Lufthansa stewardess in her nurse's uniform smiled encouragingly at him. Aubrey turned away. *Germans,* he thought. He knew Clothilde, he was on friendly terms with Sigi, he had studied Nietzsche, Schopenhauer, and *Mein Kampf,* this year he had pored over every German periodical he could lay his hands on as well as having those long conversations with refugees. Even so, Germans remained a conundrum to him. How could this nice, open young nurse and the millions of others like her have fallen for a hatemonger whose sole honest emotion appeared to be a virulent anti-Semitism?

The props were still spinning noisily as he descended the aluminum ladder.

"Aubrey!"

Käthe, wearing a belted trench-coat, was running across the wet tarmac. He splashed through the icy rain toward her. She pressed her cool, damp cheek against his, and he inhaled the delicate fragrance that he suspected was not bottled by a perfumer, like Araminta's scent, but unique to Käthe. When they reached the bargelike old Steyr, Aubrey glanced around for the neckless, officious chauffeur, Gunther.

"I've taken driving lessons," Käthe said, laughing. "Get on in. Compared to flying it's relatively safe."

The parking area was being enlarged. Aubrey suffered a relapse of nausea as the car bounced over a stretch of unfinished roadway where raincoated men wielded shovels. Large signs proclaimed DASS WIR HIER ARBEITSENVERDANKEN WIR UN-

SEREM FÜHRER—this work is being done thanks to our Führer. Aubrey had seen similar signs posted throughout the Third Reich. Citizens were kept well informed whence the blessings of prosperity flowed. They turned onto the smooth roadbed and his nausea abated.

"What about those driving lessons?" he asked. "Did you take them when you began helping Schultze?"

"He told you about that?" she asked in surprise. Schultze had maintained his original closemouthed truculence.

"Just a stab in the dark. But, Käthe, I know you."

"A few minor odds and ends—it's nothing."

"Nothing? With so many labor sympathizers in Neukölln, don't you think the Gestapo keeps tabs on every apartment building?"

"I've been to his flat once."

"What do you do, then?"

"Oh, drop off small things, drive somebody, that's all."

"God knows I'm all for Schultze, what he's doing is tremendous. But he's a man. You're a girl. And you've done enough."

The windshield wipers threw slapping shadows across her profile, and there was a set to her delicate chin. "Shall I take you to the house first?" she asked. "Or are you agog to see the collection?"

His anxieties unresolved, he said, "The shop, please."

IV

Alfred met his nephew at the shop door, beaming warmly. Despite his pleasure his innate dignity prevailed and he shook Aubrey's hand, offering congratulations on the courageous journey by air as if he were an ambassador welcoming a foreign dignitary. In much the same ceremonial tone he inquired about Euan's health and that of the rest of the family; they proceeded through the shop. The showcases were as dark and crowded as those on Bond Street, and, as in London, sprigs of holly in silver goblets signaled the season. Here, too, fur-clad matrons sat firmly planted in chairs, waiting for the scurrying clerks to place the merchandise they requested on black velvet squares.

Alfred's office in the rear overlooked a narrow service courtyard. On fine days the clerestory window didn't give much light, and in bad weather brown shadows washed the tan walls and maroon carpet. Even by this wan illumination the silver, gold, and vivid enamelwork glittered.

Aubrey sank to his knees, examining the treasure trove of antique drinking vessels. There were huge cups shaped like fantastic birds and animals, there were huge *Jungfrauenbecher,* there were medieval wedding cups, royal christening mugs, archducal goblets, drinking horns heavy with sculptured gold stags. The workmanship from various centuries was uniformly magnificent—many pieces might well have taken a master craftsman over a year to adorn.

"Rather splendid, what?" Alfred asked.

"I'm completely bowled over."

"Two generations of connoisseurs had a hand in the collecting."

"Whose is it?"

Alfred glanced around the empty office before responding. "Heinrich Leventhal."

"Of Leventhal's? He died? We should have seen something in the papers."

"He's quite well. It's not an estate sale, but you know the situation we have here, certain people needing to sell." Alfred lowered his voice and gave a little cough at this indiscretion. "There aren't many places Herr Leventhal could dispose of this lot. Still, I didn't wish to take advantage of another's misfortune, so I let him set the price. Aubrey, it's unbelievably low. Our three branches can turn a handy profit—"

"Three?"

"By a stroke of luck Wyatt lands tomorrow. It's his law school's holiday and he'd made plans to join us at Garmisch-Partenkirchen." The Alfred Kingsmiths owned a chalet in the Bavarian Alpine resort. "When this proposition came up, I cabled New York as well as London—naturally I couldn't mention Herr Leventhal's name. Wyatt had already sailed, but Humphrey and Rossie cabled back that if our branches go ahead, they were in, too, and Wyatt could make the decision about what should go to America. You and Kate had a lot to talk about on the way in from the airport, otherwise I'm certain she would have mentioned your cousin would be here too."

Aubrey used both slightly shaky hands to heft an intricately worked silver-and-gilt goblet encircled by a green enameled dragon. "Was this on the inventory, Uncle Alfred? It doesn't look German. More like late Italian Renaissance."

Alfred's eyes beamed behind the thick lenses. "You're a true Kingsmith, my boy. That particular piece wasn't offered with the rest, but Herr Leventhal evidently needs a bit more money. That cup's a gem. It's attributed to Cellini."

V

After dropping Aubrey off, Käthe had traveled another long block on Unter den Linden in the direction of Museum Island. The immense Kaiser's Palace was scaffolded for painting. The lime trees that lined the pavements and edged the center walkway were leafless. She waited as a policeman held up his hand at the busy corner of Friedrichstrasse, then parked in front of Schloss-Konditorei. This was a slow hour for the famous coffeehouse-café. Fortunately a particular table near the window was free. The waitress with the long, placid face came over. Ordering coffee and a Turk's-head cake, Käthe pretended to relax, gazing in the direction of the equestrian statue of Frederick the Great. The aroma of Schloss-Konditorei was different nowadays. A recent government regulation banned the use of butter, and now the less tempting smell of margarine prevailed.

Paying, Käthe fumbled with her purse, "dropping" an envelope that contained a badge of the Nazi Women's League. The placid-faced waitress slipped it into her leather change bag. The badge was for a Jewish woman who needed to appear thoroughly Aryan as she traveled to the Belgian border for an illegal exit.

VI

The following afternoon, Sunday, was clear and cold. Aubrey, wearing a Fair Isle pullover under his tweed jacket, sat in his uncle's dining room frowning at the inventory spread in front of him as he worked out prices for the collection—pricing was a task he particularly disliked. The car pulled into the porte cochere. This morning Wyatt had docked at Hamburg and boarded the *Flying Hamburger* to Berlin. Clothilde and Alfred, who took a weekly sabbath hike in the Grunewald Forest, acceded easily when Käthe volunteered to meet him at the Lehrte station. Feeling a sneak yet unable to help himself, Aubrey stood to watch.

Wyatt was at the wheel. *Why didn't I take the driver's seat at Tempelhof yesterday?*

Tanned, strong, and invincibly American in his broad-shouldered suit worn without a hat or overcoat despite the chill, Wyatt jogged around the tall old Steyr to help Käthe out. Hands still clasped, they gazed at one another. Though separated by double-paned glass and Mecklenburg lace curtains, Aubrey could see the oddly atypical tenderness of Wyatt's smile, the radiance illuminating Käthe's pure oval face.

Before coming inside they went down the grass and stood by the Olympic oak saplings.

"See what good care I've given yours," Käthe said. "It's taller than mine."

He linked his little finger in hers. "Did I ever tell you that you look like a sluttish angel?"

"Sluttish?"

"Hey, I'd forgotten how easily you blush. Sluttish as a compliment. Meaning I wish we were married and in bed."

"It's wonderful having you here."

"It's swell being here. The swastikas, the saluting, the *Heil Hitler*'s, those wonderful signs JUDEN VERBOTEN. Thank God we'll soon be back home."

"When will you talk to Father?"

"The minute I get him alone. Think the Kingsmith oaks will transplant?"

"Absolutely," she said.

Sigi came to the Grunewald house for dinner. After Clothilde and Alfred had retired, the four young people gathered around the logs blazing in the cavernous drawing room. Käthe returned twice to the kitchen for bottles of dark Schultheiss beer: the conversation, growing more candid, turned to the subject of Hitler.

"I don't like the man any more than you do," Sigi said, shrugging in his good-natured way. "But you must accept that a vast majority of Germans are solidly behind him. As far as they're concerned, he's worked miracles."

"God," Wyatt said.

"It's easy for you and me to dismiss him." Sigi took a drink, depositing a little foam on his upper lip. "But none of us have ever worried whether the bagful of paper marks we set out with to the bakery would be enough to buy a loaf of bread when we arrived. We haven't seen our children's legs bowed with rickets and their teeth come in black and crooked." He paused reflectively. "After the war the entire country was bankrupt, and the Treaty of Versailles was very hard on us. It's not many years since the country was lining up at the corner soup kitchens. An unpleasant number of times I saw men I knew waiting. God, the despair in their expressions, the shame when we recognized each other. At first I tried to help out, a loan or a meal. But that made matters worse. Soon I politely looked in the other direction. What a demoralizing way to live your life. At that time there was no hope things would get better."

"It's rough," Wyatt said. "We've still got a depression."

"We call ours the Slump," Aubrey added in the same bleak tone.

Käthe said, "Dr. Goebbels and the Ministry of Propaganda pour it on thick that Hitler and only Hitler led us out of the bad times."

"The Aryan Moses," Wyatt said.

Everyone chuckled.

"And now," Aubrey said quietly, "he intends to lead Germany into the promised lands of Europe."

"Aubrey, Aubrey." Sigi shook his head genially. "It's not like you to exaggerate."

"You honestly believe he'll stop with the Rhineland?" Aubrey asked.

"The Rhineland is part of the Reich," Sigi said.

No hint of acrimony had entered the conversation, yet Käthe, sitting on the ottoman, shifted uneasily. The twin loyalties were tugging at her. "Yes," she said. "All we did was march into our own country. How would you have felt if we'd won the War, Aubrey, then imposed a treaty that chopped away Cornwall? Wouldn't you have cheered your Prime Minister when he got it back?"

"One guess who's next on the list," Wyatt said.

"List?" Sigi asked. "There's no list."

"What about the demonstrations in Austria?" Aubrey asked. The fire cast red shadows across his intent face.

"Austrian Nazis," Sigi said. "Austrians in Austria, nothing to do with Germany."

Aubrey asked, "So there's no buildup for a war?"

"War?" Käthe asked. A log burned through, falling loudly, and she jumped. "Whatever are you talking about, Aubrey? There's nobody in the Reich with the least interest in another war, is there, Sigi?"

Sigi was lighting his pipe. Blowing out the match, he smiled at her. "The Bendlerblock's absolutely against any kind of combat." His uncle's adjutant, he worked with the general on Bendlerstrasse at the High Command buildings, informally called the Bendlerblock. "The top brass see war as the worst possible disaster. Even if Hitler wanted another war, which he doesn't, he wouldn't get them to agree."

"So the general staff doesn't necessarily go along with your Chancellor?" Aubrey asked.

"A few of them admire him. Most of them see him as a shoddy opportunist," Sigi responded, then gazed into the bowl of his pipe. "Still, he's confident and decisive, and we Germans have always been good followers." He gave a good-natured shrug. "Take me, for instance. Did you ever see anyone less suited for a military career? But here I am, wearing a uniform because my grandfather commanded me to follow the family tradition."

"Okay, Sigi," Wyatt said. "Granted Adolf stepped into this vacuum, this horde of obedient *volk* awaiting a man who would give them orders. Should I take that to mean the good, loyal flock, including the generals, support his racial policy?"

"God knows I despise it." Sigi's expression changed to earnestness. "Nothing's gotten any worse for the Jews since the Olympic Games."

"Wunderbar!" Wyatt said.

"We've just dug our way out of a deep, rotten hole," Sigi responded. "So don't think too badly of us, eh, Käthe?"

Käthe didn't hear her half brother. She was watching Wyatt's baffled, angry face.

Sigi glanced at her. Reaching out his thick arms to grasp Wyatt's and Aubrey's hands, he said, "We're all friends, and our countries will remain friends. So let's stop upsetting my baby sister with politics."

VII

Clothilde had put Aubrey and Wyatt in the same guest room. The red coils of the small electric heater did little to dispel the chill, and both men undressed rapidly.

Wyatt switched off the light. "Hitler's sold the Germans some bill of goods," he said.

"Not all of them."

"Bull! Sigi's a decent guy in every way, yet even he's convinced that the great leader is a staunch pacifist and in the fullness of time will come to love the Jews."

"Sigi's a German, that's all. Don't you stand up for your country?"

"Käthe thinks the Führer's pretty okay too."

"You will not pigeonhole her as a Nazi!"

After a pause Wyatt said, "Jesus, I never heard you so snippy. Does that mean what I think it does?"

"Good night," Aubrey said. "Pleasant dreams."

After a long pause Wyatt said, "So you're gone on her too? I'll say one thing for you. You sure kept your feelings well hidden."

"That's how we English are. Reserved."

"Look, you might as well know that I'm out of my mind about her. We're going to be married. I'd kill to keep her."

"No need to issue warnings, Wyatt. Any fool can see that I don't stand a ghost of a chance. Marry her quickly, take her as far away as possible from here. You have my every cousinly blessing."

Wyatt's mattress creaked. "She's half English. Why should she feel so damn obligated to the Third Reich?"

"The von Graetzes have a code of honor that's been bred in the bone for nearly a millennium. They might look modern, Wyatt, but they're still the Teutonic knights and their ladies. Sigi's got the motto in his room. Roughly it translates into 'Allegiance to country, fidelity to sworn pledge.' "

"Big deal."

"It is to a von Graetz. They give allegiance to the Reich, they never go back on a promise. Käthe can't renounce that side of her any more than she can forget the English part." Aubrey sighed. "This talk of divided loyalties is all Greek to you, isn't it?"

Wyatt turned over and his voice was muffled. "Aubrey, there's a lot you don't understand about me. Divided loyalties happen to be my field of expertise."

FIFTEEN

I

"Well, what do you think, Wyatt?" Alfred asked, gesturing at the glitter of drinking vessels.

Though Wyatt lacked both Aubrey's depth of knowledge and loving respect for antiques, his aesthetic sense told that he was looking at virtuoso craftsmanship. Whistling, he said, "Fabulous, but too rich for our blood. Mother and Dad'll back me up on this. Your average American customer wants flash, nobody'll pay the price for museum quality."

"No need to worry on that account. The collection's going cheap. The poor devil has to sell. A Jew."

"It's an ill wind."

"He set the price," Alfred added hastily. "I don't know the ins and outs of the immigration policy, but he's buying exit permits for quite a number of his people."

"Uncle, give him ten thousand marks more than he asked."

"What?"

"Translated into dollars, that's how much is in my bank account."

"That would not set a good precedent," Alfred said, regaining his equanimity. "One doesn't know what might happen to wholesale prices if it got about that we were overly generous with Herr Leventhal."

Wyatt's carelessly handsome features twisted into a strange grimace. "Who?"

"Herr Leventhal, the seller."

"Leventhal?"

"You'd recognize the name if you'd been here in the old days. Leventhal's was Berlin's largest department shop, bigger than Harrods. It still is, for that matter, only now it's under new management and called the Berliner. Herr Leventhal's family founded the company. A very decent sort, a touch sarcastic for my tastes, but a gentleman. These"—Alfred gestured at the treasure trove that covered his floor—"were collected by his father and himself."

The boy had gone quite pale under the tan. "Uncle, where's the toilet?"

"Out the door and to your left," Alfred said hastily.

After his nephew had barged out, Alfred rubbed his hands together to warm them. Pay more than the asking price? Who ever heard of such a thing? But there was an unpredictability to Humphrey's son—he was the wild card in the Kingsmith deck, full of contradictions. Alfred blew warm breath on his fingers with a trace of irritability. People with jagged character traits had always disturbed him. And here was Wyatt. He had been rudely distant at the Games, yet most kind to the girls when they were in New York. He had been graduated from university summa cum laude so must be highly intelligent, yet he forever spouted those ridiculous remarks that Americans called wisecracks. Though quick tempered, he didn't hold on to his anger —and Kingsmiths were a tenacious breed with their possessions, even their anger. Now this offer of a considerable sum— it must be his entire inheritance from Rossie's parents—to some total stranger. Yet despite his nephew being so irresponsibly complex, there was a decency, a warmth, a generosity, to the boy. Alfred felt a rush of affection.

II

"Sorry, Uncle." Wyatt had returned from the lavatory.

"You look a bit pale about the gills. That sausage must have been a bit off. The Hotel Central's dining room used to be reliable, but nowadays it doesn't matter where you are, the menu's filled with these ersatz concoctions. I'll telephone Gunther to collect you."

Wyatt shook his head. "Not yet. Uncle Alfred, I have something to discuss with you."

"No need, my boy. I've thought it through. None of us would wish to take advantage of anyone's bad luck. Kingsmith's will put in the extra amount."

"It's not about that." Wyatt paused. "Uncle Alfred, bear with me. The truth is I don't know if I'm coming or going. It's been like that since the Olympics."

"The Games?"

"Since I met Käthe."

"Kate? My Kate? What does she have to do with what you had for lunch?"

"That's just it. I can't eat, I can't sleep, that's how crazy I am about her. She feels the same way." He drew a breath. "That's what I'm asking. About marrying her."

Alfred wondered bemusedly if this was one further example of his nephew's incomprehensible American wit. "You're asking for Kate's hand?"

"And the rest of her, Uncle. It won't be a plush life at first, but later on . . ." The boy's smile was forced. "I'll make her happy, I swear it."

"Kate never said a word to us."

"We agreed that I should be the one to talk to you."

"But damn it all!" Alfred cried, breaking his decades-long, self-imposed ban against even the mildest curse. "You're cousins! First cousins!"

A muscle jumped near Wyatt's mouth. "Genetically speaking we're on good ground, then," he said. "Other than nearsightedness, which neither of us has inherited, the Kingsmiths are a healthy crew."

"She's a schoolgirl."

"Not anymore. She's eighteen."

"A child." Alfred, unable to look into the brown eyes, stared out the clerestory window. Snowflakes drifted, snow mounded high on the ledge. Why hadn't Rossie had the decency to stay home and protect her niece? Women were meant to chaperone young girls, not dash about bossing their husbands' businesses. Why hadn't Humphrey warned him something was going on?

"She'll always be the most important thing in my life."

"Let me think about it," Alfred said in a strangled tone.

III

Alfred's impulse was to rush to the mansion in the Grunewald and tell his wife—he deferred to her judgment in all matters beyond this shop. He was too much a creature of habit to detour from his routine of locking up after his employees departed. All afternoon he slumped at his desk, occasionally removing his pince-nez to wipe his eyes and blow his nose.

Arriving home, he climbed heavily to his bedroom, sliding the bolt on himself and his wife as he did for their unchanging yet astonishingly pleasurable bouts of passion. As he described his interview with Wyatt, his German grammar became imprecise and his accent stronger. Clothilde's expression retained its normal placidity, but her spine crumpled until the knobs and swirls of the chair back cut into her ample body.

She said nothing until he had finished his story. "It was a mistake allowing your father to send Käthe to America."

And they began listing the impediments to the marriage.

Unlike Alfred's, Clothilde's objections were not based on consanguinity: to her mind this was a geographical and cultural misalliance. Her daughter, from a family who had commissioned several of the works of Mozart and subsidized Goethe, who could trace her ancestry in a direct line to the thirteenth century, living in an uncultured, pistol-crazed desert!

"Impossible," they both kept repeating. Yet their expressions softened with memory. Hadn't their romance been played out against the bitterest criticism as well as a viciously devastating war?

"It's too large a decision for a young girl," Clothilde pronounced. "They must wait until Käthe's of age."

"Absolutely. In the meantime let's hope they change their minds."

"If they haven't, we'll announce the engagement at Christmas of 1940."

Alfred voiced his worst fear. "She's never had any serious entanglements, the child. He's a good-looking young chap." Alfred's close-set ears reddened. "What if he talks her into . . . ?"

"My daughter is not a scullery maid."

Alfred, who wouldn't arrive in Garmisch-Partenkirchen until Christmas Eve, had intended suggesting that his wife keep a close eye on the lovers. Intimidated, he mumbled, "No, no, of course not. Kate's a lady through and through."

IV

"Three years, Mother?" Käthe whispered.

It was after dinner on the same evening. The two of them were in the *Damenzimmer,* a small, brocade-walled room where Clothilde received her women guests.

"Three years from this Christmas," Clothilde said. "By then you'll be of age. Your father is explaining to Wyatt that you aren't ready to make such a decision." Alfred and Wyatt had just left the house—Alfred had bought three tickets to a boxing match, intending to go with both nephews, but Aubrey had disappointed him by returning to London a day early.

"We'll be on different continents—we might as well be on different planets."

"He may visit you on his holidays. And of course there'll be letters." Clothilde paused. "Listen to me. You think you're grown up, but you're very young, and so is Wyatt. He's in university still."

"Please, Mother, make it next year."

"We'll announce the engagement in 1940."

Käthe groaned. "That's forever. . . ."

"We have your word not to do anything rash?"

"Rash?"

"Elope. We prefer to trust you and Wyatt."

"I can't promise that."

"We have no choice, then. He may not visit you."

Käthe stared pleadingly into the placid, unlined face. But when did her mother ever compromise?

After a silence that was broken only by the ticking of the Biedermeier clock, Käthe sighed. "I promise."

"Say it."

"You know I never break my word."

"Käthe."

"I promise not to elope," Käthe cried, and darted from the snug room.

At this minute Gunther was driving Wyatt and Alfred through the softly falling snow.

Alfred had just laid out the rules for the delayed engagement. "Your aunt and I are in agreement," Alfred said. "Kate's far too young. After all, there is the matter of your being cousins, and that makes it much more of a decision. Besides, by 1940 you'll be a solicitor, able to support a wife—"

"I have money."

Alfred gripped the worn leather strap as the Steyr edged around a slow-moving convoy of military vehicles that included bicycles. "She's far too young. Do I have your word to wait?"

Wyatt stared out at the convoy. He said nothing.

"They agreed," Käthe whispered to Wyatt. He and Alfred had just hung their things on the coatrack and her father was heading for the dining room, where platters of bread and cold meat had been set out for their return.

"Yeah, to let us be engaged three years from now."

"Oh, how can we stand it?"

"Stand what?"

"Being apart three years."

"Who says we have to do that?"

"We'll see each other in the holidays."

"If I clerk and we're careful, we can make it."

"I promised Mother not to elope."

"You *what?*"

"They wouldn't have let us see each other."

"Once we're married, that'll be a breeze. You might even get sick of seeing me."

"I gave her my word."

"Wyatt, Kate, have a bite with me," Alfred called.

"Coming," Käthe called back. Resting her hand on Wyatt's cold cheek, she whispered, "I had to promise. I couldn't break their hearts. I couldn't bear not seeing you."

SIXTEEN

I

A blizzard in the Bavarian Alps deposited several feet of fresh powder snow but by December twentieth, when Clothilde, Käthe, and Wyatt arrived at the twin villages of Garmisch-Partenkirchen, the sky was a deep, intense blue and thick whiteness like whipped cream covered the Loisach Valley with its quaint, steeply pitched rooftops. The next three mornings Käthe and Wyatt joined the cheerful holiday crush on the trains snaking up snow-covered mountains to the gondola in the shadow of the soaring Zugspitze. They swooped down narrow, freshly covered trails until dusk.

Pleasantly weary, they passed their evenings in the snug, simple main room of the chalet. While Clothilde followed her schedule and read, Wyatt would crank the gramophone and play the records he'd brought from America—"In the Still of the Night," the Andrews Sisters' *"Bei Mir Bist du Schön,"* "I've Got My Love to Keep Me Warm."

At ten Clothilde would warm the butter-rich strudel and pour a little rum into the jug of creamy milk left by the cowherd's wife who came in to clean and cook—most of the locals ignored the government's stringent regulations about food.

Flanking the massive stone fireplace were doors to the pair of whitewashed bedrooms. Alfred and Clothilde's room was furnished with a large bed painted with worn floral Bavarian patterns; Käthe had a trio of narrow cots to accommodate female visitors. Guests of the stronger sex climbed the sturdy ladder in the corner, making do with the bunks set below the slanting pine beams of the attic. Promptly at ten-thirty Clothilde would retire, leaving Wyatt and Käthe to themselves. It was this blandly implicit trust that inhibited them from exchanging more than a few lingering good-night kisses before Wyatt climbed the ladder.

II

Sigi and Alfred were due to arrive on Christmas Eve. The night before, Käthe put on her nightgown then opened her window. The icy air cut deep into her lungs, yet instead of scurrying to bed as she normally did, she leaned her elbows on the window ledge, gazing at the blue glitter of moonlight on the majestic peaks. Smiling, she hummed the sinuous, romantic notes of "In the Still of the Night," then, moving dreamily, she climbed between the cold, starch-scented sheets, pulling the goose-down cover high. She shivered a few times, and then the feathers warmed her.

"Käthe?" Wyatt whispered at her door. "Asleep?"

"Not yet."

"Mind if I come in a sec?"

There was no doorknob. Käthe got up to pull the antiquated iron bolt, which needed both hands to draw it back. Her hair, loosened from its long braid, reached below her waist, a pale, cloudy cape silvered by the moon. The light also etched the slender curves of her body beneath the long, full nightgown.

Wyatt gazed at her. "I decided to hand over your present early," he said in a strangely pitched voice, then reached out to touch her hair.

She could scarcely breathe. "Come inside," she whispered.

"I shouldn't. . . ."

She put her arms around his waist, pressing against him. With a groan he buried his face in her hair, kissing the base of her neck. Just as she felt the drumming of his heart, so he felt the rapid beat of her pulse.

"Käthe," he murmured against her ear, "you're shivering."

"Trembling. . . ."

Lifting her, he carried her to the narrow bed.

She drew the feather quilt over his shoulders as he pushed up on one elbow, smoothing back her thick, cool hair and kissing her eyelids before he kissed her mouth. Her lips parted, the endless kiss became more and more passionate, and she drew down the ribboned straps of her nightgown. He buried his face between her breasts. A breeze rustled the tied-back curtains, faraway sleigh bells jangled. Without speaking they drew apart briefly to throw off their nightclothes. Naked bodies clasped, they were both slick with sweat. An entire orchestra of emotions played tumultuously within Wyatt. Love that was almost worship, lust, the desire to be part of her, but these were dominated by the need to bind her to him forever. The act he had forbidden himself seemed the sole bridge across the chasm her parents had placed between them—yet he couldn't quell the compunctions swirling through him.

"Käthe, love, I'd better go back upstairs."

"I want to."

"Love, I meant us to wait. . . ."

"Three years . . . ? Please, ah, please . . ."

His weight shifted onto her, and she moved her thighs apart. He caressed her until she moaned and bit his shoulder, then he guided himself into her. At the sharp pain she gasped.

He kissed her hair, her face, her throat, whispering incoherent endearments before he pressed again, and then she was moving in the same rhythm as he. A cloud passed over the moon, and neither noticed the darkness. Snow fell with a powdery thump from an eave above her window, but they did not hear. All at once Käthe was still, the same stillness that might be felt if the earth ceased its rotation, then spasms fluttered around Wyatt and his body was no longer his but transmuted into another being, their joined selves, and he raced yet faster into the mysterious darkness.

III

She drowsed. Waking, for a brief instant she imagined she was dreaming, but his body, the moisture gluing their legs together, was real.

"How long was I asleep?"

"A minute or so." He kissed her nose. "I never intended this to happen—oh, hell, why lie? The other guy, the civilized Wyatt Kingsmith, he didn't intend. The real me hasn't thought of much else since I saw you outside the Olympic Stadium." He kissed her nose. "What would you say about coming back home with me?"

She sighed. "Wyatt, it's impossible."

"Myself, I rank what we just did over their three-year plan."

"I love you so much. But they're only doing what they think is right. Besides, I gave my word."

"I didn't."

"Hush," she said, kissing him.

"I'm not going to give up, love, so be prepared." He rested his cheek against hers. He said, "Käthe, when we get another chance, I'll be careful."

"Careful?"

His chuckle was soft in the darkness. "Maybe you *are* too young. Birth control, ever heard of it?"

"In theory, not practice."

He chuckled again, rubbing his knuckle lightly over her lips. Then the mattress creaked as he rolled onto his back. "Käthe, did you have anything to do with Heinrich Leventhal bringing Uncle Alfred his collection?"

"No," she said, and though this was true, her face burned. She had told Wyatt nothing about her meeting with Herr Leventhal on Museum Island nor the activities that resulted from that afternoon.

"Just a thought." He took her hand, pressing it to his chest so she could feel his beating heart. "One thing you should keep in mind. What just happened, making love to you, was the best part of my entire life. If I live to be a hundred, it'll be the best part."

When she got up the following morning, she stumbled on a worn jewelry box. She pressed the catch. On the inset velvet lay a large oval amethyst centered with a star of tiny diamonds and seed pearls. Wyatt had folded a note inside the box. *Christmas*

1937. This brooch belonged to my great-grandmother Wyatt, who owned slaves. What's more appropriate than for you to receive it from your personal slave?

IV

Alfred and Sigi arrived on the afternoon train. That night they lit the beeswax tapers on the Christmas tree. After the traditional goose and gingerbread they bundled up and hurried through Garmisch. Candlelit trees shining in windows of the wide-eaved houses dimly outlined the scenes of peasant life painted on exterior walls.

Breath streaming, Clothilde and Sigi caroled:

> *"Stille Nacht*
> *Heilige Nacht*
> *Alles schläft*
> *Einsam wacht. . . ."*

Käthe, Alfred, and Wyatt joined them in English.

> "Silent night,
> Holy night,
> All is calm,
> All is bright. . . ."

There were two St. Martin's in the village of Garmisch. As a rule Alfred and Clothilde, like most of the holiday people, attended the newer one, the eighteenth-century onion-domed church. Tonight, however, they selected the medieval arches and faded frescoes of Old St. Martin's. The cold air smelled of sweat, heavy loden cloth, and strong Bavarian beer.

When they emerged, the church gateposts had been freshly affixed with signs: JEWS NOT WELCOME HERE.

Wyatt strode forward, yanking down both papers.

"What do you think you're doing?" Planted in front of Wyatt stood a man equally as tall but hugely thick in his clumsy mountain togs. With his feathered hat pulled low his bushy mustache seemed to divide his broad face in equal halves.

"What does it look like?" Wyatt responded, crumpling the signs onto the snow. "A hell of a birthday message."

"Is that a joke?"

"Stop me if I'm wrong, but we're celebrating Christ's birthday, aren't we? And wasn't he Jewish?"

"What sort of accent is that?"

"American."

The mustached giant glanced at the churchgoers who had gathered around them. "What can you expect from mongrel foreigners?"

"Go soak your head," Wyatt said, clenching his fists.

Alfred pulled at Wyatt's arm, muttering in English, "This is Bavaria, the politics are stronger here."

A shorter local had stepped forward. "Is he a Jew?"

The question that reverberated throughout the Third Reich.

"Are you crazy?" Sigi responded. "I'm Siegfried von Hohenau, and this is my cousin."

The burly man with the mustache glanced at Sigi's uniform topcoat, then bent for the paper signs. "Well, then, Herr Oberleutnant von Hohenau, if your American relation don't like the way we do things in the Reich, tell him to stay home, where he can put his tongue up the asses of his Jew friends."

Wyatt clenched his fists.

An unpleasant smile of satisfaction showed below the mustache. "So you want to fight, do you?"

"You're on, buster," Wyatt said, raising his fists.

Sidestepping the blow, the big man swung his enormous fists at Wyatt's stomach. The old one-two. Both blows connected. As Wyatt staggered backward, the second man gripped his right arm, twisting it behind him. The duo's movements showed a rehearsed quality. It struck Käthe that they must have provoked this sort of incident many times. As Wyatt struggled to free himself, the larger assailant landed a left hook.

Käthe didn't see the blood spout from Wyatt's nose. The churchgoers had converged on the fight.

"Where's a policeman?" Alfred shouted.

Sigi shoved through the crowd to help Wyatt. A hobnailed

boot was thrust out. Sigi tripped, expelling a dry little breath as he dropped into the snow mounded on the side of the path.

Wyatt had broken free. Shoulder muscles bunching, he landed a blow in the middle toggle of his huge assailant's jacket. The smack of the blow could be heard, then a grunt.

Fury contorted the mustached face. "You need a real lesson!"

"Enough!" Clothilde's voice rang with the command that can only be acquired through generations of unquestioned authority. "This is Christmas!"

The mustached man, who was aiming a murderous blow, stopped uncertainly. His cohort, arms raised to club Wyatt between the shoulders, lowered his hands with an uneasy smile.

"Go on home, all of you," Clothilde ordered.

The pair of fighters exchanged indecisive glances.

"Go home," Clothilde repeated.

"We'll be back," the original attacker snarled at Wyatt. "So you steer clear of trouble." He linked arms with his shorter comrade, and the two stamped along the road to Partenkirchen.

The crowd melted into the night.

Wyatt, wiping the blood from his nose, went to reach out a hand to Sigi. "Thanks for wading in."

"Wasn't much help, was I?" Sigi said with a good-natured laugh.

The following morning a wiry youngish policeman came to the chalet. Apologizing for disturbing their Christmas day, he jotted down notes about the incident, requesting to see their papers and Wyatt's passport.

"A Kingsmith family gathering," he said politely. "Herr Oberleutnant, you're a guest, I take it?"

"I have the honor to be Herr Kingsmith's stepson. Those two thugs provoked the fight."

"Well, I see that our American visitor has a black eye," responded the policeman, his face noncommittal.

Afterward, over a cup of coffee and butter *plätzchen,* he thanked them for their cooperation. "We like to keep order in the Reich," he said to Wyatt.

V

In the middle of January a letter arrived for Käthe on Kingsmith's custom-watermarked stationery with Rossie's monogram. The first page warmly told her what a delightful guest she had been the previous summer. The second page consisted of one paragraph.

> There are no married students at Columbia Law School. Wyatt is doing so well. If he makes a wrong move now, he could lose his chances to get into a top firm. He should be increasing his circle now, not settling down. As a European it must be difficult for you to understand the social influences at force here, but the friends he makes now could alter his entire life. Please don't take this the wrong way, dear. I only want what is best for Wyatt—and for you. The crux is that your parents are right. I couldn't agree more with them. Waiting three years to announce an engagement is by far the wisest course.

The writing blurred. Käthe was reading a hidden subtext. Wyatt would be far better off marrying an American girl.

VI

On March twelfth the Anschluss, the uniting of Germany and Austria, was achieved. The press was euphoric. There were photographs and newsreels of panzer divisions streaming over the Austrian border and being greeted by joyous crowds waving swastika flags and pelting flowers. In essence Austria was now a province of the Third Reich.

A few days after the Anschluss, Sigi invited his sister to a variety show at the Metropol. He picked her up, his amiable face oddly stern. Though the top of his touring car was closed, the air was as frigid inside as out. He handed her the car rug but didn't start the engine.

"What's wrong?" Käthe asked.

"Do you remember Otto Groener?"

"Isn't he the friend you went with on the walking tour of the Berchtesgadenland?"

"Yes, he's a Bavarian. He joined the Party early. At the time the Nazis were nobody—to be honest, I didn't know anything about them. Groener had been through hard times, and at school I found him a good chap. His swastika seemed harmless enough. We've been out of touch for years. Now he's over there on Prinz-Albrechtstrasse."

"God," Käthe whispered.

Himmler had taken over the School of Applied Arts and Design as well as the baroque Hotel Prinz Albrecht and other lesser buildings on Prinz-Albrechtstrasse for his terror agencies, the Gestapo and the SS, joining the basements into a prison with up-to-date torture methods. Now the street name was a synonym for dread in Germany.

"He's a higher-up in the Gestapo." Sigi inserted the ignition key. "Evidently all reports concerning visiting foreigners cross his desk."

"It's about Wyatt, isn't it?" she asked, shivering.

"Did you know Rossie was a widow when she married your uncle? Her first husband was related to the Leventhal department store family. He died only a few months before Wyatt was born."

"But how could the Gestapo find that out?"

"They'd done a preliminary check of Wyatt before the Olympics. The Kingsmith family comes and goes, they could be spies. Or so the Gestapo decided. The incident at Garmisch-Partenkirchen set them to snooping again."

"Aunt Rossie lives in New York, but her first marriage was in Boston, and her husband died there," Käthe said stubbornly. "Nobody in the family ever suspected. It's impossible for the Gestapo to have tracked down the Leventhal connection."

"Groener was very proud of the Gestapo's foreign intelligence. The bastards are nothing if not thorough."

Käthe stared at the curlicued silhouette of the porte cochere. "Don't tell anyone about Wyatt."

"Are you crazy? Of course I won't." Sigi started the motor, and it coughed violently. "Groener asked me to lunch to spill all this—as a favor to an old friend, he said."

"Wasn't he ashamed of spying on everybody?"

"Not in the least. But it chilled me to the bone. Käthe, our people probably won't issue Wyatt another visa. Even if they do, it's not safe for him to come here."

The variety show at the Metropol blurred by Käthe as if she were on a fast train. Her parents, she knew, would never permit her to go to New York. She must keep Wyatt out of the Reich. There was no way she could explain the situation. Therefore it behooved her to tactfully arrange some neutral meeting place. Yet as she sat tensed in the red plush theater seat at Sigi's side, her mind, cloaked in cold dread, refused to solve the problem.

SEVENTEEN

I

Though a mere one hundred and ninety-seven pages, C. Osmond's *Tarnhelm* (Keiffer Press, 2/6) is a major work by any standards. In light of the recent events in Austria, the novel is doubly important, for it makes a companion piece to the depressing newsreels and photographs.

The story is austerely simple. A young Englishman on a skiing holiday in Switzerland falls in love with a German girl of highly anti-Nazi sentiments. Later in the year he visits her home in Berlin to discover that she has disappeared. Her frightened family refuse to discuss the matter with him, her friends pretend nothing is amiss, insisting that she will return shortly. His search through the iron wall of the Nazi bureaucracy and then the terrible landscape of concentration camps makes the young hero realize that the Germans courageous enough to raise their voices against the current government, like the girl he loves, will disappear from sight as surely as though they have donned the title's magical helmet.

C. Osmond chooses each word with the care with which one would select a gem. The prose is lean and sinewy. There is not one false plea for sympathy nor a maudlin sentence.

Tarnhelm is a masterpiece.

II

Aubrey, at his desk in the glassed offices overlooking King-smith's, held the London *Times* of April 2, 1938, folded to the review.

He had changed the title of *The Thousand Years* to *Tarnhelm*—the cap of invisibility crafted by the Nibelung dwarfs of Teutonic myth—for the same reason that he had chosen a pseudonym: he wanted no connection to the novel. Yet as he reread the glowing review a leaden gloom settled over him. *What's the use of being down in the mouth? It's not as if you had any choice,* he told himself. But why were circumstances forever forcing him into decisions against personal happiness? From his tenth year throughout adolescence he had secretly nourished himself with the idea that Aubrey Kingsmith, skinny, nonathletic, shy, was actually the larva of a Great Author and eventually would spread his wings as one with Homer, Shakespeare, Tolstoy. It goes without saying that reviews of this ilk were part of the dream. At Oxford, when he had started to write seriously, he'd ceased indulging in such idiotic fantasies. And to be honest, writing the novel, even the inevitable frustrations, had been a kind of delirious ecstasy. *Tarnhelm* was its own reward. Yet on the other hand public acclaim of this type would have secured grudging praise from his father rather than a stream of back-biting reminders that his writing stint had been a complete and utter waste of time, not a penny brought in. Käthe, after reading the book, would have given him the glowing, dreamy smile that she bestowed on Wyatt—here Aubrey again lapsed into folly, imagining what Käthe might have done.

His telephone rang. Expecting his father with a list of commands, he hastily crushed the *Times* into his wastebasket. But Norbert Frognall, a desiccated second cousin, was on the line with an invitation to his club on St. James's Street, a club in which no tradesperson like a Kingsmith would ever be put up for membership. There was somebody who wanted to meet Aubrey. As Norbert Frognall said the fellow member's name, Aubrey's expression changed to reverent mystification.

III

As the short, rotund man with the unlit Romeo y Julieta cigar in his pudgy hand stamped across the gloomy "strangers" room, Aubrey pulled his shoulders back. Even if he hadn't known whom he was to meet, the sparse white hair, the hunch of shoulders, the scowl, the cigar, were instantly recognizable. Every Englishman knew this politician from scurrilous cartoons as well as photographs.

"Mr. Kingsmith?" A gruff yet sonorous voice. A firm handshake. "Winston Churchill."

Winston Churchill, though a backbencher, was the most controversial member of the House of Commons. An outspoken disciple of social justice, he had been born in Blenheim Palace, the grandson of the duke of Marlborough. He had held many Cabinet posts. He wrote prolifically for newspapers and magazines around the globe; his books were in every library. He had been called one of England's greatest men; he had been called a flamboyant fraud, a war lover, and a pathetic old bore. In 1916, as first lord of the Admiralty, he had been unfairly excoriated for the Gallipoli disaster. He had championed King Edward's recent ill-fated attempt to crown Mrs. Simpson his queen.

Almost alone Winston Churchill sounded the tocsin against Hitler. For this last reason he was currently being vilified as a warmonger.

Aubrey himself, during his pacifist phase, had shared the view of Winston Churchill as one dedicated to hurling the country back into the blood-soaked trenches. The Olympic summer, however, had altered vital circuits of Aubrey's brain. During their greetings he couldn't quell his admiring deference.

A butler was setting down a humidor and a bottle of Hine brandy.

"Drink?" Churchill asked.

"Please," Aubrey responded.

Waiting until the servant had scuttled to his shadowy station near the green-baize service door, Churchill took an appreciative sip. "Since we are colleagues," he said, "I shan't attempt a cagey game, but will lay my cards on the table."

"Colleagues, sir?"

"Both afflicted with the insatiable urge to put pen to paper, Mr. Kingsmith—or shall I say Mr. Osmond?" At Aubrey's start of surprise the pink, age-spotted face beamed with impish pleasure. "By either name, Mr. Kingsmith, you are younger by far than I anticipated. Might I call you Aubrey?"

"Please, sir. But how did you know about . . . ?"

"You hardly flatter me." Churchill was smiling. "There are a clear-sighted few who agree with my position on Herr Hitler, and Keiffer's one of them. When I looked into his author's identity, he gave me your name and mentioned that you were a connection of Frognall's." He raised his brandy. "To *Tarnhelm,* a fine novel."

Aubrey glanced around. Another member and his guest had their heads together in a faraway corner. "You've read it, sir?"

"Where do you think I got these reddened eyes? After I finished my own work, I stayed up the rest of the night with yours. Those scenes in the concentration camp, the smell of fear in the pulpit!"

"I didn't do either justice."

"No need to be so modest. A miraculous evocation," Churchill said. "It never fails to astonish me how blind many of our finest minds are to Herr Hitler and his goals. They consider him a rambunctious boy with his parades and his flatulent, howling bellicosity. They ignore the Saar, the Rhineland, and now Austria all under his belt. Will they keep their eyes closed until he's gobbled up the rest of Europe?"

"I'll do anything to help you, sir."

"Exactly what I was hoping you'd say. You've an acute instinct for the hidden horrors in the Third Reich. You travel there."

"Not often, and then it's a quick business jump. I'm in my grandfather's business—"

"Yes, Kingsmith's on Bond Street. Mrs. Churchill buys wedding gifts there."

"I know, sir, and we're honored," Aubrey said. "We have a branch on Unter den Linden."

Churchill showed no surprise. "Next time you're in Berlin, if you can drop me a report of what you observe . . ."

"It would be an honor, sir."

"I have no parliamentary sanctions, Aubrey. I can offer you no rewards."

"That's the last thing to worry about."

"Excellent." Churchill dropped his unlit, well-chewed cigar stub in an ashtray, then went about sniffing and lighting a fresh one with a ceremonious pleasure that reminded Aubrey of his grandfather. In this case, however, it was not an active old man camouflaging his blindness but a fisherman's ploy, giving out the line before reeling in the catch. Aubrey, aware of being the fish, felt a sharp hook of curiosity. So Churchill desired more from him than his word pictures of Berlin. But what?

Churchill took his first appreciative puff. "Is it possible for you to dine with us—myself and a friend, Major Judson Downes?"

So the line was to be stretched out farther. "I'd be delighted, sir."

IV

A male secretary telephoned with the address on Morpeth Terrace, which turned out to be just off Victoria Street, a block of bloodred brick flats opposite a Roman Catholic cathedral, within walking distance of Parliament and, or so Aubrey would learn shortly, two doors down from Morpeth Mansions, where Winston Churchill had his London flat. Major Downes, whose dinner jacket was neatly pinned at the left elbow, introduced himself with the information that Churchill could not join them until after the meal. Aubrey's ragged smile didn't hide his disappointment.

His host managed his cutlery in the one-handed American style, he spoke with an American accent, and at first Aubrey assumed him to be an American. But during dinner the major mentioned that he was Canadian and had lost his arm in 1917 at Flanders, where he had served in the trenches under Churchill. After the war Downes had returned to Canada, and though he didn't say as much, it was obvious that he had dug a considerable fortune out of his Manitoba mining venture. Three years ago, in 1935, he had retired, settling in London. He spent many of his weekends at Chartwell, the Churchill home in Kent.

Aubrey ate little. His curiosity had reached a high, whining pitch by quarter to eleven, when Churchill made his appearance. The major excused himself.

Slumping back in the largest of the armchairs, Churchill loosened his black tie and brushed a hand over cigar ash that had fallen on the cummerbund encircling his plump belly. "Aubrey, I've only met you once, but my instincts are first rate. You're a quiet, diffident man who does what must be done, not the sort to blow your own horn or sound off. In other words, completely trustworthy."

Pleasure warmed Aubrey. "That's most kind of you, sir."

"What I say now is so highly sensitive that it is known only to a few of our group."

"You have an organization, sir?"

"A small, weak one. However, we are sponsored by the highest in the land. Our monarch. King George has a small discretionary fund for secret operations if the kingdom is endangered, and it is His Majesty's belief that at this hour such is the case." Churchill's formal phraseology rumbled from deep within his slumped chest. "I'm telling you this to prove my confidence in you."

"I'm deeply appreciative, but it's most unnecessary. I've already given my word to help."

"Excellent, excellent. Then I won't be presumptuous if I asked to meet your German cousin."

"Käthe?"

"Fräulein Käthe Kingsmith, yes." Churchill pronounced it the same way Araminta did, Katy.

"But why?"

"Herr Hitler, or so I believe, was delighted with her performance at the Olympic Games."

"She won a gold medal for Germany," Aubrey said warily. "In the two-hundred-meter dash."

"Through her half brother she is connected to General von Hohenau of their general staff—"

"I won't let Käthe be involved in your group."

The interruption startled Churchill. "What?"

"The reason I published *Tarnhelm* under another name was to protect the German side of the family. Mr. Churchill, I'll do whatever you ask, I'm more than willing. But there's nothing that would induce me to put Käthe—any of my German family —in jeopardy."

"All Europe, nay, indeed all mankind, is in jeopardy." The grandiloquent words rang with rumbling undertones, as if being orated in some large, drafty auditorium. After a brief but searching glance from under his beetled brows, Churchill sat back. "Your cousin," he said in a normal tone, "has already taken sides. She's against the Nazi regime."

"Sir, I can't understand why you think that," Aubrey said. But beneath his dinner jacket he had gone cold. *Schultze,* he thought. If Winston Churchill, on this side of the English Channel, with limited resources and inadequate manpower, had uncovered Käthe's professedly minor errands for Schultze, surely the Gestapo must be aware too.

"A Jewish refugee informed us that he was helped by an Olympic medalist." Churchill exhaled a cloud of smoke. "A beautiful young lady whose photograph he recalled seeing."

"God. . . ."

"There's no need to sound so tragic. Bluntly, if Fräulein Kingsmith were suspect, she'd be of no use to us. As it is, well, who could be more perfect? Connected to the von Graetzes, close to General von Hohenau. Acquainted with that villainous man."

Aubrey fingered back his reddish-brown hair. His jaw had hardened to the mulelike obstinacy that Araminta called the Kingsmith clench. "She's put herself in enough danger."

"Why not let the young lady decide for herself? That's all I'm asking. Will you arrange a meeting when she visits London?"

"She has no plans to come here."

"Two days ago she applied for a visa."

"She has? Sir, your network is neither small nor weak."

"You will be having visitors from both sides of the Atlantic," Churchill said.

Eighteen

I

"Darling!" Araminta, waving, vigorously squirmed her way along the crowded platform at Victoria to engulf Käthe in a cloud of gardenia perfume. Brushing aside Käthe's effort to thank her for coming to the station, she cried, "The entire family's agog! I hear even indulgent New York is against Kingsmith plus Kingsmith. Is it true they sent a you're-too-young letter?"

"Aunt Rossie did," Käthe said.

"Doubtless written on asbestos to douse passion. The older generation!"

Before this, tears had come to Käthe's eyes whenever she thought about Rossie's veiled warning, but Araminta's amused tolerance made her aunt's objections seem fustily ridiculous.

"Tell me all. Does he write a million letters? Does he kiss divinely? Oh, Peter, in case you haven't guessed, this is my notorious cousin, Katy. Katy, this is Peter."

The young man who had followed Araminta was the Honorable Peter Shawcross-Mortimer, Aubrey's friend from Oxford who now squired Araminta to parties and balls in the upper reaches of Mayfair. With his chiseled profile, sooty eyelashes and eyebrows, his black hair in need of a barber's attention, Peter resembled a leading man playing at the Old Vic rather than the scion of an earldom granted in Shakespeare's days.

"This is a pleasure, Fräulein Kingsmith." He enunciated

slowly, as if she might have difficulty following. "I feel as though we've met. I've heard so much about you."

"Let's hope Aubrey's damped down the worst of Araminta's scandalous rubbish, Mr. Shawcross-Mortimer," Käthe said, realizing that though Peter's eyes were both dark, one was blue, the other brown.

"But you speak perfectly," he said, surprised.

"Why not? Uncle Alfred's as English as treacle," Araminta snapped. "And do see to her trunk or we'll be here all night." As the shortish figure disappeared into the crowd, she shook her head ruefully. "Poor Peter, I do lead him a merry dance."

"But he seems so nice. Why be cruel?"

"Oh, don't be an idiot. Because I adore him. Do you think you and Wyatt're the world's only star-crossed lovers?" A transitory grief drabbed Araminta's flawless complexion. "His family's worse than ours by a long shot—they ignore me. I'm beneath notice—I can just hear them. 'Kingsmith, a shopkeeper, don't you know.' And Peter's not the sort to tell them to chuck it all." Then she drew a breath and her vivacity flowed back. Linking her arm in Käthe's, she said, "How long is this wait?"

"Two and a half more years. At Christmas of 1940 we'll have the privilege of being engaged."

"He's sharing Aubrey's digs, isn't he?" In March, Aubrey had rented a bachelor flat in Shepherd's Bush. "Well, what could be simpler? With Aubrey at Kingsmith's all day, you'll have every chance to see each other alone." Circling a porter, Araminta repeated meaningfully, "Alone."

"That's not the point."

"Don't be such an infant, of course it is. You're running high temperatures, both of you. There's only one way to get the fever out of your systems. I'll bet that the physical thing is all either of you want, actually. Not that I blame you. He has a look as if he'd be absolutely marvelous in bed."

"Shh!" Käthe, blushing furiously, gripped her cousin's bare, rounded arm. "People are staring."

"I should hope so. We're a smashing-looking pair, if I do say so myself, you so fair and demurely virginal, me so vividly, extravagantly sensual. But to get back to you and Wyatt. It's dotty not to take advantage of Aubrey's flat."

Käthe murmured near the red hair. "Do you and Peter . . . ?"

"No, but then at heart I'm a Kingsmith, a middle-class realist. You, ducky, are a romantic. Wyatt is, too, no matter how he covers it up with that clever sarcasm of his. He has a garden-variety itch for you. But he talks weddings because you look like the damsel with the golden hair from some fairy tale. And you're prettying up the same basic urge. Take my tip and go to bed with him this summer. Oh, do stop blushing. We aren't living in the reign of Queen Vic—"

"Look, there's Mr. Shawcross-Mortimer with a porter."

"Call him Peter. Oh, I nearly forgot. Aubrey's dropping over to Grandpa's tonight to welcome you." Araminta drew Käthe to a halt. "Now, mind you, though you ought to sleep together, I agree that marriage is as wrong as wrong can be for you two. In Wyatt's heart he agrees. Why else do you think he suggested meeting you away from maternal supervision?"

Käthe looked away. After Sigi had brought her home from the Metropol, she had scribbled Wyatt a page about the Gestapo's prying, then had known her initial impulse was right. Sending such a letter would start a transatlantic battle. She had torn up the page and written about the advantages of London, away from both sets of parents. He had cabled back: *England perfect.*

The porter piled her baggage in Peter's long-hooded Humber. On the way to Porteous's house on the Bayswater Road, Käthe drowned out Araminta and Peter's bantering. *In exactly a week,* she thought, *he'll be here. . . .* Anticipation burned through her until her skin glowed like a pink pearl.

II

It was just after dawn in New York and Wyatt was driving the big Packard through the quiet streets to the Thirty-fourth Street docks. Rossie sat at his side.

Humphrey, in back with the two Mark Cross suitcases, was leaning forward. "So Katy's already there," he said.

"She should be arriving in London at this minute."

"Wyatt," Rossie said quietly, "I'm counting on you not to do anything crazy."

"Is this still on the subject of Käthe?" he asked.

"We only want what's best for you," she said. "Alfred and Clothilde are right."

"What constitutes right?"

"Watch out for that milk wagon," she said. "If this is the real thing, it'll stand the test of time."

A stop sign's arm went up. Wyatt braked. Twisting around to the backseat, he asked, "Tell me, Dad, how do you stand on time tests?"

"Alfred's always been such a stickler," Humphrey equivocated. "He's set the date. He'll never alter it for anything less."

"But say he was presented with a fait accompli?"

Rossie interjected raggedly, "Wyatt, you must finish law school."

"Hey, who said anything about quitting?"

Humphrey leaned forward to pat his wife's shoulder. "Rossie, it's all right. Wyatt won't do anything silly. And so what if they're cousins? It doubles our odds of having Olympic champs for grandchildren."

Wyatt shot a glance at his mother. Rossie was concentrating on an old brick warehouse, so he saw only her smartly waved hair and her new tilted straw hat. "Wyatt, you might as well know," she said. "I wrote to Katy and explained how impossible it was for you to be married while you're in school."

"Terrific," Wyatt said bitterly. "Did you send letters to the rest of the family?"

Rossie didn't answer.

III

"Kate," Porteous said at the dinner table, "I shan't bring up the matter again, but I do feel responsible, sending you off to New York last summer. This business between you and Wyatt must stop. Mark you, he's a very decent young chap, if a bit hotheaded. But he's not for you. Cousins shouldn't marry. And besides, you're such a tender little thing, taking everything to heart. He's all push and energy—it's the American in him. Let him racket around London with Aubrey while you and Araminta take the boat train to Ostend. Or maybe you could go down to Nice."

Porteous cajoled with alternate holidays. Käthe picked at her shrimp mayonnaise, then her saddle of mutton.

They were being served the trifle, whose peaked whipped cream was embedded with candied violets and mandarin oranges, when Aubrey arrived.

Käthe, at first delighted to move away from the personal, grew silent again as the two men explored the Sudetenland issue. The Sudetenland had been taken from Germany by the Versailles Treaty to become the western half of the newly formed nation of Czechoslovakia. Since May, Hitler had shrieked demands that the territory be restored to the Third Reich. The Ministry of Propaganda had been spewing out horror stories of Czechs persecuting Sudeten Germans. Recently panzer divisions had settled along the German-Czech border, leading Czechoslovakia to mobilize every male between six and sixty. Europe was stricken by a bad case of war nerves.

They had coffee in the drawing room.

"It's a fine night, Käthe," Aubrey said. "Are you too tired for a stroll in the park?"

"You young people don't need to rush out to have a private chat," Porteous said a little stiffly. "Go on in the garden."

The garden wasn't a garden at all but a terrace above the flat-roofed kitchen. The potted rhododendrons hadn't done well but the white roses that climbed from a pair of Italian urns spread luxuriantly across the trellis behind the marble bench. Käthe sat, feeling the chill of the smooth stone through her dinner dress. Aubrey stood with one foot on the low balustrade, gazing up at the narrow new moon as if seeking advice on how to begin a speech.

"No," Käthe said. "Absolutely not."

He turned. "What?"

"You asked me out here to tell me to forget Wyatt."

"What on earth gave you that idea?" The blood had rushed to Aubrey's face, but it was too dark for Käthe to see. "Nothing like that at all. I was wondering . . . Käthe, have you ever heard of Winston Churchill?"

"Churchill? Your politician?"

"He's in the House of Commons, yes. As a matter of fact he's held most of the Cabinet posts. Quite a well-known character here. Grandson of the duke of Marlborough. Writes articles and books."

"Our press hates him. He's against Hitler."

"Very much so." Aubrey drew a breath. "He's invited us to tea tomorrow in his chambers."

"Us?" Her long skirt rustled as she got to her feet. "The House of Parliament? You *have* come up in the world."

"I'm refusing."

"Whatever for?"

"I can see you're fagged out from the journey," he muttered.

She needed ways to hurry the interminable hours until she saw Wyatt. "I wouldn't miss it for the world!"

IV

Parliament had adjourned, and the corridors of power echoed emptily to Käthe and Aubrey's footsteps. After waiting briefly in an anteroom whose shabby Jacobean furnishings were the genuine article, they were ushered into a large office saturated with the aroma of cigar smoke.

Churchill rose from his desk. Elderly, stout, considerably shorter than Käthe, his pudgy pink face reminded her of a baby crossed with a pug dog. Yet as he stamped across the carpet to greet them, there was something impressive about him that she recognized from Clothilde. Both moved with the same patrician self-assurance, as if the ground welcomed them.

"Tea won't be for a few minutes," Churchill said, and cocked a bushy white eyebrow at Aubrey. "What have you told Fräulein Kingsmith?"

"Nothing, sir."

"Well, then, busy yourself outside while I explain." As the door closed on Aubrey, Churchill surveyed Käthe. "Your Olympic photographs didn't do you justice. Do sit down." He pulled out a chair. "Fräulein Kingsmith, I congratulate you on your involvement against the Nazi regime."

"Aubrey told you about *that*?"

"Josef Kahn, the theoretical physicist, for whose knowledge we are most grateful, mentioned your assistance to him and his wife." Frau Professor Kahn was lame. Though the couple had held legitimate emigration papers, there had been nobody to drive them from their shabby flat in Kreuzberg to the Anhalter terminal. "Don't look so concerned. You're absolutely safe."

"There are other people involved," she said.

"Professor Kahn and the rest of us are most circumspect." Churchill's gold watch chain glittered as he thrust out his round belly. "Fleet Street's labeled me a busybody and warmonger. But you obviously agree that the Nazis are a foul crew and must be stopped."

"Politics is out of my realm." The sense of owing two separate allegiances that had stirred during the conversation at her grandfather's dinner table now settled like glue in her blood vessels. The flesh around her mouth felt hard. "All I do is occasionally drive somebody or pass on an envelope."

"Helping us would involve even less."

"Helping *you*?"

"In a most minor way. For example, should you hear something unusual, like a factory taking on more workers, or see more uniforms on the streets—any such trivial information—you would pass it on to Aubrey."

"Tell Aubrey?" Her voice rose. "You're asking me to spy?"

"I'd never phrase it so dramatically. But the Nazis have a highly organized observation ring in this country while we—"

"No," she interrupted thickly.

He blinked at her. "What?"

"I'm a German."

"Of the highest type. Already you're disobeying your laws."

"I'm helping innocent people."

"I, too, wish to help them. Miss Kingsmith"—Käthe noticed the switch from *Fräulein*—"your father is British."

"My mother's German. I was born in Germany. Aubrey told

me that you have an American mother. If an American asked you to pass on information to Washington, would you?"

"Not at this time," he said. "But if there came a day when wickedness were abroad in the land, yes, I would."

"You were born here. What about your conscience?"

"My conscience would demand that as an Englishman I do my utmost to stamp out the wickedness."

V

Wyatt knew immediately that his mother had sent those letters. Possibly Alfred had dispatched warnings from Berlin. The older family members joined ranks to allow him as little time as possible alone with Käthe. Euan, now fully recovered from his heart attack and back at work, procured a box at the Duchess, taking them to see the hit play *The Corn Is Green.* Elizabeth flustered into town to give a dinner at the flat. With Araminta's help drawing up guest lists she also arranged parties at Quaglino's and lunches at the Savoy. Porteous took the family young people to dinner amid the gilt angels of the Café Royal. There was a weekend at Quarles during which Wyatt swore he could hear Euan patrolling the corridors. The rare hours they had to themselves, Wyatt found himself unable to suggest they head for Aubrey's one-roomed flat. Knowing how his host felt about Käthe, it seemed vicious to make love on the lopsided divan. After a week Wyatt set aside a large portion of his traveler's checks to take the cheapest single at the Dorchester. The hotel guests were almost exclusively American and Käthe in her New York clothes was more or less inconspicuous as she traveled up in the elevators to his room.

"What are you thinking?" she asked.

"That we should be spending the entire month like this."

They were entwined on his bed, the dusk slanting from the window to paint a blue gleam across their naked bodies.

"What, with Grandpa and Uncle Euan and Aunt Elizabeth in the wings?"

He kissed her breast, rubbing his cheek back and forth across the chiffon softness. "Käthe," he said, and broached what had been on his mind since the previous December. "Let's elope to Gretna Green and tie the knot."

A pigeon cooed on the twilit window ledge, a truck backfired on Park Lane. She kissed his shoulder, which was still damp with sweat, an aphrodisiac scent to her. "Mmm, nice and salty. Gretna Green marriages haven't been legal for ages."

"I'm sick of having an ocean between us."

"What about law school?"

A memory popped into his mind. Käthe in that white uniform, crowned with laurel, standing below the giant swastika while the crowd roared out "Deutschland Über Alles." "That sounds suspiciously like a put-off," he said.

"Your mother wrote to me."

"Yeah, I know. Look, so there aren't hordes of hitched law students. But that doesn't mean I can't swing it."

"All I think about is being married."

"Then stop thinking. Plan an elopement with me."

She sighed. "I can't go back on my word."

He had heard that damn excuse once too often, but even so he was surprised to hear himself ask in a loud courtroom voice, "How do you feel about the Leventhal side of me?"

"Wyatt, please don't do this to us."

An oppressive pain settled in his forehead, as if a hatchet were sinking into his skull. "Answer the question."

"If only you realized how much you're hurting me."

"It's no fun and games for me either. Käthe, level with me."

She turned her head on the pillow, looking away from him. "Sometimes . . . this makes me ashamed to say . . . Sometimes I think I love you more because of it." She paused, asking in the same muffled voice, "Why must you always keep picking on me for being German?"

"I love you in spite of it. So let's make an honest American of you."

"Wyatt, why won't you understand? My parents let me come here and meet you because I'd given them my word to wait. They trust me."

For a long few seconds he peered at the face on the pillow

next to his. How could this madonna loveliness hide such a diamond-hard will? Tears swam in her blue-green eyes.

"It'd be easier"—he sighed—"if I hadn't fallen for you in such a damn big way."

"So we're all right?"

He raised up to kiss her eyelids, then her breasts. "Mmm, aren't these soft and sweet, my, aren't you sweet and soft here. . . . Yes, do that . . . and that. . . . Ah, love, love, love . . ."

NINETEEN

I

That summer of 1938 Hitler continued to howl ultimatums while the far less militarized Czechs steadfastly refused to surrender the Sudetenland. By September an unendurable tension gripped Europe. The British Prime Minister, Neville Chamberlain, and the French Premier, Édouard Daladier, whirled more and more feverishly between Czechoslovakia and Germany, browbeating the Czech government, pleading with Hitler. On September twenty-ninth, Chamberlain, his grizzled mustache pulled sternly over his prominent teeth, carried his furled umbrella aboard a plane to Munich. Amid the architectural treasures of that Bavarian city he handed Germany the living, beating heart of Czechoslovakia, eleven thousand square miles that included most of the country's coal, iron, and steel as well as its defensive wall. Cheering crowds filled Downing Street on the Prime Minister's return. Chamberlain went upstairs, standing in a second-floor window to brandish the treaty that had slain another country as he proclaimed that the parchment insured "peace in our time." The *Times* declared that no hero had ever returned with nobler laurels. And when Winston Churchill told the House of Commons that the Munich pact was an unmitigated defeat, hooting shouts of protest silenced his warnings.

Parliament, like the rest of Europe, longed to believe that Hitler's territorial hunger and bloodlust were assuaged.

II

Early on the gloomy afternoon of November 9, 1938, Käthe pulled into the narrow courtyard behind the Unter den Linden shop, putting the car in neutral before she eased on the brake, which tended to work stiffly. She succored the old Steyr now that Gunther was no longer around—in early October the chauffeur's SS reserve unit had been called up for duty in the new Czech Protectorate. Stepping into the dinky, windowless cloakroom, she exchanged her heavy winter coat for the black linen coverall worn by the sales clerks, then glanced in the steel mirror to smooth her coronet of braids. Fräulein Kingsmith was ready to perform her duties.

During the Czech crisis the young clerk had been mobilized, and Käthe, anxious to bridge the sea of time until she would again be with Wyatt, had pleaded for the job. Alfred had pronounced in his most stuffy tone that well-bred girls didn't belong in the workplace. Porteous, however, had supported her. *The child has a good mind,* he had written in his odd yet legible scrawl. *And hopefully an interest will cure her of the other.* Alfred had given in, comforting himself with the truism that as more German men put on uniforms, more women were helping out. Having his daughter at the shop proved an unexpected pleasure. Despite that fey dreaminess of hers she did indeed have a good mind—an excellent mind. Soon she was balancing the books and learning the merchandise. He would hold his magnification glass, squinting with Kingsmith nearsightedness as he taught her to decipher the symbols on old silver and china. Her lovely smile disarmed customers: Fräulein Kingsmith's salesbook began to fill.

This particular afternoon, business was slow. The half-dozen elderly clerks put on gray felt gloves, dusting or rubbing fingerprints from the silver while they exchanged baleful whispers about this week's cause célèbre. Ernst vom Rath, the Reich's third secretary in the Paris embassy, had been shot in that city; it was an act of protest against the anti-Semitic persecutions. Herschel Grynszpan, a seventeen-year-old German Jewish refugee, had fired the shot. Echoing the diatribes shouted over radio, the clerks agreed here was a prime example of Jew bestiality and cunning. Käthe was grateful when closing time came.

After Alfred had locked the door behind his employees, he followed his custom of going through the shop for an eyeball inventory. Käthe was putting away a misplaced bonbonnière when loud crashes rang on the Unter den Linden.

Father and daughter hurried to the already barred shop window. The streetlamps were on. Peering through the silhouetted trees on the broad shadowy boulevard, Käthe saw a green-uniformed *schupo*—a policeman—holding back a group of pedestrians while a trio of burly young men swung iron jacks at Gottlieb's Haberdashery. Despite the stars centered with the word *Juden* that had been scrawled on the now shattered windows and the dwindling away of trade, Herr Gottlieb had remained, one of the last non-Aryan shops in this elegant part of town.

"We must stop them!" Käthe said.

"No!" Alfred warned sharply. "Remember what happened to Herr Weber." A year earlier Herr Weber, their landlord, had attempted to stop the hooligans from defacing Gottlieb's shop and for his pains had been sentenced to three months on charges connected to the Nuremberg racial laws.

As if to prove Alfred's point a tall man began waving his arms in obvious remonstrance. One of the vandals shoved him in the gutter. The policeman did nothing. The three ruffians jumped into the shop. There was a long, drawn-out cry, then shirts began flying out. As the crowd scrabbled for the loot, a truck swerved from the direction of Friedrichstrasse, screeching to a halt outside Kingsmith's. Käthe watched the half-dozen young men, all in civilian clothes but wearing military boots, jump out and charge across the broad boulevard to join the plundering.

With a shaking hand Alfred lifted his pince-nez to rub at the bridge of his nose. "The paper said there might be a spontaneous uprising because of that poor devil Grynszpan."

"Spontaneous, my foot! Come on, Father, we must help Herr Gottlieb, he's still—" She stopped with a gasp.

Alfred, who had never used physical force on her, was gripping her arm. "You'll not be anywhere near that bunch of bullies! A pretty thing like you—who knows what might happen?" He yanked her toward the rear of the shop. "We're going home."

III

The sky had a reddish glow. By this illumination Käthe glimpsed a quick, furtive movement along the rear of the courtyard. "Who is it?" she called.

There was no answer. Shaking off Alfred's restraining hand, she moved forward.

A child of maybe twelve edged into the darkest corner. She was hatless and coatless.

"It's all right, we're your friends," Käthe said gently, and when the child continued to shrink backward as if to melt into the bricks, Käthe asked, "Where do you live? We'll drive you home."

The child gasped several times, then said, "They threw him out the window."

"Who?"

"Vati—my father. We were having supper in the kitchen." The words raced. "They broke down the front door and began smashing everything. Vati went into the sitting room and begged them to stop. The big one knocked him down. The others laughed and grabbed his hands and feet, swinging him and shouting 'Heave ho.' " The child broke into a sob. "They threw him out the window. They were coming for Mother and me, but she pushed me out the back door."

"You'll have to spend the night with us, then." With an effort Käthe kept her voice calm. She glanced at her father, prepared to do battle.

"You'll be safe, child," Alfred said in his heavily accented German. "Here, take my coat."

IV

Several times on the way to the Grunewald they saw civilians and Hitler Youth standing around burning houses. Looters dashed in and out of stores where the plate glass was shattered. In Charlottenburg three SS men forced a shivering line of people into a police wagon. On Bismarckstrasse two neatly dressed old women were scurrying away from a small rooming house whose windows were systematically being smashed. Käthe halted for the pair.

As they neared their home, Alfred said in English, "Kate, how can we take them inside? The servants."

Käthe's hands gripped the steering wheel. "What about Gunther's place?" Since the chauffeur's departure, his two tiny rooms had stood empty.

"I should have thought of that myself. Yes, the garage's a good bit from the house, and the windows face the lake."

Käthe left Alfred off at the porte cochere as usual, curving down the slope to the garage. The chauffeur's quarters had none of the carved excesses of the house, and in the barren cubicle with the yellowed corner washbowl the dust-covered, cast-off table and chairs seemed like the baroque relics of a giant. Pulling the blinds and drawing the faded curtains, Käthe summoned the trio from the car. Apologizing for the dirt, she said, "I'll be back."

At ten-thirty, when the house was silent, she tiptoed down to the immaculate pantry. She gathered three quarters of a loaf of bread, some jam, a jug of milk. As she picked up the tray, the door to the dining room swung open. Clothilde, gray braid hanging over her wool bathrobe, folded her arms. Käthe lifted her chin defiantly, but dishes slid across the tilting tray in her hands.

"Take care," Clothilde warned. "Is that all you're taking them?"

"Father told you?"

"Naturally."

"Cook might miss anything more."

"Cook!" Clothilde's tone dismissed any such kowtowing. "Make some tea, bring the rum and *kompott* with *plätzchen*. Oh, and use the good cups. I'll go down to our guests."

When Käthe arrived with her heavy tray, her mother was sitting on one of the battered chairs talking to the old ladies about Baden-Baden. Käthe served the compote and passed the cookies; Clothilde poured the tea, carefully measuring a stream of rum from the tiny, long-necked crystal pitcher, the same ritual that prevailed when Clothilde summoned her daughter to the *Damenzimmer* to help entertain some titled woman visitor. The little girl forgot her grief and fear at being included in this adult rite; the neat, elderly sisters—the Fräuleins Brandsteiner —sipping and nibbling, regained their dignity.

"My daughter will bring you covers and take you home in the morning," Clothilde said.

"We are most grateful," retorted the stouter Fräulein Brandsteiner, pausing delicately. "However, our place might not be possible."

Käthe darted an assessing glance at her mother, then said rapidly, "I have a friend. Let me find out if we can find a temporary place for you."

For once she risked calling Herr Schultze from the house.

Before dawn Käthe drove the trio to a "safe house," a white cottage in the suburb of Siemensstadt, where Schultze was waiting.

Returning home, she found Clothilde bundled in heavy clothes—her ironbound schedule included a brisk three-mile walk before breakfast. Imbued with the camaraderie of the previous night, Käthe suggested she come along. Mother and daughter swung along, arms bent at the elbows, matching their rapid strides on the mulchy paths. The odor of the previous night's fires had penetrated even this refuge of quiet woods. When they reached the Jagdschloss, the sixteenth-century, stone royal shooting lodge, they turned back.

Käthe tugged her woolen muffler tighter. "Mother," she said, "have you given any more thought to the engagement?"

"That again? Käthe, nothing's changed since last week. You're barely nineteen. Wyatt's still in university."

"What about next year, then, when he's finished law school?"

"The way you keep on like this just proves that you're still a little girl," Clothilde said, smiling fondly.

"I'll be twenty then."

A straight-backed old man strode by them. Slowing, Clothilde said, "Käthe, about last night. Your behavior made me proud. These Nazis are such evil peasants."

V

When Aubrey arrived on November twentieth for a "holiday," Käthe drove him around the destroyed buildings, her voice low as she told of the pillage. According to the *Völkische Beobachter* the "spontaneous uprisings" across the Reich, born of a righteous anger against the murder of vom Rath, had destroyed two hundred synagogues, seventy-five hundred Jewish shops, and thousands upon thousands of homes. Because of the rivers of broken glass, people were calling the night Kristallnacht.

"Crystal night?" Aubrey asked. "Such a lovely name."

"Yes, for the return of the Dark Ages."

"I've heard the jails are crammed with Jewish people."

Käthe nodded but didn't tell him of the two men in danger of arrest whom she had driven to Schultze's "safe house." Instead, she described her mother, wearing her ancient wool dressing gown, entertaining the Fräuleins Brandsteiner and the little girl as if at a reception.

Aubrey chuckled. "Good for Aunt Clothilde."

"She was marvelous! I was tiptoeing around the house, but not Mother. Never Mother. She's always so sure of herself. What I wouldn't give for that inner compass!"

"You have something far more rare. A pure soul."

Käthe flushed, dismissing Aubrey's remark as a flowery holdover from his writing days. "I'm so ashamed for Germany. Aubrey, will you tell Mr. Churchill that until Wyatt and I're married he has another pair of eyes."

"I should send up cheers, but I wish you wouldn't."

"It's little enough," she said.

Aubrey stared at a burned wall, all that remained of a Jewish bakery. "If Thursday's all right with you, then," he said, "I'll arrange for dinner at Pupi's and opera tickets. Somebody I'd like you to meet will be arriving in Berlin."

* * *

Aubrey's friend, Major Downes, was one armed, with a neat, graying mustache. Käthe liked him immediately because his Canadian accent sounded American and therefore reminded her of Wyatt.

"Aubrey tells me good news," the major said.

Käthe glanced around. The stout waiter with his long apron was nowhere in sight and the surrounding tables were involved in Tower of Babel arguments—Pupi's was a popular meeting place for foreign journalists. "It's nothing," she murmured. "We already send each other letters."

"What do you write about?"

"Oh, books, the shop, music. Nothing exciting. I don't go anywhere much. I'm, well . . ."

"Käthe's engaged to our American cousin," Aubrey said.

The opera was *Der Freischütz*. Behind them sat a plump blonde and a young lieutenant in Luftwaffe blue. Before the curtain went up, the lieutenant boasted to his companion about recent maneuvers. From her voluble questions and his answering descriptions it was obvious that the exercise had taken place near the new unfortified Czech border.

Major Downes turned to Käthe. "How I envy you living in Berlin," he said. "So much going on, such a center, so much to hear about. I hope we have another chance to talk about it."

"I'll be meeting my fiancé in England next summer," she replied.

FOUR
1939

Mr. and Mrs. Humphrey Kingsmith
request the pleasure of your company
at a buffet supper to celebrate
the graduation from Columbia Law School of their son
Wyatt Kingsmith
on Saturday the twenty-third of June
at half after seven
Thirty-five East Seventy-second Street

TWENTY

I

Wyatt had graduated second in his class; he had been an editor on the law review and written articles for it; he had been offered a prestigious clerkship by a district court judge; he was being interviewed by the most eminent Manhattan law firms. Humphrey, flushed and excited, was circling the crush at the flat, informing his and Rossie's friends of these facts. Waitresses passed trays of champagne, the dining table had been extended, and the buffet was in full swing. The stoutest butler sliced the enormous golden-browned turkey while another separated pink slabs from the pair of cold poached salmons and a third ladled shrimp curry from the outsize silver chafing dish. Guests in evening clothes pressed around, helping themselves to the assorted condiments, the salads, the tiny beaten biscuits.

The younger group was carrying their plates to the jammed living room, where a black pianist was playing "Frenesi." The older guests chose to eat at the round tables set up in Wyatt's bedroom and the guest room—for tonight the furniture was being stored in the basement. Wyatt had just finished circling both rooms, laughing and chatting a minute with each couple, accepting their congratulations.

In the calm of the corridor he met Rossie.

"Terrific party, Mom."

"You deserve it," she said, patting his cheek. For a moment her smile was sad, and he wondered if she were thinking of

Myron Leventhal, who had never finished Harvard med school. "Wyatt, I don't think it's smart for you to go to England before you take the bar."

"Nothing to worry about. I've got a reasonably supple mind —and I've crammed enough to pass two bar exams."

A plumply pretty woman with white hair came toward them with a laden plate. After applauding Wyatt and praising the food to Rossie, she continued into the guest room.

"Mom, I'm bringing Käthe back with me."

"There's no need to sound so defiant, dear. You're ready to practice law, that's all I wanted."

"So we have your blessings?"

Rossie twisted her diamond wedding band. "It's quite clear that this year's separation was hard on you."

"Why the equivocation?"

She looked directly at him, and after a moment said in her most practical tone, "All right, dear, I'll tell you. The circumstances being what they are, you'd be better off with an American girl."

"Käthe'll take out her citizenship papers."

"How did she convince Alfred and Clothilde to change their minds?"

"She didn't. She couldn't inveigle them. Talk about the Rocks of Gibraltar! I decided to try my persuasive powers and applied for a visa. The German passport control turned thumbs down."

They exchanged glances, and Rossie said softly, "That exactly proves my point. An American girl would be so much better for you."

"Käthe's not like that."

Rossie looked startled. "Who ever thought she was? Good heavens, Wyatt, she's the most darling girl. Very fine and honorable. But she *is* a German. And that makes so many problems because of . . . Myron. You'll never be able to visit her country. They have those disgusting laws that make my blood boil and must do the same to you—"

"Okay, okay, I get the drift."

"I don't want to see you hurt, that's all." Rossie glanced

toward the noisy living room and the bedroom doors before murmuring, "Dear, you've been marvelous. I know it would have been way easier if you could've told them there's no problem about being related."

"Hey, come on," he said in an equally low tone. "There's no way I could tell Uncle Alfred and Aunt Clothilde without destroying Dad. Besides, they have other objections. Käthe's too young, et cetera. But my mind's made up."

"Your mind? What about Katy?"

"God, it's lousy, being apart like this! She feels the same—but I'll have to convince her."

Rossie surveyed her tall son in his white dinner jacket, his tie pulled askew, his streaked hair as usual looking attractively unkempt. "If anyone could convince a girl, it's you," she said. "Now, get on back to your friends."

Wyatt walked slowly down the corridor, halting at the entry of the hot living room where the laughter and voices all but drowned out the pianist's jazz version of "I Didn't Know What Time It Was."

Rossie was right about the separation being rough on him. This past year had been the worst of his life. Some days he had been too absorbed in his misery of impatience to pay attention to the life around him, other days he'd been so acutely conscious of people—his family, his classmates and professors—that their every action, every word, had grated on him and he would flare with sarcasm—he had gotten into a fistfight with an old friend who had made a mildly anti-Semitic joke. For the first time he'd had headaches. He'd played such vicious squash that he had torn his left Achilles tendon. He had studied as if demons were on his tail. Maybe demons were chasing him—could there be any other explanation for the doubts that had razored into his brain cells? Had Käthe refused to elope with him the previous summer because of Myron Leventhal? Had she kept that promise to her parents out of her own hidden psychological urge to avoid a lasting tie with him? In his bitterest moments he was incapable of visualizing her without the word NAZI superimposed across her chest like those place-name ribbons worn by beauty-pageant contestants. Her letters, loving and tender, ameliorated the doubts but never cured them completely.

He was constitutionally incapable of another year and a half of separation. It would be torment to break up, but a clean, prophylactic torment. Like amputating a gangrenous arm so the rest of him might survive. The group at the piano was waving and calling to him. He went toward them, thinking, *I meant exactly what I told Mom. Either Käthe comes back with me or that's it for us.*

II

Käthe halted. Heaving and gasping, she held a hand to her side. *Totally out of shape,* she told herself. She and Wyatt were in London. It was just after six-thirty on a soft, cool morning, and they had been running parallel to Rotten Row.

"Wyatt, wait," she panted, and flung herself on the clumpy grass. She could feel the reverberations of hoofbeats from a solitary early-morning horseback rider.

Wyatt jogged back to her. "Hey, we don't want you cramping up," he said. "Upsy-daisy, lady."

"I can't move."

But he took her hands, hauling her to her feet. An arm around her waist, he started her into a slow jog to cool off. Her breathing grew more normal, and the brushing of their sides sent filaments of happiness through her. This pleasure faded as they neared the clump of trees beyond which they had left their warm-up clothes. Where an hour earlier a pair of Canada geese had pecked in the grass, a sergeant paced up and down, overseeing maybe a dozen khaki-uniformed men as they dug up the park. A gnarled little private caught her expression of dismay. "Antiaircraft gun emplacements, miss," he called. "That 'itler! 'E's got another think coming if 'e tries the same game with the Poles as with the Czechs."

Käthe had written to Aubrey about the jubilant crowds sieg-heiling outside the beige-marble Chancellery after Hitler had junked the Munich Agreement and marched into what remained of Czechoslovakia. Now the Führer was once again screaming a mandate. Poland must surrender the former German port of Danzig. The Poles were refusing. Once again Europe gnawed fingernails.

Wyatt and Käthe rounded the copse to the bench where they'd left their things. He pulled on his old Olympic sweatshirt and tapped a cigarette from the pack.

"Käthe, listen," he said. "Ever since I landed two weeks ago I've been hashing and rehashing how to put this. You know me, Mr. Spur-of-the-Moment. Waiting this long proves I'm dead serious."

"Yes?"

"It's time to take the plunge."

The sweat had cooled on her skin. "There's only a year left."

"A year and a half before we're engaged," he corrected.

She pulled on her top, feeling an ostrichlike security in the brief darkness. "You mean everything to me, you know that."

"Before we go any farther, you might as well know that I decided to personally persuade Uncle Alfred." Striking a match with his thumbnail, he lit his cigarette. "It seems I'm not wanted in Naziland."

"Sigi told me you might have problems," Käthe mumbled.

"Sigi? What's Sigi got to do with my visa?"

"After that fight in Garmisch a friend of his, somebody in the Gestapo, noticed his name on the report. He had lunch with Sigi and told him that they'd looked into your background."

"Swell crowd your brother hangs around with," Wyatt said bitterly. "How come you never mentioned this?"

"We'd only have started an argument."

"Stupid of me. I should've guessed."

He smoked his cigarette while she ran a comb through her hair. The roots were wet with perspiration. After she had put away the comb, she said quietly, "The visa doesn't really matter, Wyatt. We'll meet here next year."

"One trivial complication. Those guys weren't digging up Hyde Park for their health. There's going to be a war."

"Hitler and his ultimatums."

"The salient point here is I am making an ultimatum of my own." The moment of truth was upon him, he couldn't put it off. His mouth was dry. He had feared he might actually break down and weep, grovel and plead with tears running down his cheeks. Instead he sounded quite rational. "Okay, I'm not cut out to be a monk eleven months out of twelve. Okay, I miss you until I think I'm going to pop like a balloon. It goes way beyond that. Käthe, the questions, the questions. It's the questions I can't take. When I should've been cramming for exams, I'd find myself pulling mental daisy petals. My girl is German. Does my girl love me, does she love me not?"

"Wyatt—"

"No, hear me out. I'm not saying this is your fault. It's me. I'd rather cut off my right arm than lose you, but I can't take another day of this craziness. So it's up to you. Are you coming back to New York? Or are we finished?"

"You can't mean today—"

"Don't look like that, Käthe. None of this is coming out of the blue." Tremors ran along his thighs and calves, as if from a neurological disease, and he had to force himself to continue. "Tell me yes or tell me no."

"I've tried and tried to get them to move up the date. But Mother never changes her mind. And Father's not much more flexible."

He took a long puff on his cigarette and smoke burned deep in his lungs. "This isn't their decision. It's yours."

"I love you more than anything in the world," she said.

"One syllable. Yes. No."

"It's my promise, Wyatt."

He stubbed out his cigarette. His face had drained to the frightening Atabrine yellow of malaria patients. "So it's negative?"

"Sometimes you're frozen," she flared.

They walked along the broad path, he keeping apart from her, she reminding herself of his notorious hot temper and trying not to take this argument to heart.

When they reached the Bayswater Road, he said, "So long." He prided himself on his voice. It was neither conciliatory nor bellicose. He jogged back to the Dorchester, waiting until he was in his room before he allowed himself to cry.

III

After Käthe bathed, she brushed her hair until electricity crackled, sparking, and her arm ached. She left the pale, gleaming strands loose over her shoulders the way he liked, she put on the new blue-and-green flowered Liberty blouse that he had said matched her eyes. She sat at the drawing room window. Every few minutes she would get up to touch the aspidistra plant, the Matthew Boulton candelabra, the cabinet with the silver birds, as if these relics of a bygone era were magic amulets to draw him to her. *Oh, Wyatt, don't put me through this.*

At last, a few minutes before one, he trotted up the freshly washed steps. She ran to open the door.

He touched her hair, smiling. "Rapunzel."

Unglued by relief, she leaned against him. He held her tight, then released her. "Spent the morning at Thomas Cook's on the Strand. What a zoo! People lined up everywhere and pleading for berths. The *Queen Mary* sails the day after tomorrow. As I got to the counter a first-class cabin opened up. First class being out of my range, I signed all my traveler's checks as a deposit and cabled the folks for the rest."

"You what?" she asked, incredulous.

"No choice. Everybody and his brother is heading home."

"Wyatt, be reasonable—"

"Love, I'm in total control of my reason. After lunch we'll head over to the embassy and start the paperwork for a marriage license. Lucky you, you picked yourself a lawyer who can cut through the clauses."

"At least wait until I get home and can try one more time to get them to change their minds."

A muscle jumped in Wyatt's jaw. "Offhand, isn't two years long enough?"

"I'd never break my promise to you."

"So here we are in a full circle. I take it, then, that you're staying within the legal code of the Third Reich?"

Her heartbeats seemed to cease as she gaped at him. "What?"

"The law banning marriage between an Aryan and a non-Aryan."

"God," she whispered.

He moved away from her to stand by the case of predatory silver birds. "The evidence is all in. You lie to keep me out of the *Vaterland*. I've begged, groveled, pleaded with you to marry me, done everything short of dragging you off by that beautiful Nordic hair. Okay, I'm willing to accept that you don't realize how your subconscious mind works. But whichever side of your brain makes the decisions, Käthe, the fact remains. You aren't willing to trade in that big swastika on your passport for a half Jew."

"Never say that."

"It's true."

The reverberations of a rumbling double-decker bus clattered crystals of the Waterford chandelier. Käthe's eyelashes went down. Now was the time to tell him about Schultze and Heinrich Leventhal. But would succoring his (unacknowledged) relation against his express wishes prove anything more than her further deceptions?

"I've—I've helped Jewish people," she mumbled. Boasting, as it were, of her nobility of character made her flush with shame.

He was watching her. "Oh, I imagine thousands of them," he said.

"What a rotten thing to believe of me!"

"I've cut myself open for you, Käthe. Any more self-surgery and I'll bleed to death."

"Even if you hadn't told me about your—about Myron—I couldn't marry you until my parents released me from my promise."

"Which is it, Käthe, are we going to the American embassy? Or are we forgetting the whole thing?"

She couldn't speak.

His shoulders slumped and his color drained to that awful jaundiced shade. "You're a Nazi, Käthe," he said quietly. "Whether you realize it or not, you're a Nazi."

A small involuntary sound escaped her.

As his steps dragged heavily across the parquet hall, the words bubbled up—she would go anywhere with him, she would do whatever he asked. Yet her larynx remained constricted. This inability to break her promises was part and parcel of the black obstinacy that dangled her midpoint between her English and German origins.

IV

The following morning he arrived at the usual time. The dark shadows of sleeplessness showed beneath his eyes as well as hers. He didn't refer to the previous day's battle royal, and she eagerly fell in with his plan that they hike to Hampstead Heath for lunch at the Spaniards. Working-class men drank Guinness and threw darts. Wyatt's leg pressed, trembling, against hers. Neither of them did more than nibble at the sausage rolls.

Outside he hailed a taxi, telling the driver, "Dorchester."

As soon as they were in the hotel room, they strewed their clothes. On the narrow bed, with no preliminary embraces, they joined together feverishly. Only when he was inside her did the caresses begin, the endless kisses, the murmured endearments, the groans and hoarse requests—"Yes, that, do that again. . . . Ahhh, love . . ."

The roar of late-day traffic on Park Lane had swelled when, gasping and drenched in sweat, they came together. She clasped him tightly with her arms and legs as if to bind them together always.

"I'm nothing without you," she murmured.

"I'm so wild about you that sometimes it makes me think I'm crazy."

"I'll love you forever," she said.

"Always." His voice shook.

They splashed together in the bathtub. Afterward he tucked the towel around his waist and sat on the edge of the bed, watching her draw on her sheer silk stockings.

"I got a cable from Mother this morning," he said. "It seems Carrothers, Uzbend, and Hanson have urgent need of my courtroom skills in their litigation department. They want me to start before I take the bar."

Her nail snagged the silk. "You're going home."

"They're the best of the three choices. Talk about luck. I was able to change my reservations and get a single cabin-class berth. The *Queen Mary* sails tomorrow evening."

Her heart felt swollen and sore. *You're a Nazi, Käthe. Whether you realize it or not, you're a Nazi.* Had there been a cable? Had he meant that ultimatum in the park? Was it over between them? Glancing down at the rumpled sheets, she knew only that the physical love between them had blazed with honesty and trust.

V

The following morning she saw him off at Waterloo station. Oblivious to the crowd and the noise, they embraced, arms tight around each other.

"Be happy," he said against her ear.

"I'll write to you every day."

"I love you." He pressed a kiss near her cheek. "Always remember that I love you."

"Oh, darling, darling," she whispered. "It won't be long."

"Alll aboo-ard. . . ."

He kissed her mouth hard, then pulled away. Jumping the steps, he reappeared a moment later at the closed window of the passageway. He stood there with his palms pressed against the large pane. Maybe it was the dust-streaked glass: his face seemed contorted into a grimace of mortal agony, as if he were being stabbed in the back with a curved rusty knife.

TWENTY-ONE

I

Unable to control her tears, Käthe didn't go down to dinner or breakfast. Before her grandfather left for work, he came in to say good-bye, resting his veined old hand on her head. Wordless comfort. In midmorning a summer breeze blew across the Park. She gazed with dry if aching eyes at the billowing old-fashioned lace curtains. A tap sounded and at the same moment the door swung open. Mary, the housemaid, popped her capped gray head inside. "A gentleman on the line for you, Miss Kate, a Major Downes."

Käthe, on the verge of not taking the call, told herself she couldn't keep moping forever. And here was somebody who knew nothing of her private life, somebody who would neither question nor pity her.

The major invited her to tea at the Connaught.

Outside the hotel the routine quiet of Carlos Place was broken by a newsboy shrilling, "Riots in Danzig, read all about it. Riots in Danzig."

The major was waiting on a sofa in the lounge.

"Are you all right, Käthe? If you don't mind my saying so, you look a bit under the weather."

"I'm feeling much better."

"Good. You see, I'd like for you to spend a long weekend in Devonshire."

"Aubrey's working in Dublin." Euan had sent him to an

estate sale with orders to sniff out bargains in old Belleek and Irish silver. She managed a wan smile. "And my grandfather would take a dim view of me going off alone with a strange man."

The major waited until the waiter had set down the thin-sliced Madeira cake before handing her an opened envelope with an English postmark. Her name and the Bayswater Road address were written in a Germanic hand, as was the letter. Liesl Wenders, who also had come to England for her summer holiday, was dying of boredom and begged an old school chum to save her life by visiting her uncle's house on the Devon moors for a long weekend.

II

The tall, thick hedge blocked the empty moors from every aspect of the crenellated Gothic-Victorian house and its spacious gardens. A fine afternoon, men and women were clustered on deck chairs around a short, stout woman.

"Your lecturer looks like a Berlin hausfrau," Käthe said.

The major smiled noncommittally.

Inside he led her to a good-sized library whose bow window looked out on a small herbaceous garden insured of privacy by yet another tall hedge. The upholstery was worn but comfortable; the shelves were jammed helter skelter with German books—not the matched sets of Goethe and Schiller one expected to find in this kind of mansion but new Nazi best sellers like *The Belief in the Nordic State, Socialism Betrayed,* and *So This Is Poland.* A wheeled cart was set for lunch and the major removed covers from the cold roast chicken and potato salad. Käthe was unable to down anything more than a few sips of her wine—since Wyatt's departure her throat passage had narrowed to a hair.

Her host pulled off the napkin tucked in his vest. "This is highly confidential and must go no further than these walls," he said. "England and France are ready to sign commitments to Poland."

Käthe shivered as if a chill had invaded the summer-warm

library. The major was not second-guessing when he spoke of mutual assistance pacts. "Why are you telling me?"

"If Hitler doesn't back down, you and Aubrey won't be able to write to one another. Could we set you up with a pen pal in a neutral country?"

"No," she burst out. Then into her mind came the smell of smoke, the glitter of fire on broken glass. Clenching her hands, she said, "I mean yes, at least until the Christmas after next." Were she and Wyatt still getting married? *Yes, yes, yes.*

"Your first answer was the brainy one, at least so far as you're concerned. You must consider all the angles, the guilt involved. The dangers. You'll be putting yourself in the thick of it."

"I thought you said a few letters, not blow up the Chancellery."

"Never underestimate your Gestapo."

"I don't." She sighed, suddenly remembering how they had exhumed Rossie's first marriage to Myron Leventhal. "But I've got nothing to be afraid of. I'm an Olympic gold medalist. My brother's in the Bendlerblock. Why would they suspect me?"

"That's in your favor. But there's still risk. And what about the future? Think about the future. It goes without saying that if Germany wins, you'll stay silent."

"I can't believe all of this! You're acting as if we're already aiming cannons at each other."

"It's coming, Käthe, it's coming." The major ruffled his graying eyebrow, one of his few mannerisms. "If England gets the upper hand, you won't be able to talk either. I don't imagine you've ever heard of the Official Secrets Act?" He waited until she had shaken her head. "You'll need to sign a paper that whatever you do for us will remain absolutely secure—private. Forever."

She looked down at her hands. "I keep my word," she said.

"The point I'm trying to make is that you'll never be able to tell anyone."

"Glory's the last thing I care about."

"What of your parents, your brother, your fiancé?"

"Can't I even let him know after we're married?"

"The Official Secrets Act makes no distinctions about husbands and wives. Secrecy across the board. Käthe, there might come a day when it would save your life to say you'd worked for us. How would you bear up then?"

"Let's hope well," she said with a smile.

"You're brave—cowards don't throw in with men like Schultze. But this is making a commitment to our side. And you can't expect any help from us. Ever."

"Is this what's called playing devil's advocate?"

"Aubrey's not here to do the job." Going to the library table, the major pressed a corner of veneer. A narrow drawer slid open. "Don't make your final decision until you've read this carefully." He extended a stiff, triple-folded document. "Once you sign this paper you'll be bound by the Act."

Reaching for the cart, deft with his single hand, he wheeled it from the study, closing the door behind him.

The document, headed by the British lion and unicorn, at first glance appeared much the same as any of the half-dozen visa applications she'd made out in the British Embassy on the Wilhelmstrasse. But this was pricked with a circular stamp:

CI-4

UTMOST SECRECY

It was only two brief paragraphs. She must swear by Almighty God not to divulge matters pertaining to activities engaged in for His Majesty's government. Under pain of full penalty for treason these activities must remain secret and confidential even from spouse and closest relative.

She heard a strange whirling clatter. A crow rustled its black wings while it pecked at the window. She shivered as if the harmless bird were an omen. *You're a Nazi, Käthe. Whether you realize it or not. . . .*

She unscrewed the top from her fountain pen and scribbled her signature.

III

The CI-4 code was hers alone, known only to the major and to her control, Aubrey.

She never left the library. The smaller sofa turned out to be a daybed, and she slept there, using the connecting bathroom and lavatory. She never met any of her fellow guests, she never saw a servant. The major wheeled the cart with their meals in and out. She ate little, shifting her food around the plate. Just as well she had no appetite. Over breakfast, lunch, and dinner the drilling continued. She must learn approximately four hundred phrases and maxims. *The wind is heavy now* meant that she had seen an unusual number of soldiers in Berlin. *Noisy sparrows* referred to people complaining. *Quiet sparrows* meant a large number of newspaper advertisements of deaths placed by the bereaved. The deeper she sank into memorization, the greater became her conviction that all would be well between her and Wyatt. Did intense concentration directed away from a source of great unhappiness always act curatively?

Early on Sunday afternoon, for the first time the telephone sounded.

Answering, the major said respectfully. "Yes, sir. . . . Yes. . . . Absolutely. . . . Quite a young lady. . . ." He extended the earpiece. "For you, Käthe."

Bewildered that anyone should know her whereabouts, she took the instrument.

"Miss Kingsmith?" The gruff, cadenced English voice was vaguely familiar. "Winston Churchill here."

The once scorned MP was finding more and more support: the British hated bullies, and the Nazis had been kicking underdogs for a long time, first the Jews, then the Czechs, and now the Poles.

"Mr. Churchill," she said.

"We are most deeply appreciative of what you have already done, and are even more grateful for your contribution in the future."

"I must say none of this seems completely real to me."

"Mark you me, it's real. That little dictator of yours is on the warpath." Churchill's rumble sounded jovially ominous. "Miss Kingsmith, I commend your courage."

As she hung up, she realized the major was watching her meditatively. "You're very young, you've had three days' training, not three months'. But Mr. Churchill's seldom wrong about people. Let's hope for your sake he's right this time."

That afternoon she and Downes drove back to London.

IV

During Käthe's absence Alfred had hired a deaf pensioner as a temporary chauffeur. The wizened old man drove them home from the Anhalter terminal, going fifteen miles an hour. Alfred and Clothilde asked about the family.

"All anybody talked about is a war," Käthe said. "Wyatt's worried."

"He's not normally an alarmist," Alfred said.

"Alarmist! They're digging up Hyde Park. Even the little children have been issued gas masks."

"So they have here," Clothilde said.

"This crisis is all hot air," Alfred said with a cautious glance at the deaf old man beyond the glass. "Heaven knows I'm no Nazi, but believe me, Hitler's only getting back what that ridiculous treaty took away—those French, how they insisted on their pound of flesh from Germany!"

Käthe inhaled the acrid scent of chrysanthemums, her welcome-home bouquet. "What would be so awful if we were married this year?"

Clothilde's smooth forehead creased into a frown. "We'll make the announcement the Christmas after next."

"And that's that," Alfred added. "No more nonsense."

After she had unpacked, Käthe was drawn to Sigi's room, which smelled faintly of his tobacco and the must of the decrepit von Graetz tapestry. She stood a long time staring up at the faded, near invisible medieval lettering: LOYALTY TO COUNTRY, FIDELITY TO OATH.

V

That night Sigi came to dinner. After the gala roast chicken he suggested they stroll down to the lake. The August evening was balmy, the moon almost yellow, but with the parental turn-down her earlier sense of doom had settled back with a vengeance.

"You're quiet tonight," Sigi said. "Missing Wyatt?"

"Sigi, a lot of people in London seem convinced there'll be a war."

"The Poles will cave," he said. "Their cavalry doesn't stand a chance against our panzer divisions."

"But if England and France stepped in?"

"They didn't side with Czechoslovakia, why would they with Poland?"

A bulky outline loomed in front of the lake. The straw target, stored away years ago, had been set up again. When she was twelve Sigi had installed it to practice his shooting. Wild to copy her big brother, she had pestered him for lessons. Her coordination was excellent, and despite the Lüger's heaviness and recoil she had hit the bull's-eye far more consistently than he.

"I see you've been practicing," she said meaningfully.

"Don't read anything into it. The junior officers at the Bendlerblock are being tested on marksmanship."

"Mmm."

He halted, fingering a rhododendron leaf. "Käthe, how about coming to Bavaria? The top brass has been summoned to Berchtesgaden—no, actually to Mount Kehlstein." Hitler was often photographed in the Bavarian Alps at the Berghof, his beloved summer home above the village of Berchtesgaden. Last year, however, a less public retreat had been completed for him atop Mount Kehlstein, a sanctuary so lofty that it had been nicknamed the Eagle's Nest. "I'm going with Uncle, of course, and we're expected to bring a lady." The general was a confirmed bachelor.

"The Führer makes my skin crawl."

"Of course he does," Sigi said agreeably. "But you're so perfect. A blonde of blondes, heroine of the Olympic gold.

Besides, I don't know anyone else to invite." Sigi's voice had grown awkward. Neither he nor his family ever mentioned Marga Salzwebel, the plump, comfortable, fortyish Potsdam dentist's widow, his long-term mistress. He put his thick, warm arm around Käthe's shoulder, giving her a brotherly hug. "Look at it this way. How many people get to see the Eagle's Nest?"

She pushed herself out of her depression. Surely Hitler's meeting with his generals would be momentous information for the British. They had reached the target. She picked up a metal bullet case and threw it. The path of yellow moonlight on the lake shattered. "If you swear not to leave my side," she said. Almost immediately the guilt the major had warned of swept through her with a vengeance. Not only would she be betraying her country, but also her half brother.

TWENTY-TWO

I

Perched high in the mighty outcropping of mountains that comprise the Göll massif, the Eagle's Nest, Hitler's ultimate aerie, can be reached only by a road built to be used exclusively by the Führer and his guests. This single lane, a marvel of engineering, zigzags precipitously up Mount Kehlstein, burrowing through tunnels to emerge on yet vaster, more intimidating Alpine panoramas until one can see far into Austria. Here, where winds race clouds around the roof of Europe, even in summer there is a nip to the air.

It was chilly at eleven on that mid-August morning when an escort of BMW motorcycles, headlights ablaze, swerved from the topmost tunnel, leading a line of Mercedes-Benz limousines affixed with swastika flags. The motorcade carried chieftains of the Oberkommando der Wehrmacht—the OKW—the High Command of the Army, Navy, and Air Force, which had been joined together by Hitler the previous year when he had named himself Supreme Commander.

In the fourth car Käthe, sitting between Sigi and General von Hohenau, fought car sickness by taking deep breaths from the open windows. She wore a dirndl-skirted dress with a cardigan, for this was to be a "casual" luncheon. The general's hand rested on the thick briefcase between his gleaming black boots. He had not spoken since they had pulled away from Hotel Kronprinz, the comfortable, flower-box-adorned hostelry commandeered for the OKW in nearby Berchtesgaden. Sigi had taken out his pipe, and General von Hohenau had said, "Our lance corporal doesn't care for a man with the smell of smoking on him." There had been a paternal note in the warning. Though the general never displayed open affection to Sigi, he considered his long-deceased brother's son his heir.

The three passengers jerked forward as the driver swerved around a final turn, pulling to an abrupt halt on the large oval that marked the end of the road. There was nobody on hand to greet them, no sign of the Eagle's Nest. A pair of immense closed bronze gates set into the face of the mountain seemed unreal—they might have been borrowed from the *Arabian Nights*. The heads of the OKW and their wives were being helped from cars by their aides. Each senior officer gripped a bulging briefcase. The wives, decades older than Käthe, were dressed as if for a formal garden party: mountain winds pulled at their silk skirts and hats. A large-brimmed straw blew off to be chased by a driver.

After five minutes General von Hohenau tugged the Iron Cross that dangled from a chain around his tunic collar. "The nerve of it," he muttered to Sigi. "Leaving us to cool our heels!"

Just then the bronze doors slowly swung open. A trio of black-clad SS officers emerged.

"Ladies and gentlemen," the *sturmbannführer*—the SS equivalent of major—called in a thick Bavarian accent. "If you will come this way, please."

A broad, high tunnel had been drilled into the heart of the mountain. Copper chandeliers set into the high arch of the ceiling shed receding pools of light. There were two pairs of bronze doors. As soon as everyone had walked inside, first one pair then the other clanged shut. Gleaming boots and high-heeled shoes reverberated more rapidly. After an eighth of a mile that seemed far longer, the tunnel made a sharp right turn. They were in front of a large elevator lined with Venetian mirrors. One of the SS guides barred the open elevator, another hustled inside to open a trap door, while the third directed the junior officers down an iron ladder into the service level.

Sigi started to follow the other aides, but the one-eyed general took his arm, holding him back.

"My nephew, Oberleutnant von Hohenau, stays with me."

Käthe stood pressed close to her brother as they rose silently and with no sense of motion.

II

The two-story granite and sandstone house, intended for top-level conferences, was not large, but the mountaintop had been leveled for vast terraces that looked down on scudding clouds, villages clinging to mountainsides, and green, faraway valleys.

Hitler, lumpy in a Bavarian costume, stood on the terrace surrounded by men in similar getups. Each group of OKW visitors was escorted to greet the host. When it was their turn, Käthe's legs felt rubbery. Hitler also appeared on edge, continuously touching his silver buttons, the braid of his jacket. Recalling Käthe—or primed to recall her—he inquired whether she was preparing herself for the 1940 Olympics. Repulsed yet mesmerized by the pale blue gaze, she responded that she wasn't yet in training.

"I see you're appropriately dressed," he said, glancing with malicious satisfaction at the aristocratic older women shivering in their silk dresses at the sides of their eminent husbands. He waved away Sigi and General von Hohenau, chatting with Käthe about her victory, about Leni Riefenstahl's film of the 1936 Games. Grand Admiral Raeder's group waited.

After Käthe had been dismissed with a handshake, she moved to the stone parapet where Sigi was talking to a guest in the Bavarian *tracht.*

"Welcome to Mount Kehlstein, Fräulein Käthe." Sigi's companion spoke as if they were old friends. He was about Sigi's age, but powerfully compact, and a good head shorter. "What a pleasure to see you again."

Sigi asked, "You remember Otto Groener, don't you, Käthe?"

Otto Groener? It took her a moment to connect the name with Sigi's old school-friend, the Gestapo officer who had passed on word that Wyatt's antecedents were in their files. She supposed Otto Groener might be considered handsome with his sleeked blond hair, his square chin, short nose, and keenly alert, if small, eyes. But in her admittedly prejudiced opinion, his stance, feet planted apart, head thrust energetically forward between wide, thick shoulders, made him look remarkably like a bull readying itself for a charge.

"Sigi used to talk a lot about you," she said. "But we've never met."

"Years ago we did." His smile showed the effects of early privation, jagged teeth with numerous gold fillings. "You were a beautiful little girl, and I must say that time has only improved you. No wonder the Führer honored you with so much attention." He paused. "Do you still live out there in the Grunewald?"

"The same house, yes."

"House? That's a palace!"

Sigi and Käthe both demurred.

Groener's eyes were fixed on Käthe. "No, it's true. In those days, believe me, I'd hardly been near anything that grand, much less inside. My father was a bricklayer. In Munich nothing was being built, so we came to Berlin. No work there either— but you know how it was then, the Jew contractors gave all the jobs to the bolshies. Let me tell you, we'd have starved without the soup kitchen. Still, I wanted a good education, so I pushed my way into Sigi's school. I can't count the number of times I'd have been shoved back out if my pal here hadn't come up with my fees."

Sigi looked embarrassed. "You more than repaid me with that walking tour of the Berchtesgadenland. What magnificent country you come from!"

"Yes, those days are behind me." Groener passed a hand over his hair—it grew in a peculiarly straight line across his forehead and must have been heavily brilliantined to remain smooth in this wind—and smiled at Käthe. "Now I outrank your brother, I'm a *hauptsturmführer*. A captain in the SS. I have an elephant's memory for favors."

And I bet you never forget a wrong, Käthe thought. He seemed to be waiting for a response, so she murmured, "Oh?"

"I still remember my exact thoughts when you came flying down that magnificent carved staircase. 'What else did you expect in this palace, *dummkopf?*' I said to myself. 'Of course there's a little princess with swan-gold hair.' "

A flush showed in Käthe's cheeks and she pulled her cardigan more tightly closed.

Sigi noted her discomfort. "Otto was about to show me snapshots of his boy."

Groener fished in his pocket, extending a pack of photographs of a solemn, long-faced four-year-old in various poses. "Little Otto," he said proudly. "Can you believe it, this little tyke's already met the Führer six times."

Sigi and Käthe thumbed through the stack. Groener kept up a running commentary on little Otto's achievements, omitting mention of the long-faced, long-bosomed woman clearly the child's mother. He continuously tapped Käthe's shoulder as if for emphasis. While he replaced his snapshots, she moved a few steps from him, pressing her cold, blue-tinged hands on the stone ledge.

He came to her side, pointing at a conical mountain. "That's the Untersberg. Do you know the legend? Charlemagne and an army of five thousand knights sleep inside, waiting to restore the fame and glory of the German Empire. Well, let them snooze on. The Führer's restored fame and glory to us." He gazed down at the faraway blue sparkle of the Königssee. "God, what scenery!"

"Isn't it incredible?" Sigi shifted to stand between Groener and his sister.

"Did you know the Führer comes here to meditate?" Groener's awed tone suggested that he had imparted a revelation about the nature of Christianity. "But it's just not gemütlich like his Berghof in Berchtesgaden—such jolly times we have there."

An accordionist had started to play Austrian folk tunes and the wind tore at the rollicking music in the same way that it tugged the shivering women's dresses.

Groener glanced around. Nobody was near them. "Sigi, you did tell her about that American so-called Kingsmith?"

Sigi's affable smile faded. "Naturally."

Groener ignored the cold tone. "So it seems this cousin's not quite a kosher cousin," he said, laughing at his own joke. "Starting fights at church on Christmas Eve!"

Käthe stared in the direction of Salzburg, which at this moment was hidden by a large puffy white cloud. "Wyatt was jumped by two bullies," she said.

"Loyal Party members understandably annoyed because he tore down government property—" He halted in midsentence.

Hitler was moving toward the steps that led up to the glass doors.

"Ah, lunchtime," Groener said, bending his elbow to offer his arm to Käthe.

She moved toward her half brother.

"Käthe's sitting with me," Sigi said.

"You have the honor of being near the Führer with your uncle. We lesser folk are far below the salt." Groener's wink indicated that he no longer considered himself lesser than Sigi or anyone else, including the assembled High Command. "Fräulein Käthe, you're shivering. Come on inside."

III

The long, clothless oak table surrounded by twenty-six brown leather chairs gave the dining room the impersonality of a boardroom. The highest-ranked officers sat nearest Hitler. Käthe, at the far end where silk dresses were interspersed with Bavarian *tracht,* noted the High Commands' strained expressions and wondered if the blanket tension would have been lessened by alcohol. Because Hitler was a teetotaler, no drinks had been served earlier and no wine was being poured with the meal. However, although the host was a vegetarian, stringy, pallid hunks of stewed veal were offered. Groener ate rapidly and greedily. Käthe moved her food around her plate, her mouth too dry to chew. *Wyatt,* she thought over and over. *Wyatt.* There hadn't been time for mail to arrive from him in New York, but after his other passages he had cabled immediately upon landing. Following her custom of writing before she went to bed, she had sent daily letters, none of which referred to the argument in London.

Evidently mental telepathy existed in the Bavarian air.

Groener gulped down the last mouthful on his plate. "In London, did you see a great deal of that American?"

She tensed. "How did you know Wyatt was there?"

"My department deals with foreigners who have visited the Reich. Especially the troublemakers."

Her hand shook and it was all she could do to cut off a nibble of the cream cake that had been set before her. Could the Gestapo also be aware of her meeting with Heinrich Leventhal, her activities with Schultze, the weekend in Devonshire? No, she told herself firmly. If they knew any of that, Groener wouldn't be watching her with such admiring interest. "They really did jump him," she said.

"Tell me, is there some sort of understanding between you two?"

"Are the State Police interested in gossip?"

"Fräulein Käthe, this man is connected to the Jew Leventhals in Berlin. If it were anything less than the laws against racial pollution involved, I'd never bring this matter up, but there's a report on file that you and he had some kind of relationship."

"I'm surprised at you. Believing talk of a friend's sister."

"So it isn't true?"

"Wyatt was a guest of the Reich at the Olympics—he won a gold medal. We were told to be polite to our guests."

With an unexpected sympathy Groener said, "You've set my mind at ease. I knew it was best to talk to you directly. And I understand your attitude. I'm also a loyal person. All right, subject closed." He finished wolfing down his dessert, scraping up the last bit with his fork. "Tell me about your boyfriend."

"What?"

"If you aren't involved with this so-called cousin, you must have somebody. How can such a beauty be unattached?"

"I'm not ready yet."

"Good girl. Before you trap yourself, take your time. Fräu-

lein Käthe, make sure the man's right for you. As far as I'm
concerned, the sun rises and sets on my little Otto, but my wife
. . . well, she isn't the one for me."

IV

The Führer had finished his second large slab of cake and was
looking around at his guests. The various conversations
ceased, cutlery clinked onto china, and there was only the
sound of the wind outside. Käthe was astonished how these
august officers, most of them Prussian aristocrats who thoroughly despised Hitler, turned servile in his presence.

"The Polish pigs are castrating our German *volk* in Danzig,"
Hitler said, repeating the word *kastrieren* on a rising note three
times before launching onward into his monologue. The Polish
people, like all of the Slavic races, were subhumans. To have
these *untermenschen* defiling German women and persecuting
the German men trapped on Polish soil was a cruelly unjust
situation that could no longer be borne. His voice grew
hoarsely shrill, the famous mustache wiggled like a dancing
black animal. "Those vermin were put here to serve the Master
Race, not persecute us!"

Groener and the men in Bavarian getups at Käthe's end of
the table applauded vigorously. From the OKW came murmurs
of approval.

"And this, my commanders, is your task." Hitler jumped to
his feet, hammering his left fist into his right palm. "To grind
down these crazed, dim-witted Poles. As I have brought the
Rhineland, the Saar, Austria, and Czechoslovakia into the
Reich, so I must fulfill the rest of the task and reunite all the *volk*
and punish their tormenters!" Despite Hitler's jerky gestures
and raised voice his outburst seemed calculated. He stood
glaring for a full minute. Then, hands behind his back, he
stalked into the enormous glazed rotunda that served as a
conference room. The heads of the OKW and their aides followed him.

V

"Sigi, how do your uncle and the others put up with it?"

"They're soldiers. A soldier's first duty is to his commander-in-chief."

It was after ten, and they were ambling down the dark road that led from the Hotel Kronprinz into the village of Berchtesgaden. Immediately after lunch Käthe and the other women had been brought back to the hostelry. Sigi and his uncle had just returned.

"He's terrifying," Käthe said. "Especially when he starts on that hysterical racial tack."

"He's not crazy, though." Sigi sucked at his pipe. "The discussions today are top secret, but I can tell you he's not crazy by a long shot. In fact, at times, there's a touch of military genius about him."

"Your old friend thinks he's the Second Coming."

"Did you ever see such a Party stalwart? Still, Groener has a real soft spot for his son. You can bet the boy—all his children —will have everything he missed."

"Did you really pay his tuition?"

"What choice was there?" Sigi mumbled. He was embarrassed by his tender heart, a characteristic noticeably absent in his von Graetz and von Hohenau forebears. "I can still see Groener when the whole school lined up in the yard to pay. The way he held his head down, ashamed. Well, poverty's behind him now. Before you came over he was telling me about his palmy new home in Dahlem, the servants, and how understanding his wife is."

"Women, you mean?"

"Such naïveté." Sigi chuckled. "Of course, women. He's quite the big shot on Prinz-Albrechtstrasse."

"Thank God I won't see him again."

VI

I can't tell you how thrilling it was, Aubrey, being up there above the clouds in Eagle's Nest. You feel all you have to do is reach out and grasp the entire world.

If only I could describe how marvelous the Führer is!

The other times I met him were so brief, and today I was in his presence for nearly four hours. Oh, Aubrey, he is a truly great man! So firm and yet so all knowing. When he talked about the need to reunite the German people, he held us spellbound—I wish I could think of another, less hackneyed phrase but there isn't one. It was as if nothing else existed except his nobility and will. If this sounds like girlish awe, believe me, it's not. Everyone, even General Keitel, listened with reverent attention.

The one unpleasant note of the day was the wind. The wind blew very strong out of the east.

Käthe reread the entire letter. This was the first time she had written to Aubrey since her tutorial from Major Downes. "The wind blew very strong out of the east" meant Hitler would assuredly mass troops on the east—on the Polish border. "Another, less hackneyed phrase" meant that Hitler had the High Command totally in hand, and whatever he said went. "Reach out and grasp the world" meant war. The code stuck out bizarrely to her. She visualized Haupsturmführer Groener, heavy shoulders hunched over her letter. Loathing him didn't prevent her from accepting his intelligence.

Ink had splattered onto the page. Using her blotter, she signed her name rapidly and sealed the envelope.

She started her nightly letter to Wyatt. Abruptly she put down the pen. It had come to her that if the Gestapo were indeed reading her letters to Aubrey, they would also be opening her mail to Wyatt. She sat still for a few moments, then began to write again. Hanni Trischen, her old friend, was going to Holland next week. She would ask Hanni to mail a batch of letters from Amsterdam.

Twenty-three

I

A humid breeze wafted salt odors of the Rhode Island Sound up acres of lawn to compete with the French perfume being exuded on the outdoor dance floor. The twenty-five-piece Meyer Davis orchestra was scattering inventions and riffs, the glowing lights strung in the huge copper beeches were minor moons, summer-tanned bosoms rose like ripe exotic fruit from strapless white formals. Viewed dispassionately, Wyatt admitted, the Marchains' dance should have been a magical evening rather than an ordeal.

When he had returned from England solo, Rossie had questioned him about Käthe, and he had responded in a purposefully unconcerned tone, "We decided that it's finished. 'Nuff said, okay?" Since then both Rossie and Humphrey had been urging him to get back in the swim. As old friends of the Marchains they had insisted he join them in Newport for the dance.

Now, like most of the older couples, the Kingsmiths had retired to the vast gilded drawing room, leaving the dance floor to the kinetic gyrations of the unmarried set.

Wyatt swung out the brunette whose name he couldn't recall, his knees bending lower and lower as she whirled, organdy skirts flaring to expose bronzed, thin legs. Sweat shone on his face, his smile was manic. He'd been drinking steadily all evening, but nobody could gauge how soused he was from the complicated steps that he improvised. The bandleader drove his clarinet to higher peaks, horns blared, drums raced. The dancers gathered around Wyatt and the brunette, clapping them on to greater extravagances. With the final raucous chords Wyatt bent her so far back that her spine paralleled the floor, then lifted her high in the air.

Applause burst. Then the clarinet began a bittersweet mating call. Couples melted close to one another as the male vocalist started to croon "Smoke Gets in Your Eyes." A song that Käthe had loved.

His partner was pressing her breasts against his stiffly starched shirtfront. He stepped back, bowing the polite way small boys are taught at dancing class before he led her to a table, hopefully hers. He headed for the open French door, behind which stood one of the portable bars.

A group of guys he knew were drinking and discussing— what else?—the Polish crisis.

"There's going to be a war over this mess, McAllister," somebody said. "You can bet your bottom dollar on it."

"Let the Poles get skewered, let the English and French fight the Germans. Who gives a flying fart?" McAllister responded. "Just so long as the good old Atlantic Ocean stays between us and them."

"Couldn't agree more," somebody chimed in. "So what if they have suicidal urges over there in Europe? It's none of our business."

"Don't count on that, old buddy. We've got Chosen People here and Roosevelt's their boy."

"Roosevelt's a savvy politician. A bolshie Democrat maybe, but nobody's fool. If a war develops from this Danzig screw-up, which I sincerely doubt, he'll pass."

"Double Scotch," Wyatt said.

"Hey, Kingsmith! You were just in London, weren't you? What think you? Are the British gung-ho to leap to the aid of Poland?"

"You better hope they are." Amber liquid sloshed over cut crystal as Wyatt took a long gulp. "Because if they don't, that bunch of cutthroat Nazi bastards will chew up that side of the

Atlantic. Then watch out! You know their motto, Today Germany, tomorrow the world."

"The problem with you, Kingsmith, is you've swallowed the bull that each and every German's a direct descendant of Attila the Hun. Well, let me tell you. I was over in Berlin this spring. Business for the bank. A beautiful, clean city, and you couldn't meet a more hospitable bunch. Polite, gregarious. On the streets you saw adorable kids. Everybody neat and well-fed looking. Like it or lump it, Hitler's done wonders."

"Yeah, Wyatt, what's eating you?" Fredrick McAllister swayed on his feet. "Didn't I see you mooning over that dishy German cousin of yours?"

"Shut your fat mouth."

"So she's the problem. What happened? She give you the gate?"

Wyatt clenched his fists to swing. Then suddenly he was sprawling in a low French petit-point chair.

"Enough fur and fangs," somebody was saying. "In case you guys haven't noticed, this is a civilized gathering."

"Don't tangle with Kingsmith," somebody else said. "Right now he's bad joss."

Wyatt slumped in the deep cushion, thinking of the clean city, the polite, hospitable folk who put up signs and broke windows, thinking of Käthe with her swastika Olympic badge. The band switched to "A Foggy Day in London Town," another of their songs. Wyatt lurched to his feet.

Without saying good-bye to his host or hostess, the guest of honor, or his parents, he brushed by the liveried butler at the front door.

II

Rossie and Humphrey had given him a red Packard convertible when he had graduated from law school. He sobered up a little as he jogged to the immense oval courtyard, where he'd parked it amid the other nonchauffeured cars.

"Wyatt," Humphrey called, puffing after him.

Wyatt stopped. "Oh, hi, Dad."

Humphrey caught up. "Aren't you staying for the supper?"

"I've a living to make," Wyatt said. "It's time for me to head back to New York and get to work."

"Work? But you're staying at the inn with us."

Wyatt was moving toward the tightly packed lines of cars. "Sorry, Dad, but a client wants to contest his long-deceased grandfather's will. He's tried before. And I, as newest associate, have been given the job of finding a loophole in one of the clauses."

An elaborate ironwork torchère lit Humphrey's full-cheeked, concerned face. "Wyatt, listen, maybe I should go over there."

"To Carrothers, Uzbend, and Hanson? Dad!"

"I meant Berlin. Even as a boy Alfred was set in his ways, a stodgy type, but he's not like Euan, he's not hard as nails. I'm sure I could convince him to move up the wedding date."

"Dad, how many times do I have to say it? There's not going to be a wedding."

"If only Katy could see how unhappy you are."

"Hey, you're barking up the wrong tree. I'm doing great, if a bit overworked. And the split was by mutual consent."

"She still writes to you all the time."

"We're friends, Dad, good friends." Wyatt concentrated on rubbing a bird speck from the convertible hood. "As cousins should be, right?"

Teetering on his patent leather pumps, Humphrey peered into Wyatt's taut smile. After a moment he touched Wyatt's sleeve. "Drive carefully, son."

III

Leaving Newport, Wyatt recalled this advice. He pulled over and slept. It was morning when he finally reached Manhattan. Without thinking it through he headed for the Lower East Side, parking on Delancey Street. The signs of the dark, narrow shops were in Hebrew. No Sunday quiet here. Pushcart vendors argued vociferously with their customers. A group of gray-bearded men shouted with swooping gestures. Children shrilled as they circled around some sort of game with a top, a pair of girls pointed upward to indicate one of the bright coats that dangled like flags from the poles jutting out into the streets. A pickle seller thrust his burly red arm in his barrel, next to him a vendor hawked big, soft pretzels. Shawled women lingered gossiping outside a butcher shop. Men and little boys in ankle-length black coats and black hats hurried down steps into a basement whence came the sound of dissonant liturgy.

I should know more about the religion, he thought. *More? That's a laugh. I don't know one damn thing.*

But which Judaism should he study? The coarse, exhilarating version around him? Its opposite, the decorum and unrelenting stiffness within Judge Leventhal's brownstone?

And why had he pushed thoughts of learning about his father's people from his mind while he was bound to Käthe? Had he feared seeing them through the eyes of a citizen of the Third Reich?

There was a tap on the rolled-down window. A little boy in a skullcap and ragged trousers held up a newspaper printed in Hebrew. Wyatt shook his head. The boy glanced shyly at him. Wyatt realized that, wearing his rumpled white dinner jacket in midmorning, he must be a bigger curiosity than the people around him. The boy reached into his canvas satchel for the fat Sunday edition of the New York *Daily News*.

FRENCH BEEF UP MAGINOT LINE

Wyatt handed over a coin.

IV

Unlocking the apartment, Wyatt dropped his overnight bag on the chair, then bent to retrieve the Saturday mail, which the super had pushed under the door. Fanning the envelopes, he saw a half dozen addressed in the familiar delicately spiked hand but postmarked Amsterdam.

Puzzled, he dropped his parents' letters in the salver, carrying Käthe's to his room. He forgot about the postmarks as he read the tender passages.

She was in Bavaria with Sigi, and the scenery was magnificent. She was back in Berlin. And she missed him. And she loved him. She loved him.

The silence of the empty apartment engulfed him. If she loved him this much, would she be writing about it in Germany? Wouldn't she be here in his bed telling him? Why did she insist on playing out the farce that she was obeying a parental injunction? If she ached the way he did, would she give a damn what she had promised?

She still writes to you all the time, Humphrey had said.

Wyatt tore up the letters, the tendons of his hands standing out as if he were strangling a rabbit. He yanked open the narrow top drawers of his bureau, shoving the mass of German-stamped envelopes into his wastebasket.

Sitting at his desk, he took out his stationery, writing the date:

8/20/1939

He stared at the numbers for nearly five minutes, then blew his nose and began to write rapidly.

Dear Käthe,

This isn't the sort of thing I'm good at, so forgive me if I use the wrong wording. The simple truth is there's no correct way to write this letter.

Ever since I left you in London it's become even more clear to me that we can never make a go of it.

I'm what I am, haunted by ghosts that cannot be laid to rest. And you're on the other side of the fence, a German. The world is the problem between us, but that doesn't alter the situation. In your heart you must know as well as I do that the difficulties are insurmountable.

Even the family, seeing only the surface, knew the truth. You and I aren't made for each other. That's one lucky thing about not being officially engaged. The breakup is less formidable.

I've already been stepping out.

At the lie his pen stopped. It took a minute or so before he was calm enough to write again.

> I'd feel far less of a heel if you were dating and enjoying yourself too. Let a few guys wine and dine you, Käthe Kingsmith, and you'll make the same discovery I have.
> You've been boxed up and housebound long enough.
> This is not to belittle what we had. The romance was a very special part of being young. Let's not ruin it by dragging things out. This way we can keep on being friends.
>
> Wyatt.

He folded the sheet unevenly, slashing the Grunewald address across the envelope. He trotted to Madison Avenue, getting to the mailbox just as the first Sunday pickup was being emptied into the leather pouch.

Returning to the apartment, Wyatt glimpsed himself in the elevator's gold-veined mirror. Once he had witnessed the death of a man hit by a delivery truck, and the luckless pedestrian had worn this same expression, lips drawn flat against his teeth, eyes wet and bewildered by the terminal agony.

FIVE

1939

TWENTY-FOUR

I

Araminta could feel the grit of the perfumed salts beneath her, and the water of her predinner bath was nearly cold, yet she didn't move. She lay brooding about her latest argument with Peter. She had lost her temper often enough with him, a redhead's prerogative, but before this afternoon none of their rows had attained a physical dimension. The explosion had occurred when he told her that his parents were inviting her—finally—to spend the last week of August at Mainwaring Court, their estate in Buckinghamshire. A sharp burst of pain had shattered her thin, if skillfully applied, veneer of uncaring sophistication. "Can't you see?" she had shrieked. "I'm a goddamn going-away present before you join that RAF squadron of yours!" With that, she had hit him. Even as she had delivered the palm-tingling blow to his cheek, she was aware that her actions proved the earl and countess of Mainwaring correct. Araminta Kingsmith, whose patronym was smeared across the top of newspaper advertisements, whose great-grandfather had started out his career as a ragpicker, whose grandmother had been a parlormaid, was irrevocably common. What could be more common than making this scene in full view of everyone on the Strand? Nevertheless, those red splotches on Peter's pale cheek had brought an exultant relief, and she had yelled, "I'll tell them what they can do with their bloody week!"

Peter's the third son, not the heir, she thought, a rebellious kick sending perfumed splashes onto the new bathroom tiles—all

three upstairs bathrooms at Quarles had recently been renovated. *What the devil difference can it make to the earl of Mainwaring
who Peter spends his time with—or marries?*

There had never been a hint of proposal from him; she still
saw her other young men. Peter, although transparently besot-
ted with her, was in no position to take on a wife without his
parents' approval—and the lack of invitations to any one of the
five Mainwaring homes certainly didn't signify approval. He
didn't have a bean other than the generous income his father
allotted him. In her top drawer was the *Times* with the Honorable Peter Shawcross-Mortimer's First printed amid the Oxford and Cambridge examination results—but alas, a First in
Classics wasn't a commodity high in demand on the labor market.

And all I've got is the pocket money Daddy gives me.

Sighing, she reached for the big soft towel and caught her
reflection in the mirrored door. Long slim legs, large firm
breasts, deeply indented waist, gracefully curved buttocks.

God, I lead the poor darling a merry waltz! she thought. *We're both
a bit dotty from the sheer weight of all this sexual frustration.*

Araminta behaved and felt virginal. That German lapse was
buried like a prehistoric shard beneath layer upon layer of
lightly but determinedly fended-off passes made by numerous
young men, including the Honorable Peter Shawcross-Mortimer.

II

At the dinner table she reconsidered the invitation. Of course
she would accept. Once at Mainwaring Court she would charm
her host and hostess. Yes, she would win them both over. If
they wanted ladylike, she would be ladylike; if they wanted
vivacity, she would effervesce. More important, they would see
for themselves how essential she was to their son's happiness.

Engrossed in her plans, she slowly became conscious of the
rise and fall of Euan's voice.

"Poland!" he was shouting at Aubrey. "Why listen to a pack
of war lovers, why not get it straight from the horse's mouth?
Herr Hitler states categorically that he has no interest whatso-

ever in Poland. Germany only wants the Free City of Danzig, which, as you might recall from your geography lessons, belonged to them in the first place!"

"Can't you see it's the same old story." Aubrey drew a calming breath. "Hitler said he didn't want Austria or Czechoslovakia. We should've stopped him then."

"Thank God Prime Minister Chamberlain has the brains to keep peace! That's why England backs him solidly!"

"What about the movement to get the Prime Minister to resign in favor of Winston Churchill?" Aubrey responded.

"This Churchill of yours! Who is he? The crackpot voice for armament salesmen!"

"He's—"

"Please, Aubrey dear," Elizabeth interrupted anxiously, one hand on the decanter. "You know your father hasn't been . . . himself."

Euan, as always when his wife brought up his heart attack, responded furiously. "Stay out of this!" Half rising from his chair, he shouted at his son, "The trouble with you, young man, is you've never lived through the trenches, never seen your friends slaughtered!" His face was red and swollen.

Araminta, from a lifetime's experience, knew that at this point anything Aubrey or Elizabeth said would inflame him further. "Daddy darling, you old fraud," she cooed. "When were you near a trench? You weren't fool enough to let Kaiser Bill's boys take potshots at you."

Elizabeth drained the glass. "Neither of my brothers were fools," she said with a forcefulness that made them all turn to her end of the table in surprise.

They finished the raspberry tart in silence.

III

"What was all that about?" Araminta asked her brother when they were alone in the shabby, comfortable library.

"I'm leaving Kingsmith's."

Araminta, who had been cutting Málaga grapes, dropped the dark cluster back into the fruit bowl. "You're what?"

"I told him on the way down this was my last month."

"Trying your hand at another novel?"

Aubrey glanced around the tiers of Frognall bookcases with their small, irregular-shaped wormholes. "No. The army."

"You're enlisting? No wonder poor Daddy was so keen on appeasement. Which regiment?"

"Seventh Artillery."

"You shooting cannons? With your Kingsmith eyes?" Her mouth pulled in shrewdly. "I supposed you'd end up in some hush-hush planning job with that one-armed major of yours."

"Surely you've heard of the Seventh Artillery's famed seeing-eye-dog division?"

With a high, pretty laugh she began peeling a grape.

"Seriously," he said. "With my glasses I have twenty-twenty vision."

"Another Oxford Union pacifist has heard the call to arms."

"Peter?"

"Yes, Peter."

"Tell me another!"

"It's not all that incredible. Those Nazis are a bit sick-making. Open your mouth and close your eyes and see what God'll send you." She popped the juicy grape in her brother's mouth. "Did you know he can fly a plane? I didn't, either, until lunch this afternoon. He's like you in that respect. He never toots his own horn."

"I can't get over it. Peter in the RAF?"

"The belted earl and his countess are expressing their gratitude for his willingness to serve king and country by allowing me within the sacred confines of Mainwaring Court. I'm going up there for a week."

"Araminta, don't pin your hopes on the invitation."

"Am I that transparent?"

"Only to me." He gripped her hand. "Neither of us has much luck in love, do we?"

"Once inside Mainwaring Court," she said, "I'll make my own luck."

IV

With its hundreds of peaks, gables, oriel windows, and fantastically clumped Tudor chimneys floating above centuries-old trees, Mainwaring Court deserved its reputation as one of England's most beautiful country homes. Ancestral portraits by Romney and Gainsborough hung along the length of the lead-glass-windowed gallery. A pair of gold saltcellars made in the reign of Charles I graced the Sheraton dining table, as did a vast Ming Dynasty bowl.

But when it came to creature comfort, little Quarles won hands down.

Though the week that started on the twenty-fifth of August was exceptionally fine, Araminta's bedroom was so dank that she bought a hot-water bottle at the village to surreptitiously pop into her curtained Tudor bed. Only half jokingly she told Peter that she needed to drop bread crumbs along the bewildering maze of corridors that led to the loo. The nearest bathroom (there were only two in the vast structure) was miles away down another drafty labyrinth. By night mice and rats scurried within handsome wainscoting. By day she could see the water stains that brought the perpetual chill to the room.

The thirteenth earl of Mainwaring, short, thickset, with the bulbous pink nose and receding chin of the Hanoverian kings to whom he was somehow related, spent most of his waking hours astride a massive roan stallion. He spoke mildly enough to Araminta, but roused her hackles by barking at Peter as if his youngest son were a dim-witted tenant farmer. His countess, from whom Peter had inherited his dark, dramatic good looks, wore her magnificently fitted Paris summer frocks with an assortment of floppy straw hats apparently left over from a local jumble sale. She chatted with her other guests, three titled couples whose families quite literally had known the Mainwarings for centuries, her expression animated. But the skin around her melting brown eyes grew taut when she addressed either Peter or Araminta—the most common remark Araminta heard from her hostess was a vaguely irritable "You don't want us old fogies casting a blight on your fun. Do run along."

The first evening Araminta remained demurely quiet, but when she realized Aubrey was right—as far as her host and hostess were concerned it didn't make any difference what she did—she reverted to her usual vivacious self. The table laughed heartily at her jokes before drifting back into conversations about mutual friends. Peter gazed through candle flames down twenty-odd feet of table to her.

V

"But what about new toys?" Araminta asked.

"Never got any."

"Not even at Christmas?" It was the third day of her visit, and by now she had a place rubbed raw in her heart for the child Peter had been. They were in the day nursery. On this glorious August day the narrow windows, sheltered as they were by ancient oaks, threw such a wan light that she'd needed to go over to the corner toy-case to inspect its contents—one battered squad of wooden hussars and a dented metal train from Victoria's era.

"Books," he said, shrugging. "I remember *Westward Ho!* in unspeakably tiny print."

She touched her lips to his cheek, gently rubbing away the lipstick mark. "We bourgeois are sensible about our creature comforts, including our toys."

"I'll remember that," he said, holding her hand to his cheek. "Araminta, listen, we do get along rather well, don't you think?"

"When we're not battling."

Peter kissed her palm. "Oh, I rather like our fights, especially the making-up part," he said, his lips moving up to the veins in her wrist.

Hoping he couldn't feel the violent leap of her pulse, she said, "What would Nanny Hogwood say of this sort of behavior in her nursery?" Earlier that day they had ridden over to one of Mainwaring Court's grace-and-favor cottages, where the whiskered nurse puttered around preparing elevenses.

" 'I do rather fancy your young lady, Master Peter,' " he quavered in a close approximation of the old woman's voice.

"Oh, how I adore you!" Araminta said, laughing.

"Good," Peter said earnestly. "Good."

VI

That warm August, while nonaggression and mutual assistance pacts were signed across the map of non-Axis Europe, Hitler remained determined to gather up Poland. Aware that a majority of his people were dead set against another war, he insured their loyalty with an incident code-named Konserven—canned goods. As cynically planned as it was named, Konserven was carried out when night fell on August thirty-first. SS storm troopers dressed in Polish uniforms attacked the German radio station at Gleiwitz, shooting drugged concentration-camp prisoners dressed in German uniforms, photographing the corpses as evidence of Polish bestiality. But already a million and a half troops were streaming across the Polish border while sixteen hundred Luftwaffe planes with laden bomb bays headed toward the sleeping cities of Warsaw and Cracow. The darkness that had descended upon Europe that night would last six blood-soaked years.

"Araminta? Aubrey here."

"What's up?" she asked into the telephone mouthpiece. Her voice echoed in the bare, seldom used little antechamber off the great hall. The Mainwarings, like their corps of friends, clung to the leisurely habit of communicating via the post. "I'll be home tomorrow evening—is it Daddy?"

"Haven't you heard the wireless?"

"Not since I arrived. Who knows if there is one. Aubrey, this place is firmly mired in the Tudor period."

"German tank divisions are well into Poland." Aubrey's voice was rapid. "Whitehall's sent an ultimatum telling them to get out."

"Is it any of our business?"

"It seems we signed a mutual assistance treaty with the Poles on August twenty-fifth. I'm in London, and the stations are madhouses. Children are being evacuated. The Irish and Germans are heading home. Men're everywhere—the radio's been announcing that Army, Navy, and RAF reservists are called up."

"Oh, my God." Araminta leaned against the paneling. "Do you think the Germans will listen to reason?"

"The Germans might. Hitler won't."

VII

"Are you positive Aubrey said we'd issued an ultimatum?"

"Eh?" she said, cupping her hand to her ear. "What was that?"

"You're not deaf, darling, but you might have misunderstood—"

There was a loud tap. Araminta darted into a corner, standing discreetly out of sight as a footman opened the door to tell Peter he was wanted on the telephone. Alone, she moved to the window, where heavy handmade lace curtains made her invisible from outside. She watched one of the maids moving around the terrace to retrieve whiskey glasses. Mainwaring Court had forty-seven inside servants, exactly half the number there had been before the Great War.

War . . .

War brought change even to aristocrats. . . . The old order changeth . . . the Mainwarings would come to accept her. A thread of excitement wound through her. The door opened. Peter's eyes held a gleam that matched her own.

"Aubrey was right," he said. "That was my orders. I'm to report to training camp tomorrow morning. I won't be there long."

"Why not?"

"I already have my pilot's license."

"You've never flown a combat plane."

"The RAF has damn few qualified pilots."

"But, Peter . . . You could be . . . hurt."

War . . . Suddenly she thought of the sepia photographs of those eternally boyish young officers, her uncles, whose bleached white bones lay beneath fertile French soil near Château-Thierry. Running across the creaking, magnificent Elizabethan parquet, she clasped Peter. The tightness of her embrace had much in common with her binding grip that summer night three years earlier (O banned memory) when after speeding tipsily through Berlin with Jürgen von und su Gilsa, she had awakened in a ditch to the irrefutable fact of humankind's mortality. *Jürgen was in the Luftwaffe,* she thought. *Maybe one day he'll down Peter.*

Before this she had not allowed Peter to caress her below the waist. Now she abandoned herself to him.

"Araminta . . ." His hot whisper against her ear aroused her yet more. "Darling, sweetest . . ."

While Peter locked the door, she yanked off the heavy, worn tapestry that served him as a bedspread. The late afternoon sun dappling them with the lacy patterns of the curtains, they made love on the Tudor four-poster bed.

VIII

On September third Araminta, Euan, and Elizabeth sat around the radio in the lounge. On this hot, muggy day, the windows were open, admitting a lazy buzz of bees that had as much emotion as Neville Chamberlain's flat voice. "I am speaking to you from Number Ten Downing Street. This morning the British ambassador in Berlin handed the German government a final note stating that unless the British government heard from them by eleven o'clock that they were prepared at once to withdraw their troops from Poland, a state of war would exist between us. I have to tell you now that no such undertaking has been received and that consequently this country is at war with Germany."

"War!" Euan reached to turn the switch. "I suppose that young flyer of yours will be seeing action," he said, irritably pulling at his tie. Though secretly delighted by Araminta's friendship with the son of an earl, he often advised her to concentrate on ordinary businessmen like himself. "Well, it seems that Aubrey did the right thing, enlisting."

"We'll do *our* bit," Elizabeth added.

"Yes, of course," Euan said testily. "I'll be working all hours now to relieve Aubrey, so it's best to stay up in London. You'll stay down here in Quarles and take in some of those evacuees."

"I'll find a war job," Araminta said.

"Poor old Alfred, over there in Germany." Euan thumped a fist on his thigh. "I shouldn't want to be in his shoes."

"Or Katy's either," Araminta said. "She'll have the worst of it."

TWENTY-FIVE

I

On August thirty-first Käthe found a letter from New York on the ornately carved hall table. Snatching up this, the first mail she'd received from Wyatt since the debacle in London, she raced up to her room.

It was dated 8/20/1939. As she read, her lips moved, as if she were a small child puzzling out the words. Finishing, she read the letter over again, then closed her eyes. *He's been taking out other girls while he got my letters. That idiotic, adoring pap! How could I have written such trash?* Her mind clenched tight around her humiliation, and it took several minutes for reality to hit.

This was a good-bye letter. Wyatt was saying good-bye to her.

She dropped face down on her bed, breathing unevenly. A watery pressure filled the cavities around her eyes. Excusing herself with illness, she didn't go down to dinner.

The windows showed a gray dawn light when she heard the voices. Alfred's rumbled queries, Trudi, the downstairs maid, and Frau Milch, the cook, shouting that berserk Poles had attacked the Reich. By the time Käthe ran into the hall, her father was alone. She seldom saw him in his nightclothes. How vulnerable he looked in the ancient, sagging plaid dressing gown with his gray hair rumpled. He held a newspaper. From twenty feet away she could read the huge headlines:

POLES STORM GLEIWITZ RADIO STATION
FÜHRER ORDERS COUNTERATTACK!
WILL ADDRESS REICHSTAG AT 10

Breaking his habit of speaking English to her, Alfred used his heavily accented German. "We've got a nasty business on our hands."

Nastier than he knew, she thought, recalling what Major Downes had told her of England's secret treaty with Poland. "How can we be sure the Poles attacked?" she asked.

"You know as well as I do that the Poles've been on a rampage against every German trapped in their territory. The Chancellor's been more than reasonable." Alfred's tone of rectitude told her he was not voicing his own convictions but what he preferred to believe—or wanted others to hear. "It's high time we showed them a firm hand." He stopped as she gave three staccato sneezes. "Kate, that's a nasty summer cold you've got. Under no circumstances are you to come to work this afternoon."

"I'll call Sigi and find out what's going on."

"Call Siegfried about what?" Clothilde emerged from the bedroom, wearing a wide-brimmed hat, her summer coat, and laced oxfords for her walk.

Alfred held up the newspaper.

Clothilde gave the headlines a cursory glance. "Didn't I mention that Siegfried telephoned two days ago? He's gone on maneuvers."

"At the Polish border, of course. He and the rest of the army had to be on the ready for this 'surprise attack.' " Käthe's wan sarcasm ended in another sneeze.

"Go back to bed, dear." Clothilde glanced at her lapel watch. "Trudi will bring you up something."

Käthe didn't touch the roll and margarine. She had developed a sick cold. Sipping tepid coffee, she stared out the window. The sunlit morning was sultry. Across the small still lake the Bolle Dairy horse waited docilely while the milkman chatted with a laundress hanging out sheets. From here the pair resembled miniature dolls in the serene landscape. *Could war seem more of a delusion?* Käthe wondered. *But if it comes, we'll be cut off from the English family. And already I'm cut off from the American.* Returning to the affairs of her aching, intransigent heart, she began to cry hot, sparse tears.

While she wept, Hitler was delivering an announcement to the Reichstag. His attempts to keep the peace were over, his patience was exhausted. From now on Polish bombs and bullets would be met with German bombs and bullets. The venomous speech entirely ignored the panzer divisions that were already deep into Polish territory.

At six Käthe dressed for dinner.

II

Because of stringent gasoline rationing Käthe and Alfred now took the S-Bahn to work, returning on the train that stopped at the Grunewald station at six thirty-three. Tonight, when the hall clock chimed seven strokes, Alfred still hadn't returned.

The tense silence was punctuated by Käthe's sneezes and the rattling of her outdated English *Vogue.* When double chimes indicated seven-thirty, Clothilde folded the sock she was mending and replaced the darning egg in her sewing box.

"Dinnertime. We'll have to go ahead without your father." Her voice was uneasy. Alfred was the embodiment of promptness, and deviations from routine disturbed them both. "What's that?"

An ululation had started, rising and falling like the howl of distant wolves.

The fine, pale hair of Käthe's arms prickled. "The air-raid alert."

Frau Milch and the new maid barged into the hall, clutching their gas masks, both shrilling at once. "Those sneaky Polacks!" "They're bombing us!" "The cellar!" "Yes, the cellar—hurry!"

"Turn out the lights," Clothilde commanded calmly. "For the blackout."

No Polish planes appeared, but the all-clear didn't sound until the small hours of the morning.

Alfred did not return home.

* * *

At dawn Käthe drove the old Steyr to the nearest police station. When she returned, she found Clothilde dressed for her walk.

"The *schupo* in charge was very kind," Käthe reported. "He called headquarters in the Alexanderplatz. No accidents were reported in Berlin."

"Accidents? Käthe, you're far too imaginative. Your father decided to stay in town, that's all. I'm certain he's at the shop."

Normality reigned on Unter den Linden. Nobody hurried to buy the newsboys' extras; sunlight reflected on the freshly washed pavement outside the Hotel Bristol. Kingsmith's window, however, remained barred. The employees were congregated in the narrow rear courtyard. The last anybody had seen Alfred was as he locked the door the night before.

Suddenly light headed, Käthe held on to the wall and went into her father's utilitarian office, sinking into the deep indentations of his leather desk chair.

"Fräulein Kingsmith?" Herr Knaupf stepped inside. His lips quivered on his overly white dentures. "There isn't anyone more loyal to the Reich than Herr Kingsmith, mind you, but there is the consideration that, uh, well, that the authorities might be rounding up certain foreigners."

Hearing her own fears put into words increased Käthe's apprehension. "He's not Polish," she snapped.

"This has nothing to do with anything," Herr Knaupf's tone grew yet more placating. "But those bloodthirsty Poles might easily drag in the French and the English."

As the door closed behind him, Käthe buried her head in her folded arms. *If only Sigi were here he could find Father with a single phone call. He has high connections.* Then, clear as if a snapshot had materialized on the desk, she saw the brilliantined sleekness of blond hair, the bull-like stance.

Otto Groener.

Her upset stomach rebelled. She sat tensed for over a minute, then blew her nose and reached for the telephone.

III

An instant after the secretary buzzed him, Groener stamped into the windowless waiting room. The Bavarian *tracht* was replaced by a meticulously tailored black uniform. There must have been lifts in his glossy jackboots, for he was several inches taller.

"Fräulein Käthe," he said, beaming. "Come inside."

This new wing of Gestapo headquarters at Prinz-Albrecht-strasse 8 had just been completed. Morning sunlight flooded through the large modern windows to polish the chestnut-brown leather sofa, cast a white glaze on the heroically scaled marble of a male nude, and glint on the glass that protected the enlarged wall-hung photographs of Groener posed informally with Hitler. Everything in the spacious, up-to-date office shouted, "I'm at the top of the ladder."

"Sit here, Fräulein Käthe—no, I'm going to call you Käthe. And you must call me Otto. Now tell me about your father. I didn't catch everything on the telephone."

Going through the story of her father's disappearance, she blew her nose twice.

"That's a rotten cold you have there. Let me get you a schnapps." Ignoring her refusal, he moved to the credenza. "Drink up," he said, and stood over her until she had choked down the brandy. "That'll cure you."

And her sinuses did feel less clogged.

"Now, about your father." He sauntered back to his desk. "Does he often stay out late?"

"Never."

"Never? Between us, a lot of very high-class ladies frisk in and out of Kingsmith's. Take it from one who knows, Käthe. Very few men can resist those ladies."

"He's missing!" she cried. She hadn't eaten this morning, she'd had no dinner the previous night: taken on an empty stomach, the massive dose of brandy was working instantaneously. "I tell you he's missing!"

"Stop breathing fire. In my line you learn it's always best to look for a simple explanation first. All right, I'll start tracking him down. But you must understand it'll take time. Everything's in an uproar. . . ." His voice grew hollow, then roared loudly, reverberating against her eardrums. She noticed haphazard details about Groener: the death-head insignia on his black uniform, the hairs clipped on his earlobes, the broad fingernails that were buffed and kept long as a woman's. She missed several sentences, jolting to attention as he said, "I'll do whatever's in my power to get to the bottom of Herr Kingsmith's disappearance."

"Very kind of you." Her tongue felt oily, and she had difficulty holding on to the words. "Sigi and I, very grateful."

"I'm doing this for you, Käthe."

He was coming around the desk. A box inside her brain warned her she would vomit if he touched her and she pushed out of the chair. The motion was too rapid. Dizziness overpowered her. Her head seemed to rise to the faraway ceiling, her body and legs dwindled into mush.

"What is it?" a receding voice asked.

Groener's massive head, the desk, the marble statue, goldframed photographs, the big office, circled around her. Then the vivid sunlight dimmed and went out.

IV

She was floating on something slickly comfortable, and a cool wetness was being held to her temples, then to the pulses in her throat. She could hear a man calling her name, but everything felt loose and comfortable and she didn't want to open her eyes. As the coolness touched between her breasts, she stirred feebly. Groener had unbuttoned her cotton dress and was pressing a balled wet handkerchief beneath her freshly ironed slip.

"Stop it." She meant to shout, but her voice was a thin, dry whisper. She flailed weakly at his hand. He kept the wet cloth firmly between her breasts.

"Just rest," he said in a low, hoarse voice. "No need to be embarrassed. My God, you're beautiful; I never saw any woman so beautiful."

After that the sequence of events was never quite clear in Käthe's mind. Had he cupped her breasts before he stuck his tongue in her mouth? Did she punch his arm after he sprawled on top of her? His fingers with those long, elegantly manicured fingernails were shoving under her panties. Had she twisted too vehemently or were his scratches on her vagina intentional?

He jammed her knees apart, shoving his penis into her. Pain, intense, corrupting pain. The sensation of betraying Wyatt and defiling love. Groener's mouth stayed clamped over hers. She snorted and bubbled in her struggle to breathe as he rammed at her.

She was gasping and sobbing when he got to his feet.

"Blood," he said repentently, wiping the leather couch.

"You pig," she said thickly.

"No wonder you were fighting me off," he said. "Don't cry, little princess, it had to happen. I couldn't help myself. Don't cry. The instant anything turns up on Herr Kingsmith, I promise you I'll be in touch."

Her left thigh twinging with every step, she limped down the broad, arched marble hallway. The busts of Party deities and the waiting petitioners gazed at her with equally dead eyes. *He's going to look for Father and what else matters?*

She went directly home. Crawling back in bed, she told Clothilde that her cold was worse and Alfred wasn't at the shop. "But Sigi's old friend Otto Groener has promised to track him down. We should hear any minute."

They had heard nothing about Alfred by nightfall.

The following morning, Sunday, September third, Käthe used her cold to beg off church. At lunch, whenever the kitchen door opened they were assaulted by excited radio reports of England's declaration of war. Clothilde's eyes were rimmed with shadows and a strand of gray-blond hair had escaped the neat knot to dangle on the collar of her Sunday silk blouse. Käthe patted her mother's large trembling hand.

At five, soon after the announcement that France had declared war on the Reich, Clothilde opened the grand piano for her Sunday Bach. A car pulled into the driveway and Otto

Groener emerged. The stately chords faltered as Käthe rushed to open the front door.

"I'd better see your mother," Groener said.

His unctuous gravity told everything.

Alfred, caught in the pitch darkness, had been killed by a car or truck. The police were not yet permitted to release news of blackout accidents.

<h1 style="text-align:center">V</h1>

The warm rain had stopped an hour earlier, but wetness still darkened the old tombstones and turned the sides of the open grave to slick mud. *Man that is born of woman hath but a short time to live.* . . . Sigi, on compassionate leave from Poland, was one of the pallbearers. His boot slipped as they lowered the coffin. From inside came a muffled yet heavy shifting sound, evocative of Alfred's imposing size.

Käthe shuddered, her nausea returning. *We therefore commit his body to the ground* . . . The coffin settled in the grave. Sigi stepped back between Käthe and his mother.

Clothilde's immense black hat, resurrected from her widow's weeds of thirty years earlier, had a dense chiffon veil that hid her face so it was impossible to see whether or not she was weeping. Käthe kept drying her eyes. Sigi let the tears slide down his good-natured face.

It was a sparse group gathered at the muddy grave. The household servants, Kingsmith's staff, and three old friends. Everyone else had stayed away on the probably accurate assumption that the Gestapo would have neighborhood snoops to report on anyone paying last respects to an Englishman. As far as Käthe was concerned, though, the absentees were all named Kingsmith. How awful for her father to be laid to rest without his family. Communications with England were out of the question, but Käthe had gone to the main telegraph office on Oranienburgerstrasse to send a cable to New York. Thus far there had been no response. . . . *in sure and certain hope of the Resurrection to eternal life.* . . . She willed herself not to think of Wyatt's letter. Sigi's comforting arm was removed from her waist. Chief male mourner, he spaded mud onto the coffin. As the first clod fell, she recalled that her period had been even more irregular than usual. She was several weeks late.

An incandescent brilliance lit her mind.

I'm pregnant.

VI

Dear Wyatt,

I do not know how to tell you this. . . .

Käthe crumpled the sheet with the other balls of paper in the wastebasket. It was after nine, and she had been at her desk since late afternoon. Each time she got to the first sentence, she would recall *his* letter and could write no further.

The rain had started again, and through the light hush she heard a car turn in the driveway. Writing *Dear Wyatt,* she stared at the two words. By now they seemed without shape, form, or connection to another human being.

Could I get to New York? Yes. I must. It would be possible to tell him in person.

There was a tap on the door. "Käthe?" Sigi called. "You in bed?"

"Not yet."

Sigi came in. "Otto's here. He'd like to give you his sympathy."

A visible shudder passed through her. "It's nearly ten," she said.

"Look, I don't like what he's become either," Sigi said in a low rumble. "But he went out on a limb to find Father. He went right to the top, to Himmler himself, and with the war, I can promise you that getting through to Himmler is no mean feat." Sigi took his pipe from his mouth, coaxing, "He's in a hurry. It'll only take a minute."

After letting Groener briefly clasp her icy hand, Käthe moved to the fireplace.

"I wanted to be at the funeral," he said. "But you know how it is, briefings every hour on the hour. This is the first I could break away. And tomorrow morning I'm taking a special detachment to Poland."

Sigi, tamping tobacco into his pipe, looked up. "The front, hmm? You're one up on me."

"We'll be just behind the lines, a cleanup police action. And now we've taken Cracow—"

"We have?" Sigi asked.

"An hour ago. There'll be a special announcement on the RRG any minute. Cracow's one enormous ghetto. Think of trying to restore water and electricity while those *untermenschen* are shooting at us. Enough to make you see red, isn't it? German boys losing their lives helping the Yids?"

"We haven't heard about sniping," Sigi said.

"The general staff's job is to conquer, ours is to rule the occupied territory. But enough war talk." He looked at Käthe. There was warmth, solicitude, and a hint of pleading in the small eyes. "You do forgive me for—for missing the funeral?"

"Nobody could've been more helpful," she said tonelessly.

"I met Herr Kingsmith so many years ago, but I've never forgotten the way he showed me, a nobody, how to identify our fine German silversmiths by their stamps. I would have paid tribute to him, but I just couldn't make it. Aside from my new assignment I've been working like a dog with the committee on travel policy."

"What, tours of Poland?" Sigi asked.

Groener didn't smile. "Poland will soon be part of the Reich, and the committee's concerned with Germans visiting neutral countries. We can't have civilians taking off to wherever they want. Anybody traveling to a neutral country will need to give us a damn good reason. We're setting up guidelines. But there I go, talking shop again."

"We do appreciate the visit when you're so swamped." Sigi lumbered to his feet. "It's been a hard day for Käthe, she looks all in."

Groener bade her good night, adding, "If Frau Kingsmith or you ever need anything, you know the way to my office. The secretary will contact me."

Käthe stood absolutely still until the front door closed, then she ran upstairs. Darting into the lavatory, she knelt to vomit. There was no food in her stomach and only clear, sour bile came.

Anybody traveling to a neutral country will need to give us a damn good reason.

She wouldn't be able to go to America. But how could she have the baby here? Wyatt's background was in the Gestapo files as well as the recent trip to England that coincided with her holiday. *They'd know the baby's his.* Into her mind came the Nazi term *mischling. Mischling* meant a person with mixed Jewish blood. A *mischling* was a non-Aryan. In 1935 punitive laws had been enacted against non-Aryans.

Oh, God, God, what shall I do?

She remained in front of the lavatory in a position of prayer but no answer came.

TWENTY-SIX

I

"Is this Fräulein Kingsmith?" asked a shrill woman's voice.

"Yes, speaking."

"This is Captain Groener's secretary. The captain is in Poland but has asked me to tell you that he will return to Berlin the day after tomorrow. He requests the honor of lunching with you."

"Tell him I'll be delighted."

"The captain has suggested you meet at one at Restaurant Kranzler on the Kurfürstendamm."

The invitation did not come as a shock. After three weeks of alternating between tears, aimless thoughts, and naked terror for her unborn child, Käthe's mind had abruptly hardened to a cold mechanism rather like the steel springs of a watch. With none of the hesitation that had beset her during her attempts to write to Wyatt, she had sat down and composed a note to Groener. First thanking him for his assistance and many kindnesses (he had sent her two sympathetic letters and a black lace scarf from Cracow), she had requested to see him as soon as possible. She had printed *Rohrpost* in the upper-left-hand corner of the envelope, leaving herself no chance to change her mind. In less than two hours the pneumatic post had delivered her message to Prinz-Albrechtstrasse 8.

II

In the weeks since her father's death she had managed King-smith's with the assistance of the elderly employees. Fortunately—or unfortunately, whichever way you chose to look at it —there was no new merchandise suitable for gift giving in the Third Reich, which made Kingsmith's antiques a popular item. The morning of her lunch date with Groener she helped an overbearing if extravagant banker's wife who kept her until almost one. Käthe ran for her tram, jumping off at the many-spired Kaiser Wilhelm Memorial Church on the Kurfür-stendamm. It was a pleasantly warm autumn day, but her hands were clammy and she was shivering. Groener was waiting for her at Kranzler's. As they climbed the elegant staircase, a peculiar nerved-up fatalism enfolded her—was this how a gambler felt placing his last mark on the roulette table?

The restaurant was crowded with high-ranking officers and well-dressed women. Swooping waiters, all of them well beyond military age, balanced massive portions of beef, ham, and veal on their arms. A double-tiered trolley held rich-looking tortes and cream cakes. With legitimate use of the recently issued rationing cards, a German could buy under a pound of meat per week, a quarter of a pound of sugar.

Käthe, sipping a few mouthfuls of the buttery pea soup, reminded herself to nod at intervals to Groener's conversation. She waited until they were served their fish. The notes of a waltz playing in the background, she took a long, shaky breath.

"I'm pregnant."

"Isn't this too soon to be sure?"

"It comes regularly as clockwork." For once she hoped that her blush showed.

"Why so forlorn? Myself, I'm delighted."

His immediate acceptance took her breath away. Having been positive he would grill her about London and Wyatt, she had spent hours rehearsing her arguments. Could a few drops of blood on the brown leather sofa have totally convinced this hard-nosed Gestapo officer that he had deflowered her? Or was masculine vanity also involved?

"Delighted?" she blurted. "But you're married."

"What has one to do with the other? All that matters is that we're both of pure blood."

"All that matters to you," she said, allowing a quaver of bitterness into her voice.

"Käthe, I explained," he muttered. "I never meant to harm you. I was carried away. Certain things are out of a man's control."

"Can't you imagine how a girl like me, from my family, might feel? A bastard? There must be a way . . ." She let her voice fade.

Groener's nurturing expression disappeared. Thrusting his head toward her, he snapped, "If you're talking about what I think, the Führer's declared it a capital crime."

"An illegal operation?" She stared at him, aghast. "I never considered getting rid of the baby."

"Then what's on your mind?"

"I'm so confused I don't know. But the shame. My mother, Sigi—everybody will know. The shame, Otto, the shame."

"There is none, but unfortunately not everybody has caught up yet with the social changes in the New Order." As if embarrassed to meet her eye while he spouted this bit of Party philosophy, he looked away. Then he lowered his voice. "Have you heard of Lebensborn?"

Lebensborn, which meant "fountain of life," was kept well hidden in the shadows of the Third Reich and whispered about with titillation or righteous condemnation. Lebensborn was SS Reichsführer Himmler's project to produce a blond superrace by selectively breeding his SS officers with qualified Aryan girls. Lebensborn was precisely where Käthe had been leading the conversation. She summoned the innocent expression that she had practiced in front of her bedroom mirror. "Lebensborn? Isn't that a home for unwed mothers?"

"Why should a girl like you feel shame for giving birth to a racially sound child? The Führer asks it of you. Lebensborn maternity centers are secluded, private—each has its own registry office to record the births."

"And what happens to my baby?"

"*Our* child," he said tenderly. "Käthe, Käthe, little princess, there's nothing to worry about. Ideologically sound couples who can't have kids of their own are battering down the doors to adopt Lebensborn children.''

She took out her handkerchief. Her hand was trembling. Diehard Nazis would raise Wyatt's baby. But what other way could a *mischling* be absolutely safe in Hitler's Germany? She dabbed at her eyes. "How can I be gone for months?"

"Just leave it all to me. Now, stop looking so like the world's coming to an end. Try the trout. It's delicious."

"I'm not hungry."

His smile was tenderly proud. "So, the nausea. My poor little girl, the last place you want to be is a restaurant. I'll drive you back."

As they were chauffeured through the Tiergarten, he took her hand, pressing it to his thigh, keeping it there despite her attempts to pull away. "Käthe, do try to think a bit kindly of me. When I saw you at Eagle's Nest it was as if a mule had kicked me in the stomach. To be honest, if I weren't married, I'd have proposed on the spot. In a million years I never intended to take advantage of you."

She believed him. And though her loathing had in no way diminished, she perceived him differently. Groener was an emotional centaur, part a normal, even sentimental human being, part a creature nourished on the inverted Nazi morality.

The long black car pulled up in front of Kingsmith's. "How about a manager?" Groener asked. "D'you have a reliable man to take charge?"

She had already given the matter consideration. "Herr Knaupf, the chief clerk."

III

Groener's arrangements required far less ingenuity than she would have believed possible. A couple of days later Standartenführer von Rudorf, gray haired and courtly, one of the rare members of the Prussian officer caste wearing an SS uniform, arrived at the house. Clicking bows to Clothilde and Käthe, he expressed regret at disturbing them at the time of mourning, but his business was urgent. An English translator

of unimpeachable loyalty was needed immediately for a job
that would last from six months to a year. Should Fräulein
Kingsmith agree to serve the Reich in this vital wartime service,
her mail would need to be routed through Prinz-Albrecht-
strasse 8: she would be stationed the entire time at a secret
base.

TWENTY-SEVEN

I

Villa Haug, ten miles from Munich, had been purchased for its secluded grounds. The house itself was large but eccentric. To the original torso of a three-hundred-year-old Bavarian farmhouse later generations had added limbs of freakishly opposing architectural styles—a chalet that dripped wooden stalactites jutted from the front, a classically elegant Palladian wing receded toward the back gardens. To the left of the kitchen rose a four-story crenellated Norman tower. Not far from the Gothic gatehouse—manned night and day by SS guards—was hidden a lodge where SS officers and young women sometimes passed a few days and nights. For the most part, though, the girls arrived already pregnant.

Villa Haug was run along the same lines as a top-notch boarding school. The mothers-to-be were called by their first names, the matron checked their drawers and closets for neatness. Meat, milk, and butter were plentiful, the cooking dull. Weekday mornings were given over to classes on Party ideology, and in the afternoon, no matter what the weather, they walked two by two along the gravel paths. During Käthe's stay there were between twenty and thirty expectant mothers, all of them blue eyed, blond, and over five feet four inches tall, all able to prove Aryan ancestry back to 1750. For the most part they were fresh-faced adolescents who giggled and whispered ribaldly about the young men who had fathered their expected children, holding out hands to exaggerate the size of the man's sexual organ. They compared bellies, they seldom spoke of the girls who had babies and disappeared. When radios blared trumpet fanfares, they clutched each other, waiting breathless for announcements of victory. Yet their stupidity was imbued with sweetness. When doldrums or the ailments of pregnancy beset a girl, the others gathered around to comfort her; when a rule was broken, the transgressor was protected.

Käthe had been given the top room of the square Norman tower, which had narrow windows on all sides. From here she perceived Villa Haug through the distortion of the old glass. During the classes on Nazi ideology she daydreamed of Wyatt. She stared ahead with crossed hands, her face so white and exalted that Fräulein Scheldt, who taught the class, remarked to the matron that of all the empty-headed crop, Käthe alone had true commitment to the Führer's plans.

II

Mail came every Monday from Clothilde, and in bursts from Sigi. Groener wrote often. The two times he visited Villa Haug, he eyed her waistline with an odious hangdog egotism that made her shiver for days after.

In January, Clothilde forwarded a censored letter with a Swedish postmark. Käthe turned the envelope over. Hand-printed on the flap was

Ulla-Britt Onslager
Nybrogatan 55, Stockholm

Dearest Käthe,

I have only just heard the sad and terrible news. The entire family joins me in sending deepest sympathy on the loss of your father. It goes without saying that I would have written sooner had I known. Even though we are apart now, I think often and fondly of our pranks at La Ramée— oh, what fun we had "finishing" in Switzerland. Käthe, it's a disgrace how seldom we write. I realize that you are busy with the war effort, but surely there is still time for friendship. As for me, the big excitement is that everybody in the family came to Stockholm for Christmas. Karl was so smitten with the Onslagers en masse that he proposed. Yes, dear friend, he actually popped the Question. . . .

The remaining two pages were given over to effusions about Karl's proposal, a letter so girlishly banal that the censor had not inked out a word. Käthe stared out one of the narrow windows. White flakes drifted slowly from a white sky. At the Swiss finishing school there had been a Swedish girl named Ulla-Britt Onslager, a tall, exquisite redhead. Was this actually from her? It didn't matter. The code phrase "time for friendship" meant the sender was Aubrey's replacement.

Käthe shook her head, forcing herself from her numbness. She recalled one of the girls chattering about a brother studying the Norwegian language, another girl whispering over breakfast that her father was working on a new tank that would crush the French and English.

I must pay attention, she thought, taking out her notepad.

III

On April ninth the chaste calm of Villa Haug was battered by continuous trumpet blares and announcements. In the morning victorious troops of the Reich swarmed into Denmark, in the afternoon all strategic cities and ports of Norway were taken. "In this single day we have protected the freedom and independence of both our sister Nordic nations" set the tone for the rest of the speeches. Käthe felt as if she were drowning in the successive waves of poisonously triumphant gobbledygook.

Sweden was spared, and remained neutral territory.

As her pregnancy had progressed, Käthe had found it more and more difficult staying alert to the conversations around her. She had fallen deep into reveries of Wyatt, daydreams as unrelated to reality as smoking opium—and as addictive. No matter how often she reminded herself of his last letter, it was impossible to break herself of fantasizing a future in which they were united. Even worse were the unwilled night dreams—how could such crazily erotic dreams possess her swollen body?

On April ninth, the night of the Scandinavian coup, she found herself in a familiar yet altered landscape. The grounds of Villa Haug sloped down to a small lake, like the garden in Grunewald. Somewhere a gramophone played "Mi Chiamano Mimi," the liquid soprano notes falling around her like background music in a film. Wyatt came down the path to meet her, and she had a vague recollection that it was wrong for him to be in Germany, but she couldn't remember why. "What are you doing here, love?" he asked. She explained that Villa Haug was the only safe place to have their baby. "What baby?" he asked, and then she looked down at her body. Her stomach was flat. "But I'm pregnant!" she cried, her joy dwindling to apprehension. Then he took her in his arms, his hands caressing her backside, and she forgot everything else. Melting like the lusciously seductive Puccini aria, she drew him down. As they stretched on soft new grass, they were suddenly naked. Dizzy with desire, she rushed faster into the fleshly currents. The music ceased. Shouted announcements echoed around her. *"Achtung! Achtung!* All children and infants without certification of racial purity must report immediately!" Wyatt had vanished and Groener was piling stones on her stomach.

"Wyatt! Help me!" she cried.

Käthe awoke to a drumlike tension in her lower abdomen.

When she had arrived at Villa Haug, a septuagenarian doctor had examined her with shaky hands, then had unquestioningly entered the false dates she gave him on her chart. Until now she had successfully pushed out of her mind any problems. But as the tension began coming at regular intervals, she was forced to admit that the moment of truth was upon her. Around five o'clock, long after the tautness had turned into pains, she pulled on her robe and clumsily descended the stone staircase.

Nurse Weber, thin hair straggling under her cap, stood at the stove heating coffee. Her pathetically plain face kind and sympathetic, she asked, "What is it, dear?" Käthe, grateful one of the sieg-heiling, badge-wearing Nazi Brown Sisters wasn't on duty, explained about the pains. Nurse Weber used her apron on the steaming pot. Pouring them each a cup, she said, "You're not due, are you, Käthe?"

"Not for weeks, but—" The deep, cramping pain cut off Käthe's words.

The nurse pressed a hand to Käthe's stomach. "Mm, yes. Well, the first is unpredictable. Have a little breakfast."

As Käthe sat down at the scrubbed table, the bleakness and dreaminess of the last months vanished. A purposeful dedication filled her. The task was at hand and she couldn't waste energy on extraneous emotions like fear. Between pains she ate what was set in front of her. Nurse Weber left to telephone the doctor, then returned. "Dr. Stahl's unavailable. But I've delivered more than fifty babies. You mustn't worry."

Käthe looked at the steady freckled hands. "I'm glad," she said gratefully.

Lebensborn philosophy banned any type of anesthesia. In the bright, sterile delivery room Käthe sweated, thrashed, and groaned. Yet the sense of purpose never deserted her. During the pain she blew out breaths; between, she prepared herself for the next onslaught. Around six in the afternoon of April tenth, when dusk was falling and the other girls were assembled to hear the radio announce further Scandinavian victories, a terrible agony ripped her apart. There was something exhilarating and fervently elemental in this pain, a pain so intense that it dimmed her past and future, encompassing everything else in her life. She couldn't control her long, high-pitched shriek. When her scream faded, she heard another sound.

A thin wail.

"It's a boy!" Nurse Weber's homely face glowed with triumph. "Käthe, you have a son."

"Is he all right?"

"Fine and healthy."

"You're positive nothing's wrong?" Käthe gasped, forcing herself to add, "He's early."

"A fine, healthy little fellow."

"You're not lying to me, are you?"

"A perfect baby," Nurse Weber reassured. "Here, look at him."

The flannel-wrapped infant was laid in her arms. His pink face was the size of an apple and just as plumply round. A miniature version of Wyatt's full, well-delineated mouth yawned up at her. She couldn't help smiling.

"See? Isn't he a lovely boy? He'll have his naming and be inducted into the Black Order tomorrow." Nurse Weber turned away, gathering up the bloodied and soiled sheets. "You Lebensborn mothers think it's lucky to have a boy, don't you? Girl babies only get a speech. But the boys have a fine ritual." She paused. "The parents were notified when your labor began. By tomorrow night our young man'll be safe and snug in his home."

The parents . . . His home . . .

Reality overtook Käthe. She clasped the baby tighter. The hedge of secrecy that surrounded Lebensborn became impenetrable when it came to adoptions—the SS hid adoption records with fanatic zeal. Once her son left Villa Haug, it would be impossible to track him down. He would be lost to her. Her tears dripped onto the small fuzzy head. Nurse Weber, evidently accustomed to this response, maneuvered the infant from her arms, whisking him into the nursery.

IV

The Lebensborn naming ceremony was one of the Nazis' cultic, quasi-mystical curiosities. With a remarkable lack of insight into the feminine psyche the SS believed the Villa Haug liturgy so inspirational that if the mother were allowed to be present she would produce more children for the Reich. Before breakfast Nurse Weber helped Käthe down the stairs and into a wheelchair, pushing her to the ancient core of the house, where the walls were several feet thick. The single window piercing the small room was heavily shuttered. The shadowy light came from four thick candles set at the corners of the room's only furniture, an altarlike table on which had been set a pillow embroidered with a huge black swastika and the runic, lightning-flash SS symbol. In the shadows behind the table hung a framed print of Hitler in medieval armor gazing with noble pensiveness into the next thousand years.

This bizarre little chapel was the last place she would see her son. Käthe made a small choking sound. The three SS officers lounging against the wall had crushed out their cigarettes in a saucer and were positioning themselves to the right of the pseudo-altar. The tallest, an *untersturmführer* with a fleshy, knobby face, called out, "Who brings the manchild and for what purpose?" His booming voice had an artificial ring, as if the mumbo-jumbo embarrassed him.

"I, Otto," came the response. Late the previous night Groener had arrived at Villa Haug. When he'd come up to her room, Käthe had closed her eyes as if too weary to speak, and he had retreated, obviously to celebrate the birth with these friends. The trio raised their arms in a Nazi salute. Groener carried in the naked infant. His handsome face was sternly tensed, his black boots moved gingerly. With an audible sigh of relief he set the baby on the swastika-covered pillow. "I bring my son. I name my son. I dedicate my son to the Black Order and to our Führer."

"It is an honor to be an SS man," chorused the others. "We dedicate this, our newest brother of the Double Lightning, to our Führer."

"It is an honor to be an SS man," intoned the knobby-faced *untersturmführer*. "Touch him with the gleaming wolf's tooth that he might never know fear."

Groener reached to his belt, and the candle flame glinted on a silver dagger. With both hands he raised it above the baby.

Käthe started to her feet. *"No!"* she shrieked.

Turning to her, the four men showed their teeth in conciliatory smiles.

"It's a little tradition of ours," Groener said. "If you're worried, I'll put the point on my own finger."

The baby began to cry, jerking his small arms and legs. Water arced up, wetting Groener's sleeve. The men laughed, Groener the loudest of all.

"See, Käthe?" he said proudly. "Our boy can already handle his own battles." He touched the wrinkled, pulsing, angry red forehead with the dagger. "May you march forward into the future with the duties, obligations, and privileges granted unto you by membership in the Black Order."

The clear baby urine had melted awkwardness. The others repeated his words, their voices deep and reverent.

Groener touched the dagger point again to the baby's forehead. "Your name is Erich,"

"Erich . . ." Käthe murmured.

"Welcome, Erich, son of Otto. We welcome you to the honor of belonging to the brotherhood of the Black Order," the four men chorused. "So, Erich, shall you join us in the Fatherland's holy crusade against lesser races."

Flickering candles threw shadows on the men's faces as they, softly and not very tunefully, began singing the "Horst Wessel Lied," the Nazi anthem.

"Die Fahne hoch, die Reihen dicht geschlossen. . . ."

Her breasts ached to nurse Erich as he continued to kick and scream. Was it possible that the newborn infant retained some primordial ancestral memories? Was this descendant of Jewish Leventhals, working-class English, southern Americans, and proud Teutonic knights protesting the spooky Nazi ritual? His cries rose over the singing.

"Die Knechtschaft dauert nur noch Kurze Zeit. . . ."

V

After the naming ceremony Groener carried her up to her tower room, kissing her good-bye. He must return, he said, to "cleaning up the Polish ghettos," the meaning of which would later horrify the world.

At lunchtime Käthe heard a car crunching over the gravel. She pushed aside the untouched tray, moving unsteadily to the window that opened on the front.

A thin, well-dressed civilian was helping a stout brunette from a large Mercedes. After they hurried inside Käthe continued to stare at the car. The license plate number was FM 798. FM meant the car came from Frankfurt am Main. To obtain gasoline for so long a journey meant that the owner was a golden pheasant, a Nazi with a gold Party badge. Yes, now she could see the swastika medallions that marked the Mercedes as belonging to a high-ranking official.

After a few minutes the couple emerged. The man's arm circled protectively around the woman's plump shoulders. She carried a small, blanket-swathed bundle. They paused at the bottom of the steps, homburg and blue felt hat bending over the baby.

If the day ever came when it was once more safe for a German to be a German regardless of the racial laws, Käthe told herself, she would storm the city of Frankfurt searching for a boy named Erich, born on April 10, 1940.

She clenched her right fist. "I'll get you back," she said in a low, clear voice. "I swear I'll get you back."

SIX
1940–1941

September 10, 1940
Even before England is brought to her knees, we must be prepared to crush Soviet Russia in a quick campaign.

It is of decisive importance that our intention to attack be kept secret.

> —from Hitler's private papers, predating by two months his Directive 21 to draw up plans for an invasion of Russia code-named Operation Barbarossa

Unlike the SOE, MI-6, and the other British intelligence networks within German-conquered Europe, the actions of the small organization known as CI-4 have remained under fixed restraint. CI-4 is still operational, yet even to this day only a handful of ministers are privy to its wartime files. Many of the British agents and the German resistance fighters lie in mass graves with the other victims of the brutal, totalitarian Nazi regime. The survivors, gallant men and women who risked everything, can never be honored nor repaid.

> —from *Most Secret: A History of British Espionage,* by Sir Aubrey Kingsmith, published by Oxbridge Press, 1991

TWENTY-EIGHT

I

Lieutenant Aubrey Kingsmith halted to wipe his glasses outside double doors affixed with brass plaques:

BRITISH PASSPORT CONTROL

And the people who were still filling out forms at the counters had indeed come to this suite on the thirty-fifth floor of Rockefeller Center for visas and passports. Others like Aubrey, though, slipped through doors with the small, black painted warning: RESTRICTED TO AUTHORIZED PERSONNEL ONLY. These men and women were woven into the loose web of British intelligence organizations in the Western Hemisphere.

Both Aubrey and Downes were in the SOE, the Special Operations Executive, the spy network that Churchill had founded as one of his first actions as Prime Minister. Downes, however, also was top man of a far smaller and yet more clandestine group. CI-4. Reporting directly to Churchill, he had a scant half-dozen agents, all with German underground connections. Aubrey, one of the tiny network, had been dropped into the Reich twice.

Downes's business in the United States, however, was for the SOE. For two weeks the major had been conducting briefings while Aubrey unobtrusively took notes. This was Aubrey's first free evening in New York.

Emerging into the wall of late afternoon heat, he detoured

around Rockefeller Center, an unobtrusive maneuver to ensure that he wasn't being followed—not that he expected to be, but his training had tattooed the necessity of caution on an already thoughtful nature. Having reassured himself that nobody was paying the least attention to him, he gave himself up to the sweaty pleasure of walking through a city at peace.

At the Kingsmith apartment Humphrey greeted him with an avuncular hug and a barrage of questions about the British family. He kept interrupting his nephew's responses. From letters he knew about Elizabeth's evacuees, Euan's buying trips, Porteous's incredible stamina on the job, and of Araminta's adventures with London's Auxiliary Fire Service— she was one of the few women drivers in the AFS. "She's at the Knightsbridge station on Basil Street, conveniently near Harrods," Humphrey said archly.

"Not much to buy at Harrods," Aubrey said. "Just as well. She doesn't have much to spend. She gets two pound two a week, then kicks back fourteen bob for her meals."

"Let's hope Hitler never takes it into his mind to blitz London the way the Luftwaffe's been pounding Coventry." Humphrey's jowls trembled sadly as he shook his head. "How's that young RAF pilot of hers? Safe, I hope."

"Absolutely." Aubrey wasn't so positive as he sounded. Since the fall of France, when the Luftwaffe had been able to take off from the French coast, an RAF fighter pilot might sometimes go up as often as a dozen times a day. The casualties were staggering—when he'd left England, Peter had been the sole pilot left in his fighter squadron. "He's given her a diamond ring."

"My niece marrying into the peerage!"

Aubrey, not wishing to mar his uncle's harmless, snobbish pleasure, didn't mention that the earl and countess of Mainwaring had ignored their youngest son's engagement as well as the Kingsmiths' letters.

"Dear, Aubrey looks like he could use a drink." Rossie, changed from her workday girdle and silk suit to a floor-length hostess coat, swept in. "I could too."

Aubrey requested soda water.

"Well, well," Humphrey said. "From Euan's letters it seems to me you should have acquired a taste for Scotch." Aubrey's cover was a desk job in supplies at a nonexistent artillery school in the Highlands. "I must say it gave me quite a start when I heard your voice. What brings you to the States? Our new lend-lease program?"

Aubrey pressed the cold glass against his forehead and changed the subject. "When Dad heard I was coming, he sent me this." He fished out a folded paper curved by his body's heat. "It's a list of plated biscuit barrels and salvers, egg holders, secondhand Victorian things. He wants you to let him know if you're interested."

"Then it's possible for Euan to ship goods?" Rossie asked.

"The boats coming in this direction have space. And England's rather in need of dollars."

Humphrey sighed and glanced toward the wall, where he had taped a large map of the world. Red-topped pins marked the forces of the beleaguered British Empire; black, Hitler's expanding territory. "It's dreadful, dreadful. What do you think of this talk of the Nazis invading England?"

"We'll be ready for them," Aubrey said.

Rossie had been reading the letter. "We can sell however much Euan can ship. Victorian plate's considered antique here and sells like hotcakes."

"Our business is up fifty percent over last fall." Humphrey thrust out his chest. "Oh. And, Aubrey, Wyatt sends his apologies. He'll be late for dinner. Work. No case handled by the firm goes to trial without his opinion. That's saying a lot. Carrothers, Uzbend, and Hanson are the absolute tops."

Over an enormous rib roast—Aubrey couldn't accustom himself to the American profligacy with food—Humphrey brought up the subject of the Berlin Kingsmiths. Käthe, it seemed, wrote intermittently to her uncle and aunt.

"But we've only sent them a condolence note," Humphrey said. "Under the circumstances, she and Wyatt breaking up, the war, it doesn't seem the right thing. Seconds, either of you?" He clashed the sharpener against the carving knife, then burst out, "Damn it all! I can't get over a niece of mine—and a stepnephew—being on the other side."

"Humphrey, we're not on any side," Rossie pointed out. "You've been a citizen for years, and we're neutral."

"Hitler's a swine. And one hears awful stories about the occupied countries. Well, I suppose we should thank God for neutrality. Otherwise Wyatt would be in the thick of it."

II

Carrothers, Uzbend, and Hanson had their offices on the twentieth floor of the Dejong Plaza, the same huge complex that housed Kingsmith's. Wyatt's window overlooked Fifth Avenue. He had just returned from the conference room, where Joseph Broadmore, founder and CEO of Broadmore, Inc., had pounded on the table and demanded they resort to litigation to recover monies owed the company. Wyatt had suggested a compromise about payment and Broadmore had calmed a bit. Wyatt held an agreement that he had drafted earlier in the day to this end. Taking off his jacket, he unknotted his blue rep tie and picked up the long yellow legal pad to redraft the clauses in light of the marginal notes he had jotted during the meeting. After a few minutes he looked up at the dark window. His tan had faded, and maybe because of this, he appeared thin.

Why am I so lonely?

Why indeed? Certainly it wasn't from isolation. He dated a number of girls, and slept with two, a stunning redheaded divorcée and a very pretty legal secretary from a firm on the next floor. He was invited to the right dances and the right weekends, his parents insisted he live at home. The partners and associates in his firm asked him to join them for lunch and invited him to their dinner parties. Yet at heart he felt set apart. A fraud, a phony, a ringer. Possibly if his mother had called him Wyatt Leventhal he would have felt more attuned with himself.

Käthe . . .

Sighing, he opened the top drawer of his desk and rummaged in back for a photograph he had snapped of her in Hyde Park. The black and white didn't do her fair coloring justice, and a shadow fell across her left cheek, marring the perfect oval, yet her face blazed with happiness. Her arms were raised, as if she were reaching out to embrace him. Far away in the deserted offices a telephone rang. With an angry frown he shoved back the snapshot. If he were forced to dissect his predominant emotion toward Käthe, he would have admitted to a hot and ugly sensation akin to hatred.

He read through the four pages rapidly, slashing out two clauses, scribbling several paragraphs, then put the letter in the open box for his secretary to retype.

He shrugged on his jacket but didn't reknot his tie. Carrying his briefcase, he went down the hall. The light was on in Harper Uzbend's office, and as he passed, the senior partner called out, "Kingsmith, step inside a minute, will you?"

A single light threw its beam down on Harper Uzbend. He had the sparse white hair and gaunt face that seemed bred on a rocky Maine farm, but in fact he came from a cultivated Virginia family and spoke with the softness of that state. "We think highly of the way you're handling the Broadmore account."

"Thank you, sir."

"This might be a bit premature, but we have been considering making you a partner."

"I'm honored." If this were true, why did he feel so heavy and joyless? He thought of Aubrey, whom he would see in a few minutes, and of the embattled British Kingsmiths. And yes, he thought of Käthe in Germany. "But I won't be with the firm much longer."

"What?"

"I'm enlisting." The decision seemed preordained.

Uzbend laced his fingers and rested his hands on the desk. "Believe me, there is nothing more rash that you can do."

"Sir, sooner or later we'll be in it with the British."

"The Germans have a great deal to be said for them."

"My father's English."

"Balderdash. Nobody would be more shocked than he at the way you're throwing away your chances. I've shopped at Kingsmith's downstairs. He's an American."

"Naturalized. And frankly, sir, I can't think of one damn thing to say for the Germans." Wyatt stepped out of the pool of light and left the office.

III

When he arrived at the flat, they were finishing the richly sweet pecan pie and ice cream. They stayed at the table while he mechanically downed the food that had been kept hot for him. Twice he got up to freshen his drink. Rossie raised her eyebrows, but she had already commented on his alcohol consumption and was too sensible to waste her time broaching the subject again.

The drinking was something new, Aubrey reflected.

After dinner he said, "Wyatt, this is my one free night. Care to show me a bit of New York's nightlife?"

*"The Great Dictator'*s still running," Humphrey said eagerly. "I wouldn't mind taking it in again, would you, Rossie?"

"Let the boys enjoy themselves," Rossie said, patting her husband's hand tenderly.

IV

"Uncle Humphrey tells me that none of you write to Berlin."

"I sure as hell don't. Is this why you wanted to be alone? To pump me about *her*?" Wyatt's brief spurt of anger faded, and he slouched back in the booth. They were at Stella's Place, a narrow, dimly lit drinking establishment on Lexington Avenue. "Sorry," he said after a few seconds. "But it gives me acute colitis to think about my correspondence with Germany."

"So you do write?"

"Did. Past tense. Did. My timing stinks is all. When I left London last year, our big romance was finished. She knew it was over, but she kept on sending me letters. And you know me, never one to leave dry wash on the line. I wrote to reiterate that we were kaput. The letter must have arrived around when poor old Uncle Alfred bought it."

"It *was* rotten timing. Are you sure she knew it was over?"

"Christ, Aubrey, she made the choice. She went back to Germany instead of coming to New York. And in case you're wondering, I get around a lot. And my guess is she's dating the cream of the Wehrmacht. If you're still interested in the enemy when the war's over, the coast is clear."

Aubrey took a handful of peanuts, eating them slowly, then licking the salt from his fingers. Neither of them spoke until the waitress had set down Wyatt's shot glass and a tumbler clinking with ice.

"The folks have no idea of this yet, but tonight I gave old man Uzbend my notice." Wyatt threw his head back, belting down the liquor. "Sooner or later we'll be in this mess. I'm jumping the gun and enlisting."

"Because of Käthe?"

"Sure. Hitler's such a sweet, thoroughly decent person, why else?"

"She never was a Nazi."

"Quit staring at her through rose-colored glasses. Our *mädchen's* in the land of swastikas and racial laws by choice." Wyatt's voice grew louder, then cracked. He pressed his thumb and forefinger over his forehead, gouging into the bone. His breathing grew strident, his shoulders shook.

Aubrey was astonished at the extent of his cousin's misery. After all, it had been a full year since the breakup. He longed to say something comforting, but of course the last thing he could do was give reassurances that Käthe, rather than being a Nazi, was risking her skin for her father's country. A mean, petty voice inside him crowed, *I know her better, she's more mine.*

V

By the time Major Downes and Aubrey returned to England, all hell had broken loose over London. On September seventh 625 Luftwaffe bombers protected by 648 fighters had roared up the Thames Estuary. High explosive bombs, incendiary bombs, delayed action bombs, rained down on the civilian population. Thoroughly frightened for his family, especially for Araminta, whose job was to drive her station officer through the worst of the London Blitz to burning buildings, Aubrey requested and received a thirty-six-hour pass.

* * *

"Aren't I smashing?" Araminta asked.

"Rather." Aubrey had never before seen her in the Auxiliary Fire Service uniform. Her navy-blue peaked cap tilted on her vivid hair, her tight-cinched belt denying the masculinity of her navy-blue trousers, even the wellington boots somehow adding to the overall effect, she might have been posing for a recruiting poster as she leaned against the sandbags that protected the brick and limestone Knightsbridge station. "But this job of yours has me worried."

"The way Jerry's pounding, it's safer than being stuck in some Anderson shelter, so stop singing Daddy's tune."

"He's right."

She fingered the large diamond on her left hand. "In a small way this helps me understand what Peter's going through day after day, poor darling." Her tired eyes gave him a quick look. "But you know exactly what I mean."

"Me? I'm planted behind a desk, thank God."

"Use that cowardly line on somebody else, it doesn't convince *me*. You're no quartermaster in Scotland. I might be the more reckless, but you've never funked out of a fight."

"In this case my sight did it for me."

With a snort of disbelief Araminta looked in the direction of the London docks, the East End, the poorest section of London, where a lurid reddish haze darkened the morning sky. "Talk about bravery. It's a marvel the way the East Enders stand firm while those Luftwaffe bastards keep dropping bombs on them."

Then suddenly from that direction came the sharp clatter of antiaircraft guns. While puffs exploded between the massive silver barrage balloons, the air-raid sirens sounded. There was a clangor inside the station house.

"The bells go down," Araminta cried. "Duty calls."

She darted to the white-tiled interior where men already were sliding down the polished steel post. Moments later two big fire engines raced out, the men in back ringing the bells. Araminta, in a steel helmet, whizzed by at the wheel of a commandeered London taxi, the steel-helmeted station officer in the rear seat.

VI

Euan was off in Wales and Porteous was working at a young man's pace on Bond Street—Kingsmith's windows had been broken and boarded over. Aubrey shared his grandfather's luncheon thermos flask of meatless oatmeal soup in the offices, whose fishbowl windows were also hors de combat, then went to a borrowed flat. His convoy had been battered and he was tired enough to sleep through the night's air raid.

The doorbell awoke him around nine in the morning. He stumbled over his shoes, cursing the blackout curtains on his way to answer.

An ATS sergeant swathed in a mackintosh saluted crisply. "Lieutenant Kingsmith?" she asked.

He nodded, puzzled. Only Downes, who had arranged for the flat, knew he was here, and Downes would have telephoned.

The sergeant handed him a note written in blue ink. "I'm meant to wait, sir," she said.

Still at the door, Aubrey slit the envelope.

Pray join me at 9:15 this morning.
WSC

Beaming with undiluted pride, Aubrey carefully stowed the folded note from Winston Churchill in his billfold next to his favorite snapshot of Käthe, then hurried to shave and dress.

The sergeant marched duckfootedly and in silence through the light rain to Great George Street, turning at the sandbagged pillbox. At the classically pillared New Public offices, where steel shutters hid the ground-floor windows, she showed passes to a Royal Marine orderly. Inside more passes were shown. She led Aubrey along a hall to where another Royal Marine stood at attention on a rubber and coconut mat outside a steel door. After the display of yet another pass the door was opened. Aubrey followed the ATS down a flight of stone steps to the bustling underworld about which he'd heard. Uniformed men and women hurried beneath signs warning WATCH YOUR

HEAD. Crude timber, steel, and cement buttressed the ceilings. Lights dangled from wires. Typists clicked outside closed doors, ventilators whirred. Hurrying along the corridor, Aubrey glimpsed faces familiar from photographs: Lord Beaverbrook, Clement Attlee, Neville Chamberlain. This makeshift cellar warren was the Cabinet War Rooms.

The sergeant came to attention outside a door marked 65A. "Wait here, sir," she said, marching off.

After several minutes a slightly built male secretary in a morning suit opened the door. The familiar smell of cigars emerged from the small underground room. This, the innermost heart of the British Empire, was furnished with a narrow bed, a large desk, and a small desk. Curtains had been drawn behind a pair of crossed beams.

The Prime Minister, nodding to dismiss the secretary, remained hunched over the big desk, his plump hands braced on an immense map. Standing there with his head drawn down, wearing his one-piece zippered siren-suit, he was a Humpty-Dumpty figure, yet far from ridiculous. Aubrey, who hadn't seen Churchill since that August afternoon when he'd brought Käthe to tea at the House of Commons, felt his original awe swell.

"Kingsmith." His host took off his half-spectacles. "Here, take a look at this."

Aubrey moved the few steps and saw that the map was of Russia.

"Where d'you suppose the Nazis are going to attack?" Churchill asked.

"Attack?" Aubrey coughed to relax his throat muscles. "Sir, that *is* the Soviets, isn't it? Stalin and Hitler are allies."

" 'The dragon's nature is that it must devour all other animals, then make a supper of its own tail.' Wasn't that how you put it in your book?"

Aubrey's astonishment at the news about Russia faded briefly at the accuracy of the quote from *Tarnhelm*. The stories of the Prime Minister's photographic memory evidently were true. "Word for word, sir."

"I have no brief for Stalin, mark you, he's the same wicked

breed as Hitler, a bear gobbling up half of Poland, Finland, the Balkans, but at this moment in our history I'd sign a mutual assistance treaty with Beelzebub himself. A Russian front would take the Luftwaffe off our necks and give our war production a chance to gear up."

"But sir, the OKW wouldn't be that insane."

"Their general staff certainly wouldn't. But Herr Hitler's Supreme Commander." Churchill tapped the unlit cigar against his forehead. "A bit mad, that gentleman—clever, mind you, but mad. Barbarossa."

"Barbarossa, sir?"

"We have reason to believe it's the code name for plans of the sneak attack. You will bring Barbarossa to us."

"Me, sir?" Aubrey couldn't control his incredulity.

"Of course not you," Churchill responded. "What British agent could penetrate their general staff headquarters? It's that delightful young cousin of yours we're counting on."

"Käthe?"

"Yes, Miss Kingsmith."

Aubrey forgot self-control. "She's already risking far too much with those letters to Sweden!" he cried.

"I don't need to remind you that our cities are being destroyed and that our convoys are fighting losing battles, that the RAF is on the ropes."

Oh, God, now he's going to say that the fate of the free world hangs in the balance, Aubrey thought. During the ensuing pause he recalled the afternoon queues waiting with blankets and pillows outside the tube stations that were used as air-raid shelters, he saw the ugly clouds of smoke above the East End, saw Araminta's tired but determined face as she spoke of Peter's danger.

Churchill sat wearily at his desk, indicating that Aubrey should take the tubular metal chair opposite. "Now, about your cousin."

"Sir, with all due respect, let's assume that there is a plan. Käthe's managing my late uncle's shop on Unter den Linden, she doesn't have access to secret war plans."

"Arrangements are being made to drop you into Germany."

Aubrey breathed shallowly. Again? The force of his fear during his two missions inside enemy territory still astounded him, as did his moments of command.

Churchill's glower added to his often mentioned resemblance to a bulldog. "There, you will convince Miss Kingsmith to help us learn about Barbarossa. With that half brother an adjutant to General von Hohenau of the OKW, she should have no difficulty landing a position in the Bendlerblock."

"I refuse to—"

"You're in uniform, Kingsmith! You will refuse nothing, do you hear?" The desk shook as Churchill's small, plump fist slammed down.

"If Käthe's caught, they'll torture her until she gives way. Then they'll kill her."

The Prime Minister continued to glare, but Aubrey didn't wilt.

Churchill's chin slumped on his round chest, then he smiled. "You'd be surprised at how rarely I get arguments from that particular chair. You're a spunky lad, Kingsmith."

"Sir, I'm quaking," Aubrey retorted honestly.

"Stop worrying about your cousin. The girl's half English, she'll muddle through like the rest of us."

Twenty-nine

I

At one o'clock on an overcast Saturday afternoon in late November of 1940, Käthe stood at the doorway of the barred shop, saying good-bye to her elderly employees. Herr Knaupf, the last to leave, gave her his mummified smile, which managed to be both subservient and superior. He remained the shop manager. When she had returned from Villa Haug last April she had not possessed the mental equilibrium to run Kingsmith's. She didn't have the heart to displace him although she felt better now.

Käthe had recovered by the old trick of burying herself in activity. She worked long days, spending evenings with young officer friends of Sigi's, gathering conversations of every sort like a child picking great armfuls of wildflowers, news that she later distilled to code for Ulla-Britt Onslager. This August she had scrounged up food for two silent adolescent Jewish boys whom Schultze had asked her to hide until the pair could be spirited out of the country to Spain. She tried to leave herself no time to think. But the brain moves far too swiftly to be harnessed, and she could never completely banish the feel of the light weight in her arms, the milky smell, the tiny mouth that replicated Wyatt's. Her vow still held. If ever the day came when Erich's *mischling* status could be safely known, she would rush to Frankfurt and move heaven and earth to get him back.

Going into the office, she moved back the silver-framed photograph of her father and the telephone to spread invoices across the desk. Laying out the bills to be paid with the Reich's foreign currency, she sighed. When it came to dealing with the Protectorates, the government's euphemism for conquered countries, no matter how often the brokers assured her they were delighted to deal with Kingsmith's, she felt a plunderer. Herr van Roophuis from Holland had actually said, "Better to sell our fine antiques than be robbed." The topmost Nazis in the Protectorates commandeered whatever they wanted.

Käthe was jotting down the sums she owed when a tap sounded on the glass. Jumping, she looked up.

A soldier who must be at least six feet to be visible in the mud-streaked, tape-crossed clerestory window was smiling at her. His field-gray cap was slanted at the prescribed military angle above a bony, sensitive face.

A wave of dizziness overcame Käthe. For several moments her mind refused to accept the evidence of her eyes.

The soldier was Aubrey.

II

She fumbled with the rear door bolt, he slipped inside. Wordlessly, they clutched each other. He pulled back to gaze at her as if memorizing her face. "I've been watching the shop. You're alone, aren't you?"

"They left ages ago. Oh, Aubrey, Aubrey! Am I dreaming?"

"You're awake. Now pull down the blackout blinds."

She obeyed, then lit a candle, explaining that the electricity wouldn't come on until dusk. "It's impossible—you in Berlin!"

"Corporal Adolf Bader at your service." Clicking his boots, standing at attention, he flung his arm up in the Nazi salute. "Serving my Führer in Corbiel, a small town just south of Paris. Poor Vati, may God rest his soul, just passed on. I have a compassionate leave."

It had taken Käthe this long to realize that Aubrey's German was flawless. Though his syntax had always been above reproach, his intonations had been pure Oxford English. Now he spoke in a *Berlinische* accent—he might have been born and bred in a Berlin working-class district.

Aubrey, on his part, could not take his eyes from her. Tall

and slender as a ballerina, her hip tilted in that well-remem-
bered artless sensuality, her hair drawn back into a nugget of
pale gold, she was the same yet somehow altered. *It's the expression,* he decided. When her joyous smiles faded there was a
sadness about her lips that hinted of mortal wisdom, of mysterious, unexplored continents within her, and he was yet more
entranced.

"I'm a dud at compliments," he said. "But you do look
smashing."

"Candlelight works wonders," she said, then laughed excitedly. "But you're here, you're here. Tell me, how are Grandpa
and Araminta? Uncle Euan and Aunt Elizabeth? Is London
destroyed the way the Ministry of Propaganda says?" Her voice
faded. She longed to ask about the American branch, about
Wyatt, but was terrified she might discover that he was married.
"Has Dr. Goebbels been doctoring up the films of the Blitz? Is
London destroyed?"

"I can't tell you anything you wouldn't hear through normal
channels."

"You call this normal?"

After a momentary hesitation he said, "London's not in the
best of shape, but the morale's tremendous. Kingsmith's has
just been bombed out. Temporarily, until they lease another
shop, they're using the Bayswater Road house. And Grandpa's
the eighth wonder of the world. Working all hours, leading all
of us around during the blackout—"

"He knows the darkness."

"He takes the reins when Father goes on buying trips to
scrounge up merchandise. And Araminta's with the Auxiliary
Fire Service—she drives the station officer through terrible
fires in the worst of the Blitz. She jokes about it, but she's quite
the heroine. She's engaged to Peter."

"Tell me another!"

"His parents are still dead set against it, but he produced a
diamond anyway. And that's your ration of gossip. How's your
side? Where's Sigi?"

"Here in Germany." Her turn to hold back information. For
a fleeting moment she wondered what mechanism in her eter-

nally divided loyalties acted as a sluice gate, permitting her to write those spy letters to Ulla-Britt yet refusing to let her divulge that Sigi, as his uncle's aide, was stationed twenty miles from Berlin, at Zossen, the camouflaged buildings and underground chambers that made up the OKW's ultrasecret headquarters. "He's a captain now."

"Good old Sigi. What about Aunt Clothilde?"

"Managing with one rather dim-witted maid—Mother never changes. I admire her, but she's so *irritating*. Those eternal schedules! She now sets aside hours to cook and queue for food. Aubrey—"

"Try getting used to 'Corporal Bader,' " he interrupted.

"I can't tell you how much it means, Corporal Bader, seeing you even for a few minutes."

Aubrey held his long, narrow hands near the candle, examining his palms like a fortune teller trying to predict his own future. "You *are* my mission, Käthe."

"Me?" Her voice rose in astonishment. "Aren't my letters to Sweden getting through?"

"Yes, and they're wonderful, but we need more information." He paused. "The Prime Minister's convinced there are plans afoot for Germany to invade Russia."

"Russia? You can't be serious! Why would we attack Russia? They're our allies. I never heard anything so potty! Surely Mr. Churchill knows that they're supplying us with oil and grain—it was in one of my letters, even."

"At first I thought Russia was ludicrous too."

"Ludicrous? My God, every schoolchild knows what happened to Napoleon. General von Hohenau would laugh his head off! And so would the rest of the OKW. Russia's sheer wishful thinking on Mr. Churchill's part. All this Luftwaffe pounding—could the High Command's intentions be clearer? They're planning to invade England."

"The OKW doesn't run your armed forces, Käthe. Hitler does. Have you read *Mein Kampf*? He says that Germany must look to Russia for additional territory. Before his pact with Stalin he couldn't rant enough against communism. The more I thought about it, the more sense it made."

"I've been going to quite a few parties and receptions. I've heard staff officers after a few drinks. Surely one of them would have blurted out a hint."

"The plans are code-named Barbarossa. The Prime Minister himself briefed me on this. My orders are to ask you to try to find out if Barbarossa is operational."

"But I already told you. I haven't heard a peep."

"The Prime Minister mentioned that you could get inside the Bendlerblock with Sigi's connections."

"Sigi? Use Sigi?"

"If you want my advice you'll refuse."

"What choice do I have? If I were caught sneaking through desks, Sigi would be swept up like a pin. Maybe the general—maybe Mother too." *Would they track down Erich?*

"No arguments from me. The last thing I want is to put you at further risk." In the chiaroscuro shadows Aubrey's face was white. "Käthe, that brings me to Schultze. Are you still involved?"

"You've no idea how much worse it is than when you were here. The Jews are all being resettled in Poland. According to newspapers, to work in war plants. You can imagine conditions in those factories. People who are quite decent otherwise are terrified to help them. I'd a thousand times sooner throw in with Schultze than be a spy—" The phone rang. Käthe's hand flew to her throat as if the person at the other end could see her with her English cousin. At the second ring Aubrey picked up the old-fashioned instrument, holding the speaker to her mouth.

"Kingsmith's," she said.

"Is that you, Käthe? Armin here." First Lieutenant Armin Lamm, her escort for this evening. "I'm checking that you expect me to pick you up at Kingsmith's at six."

"Perfect," she said automatically.

"This reception's turning out to be quite the event. Field Marshals Brauchitsch and Keitel are definite, and there's a rumor that Göring will put in an appearance."

"Göring himself? I'll be ready at six on the dot."

Aubrey had overheard everything. A beat after she hung up, he said, "Sounds like an interesting evening."

"Poor Armin, he got terribly burned in France. He's studious and shy and the scars embarrass him. Oh, God, if only one could line up the good people and separate them from the awful ones."

"Wouldn't that be lovely."

Staring at the silver-framed photo of Alfred, she said slowly, "Tell the Prime Minister I'm declining."

"I'm glad."

She turned away, unable to hold back. "What do you hear from America?"

"I was over there this September."

"Is Wyatt . . . Is he still single?"

Aubrey understood her quaking tone. He had been fearing that she would ask this very question. "Very much so. He's in their army officers' training program."

"So he's enlisted. Did he tell you that it's over between us?"

"He told me."

"God, Aubrey, what's the matter with me? Why didn't I marry him in thirty-nine?"

"You promised Uncle Alfred and Aunt Clothilde that you wouldn't," Aubrey said. "Why blame yourself?"

"You're blaming *him!*" she snapped, and began to cry.

Aubrey reached his arms around her. Her fragile body shuddered against his field-gray uniform and he held her tight, resting his cheek on that marvelous silky hair. He treasured every second of the couple of minutes that he held Käthe—but why did the embrace have to be like this? Consolation for the loss of Wyatt? When she pulled away, his expression was rigid.

III

Lieutenant Armin Lamm held the umbrella over Käthe as they hurried along Unter den Linden. A line of long black cars affixed with swastika flags were circling the wet cobbles of Pariserplatz and drawing up at the Adlon. Inside the hotel Käthe and Armin joined the crush of bejeweled women and high-ranking Wehrmacht, Luftwaffe, and Kriegsmarine officers waiting resignedly at the foot of the staircase while two rigid-backed Gestapo officers checked and double-checked their invitations. A voice near her ear said, "My luck. The best-looking girl here has to be my sister."

"Sigi, you stranger!" She laughed, hugging him. "What are you doing in Berlin?"

"Staff meetings," he said, again speaking into her ear. "With our liege lord himself. Big doings."

Shortly after they reached the private banquet hall, Göring arrived. Grossly corpulent, bulging like a barrage balloon in his bright-blue Luftwaffe uniform, he waved his fat, beringed hands so that his diamonds glittered all during his brief speech to open the buffet.

On long, linen-draped tables food unobtainable to ordinary Germans was displayed like jewelry. Golden French pâté de foie gras set off the darkness of French truffles. Polish ham gleamed pink between a salad of Danish eggs, and rosy, translucently thin slices of Norwegian smoked salmon were flanked by the emerald of Czech hothouse asparagus.

Armin kept his burn-stunted left hand in his trouser pocket, removing it reluctantly to hold his buffet plate. Diverting her attention from his disfigurement, he said, "A culinary map of our conquests, eh?"

Göring was standing nearby amid a clutch of toadies. He overheard. "Well said, Lieutenant. All our table lacks is English roast beef, and that won't be long coming."

Käthe fluttered her lashes. "How exciting, Herr Field Marshal. Is that true?"

"You wouldn't even ask that question, fräulein, if you'd seen the merry blaze of bonfires my Luftwaffe has set in London." At a smile from the cruel, thin mouth, the field marshal's sycophants whinnied with laughter. "Those Tommis are on the ropes. I haven't a single doubt that pig Churchill will be singing surrender carols for Christmas. Early next year, my pretty young fräulein, you'll be enjoying roast beef of old England."

Long after she went to bed she could hear Göring's arrogant certainty. The image of the bloated field marshal presiding over a similar party at Claridges kept running through her brain.

That Sunday morning she arrived at Kingsmith's before eight. "I've changed my mind," she said to Aubrey. "Tell Mr. Churchill I'll try to find out about Barbarossa."

THIRTY

I

After Aubrey had slipped out the back door into the courtyard, Käthe sat with her hands tightly clasped, waiting for the earliest hour on a Sunday morning that she could telephone the Westfälischer Hof, the hotel where Sigi kept a room.

Even so, she woke him. Apologizing, she said, "Where were you after the buffet opened? I looked everywhere."

"Another commitment," he said, and from his embarrassed cough, she knew he had sneaked away to Potsdam to visit his overage mistress, the dentist's widow.

"Any free time today?"

"Uncle's got me completely tied up."

"But this is *Sunday.*"

"Käthe, you're not in any mess, are you? The evening's free. As a matter of fact, I ought to see Mother."

He came to dinner. After they had savored his gift, real French coffee, Clothilde excused herself—it was her hour to read. Käthe and Sigi moved to the *Herrenzimmer*. He piled three logs above a messy heap of pinecone kindling. When the fire caught, he rose to his feet, brushing his hands clean on his tunic.

"Tell old Sigi your problems." He sounded like a warm-hearted priest ultimately ready to absolve every sin. "What's wrong?"

"Work." Her cheeks were pale and she had never felt more of a Judas. "I'm just not cut out for business."

An aristocrat on both sides, Sigi readily accepted that no sister of his would enjoy being a shopgirl.

"I've been thinking. . . ." She looked into the fire. "They hire civilians at the Bendlerblock, don't they?"

Sigi looked up from filling his pipe. "You want to work for the OKW?"

"Look at you, in the thick of it." How could she be involving Sigi, her beloved clumsy bear of a brother, in her web of lies? "Rushing off to Poland, Norway, Austria."

"I'm a soldier. You'd be stuck in an office."

"At least I'd be doing something for the Reich."

"You're positive the Bendlerblock's what you want?"

"Would you—could you put in a word for me?"

The broad space between his eyes, the one feature he'd inherited from Clothilde, creased in a frown. He gnawed on his pipe for what seemed an endless pause. "Let me see what I can do."

Late the next morning Sigi called Kingsmith's. "The woman at civilian personnel told me there were vacancies for clerks!" he burst out. "My sister, a filing clerk!"

Who could have better access to military documents? "Sigi, don't get excited—it's not your style. If that's what they need, where's the insult? I'll go over before lunch."

It was a cold, clear morning. In her beige felt hat and lynx-collared coat, she walked briskly down Unter den Linden and cut across the Tiergarten. In twenty minutes she reached the complex of massive buildings that was the Bendlerblock. Staff cars were pulling in and out of the courtyards. Stern-faced sentries stood at attention or goose-stepped back and forth.

The basement of a brick building across the street housed the offices of civilian personnel. The supervisor, a harried-looking, fiftyish spinster, personally interviewed Käthe. "So you're Captain von Hohenau's sister. I can't tell you how grateful I am that he steered you here."

"Then I have a job?"

"That goes without saying." The older woman touched the sickly-looking fern on her desk. "I'm presuming that since you're related to General von Hohenau, the Abwehr"—Army Intelligence—"will grant you top clearance. We're terribly short handed in Hall Six."

"Hall Six?"

"That's where the sensitive documents are kept. Report to me next Monday at seven forty-five. By then I should know if you've been cleared."

II

Every day that week Käthe arrived at the shop before six, staying late in the evening so Aubrey could train her. She explained to her mother that she was once again changing to a job that helped the war effort, and must put the books in order for Herr Knaupf. Not that Clothilde inquired: having passed her married life as though her source of income didn't exist, why would she question it now?

"I still can't see one single thing." Käthe groaned.

She was squinting into the minuscule lens of a tiny camera that Aubrey had assembled from fragments sewn into his uniform coat.

"Keep the other eye closed."

"I am, I am. It's hopeless."

"Käthe, believe me, if I can snap pictures with it, you absolutely can. Have another go-round."

Squinting fiercely, she again raised the camera between her thumb and forefinger. This time, miracle of miracles, she saw newsprint through the lens. "Hooray!" she cried, triumphantly tapping her fingernail to the pin-sized button. Within an hour she had photographed a dozen pages of the *Völkische Beobachter* and was adept with the tiny mechanism.

"You're ready for a surveillance tutorial," Aubrey said. He had already taught her the trick of moving without a rustle of cloth, a jingle of jewelry, without a footfall. He had considered teaching her a few close-combat techniques, but then decided she was far too slight to prevail in a physical clash.

"You mean I learn to follow somebody?"

"The reverse," he said. "See if you know when somebody's

following you. Take a walk wherever you want, and I'll catch up."

"How long a head start do I get?"

"Fifteen minutes."

"You'll never find me."

III

It had snowed heavily the previous night, but now the sun was out. On the Unter den Linden the snow had turned to slush, and pedestrians stayed close to the buildings to avoid the muddy spray raised by a military convoy. From the Pariserplatz came the cheerful, brassy notes of a military band playing "O Tannenbaum" as crowds streamed through the Brandenburg Gate into the Tiergarten. He decided Käthe would join the Sunday strollers. In the park apple-cheeked children pelted snowballs, laughing adolescents sledded down hillocks, and golden Victory glittered atop her marble-and-gilt column. He caught sight of Käthe as she jumped across the wet hoof-holes of a bridle path. Following at a distance he was on the verge of losing her. He hurried forward, barely avoiding a galloping mare. The gray-haired rider, reining with a cavalry officer's rapidity, peered haughtily down. "Don't they teach you men to get out of a horse's way nowadays?"

It was one of the rare times anyone had noticed Aubrey.

In his uniform he had moved through the heart of enemy territory noticed only by two nervous Berlin whores—the weird moral code of the Third Reich demanded that prostitutes who serviced the armed forces should come from the lesser nationalities. In crowded beer stubes the sweating waitresses had barely glanced at him as they slammed down his orders of weiss beer and brockwurst. He was one more faceless soldier at the *soldatenkino*—he spent a lot of time at these free cinemas for servicemen. German films, churned out by the Ministry of Propaganda, were universally bad, their anti-Semitism blatant and sickening, but at least he had a place to get out of the rain or snow.

He watched Käthe's slight, graceful figure veer in the direction of the zoo. Quite a number of men turned as she passed.

Beauty, he reflected, is no asset to a woman who needs to remain incognito. She kept glancing from side to side and looking back. He had fallen in behind a couple of privates in Wehrmacht uniforms, and she didn't notice him. He checked his watch, following her along the crowded paths for ten minutes before catching up.

"Fräulein," he said, "I believe you dropped this?" He handed her the handkerchief that he'd discovered that first night in the office and had kept with him, inhaling the scent of her to help blank out those horrible racist films.

Her face flamed, and she mumbled, "Thank you, soldier."

"Try again," he said without moving his lips. "I'll wait here a quarter hour."

He found her sipping hot ersatz chocolate as she peered around Aschlinger's on Potsdamerplatz. The café was full, and he waited to be seated with a group of noncoms. Käthe didn't see him until she left.

"How on earth do you do it?" she asked.

She had led him back to Kingsmith's.

"Elementary, my dear Käthe," he said. "I pay attention. Tomorrow you will notice everything, the way I taught you. You will not keep turning like a windmill."

"That bad?" she asked. "Don't you ever look around?"

"All the time. I've learned to hide doing it." He reached out to touch her cheek, the sole physical contact he had permitted himself to initiate.

IV

Monday, when she reported to the basement offices, the pressured-looking supervisor actually gave a rusty little smile. "As I expected, you were cleared for top-secret. Here's your pass and badge. Go through the courtyard and the desk clerk'll direct you to Hall Six."

Across the bustling corridor from Hall Six was a cloakroom. Here, a gray-uniformed *Blitzmädchen*, one of the Wehrmacht's women's auxiliary, was permanently stationed. She gave the clerks body searches whenever they entered or left the hall.

Handbags were emptied and gone through. The guard at the dark-jambed door examined Käthe's pass and badge. Inside, soldiers patrolled the narrow aisles. The cabinets were double locked, and the nasal-voiced supervisor explained the system to Käthe. One key was universal. The other was fished out of a large cracked pottery bowl at random by the clerk when she reported to work in the morning.

"Every meaningless memo is saved, sometimes in duplicate or triplicate. You'd never believe what idiotic stuff. Memos whether or not to ban mazurkas in Poland." She had come directly to Kingsmith's after leaving work: should her movements be questioned, she could give the perfectly normal excuse of checking up on her manager. "Mazurkas! Really top-secret stuff."

"This was only your first day, don't get the wind up."

"Wind up? That's a gross underrepresentation. But at least I'm a German, in my own country. Aubrey, you're a man with nerves of steel."

"You don't know how funny that is," he said, overjoyed that she believed him intrepid.

"Must you stay until I get the photographs?"

"Käthe, it's best for you to know as little as possible about my orders."

From this she surmised he was indeed trapped in Berlin until she could either smuggle him out a copy of Barbarossa or prove that such a plan against Russia had never existed.

On her third day Käthe fished out an *S* key and therefore worked in the *S* archives. She had the opportunity to glance at a month-old MOST SECRET directive from the Führer to General Keitel. *Sea Lion will be discontinued. Sea Lion formations will be released for other duties, but these movements must be camouflaged so that the British continue to believe we are mounting an attack against them.*

V

On her nightly visit to Kingsmith's, Käthe passed on this information.

"Thank God for that," Aubrey said. "Sea Lion's the plan to invade us."

"I still can't believe Hitler's sending those troops to Russia."

"Here's your shoe." Aubrey had asked for a pair of the shoes she wore to work. Now he pressed his thumb on the left heel, and it swung aside, revealing the miniature camera nestled into chamois polishing cloth.

"Just like a jewelry case—you're a miracle worker."

"A nail file and a couple of little hinges, that's all. It should hold. Just don't stamp down hard."

"No Spanish dancing." She slipped on the shoes.

"Käthe, promise me you won't rush into anything. All that matters is you don't get caught."

The air-raid sirens began howling.

"Our boys're making themselves known," Aubrey said. Every once in a while RAF bombers and their fighter escort braved the long flight to Berlin on a so-called nuisance raid: they could wreak only a fraction of the Luftwaffe's damage but British leaders wanted to remind their own countrymen that the battle wasn't entirely lopsided, wanted to unnerve citizens of the Third Reich.

"Usually it's a false alarm."

Aubrey listened with his head tilted. The candle stub on the desk threw a highlight on one side of his face. "No," he said. And after a minute she, too, heard the faraway hum of airplane engines. Footsteps rang on the courtyard cobbles, and she recognized the gravel tones of Herr Herbst, the air-raid warden. "Turn off that goddamn flashlight and get the hell to the shelter!" "Without a light how'll I find the goddamn shelter?" The drone of planes was becoming a roar. Antiaircraft guns snapped. Explosions grew closer. The huge emplacement in the Pariserplatz opened fire with a series of throaty roars.

And all at once Käthe heard a sound she'd never heard before. A strange shuffling as if a metal box were racing down a slide directly above her head.

Louder, louder.

Without realizing how it happened, she found herself with her nose pressed to the dusty Oriental carpet. The window-panes were rattling, the blackout curtains flapped like ravens' wings. The warped doors of the heavy outdated display case sprang open. Silver and china clattered. Time seemed to slow as she watched the display case teeter back and forth. The candlestick toppled from the desk, dropping languidly, and a tongue of fire touched the old rug. Aubrey's hand clamped over the flame. It was doused, and the odor of burned cloth filled the darkness. The case crashed down. Instinctively she flung her arms over her face to protect herself.

"Käthe?" Aubrey's voice was close to her ear, then his hand was traveling up her spine. "Käthe, are you hurt?"

"God, that was close," she said breathily.

The near-hit had set off a strange reaction in her. Her brain held no hint of fear. However, her skeleton seemed to have liquefied. She was completely limp. Aubrey put his arms around her. His breath against her eardrum drowned out the barking ack-ack, the roar of planes, the more distant whistle of bombs. Disoriented, she clung to him. His arms tightened and she was briefly positive that Wyatt held her. But this body was too narrow, and the cheek pressed against her own too lean. The smell of him was different, less salty. *It's Aubrey, you idiot, and he has an erection.* She tried to pull away, but he held her close.

"You know I love you, don't you?" he said.

She had known subliminally for years. Because of her abiding affection for him, the knowledge saddened her, so she had banished it from her mind. "Aubrey—"

"No, don't stop me, I may never get my nerve up again. I've always loved you, I always will love you."

"Please—"

"If anything happens to you, Käthe, part of me would die."

"Trust me, we're both going to make it."

"Yes, and someday, someday when we're very old, I'll remember tonight, and the way you fit in my arms."

"You're part of me, too, Aubrey, but—"

"But you're still in love with Wyatt," he finished.

"It's so ridiculous." She sighed.

Striking a match, he lit the candle. "All I ask," he said, "is that when the war's over you put me at the top of the list of replacements."

She brushed plaster dust from his crisp, German-cut hair. With his sensitivity he must be aware that she also had inherited an adamant heart.

A few minutes later the all-clear wailed. Käthe hurried around the shop to mingle with the people emerging from the shelters. The pavement was dangerous with broken plate glass and bits of rubble. Fires gave off black smoke and a reddish light; firefighters aimed hoses at blazing buildings. A crater yawned in the middle of the broad boulevard. The tall, rather unmilitary-looking corporal was winding his way around the rubble and branches that surrounded the hole.

"Don't you worry," Aubrey said to nobody in particular. "We'll pay the terror-bombing bastards back."

THIRTY-ONE

I

Raid or no raid, tardiness was not tolerated in Hall Six. The following morning Käthe arrived at work promptly. She took a universal key from the rack, fumbling in the mass of metal for her second key. She had gone a few steps before she glanced at the manila tag. She would be filing archives in *"Ba."* It took a moment for the letters to sink in. Ba—Barbarossa.

She rushed down the narrow, linoleum-floor aisle. The bottom drawer of this cabinet had one of those red-type warnings:

TO BE OPENED BY AUTHORIZED PERSONNEL ONLY

Heart pounding, she forced herself to move at a normal pace to the lavatory. As usual the white-haired attendant was pushing a sodden mop over the floorboards—the other clerks swore the crone was a Gestapo plant. Käthe used one of the two open stalls. Under the pretext of changing the knitted bands used for sanitary protection, she managed to slide the camera from her heel into her palm. Looking up, Käthe saw the rheumy old eyes fixed on her.

Her mouth dry, she said, "Thank heavens! Five days late, but I finally came around."

The old woman stared at her for another moment before she went back to her mopping.

A great heap of memos between august officers of the OKW and Hitler regarding the Baltic States—Latvia, Lithuania, and

Estonia, all three seized by the Soviets earlier in the year—were Käthe's task to file. Each time she weaved back and forth, she eyed the forbidden drawer. But evidently the guards had been delivered a pep talk. The new, round-shouldered private kept lumbering up and down the aisles near her. She had no chance to see whether her key would open the forbidden drawer.

Lunchtime in the basement canteen was staggered. Käthe had been assigned one o'clock. As the hands of the electric clock jumped inexorably toward the hour, the miniature camera weighed down her pocket as though the tiny object had the specific gravity of a heavier planet. She would never be able to smuggle it through the *Blitzmädchen*'s search. She dared not risk repeating her lavatory maneuver.

"Fräulein Kingsmith," said the wen-nosed supervisor when Käthe went for a fresh batch of papers to file, "you eat now."

"I forgot my money," Käthe muttered.

"Here, take a mark until tomorrow." The tone was magnanimous.

"Thank you, but . . . Uhh, well, I'm not hungry. . . ." Käthe stared up at Hitler's sepia photograph, hoping that others saw her blush as a sign she was too impoverished to repay a single mark. "I'll just keep on working."

Among those who trooped out was the new round-shouldered private. With her watchdog gone Käthe returned to the big oak filing cabinet. Kneeling at the forbidden drawer, she made a prayer.

II

Her fingers trembled, and she had difficulty with the keys. Turning the universal one in the lock, she dropped the single key. Sweat broke out under her arms. She fumbled with the key and then heard the metallic click. Her lips parting, she slid the drawer open.

These documents were not slipped into manila files but stored in large brown envelopes without any apparent designation. *It'll take days to search through them all.* Her body temperature plummeted, and for a full minute she wondered about the OKW's purpose in filing unmarked envelopes when there was no way to retrieve the papers inside. Then it hit her that in each left-hand corner was a lightly penciled, parenthesized number.

The files marked with the nearly invisible (1) might be connected to the Reich's Supreme Commander. Hitler.

She pulled out the first (1) and hit pay dirt. Three typed pages topped with Hitler's eagle and swastika seal.

Most Secret
The Führer's Headquarters
November 25, 1940

The Armed Forces must be prepared to crush Soviet Russia in a quick campaign. All available units will be deployed except those necessary to safeguard occupied territories. Great caution must be used that this attack surprises the enemy. The campaign must be ready to start in early spring. The date will be the decision of the Supreme Commander—

Käthe flipped through the other papers in the envelope, glimpsing maps with arrows for the disposition of troops against Leningrad, against Kiev in the Ukraine, Odessa in the south. Hunching over the drawer, she slid the camera from her pocket. Swiftly she photographed the pages, then replaced them, opening another file, also about Barbarossa.

III

"Fräulein?"

She jumped. God, God! How could she have forgotten Aubrey's surveillance lessons? She pressed the camera to her palm, somehow managing that expression of bland assurance she'd seen so often on her mother's face. "Yes?"

The round-shouldered private edged closer. "I thought you might like a nibble." He extended a small slab of brown cake.

Security was no tighter than normal. The new soldier had been trying to make contact, that was all. Sliding the drawer shut, she locked it with surprising ease.

"What an angel!" Smiling, she took the cake in her free

hand. The underbaked dough tasted as if kerosene had been used instead of fat. "Delicious."

He introduced himself as Lothar Raeder.

"Any relation to Grand Admiral Raeder?"

"Yes, but distant," he replied, his long-lobed ears reddening in a way that told her he was lying to impress her.

"I'm Käthe Kingsmith."

"Yes, I recognized you," he said. "I was an usher at the Olympic Games. You made the entire Reich proud."

His timid admiration brushed across her brain like a primary color. Here was the instrument of her deliverance. Fluttering her eyelashes, she asked if she could repay him with a cup of coffee after work. He beamed. Just then the supervisor came over to ask what all the noise was about.

As they filed out, Käthe moved very close to Private Raeder. With the other clerks she crossed the hall to the cloakroom, spreading the contents of her purse and pockets on the long table. She submitted to the wandering hands of the *Blitzmädchen.* All the time she was clenching her back teeth. When she emerged, Private Raeder was leaning against the wall.

She forced herself to wait until they turned onto Lützow-strasse.

With a little shiver she said, "I swear it's too cold to snow tonight. Lothar, do you mind?"

And without waiting for a reply she slipped her hand into his pocket. The tiny camera was still there.

IV

"Käthe, you never should have risked it." Aubrey slid the exposed film from the tiny camera. "What if he'd needed his handkerchief? What if he'd worn his uniform coat? What if Sigi had come along?"

"He didn't, he didn't, Sigi didn't." Success had keyed her up. "The question is, how's my photography?"

"I won't know until I get home."

"When are you leaving?"

Instead of answering he dropped the camera in her hand

with fine strips of film wound around a pin. "Hide it in the safest place possible, do you hear? I hope there aren't any further orders, but if there are, you'll be contacted by the bald ticket-seller at the Grunewald station."

"That old martinet? Is he a British agent?"

"A loyal German whose son was killed in Flossenburg concentration camp." Aubrey blew out the candle flame and opened the door. "I meant every word I said last night. I'd rather lose the war than lose you. Be careful, Käthe, be very, very careful, darling." He kissed her lips, a light gentle touch in the darkness.

She heard a single light footfall in the darkness, then there was only the rustle of the wind in the night.

Two months later, in February of 1941, Winston Churchill dispatched a secret letter to the Kremlin outlining all that he knew of the German invasion plans, including the blurry photographs Käthe had taken.

Josef Stalin, smug in his belief that he could swallow up the countries of Europe that his ally, Adolf Hitler, didn't want, ignored the letter.

SEVEN

Yesterday, December 7, 1941—a date which will live in infamy . . .

—opening of President Franklin D. Roosevelt's speech requesting that Congress declare war against Japan

SEVEN

THIRTY-TWO

I

Six days after Pearl Harbor, First Lieutenant Wyatt Kingsmith strode briskly up West 102nd Street. As he reached the brownstone with the elegant ironwork door, he tucked his cap under his arm. His ring was answered by the Leventhals' elderly butler, who stared at him in consternation. Wyatt hadn't been here since that long-ago summer afternoon when he and Käthe had come to tea. He wasn't expected. As a matter of fact, until fifteen minutes earlier it hadn't crossed his mind to come here. He had been visiting one of his professors at Columbia and, realizing how near he was to the Leventhals, had decided that tying up loose ends was appropriate. This was his last leave before shipping overseas.

In the drawing room, assailed by memories, he went to the bow window, watching a driver in a heavy overcoat lug packages from a UPS truck into the service entrance of the house next door. The truck had moved up the street before he heard slow footsteps.

Mrs. Leventhal was yet frailer, her spine more bent, the professionally waved white hair thinner. Her black wool dress was sizes too large, her softly sagging throat lapped over the uppermost strand of her pearls. Nothing about the stern, stiff judge had changed. His jaw was set as unyieldingly, the rheumy eyes were as lacking in humor, the spinal column as fused.

"Ahh, so you're a soldier, Mr.—no, Lieutenant Kingsmith." The judge held out his hand.

As Wyatt took it, he said, "Wyatt."

"What a pleasant surprise, Wyatt," Mrs. Leventhal whispered in her rustle of a voice.

"I was at Columbia, so it was no big deal to drop by." Wyatt paused. "I'm shipping overseas."

Mrs. Leventhal sank into a chair. "So soon?"

"Eleanor, there's a war on now." The judge pulled up his trouser knees as he lowered himself into a nearby chair. "It's extremely difficult to accept that the two countries are at war again. Naturally my loyalties are all with the United States; still, Germany's the land of my birth."

"You're lucky you moved here," Wyatt said.

The judge and his wife glanced at each other.

"I was born in Manhattan, and so were my parents," Eleanor Leventhal said. "Still, all four of my grandparents came from Germany. We were raised to believe that made us superior."

"You feel that way about Germany, even being Jewish?"

At the final word the judge's nostrils flared.

But Mrs. Leventhal nodded. "Wyatt, you'd have to understand what it was like. When we were young, younger than you are now, millions of immigrants poured in from Eastern Europe. Good people, but crude and uneducated. We had standards. We didn't wish to be lumped with them, so we held ourselves apart. We had always been kept apart from the gentile world. It seems ridiculous to me now, ridiculous and sad, all of us squandering the little time we have on earth to build up barriers." The thread of voice frayed. "We're old, my husband and I, and not flexible. We find ourselves unable to bridge the gaps. Can you understand what I'm saying?"

Wyatt understood perfectly, but he said, "It's pretty oblique, Mrs. Leventhal. What do you mean, kept apart from the gentile world?"

"In many parts of Europe during the Middle Ages and the Renaissance it meant death for any Jew who married a gentile. The rest of the community suffered too. Often there was a terrible pogrom. That danger has been bred into us. Then, too, prejudice has made us touchy. Besides, there are the tenets of our religion. What I'm trying to say is that we don't intermarry." She whispered the last sentence as if the effort of using her thin little voice had been too much.

"Eleanor, you mustn't excite yourself."

At a tap on the door the butler wheeled in the tea cart with the same delicate Dresden china as before, similar pastel petit fours. Wyatt accepted coffee and a pastry, finding it impossible to banish the remembrance of Käthe.

"What about your German relation, Judge?" he asked. "Ever hear from him?"

"We received a note, it must have been a month or so after you and Fräulein Kingsmith visited us. He didn't mention being in a camp, so we assumed we were falsely alarmed. Since then he hasn't been in contact."

"We can only hope for the best," Mrs. Leventhal added.

"Being a lawyer," Wyatt said, "what you said about the old law against intermarriage interested me. I never knew it had been a capital crime. As a matter of fact, I'd like to learn about the history and religion."

Judge Leventhal's expression indicated Wyatt had produced inadmissible evidence. "Is that so?"

All at once the circumlocution in this formally arranged drawing room was more than Wyatt could take. "Look, neither of you will say it, so I will!" he snapped. "My father was your son."

The delicate folds of Mrs. Leventhal's throat trembled. "Myron . . ."

"Then what's so peculiar about wanting to know a bit about that side of me?"

The judge cleared his throat. His lips had gone pale, yet he spoke in the same ponderous tones. "Since you're being open, let me be equally blunt. My wife would prefer to have you in the role of family member. But on my part that's an impossibility. Having reached a decision years ago, a decision I must add that caused my wife and me untold pain, it's too late in the day for me to reconsider. You must understand this is not personal but a matter of the faith we live by. You seem like a fine young man." He drew a quavery breath. "It is difficult to say that you are nothing to us—"

"Abraham . . ." Mrs. Leventhal murmured.

The judge ignored the interruption. "But that is how it must be, Lieutenant. And on your part you have a set of parents. How would we fit into your life?"

Wyatt took a sharp breath. After a moment he said, "Score one for you."

"If that means I've won," said Judge Leventhal, "I can assure you that's not true. We had one child, and he was everything to us."

"Cutting him loose was your decision."

"We acted according to our faith."

"And Myron died. . . ." Mrs. Leventhal held a lacy handkerchief to her white lips.

"There was no choice, Eleanor."

After a silence Wyatt said, "Listen, I'm sorry about the whole mess. Everybody seems to have suffered. I didn't mean to harry you about it, but it seemed right to drop by before I went overseas."

"We're glad you're here," the judge said. "And we would like to see you when you return. Just so long as you understand how it must be."

"Friends," Wyatt said, glancing at his watch. "I better be shoving off."

Mrs. Leventhal managed a smile. "I wish you every sort of good luck, Wyatt. Return safe."

The judge looked at him with age-blurred eyes, a look that was searching and incomprehensible, then he said, "If you'll wait a minute."

He trod in his old man's short, hitching steps across the hall. Wyatt glimpsed a large, dim room furnished with what appeared to be a complete legal library. After a minute the old man returned with a black leather-bound book. "Please accept this as a going-away gift," he said. The veined hand shook as he held out the book.

The worn gilt lettering read: *The Story of the Jewish People.*

As Wyatt left the brownstone he gripped the book tightly. He kept seeing Judge Leventhal's trembling hand and the bluish white of Mrs. Leventhal's lips. His eyes blurred with tears for the shrunken old woman who longed to embrace him, the lonely old judge who clung so adamantly to laws he believed fixed and immutable. Yet even in his sadness for them—and for the young couple who had been his parents—Wyatt felt a lift of spirit. He had made a peace of sorts with his past.

It wasn't until he was in a taxi that he flipped open to the title page. *This is the property of Myron Leventhal.* The rusty ink slanted boldly up, sprawling across the page. Precisely how he inscribed his own books. The writing was enough like his to be a skilled forgery.

II

It was three days before Christmas of 1941 and the Yanks had not yet been shipped to the British Isles. At Waterloo station quite a few people—especially women—turned to look at the unfamiliar khaki uniform. Wyatt, on his part, was taking in the English as they hurried to catch trains. The housewives in shabby raincoats lugging heavy cloth shopping bags, the service men and women in uniforms that looked too bulky, the overage men with slumped shoulders and dripping umbrellas. Everyone seemed . . . gray. Yes, gray was the color of the determination-knotted faces.

There was no available taxi. Slinging his duffel to his shoulder, he crossed Waterloo Bridge, zigzagging toward New Bond Street. From censored family letters, newsreels, and press coverage as well as Edward R. Murrow's nightly CBS reports he knew the battering that London had taken, yet he was unprepared. Blackened walls rose like tombstones from the rubble that had been dock warehouses. Barriers surrounded gaping, water-filled craters. Once-handsome buildings were husks plastered over with warnings: DANGEROUS PREMISES. DANGER. KEEP OUT. Three men wearing goggles to protect their eyes from flying orange sparks aimed ferociously noisy metal cutters at the eighteenth-century wrought-iron rails that fronted an undamaged cream-colored house—all ironwork was coming down to supply much-needed metal to the British war industry. Women patiently queued under their umbrellas outside shops whose windows were boarded over to display a few inches of merchandise. The only external sign of the season was a Fry's chocolate poster wishing a Happy Christmas to all who had so bravely endured the Battle of Britain.

His khaki topcoat was dark with rain by the time he turned off Piccadilly onto Old Bond Street. Kingsmith's had been bombed out twice, and he halted at the original premises, staring bleakly at the twisted girders. The current Kingsmith's, leased after a brief relocation at Porteous's home, was on New Bond Street; it was in none too great condition. The top story had been burned and the door was a badly carpentered make-shift. The old sign, however, had been rescued, and angled outward. Wyatt smiled. It was the same logo used at the American branch. *P. Kingsmith and Sons* in cursive writing above the gilded rampant lion crest and proud, ribboned phrase *By Appointment to Her Majesty, Queen Mary.*

III

Inside, the Christmas spirit prevailed in the form of spicy-smelling fir branches and holly swagging the unpainted, knocked-together shelves. A half-dozen customers queued at the front table, waiting for the motherly-looking woman to write up their selections. Wyatt couldn't repress a smile at this sign of the times. Before the war no mere female had gained admittance to the Bond Street Kingsmith's employment rolls.

"Might I be of assistance, sir?" inquired a narrow-shoul-dered, seventyish clerk.

"Is Mr. Kingsmith about?"

"Wyatt! Is that you?" called Porteous.

Only then did Wyatt see the white-maned head. Edging around customers, he embraced the thin old man. *This,* he thought, *is my grandfather.*

"My boy, ah, my boy." Porteous blew his nose emotionally. "Lady Coombes, may I present my American grandson, Lieu-tenant Kingsmith. He's just arrived this minute. I'm sure that under the circumstances, you'll pardon me."

Porteous led Wyatt to a narrow cluttered office with a desk at either end. "Euan's laid up with a cold," he said. "Nothing serious, mark you, but since that spot of heart trouble it's best not to tempt fate in nasty weather like this." The twisted veins showed through the transparent skin of his domed forehead. "Well, now you Yank chaps are in, the war's as good as won."

"Attaboy, Grandfather, that's the spirit." Wyatt hung his wet khaki things on the coatrack. "But what about Herr Schicklgruber? He's squatting on most of Europe, a hell of a lot of Africa, not to mention the best Russki real estate."

"Spread himself a bit thin, our Hitler, what?" Porteous said with a smile.

Wyatt brought his grandfather up to date on Humphrey's newest diet and Rossie's negotiations with the Dejong Plaza leasing agent: additional space was needed to enlarge and ride the wave of prosperity sweeping the United States.

Porteous pulled at his limp shirt cuffs—starch was a wartime casualty—and asked, "Any word from Berlin?"

"There's a war on, Grandfa—"

With a blow that sounded suspiciously like a kick, the door burst open.

"Darling! They said you were here!" Araminta embraced Wyatt in a bounty of prewar perfume. "Don't you look magnificent in uniform!"

"And aren't you something," Wyatt said. And so she was, in her smart tweed costume (tailored from an old lounge suit she'd wheedled from Euan) with a few drops of rain sparkling like diamonds on the beret that sailed jauntily above her vibrant red hair. "But what about *your* uniform?"

"In the Auxiliary Fire Service we're on trips, which are like watches in the navy. On duty forty-eight hours, then off twenty-four hours. This is my trip off, and the moment I'm off I shed uniform and wellies. Grandpa, would you mind if I tear Wyatt away for a few minutes? Coty's is open, and he can queue with me. We'll be back for tea." An easy enough promise for her to keep. The official closing hour for shops was four o'clock.

IV

"This damn wartime secrecy," Araminta said when they were a few doors up on New Bond Street, standing outside Coty's. (He, the only male in the queue, held Araminta's umbrella high so it protected her as well as a sweet-faced Mayfair matron who vaguely resembled Queen Elizabeth.) "If only I'd known you were shipping over! These horrible shortages—you have no idea how desperate I am for lipstick and mascara and your marvelous Dreen shampoo. Ahh, wouldn't it be lovely, using proper eyebrow pencil! With ordinary lead my face looks positively bald."

"You're a knockout and you know it."

"A little bit of powder and paint make a woman what she ain't. And I'm running short of the above requirements."

"Write out a list. Let me see what I can do."

"Would you? Oh, thank God for Yank cousins!" They moved up a few steps.

"What's the dope on Peter?" he asked.

"He's someplace blacked out by the censors, but methinks it's Malta," she whispered. "He might get a leave soon. Last week his oldest brother, the viscount, was killed in Burma. Peter's second in line now." As Araminta spoke of death, the vivacity drained from her expression: her nose and chin seemed sharper. They moved up again. "Wyatt, I want you to close your eyes and remember exactly what the women are wearing in New York."

By the time they reached the counter at Coty's, only the leg makeup that stood in for silk stockings was left. Araminta took a jar. "Might as well hoard it until summer," she said cheerfully.

V

The tea served at Porteous's Bayswater Road home was strictly Austerity: dark, heavy scones made of National flour were lightly smeared with margarine and rose-hip jam.

"And now if you two will excuse me," Porteous said, "I need a bit of a rest."

Araminta smiled fondly as Porteous held on tightly to the banister, edging up the staircase. When the first-floor door closed, she said, "He's been going to bed right after tea, the sweet old love. Isn't he a marvel? Well over eighty and working a full day when Daddy's not around. What splendid genes we've inherited, you and I."

Wyatt fixed his gaze on the dried pampas grass in the China Export vase. "What are your plans for the evening?"

"I was hoping you'd ask. My trip doesn't start until ten. Shall we have dinner? Good. Let's hurry to the flat. While I change, you can look in on Daddy and tell him what's happening to the Fifth Avenue branch. Then we'll go to this lovely place in Piccadilly—they have a band. They get around the five-shilling limit for a meal by charging outrageously for the wine."

Tonight the crowded restaurant served Yorkshire ham. There was a tiny dance floor where, packed amid wiggling, noisy officers and pretty girls, Araminta taught Wyatt the Lambeth Walk. "Hoy!" she cried, flinging up her hand.

VI

Euan still had his cold on Christmas Eve. Araminta telephoned Elizabeth to explain that she was staying in town to see that the poor darling had some sort of holiday dinner. Porteous went along to Quarles as planned, a porter hauling the valise heavy with American chocolates and toys that Wyatt had brought for Elizabeth's evacuees, a half-dozen bombed-out waifs who rampaged through the gracious country house.

Wyatt, though, stayed in London. He and Araminta attended matins at St. James's Church in Piccadilly.

Christopher Wren had designed St. James's Church. Now only the south aisle remained standing. Debris mounded in the sunken churchyard. A sullen odor of burnt wood and dank earth clung to the anteroom, and the same dour smell pervaded the bricked-up south aisle. A strip of cheap, shiny blue fabric covered the damaged wall behind the altar, and netting flapped where the stained-glass windows had been. Inside the gallant shambles Araminta and Wyatt shared a prayer book. The pages were singed at the edge and the cover was warped from firemen's hoses. Instead of the reverberating chords of the Grinling Gibbons carved pipe-organ with its golden cherubs, a fur-coated woman energetically thumped at an off-key upright piano. Clouds of breath hovered about the choirboys as they swectly sang of joyous tidings. On the way out Wyatt shoved crumpled banknotes into the offertory box.

Araminta moved closer to him. "Darling, have you noticed that I've been positively the heart and soul of discretion? Not one single tactless question about you and Katy cutting off the engagement."

"We never were official," he said. "And no need to avoid the subject. Call it part of the growing-up process. It's over."

Araminta's brightly lipsticked mouth curved in a Mona Lisa smile. Wyatt's forced laugh told her that he hadn't quite doused the torch for their cousin. She touched her gloved finger above her engagement ring. Well, she adored Peter, but that didn't mean she might not have a quiver or so to spare for this large, sexy body close to hers.

THIRTY-THREE

I

Hitler, after conquering the west coast of Europe from the Arctic Ocean to the Bay of Biscay, set out to protect his new empire. German engineers, with an unlimited labor supply from occupied territories, worked their underfed, ragged "recruits" a minimum of twelve hours a day, seven days a week. Cement bunkers, pillboxes, observation towers, and heavy artillery embankments bristled along the twenty-four-hundred miles of coastline. To further fortify the beaches that faced the English Channel the engineers installed twisted steel formations called hedgehogs and sowed four million mines deep in the sand.

Across the narrow strip of seawater from this formidable barrier, in southern England, American officers whipped around in jeeps and staff cars as they selected sites for air bases and encampments. Wyatt was attached to one of these units.

That winter of 1942 the reports from all Allied fronts, though vetted, were inescapably edged in black. South Pacific strongholds fell like ripe plums into Japanese hands. Rommel, the Desert Fox, swept deeper through British forces into North Africa. Hitler's fanatical refusal to allow his armies to retreat in Russia had been steeply paid for in German blood, but his forces remained poised at the heart of the Soviets. Wyatt, like most civilian and armed forces personnel in England, heard the news with a grim expression but was too busy to fret. His legal surveys and suggestions occupied him. His small amount of free time was filled by an attractive, sexually innovative ambulance driver. He didn't return to London until the last week in April.

A few days before his leave he mailed a note inviting the Kingsmith clan to dinner at the Trocadero in London.

Araminta responded: *Mother never leaves her evacuees. Daddy's foraging around in Hampshire attics to gather up the so-called antiques your branch devours. And you know Grandpa, he never goes out at night. Which leaves only me. You can beg off with no hard feelings.*

Wyatt sent a note by return mail. *Pick you up at the flat at seven on Saturday.*

II

Araminta opened the door, wearing a form-fitting black silk dinner dress. Her cheeks were pink, her eyes glittered. "Look who's here!" she said, drawing him into the lounge hall.

Peter, his feet up on the ottoman, a bottle of malt whiskey on the table at his side, looked like an RAF pilot in a Hollywood film. Wyatt didn't sit down. After a couple of pleasantries he said, "The last thing you two lovebirds need is a third wheel."

"We're pub crawling. The more the merrier when it comes to pub crawling," Peter said. Despite his relaxed smile his left eye blinked rapidly.

"Absolutely," Araminta said, holding on to Peter's arm. "We can't leave you high and dry."

"Just for the first round of drinks, then," Wyatt said.

The headwaiter, effusively greeting Peter by name, led them through the noisy, smoke-hazed West End café to a tiny round table by the dance floor. As they sat down, Peter said that in the old days this table had been reserved for the Prince of Wales and Mrs. Windsor. "I joined them once or twice." Swank of this type was utterly alien to Peter—but then he was sozzled. He had put away most of the bottle before they left Euan's flat, and since then had been steadily belting down whatever alcoholic beverage was available. From guarded allusions it was obvious that Araminta's guess had been correct: Peter was stationed on Malta. Malta, Britain's Mediterranean island, nicknamed by the

BBC "Our unsinkable aircraft carrier," was used by the RAF to take off on raids over Rommel's heavily guarded North African bases. In return Malta was bombarded so mercilessly that a few days earlier King George VI had awarded the entire island the George Cross for heroism. No wonder Peter drank and his eye twitched.

They ordered *pommes de terre à la reine* and *boeuf à la maison* with a red wine. They were served an excellent Beaujolais with reddish salt meat and sauted potatoes.

"But, Adolf, I can't bear Spam and chips," Peter said in a heavy German accent.

Araminta held her fork over her upper lip to simulate a mustache. "If this is all they eat in England, so why are we winning the war, then?"

"You *dummkopf*, Adolf," Peter responded. "We aren't winning."

It didn't seem funny at all to Wyatt, but Peter and Araminta laughed frenziedly.

Wiping her eyes, she said, "I have to find the loo. Go ahead and eat, I'll be right back."

Peter, Wyatt, and most of the nearby males watched Araminta's curved hips swing provocatively in the black silk.

"On this leave I'd rather thought we would marry," Peter said ruminatively.

"Great idea there."

"Doesn't seem the fair thing, though."

"Because of your parents?"

"Bugger them." Peter poured another glass of wine. "Because the grouse season's open."

"Time to lay off the sauce, Peter. You're not making sense."

"Aren't I, though? In season the grouse are fair game. The hunter's there with his gun. The grouse take flight. Bang, bang, bang. Doesn't care which feathers the birds have, the hunter aims and pops away." The mismatched eyes, blinking and bloodshot, fixed on Wyatt. " 'There's another one,' says he. Bang, bang, it's dead. Bang, bang again. Another bird drops out of the sky. Quite an impartial fellow, the hunter. Sometimes an unlucky grouse buys the farm the first season, sometimes one lasts a bit. But it's a law of nature. Long enough in the air, and every grouse is bagged. No, don't try to contradict me. There's no arguing with natural laws. Eventually the hunter has us all, whichever side. Talk to Luftwaffe prisoners and you'll hear the same story in a different language."

"Sounds like total bullshit to me."

"The season's open and we're all fair game."

"Like hell," Wyatt said without conviction. What right had he, unbloodied in battle, to argue with the Honorable Peter Shawcross-Mortimer, whose chest was covered with fruit-salad ribbons?

"Doesn't seem fair to Araminta to make a widow out of her. At least this way she has her own family. Mine can be turds, y'know. Except for old Shawcross—" He raised his glass to his late brother, the viscount, the heir. "And he, poor bugger, he's gone."

"I'll order us some hot coffee."

"After . . . You'll help her get over it, won't you?"

"Jesus, Peter."

"Good. Knew you would." Peter's head fell forward into the plate of fried potatoes and Spam.

He had passed out.

III

Araminta telephoned the station officer, asking for leave because her fiancé was in town: the station officer, a bulky ex-navy salt who fondly called his redheaded driver Carrots, noting that the Luftwaffe was not waxing heavy, granted her request.

She spent all of her time with Peter. He drank steadily. He did not make love to her. On the third evening he obtained tickets for *No Time for Comedy.* He laughed loudly at Rex Harrison and pretty young Lilli Palmer, and during intermission gulped down four glasses of a raw, biting sherry, the only drink available. When they emerged from the theater, a narrow crescent moon rode high above them.

"What a divine night," Araminta said, hugging him. "Look at that moon! That's the one good thing the blackout's done, given us back our night sky."

"Let's feel our way to Rupert's on Shaftesbury Avenue. Share a bottle of champagne."

"No champers," Araminta said firmly. "We're going to your room and I don't care if the entire staff and every guest at the Savoy sees me."

"Darling, what's the difference?"

"Another problem between us."

"One minor lapse does not constitute a problem."

"In the great scheme of our dark globe, possibly not."

They were side by side on the single bed. Her hip nudged his gently. "Oh, Peter, you silly mutt. D'you think I don't know you've had a ghastly time?"

" 'I myself have often babbled doubtless of the foolish past: babble, babble; our old England may go down in babble at last.' "

"Righto. At Eton you had to memorize reams of Tennyson."

He ran his hand down her side, his fingers tracing the perfect curve of her buttocks. "What a waste, what a reprehensible waste." He switched on the bedside lamp. "Well, better get you home."

She did not move. One full, glowing breast showed above the sheet; the light caught disarranged strands of her thick, brilliant hair. "Why are you being so tiresome? I'm sleeping here tonight."

"What about your father?"

"He thinks I'm going back to the Knightsbridge station."

Peter's eyes appeared sunken in purple greasepaint. "Haven't we just conclusively proved there's no point to you staying?"

"Stop arguing, darling. You're not getting rid of me." She reached for the light, pulling the little chain.

He put his arms loosely around her.

IV

Awakening in the darkness without any sense of disorientation, she knew immediately that she was in Peter's hotel room. She reached out her hand, encountering cold, rumpled sheets.

Turning, she saw the tiny orange circle of a cigarette and a dark shadow. He had opened the blackout curtain and was gazing out at the Thames.

"What're you doing over there?" she murmured drowsily.

He returned to sit on the other bed. "Remembering why I learned to fly," he said.

"Somebody put salt on your tail?"

Not responding to her joke, he said, "The stories of those Great War dogfights over France always seemed the epitome of chivalry. What a silly little chump I was. There's the smell of burning meat, skin that peels off, a dying friend screeching over your radio." His voice wavered, then he said, "Well, chivalry wasn't all it was cracked up to be either. Sweltering in a tin can, vital pieces being lopped off with broadswords."

"If the mountain won't come to Mohammed," she said.

Kneeling in the darkness between the beds, she took his cigarette to stub out in the ashtray. She pressed his cold thighs apart. She had never sunk to practicing oral eroticism, but this was her love, her poor, pushed-to-the-edge love. He had drunk himself sodden and found every excuse to put off making love to her because he'd anticipated failure. Another failure would shatter him. Her kissing and light caresses soon made him huge. His hands pulled her hair, gripping her to his groin, and to maintain her balance she clasped his thighs: the tendons were like taut wires. Then, surprisingly, her pulses began to beat violently and her skin heated. Although she did not reach orgasm, when she heard his triumphant shout a serene and unselfish kind of joy spread through her. She had succeeded in giving her poor beleaguered darling what he needed.

For a long time neither of them moved: he remained bent over her with his lips pressing against her thick hair, she rested her cheek on the inside of his wet thigh.

Later that night he was able to make love to her in the conventional way.

V

"Will you be stationed in England?" she asked.

He had been in London six days, and they were in the flat, sitting decorously apart because Mrs. Hawkins, the charlady, was ironing in the kitchen. This was the first time Araminta had permitted herself to question Peter about the future. Pure superstition. In wartime everyone succumbs to some form of superstition, and she nursed a primitive fear that broaching the subject of Peter's future would hurl him back to combat. (In much the same spirit she had stayed clear of the little lover's jokes that in the past had sprinkled her conversations, lest such quips mark an end to their swift, erratically successful intercourse.) But she could no longer bear her ignorance.

He stared at the vase crowded with daffodils he'd brought her. "I'd rather hoped so," he said.

"Then you won't be?"

"There's talk Rommel's planning a major offensive."

She made an inarticulate sound. If Rommel and his Afrika Korps were on the attack, Peter's wing would remain on Malta, or worse yet, be posted to Libya.

"My parents are coming down to London," he said.

She swallowed sharply. "When?"

"Tomorrow." He looked at his hands. The well-shaped nails were bitten to the quick. "Mother's letter said they wanted to spend the day."

"Alone with you?"

"Alone."

"They want to talk about your brother."

His eyelid fluttered. "Possibly."

"It must be a very difficult time for them."

"Tomorrow," Peter said, "is the last day of my leave."

She rose from the chair, her face wild. "But . . . I assumed you had a fortnight."

"I report at six the day after tomorrow."

Her stomach lurched sickeningly, and she felt sudden tears prickling. She knew in all decency she ought to urge him to spend a day with his bereaved parents. Instead she found herself saying in a rough tone, "I can't help if I'm greedy. Have lunch with them, darling. The rest of the time belongs to me."

THIRTY-FOUR

I

Spume gusted out of the darkness against the prow of the *Burnsville.* Wyatt, using his sleeve to dash the salt water from his eyes, continued to peer ahead. He saw nothing but the faintest hint of luminosity that shone from microscopic sea creatures embedded within cresting waves. Clouds covered the June night. The French shoreline was blacked out, as were the nine small British boats chugging along parallel with the ship. Silence was being maintained and the rumble of the choppy sea was loud in his ears, that and the uneven vibration of the old destroyer's engine. The *Burnsville,* obsolete long before she plowed across the Atlantic as part of America's lend-lease program, had been chosen for this commando operation because of her unseaworthiness.

"Well, Kingsmith, what do you make of the operation so far?" whispered a voice burred with Scotland.

"Can't tell yet. Have to wait until Edward R. Murrow gives out the scoop."

It wasn't much of a wisecrack, but stifled laughter came from the nearby darkness. "Edward R. Murrow—that's a bloody good one, Yank."

Wyatt felt slightly less seasick.

Since they had left Portsmouth he'd been making a supreme effort not to vomit—to his mind seasickness would expose his rising barometer of fear. But of course he had only himself to blame that he was on a commando mission. British and Canadian commando units were trained to swoop across the Channel with a dual intent: to inflict strategic damage and to test the coastal defenses. Wyatt had suggested that the U.S. forces needed firsthand information for the future invasion, volunteering his own services. So here he was, scheduled to take part as an observer in the Sixth British Commando Unit's surprise attack on the immense dry dock that the Germans had constructed just south of Dieppe. At times he felt as if this were all happening in a movie and he could no more be harmed than if he were sitting in a Fox theater. Then the terror phase would sweep over him and he would recall that commandos with their shoe-polished faces deserved their status as heroes. Casualties on these raids were horrendous.

The boat lurched again, and another burst of icy spray blew spume at him. *Unusually cold for June, Käthe,* he thought, then wondered why he should be mentally addressing anyone in Nazi Germany.

Sshthwump!

All hell's about to break loose, he thought, grateful that he was thinking lucidly, without panic.

Wyatt was one of the handful aboard aware that the mission's true weapon was the *Burnsville* herself. Hidden above her fuel compartment were tons of high explosives with delayed action fuses.

The shore erupted with red tracer shells and glittering orange arcs. Shells resonated noisily, slamming against the *Burnsville*'s armored hull.

The deck jerked and shuddered, rearing up. "Here we go!" shouted a boyish voice near Wyatt. "We've broken through Jerry's antitorpedo net!"

Wounded skittered like toys. Wyatt grabbed the rail, reaching out to prevent a shrieking sailor with a chest injury from sliding overboard. The sloping deck was lit by a red, pink, and yellow glare. One of the small boats was ablaze.

Soon, with another thudding dislocation, the *Burnsville*—as planned—smashed into the dry-dock gate. It seemed like pandemonium with garbled shouts rising above the roaring and popping sounds. Yet there was an order of sorts. British sailors were returning the fire of the German sailors who knelt on the dock aiming rifles. Other British seamen hastily shifted the wounded. Commando units were leaping ashore. Stukas already howled down, strafing. Bullets thwacked on the deck.

Wyatt's assignment was to remain aboard to watch the time bombs being set. He considered himself an agnostic, yet he was muttering a prayer to the Episcopal Christ of his childhood as he struggled along the slanting companionways to the fuel compartments. He would have offered up a Hebrew prayer to his father's God, if he'd known the language. All possible invocations were required. One mistake in setting the charges or one lucky German bullet and they'd never find the pieces of anyone aboard the *Burnsville.*

The two hours in the dry dock jumped without regard to the normal passage of time. Minutes raced as Wyatt watched the intricacies of setting delicate mechanisms, slowed when he heard the shriek of a Stuka.

At oh-oh-two-hundred, departure time, Wyatt, bulky in his life jacket, was slithering down a rope. His gloves had gone overboard when he helped with the wounded, his palms were coated with some kind of acid from the engine room. The rough, wet manila hemp abraded his palms, yet there was no pain whatsoever. The icy saltwater stung pleasantly like aftershave. Striking out in his powerful Australian crawl, he headed for the nearest small boat. Shrapnel and bullets splashed into the dark sea around him.

He heard a feeble cry.

Veering through oil globules toward the sound, he reached a barely conscious commando floating in a Mae West. As he paddled with his burden toward the boat, he heard others shouting for help. Fixing the locations in his mind, he dragged the now unconscious man to waiting hands. He had rescued two others, a badly burned petty officer and a bald demolition man with blood streaming down his forehead, and was about to set out to where he'd marked another cry from mutilated humanity when a loud, precise British voice called from the deck above him. "You down there! Get the hell aboard! And that's an order."

On deck a drenched commando slapped him on the shoulder. "If all Yanks are like you, ruddy 'Itler's goose is cooked."

He was handed rum-laced tea. As the mug slithered to the deck, breaking, Wyatt saw that his palms were raw meat.

II

Of the three hundred men who had set out on the raid, half were killed, and another thirty taken prisoner.

Predictably, Goebbels's Ministry of Propaganda immediately brayed the successful repulse of the "British invasion." The following afternoon German and collaborationist French journalists were escorted through the destroyer. A smartly uniformed German naval press attaché explained that this old scow was proof that the enfeebled British Navy had no teeth left. He was winding up his speech when the delayed action fuses detonated the hidden explosives. The obsolete destroyer shuddered and arched. With a thunderous roar it came apart. Bodies and debris flew upward like so many smashed toys. The *Burnsville* had ripped in half. The blazing bow swept far inside the dry dock. The smoking, burning stern firmly blocked the entry.

The vast German dry dock facility was demolished beyond all repair.

III

"What makes you so very cheerful?" Araminta said.

"Seeing you. Oops! Sorry," Wyatt said. He had been sneaking bourbon into her Coca-Cola, his right hand awkward as a paw because of heavy bandaging and the unusable thumb. He'd already suffered two lengthy, painful operations on the tendons of each hand, and in a couple of days he would go under the knife again.

"A few drops won't show with this pattern," she said, brushing at her skirt.

She was visiting him at an American military hospital, a renovated Victorian mansion not far from Hampton Court. They sat in deck chairs on the lawn, he in pajamas and hospital robe, she in a blouse with a pink-checkered cotton skirt. Her legs, gleaming with the Coty's makeup she'd bought the previous Christmas, attracted a foursome of convalescent bombardiers: they kept looking up from their poker game to ogle her.

"Darling, aren't you going to tell me how it happened?"

"This is a warning. Never, never try feeding those damn ducks in Hyde Park."

She laughed. "Whatever it was, you're extremely chipper about it."

"I behaved okay," he said quietly. "I surprised myself."

"What rubbish. You're the very stuff heroes are made of. A true man of action." She added in a whisper, "My feminine intuition tells me you were somehow connected to that big commando raid."

He looked at her, startled.

"I'm as secret as a tomb," she murmured. "But what I can't understand is why *you* were with the commandos."

"An American observer," he said quietly.

"And you did more than observe?"

"Nothing much."

"Don't be modest. You Americans are born to swagger— that's your charm."

"I helped a few guys get to the boats—" He stopped.

A one-legged poker player who appeared about seventeen was struggling over on his crutches. "My buddies've staked ten bucks that you're not Rita Hayworth's sister."

"You Yanks," she said, fluttering her eyelashes. "How you do lead a poor girl on."

"Win me my bet. Come over and make like you're her English sister."

Wyatt watched Araminta chaff with the wounded boys. There was a hectic edge to her flirtatiousness. He knew this antic gaiety. It had been his when his heart had sent out messages to weep.

THIRTY-FIVE

I

At slightly past one on July seventh Wyatt pressed the bell of Euan's flat. His plan was to read and relax here, then, before teatime, when Araminta's trip at the fire station ended, take a long stroll to Basil Street in Knightsbridge and pick her up. He buzzed again, expecting the tough, diminutive charlady, Mrs. Hawkins, to let him in.

To his surprise Araminta answered the door. In her crumpled pink Viyella bathrobe, her tangle of red curls draining all color from her face, she looked weary if not downright ill—but then again he'd never seen her without any makeup whatsoever.

"I figured you'd be on duty," he said.

"A touch under the weather. What's the time?"

He glanced at his watch. "Five past one."

"That late?" Araminta glimpsed herself in the hall mirror. "Good Lord, what a fright!" Her vivacity canceled out her look of sickness. "Let me primp. You find out what evil Mrs. Hawkins hath wrought on that lovely coffee Aunt Rossie sent."

Used grounds had been put in the top of the percolator, wartime style. Wyatt dumped them in the rubbish bin, measuring out three tablespoons of fresh Chase and Sanborn. His palms were a bright pink, but the tendons worked again, albeit rustily: he was able to saw a few slices from the heavy brown loaf—this past April white bread had gone the way of other peacetime delicacies.

"Did you bring along a paper?" Araminta called from the bedroom corridor. "Daddy takes ours to work."

"I'll run down and grab one for you."

The placard leaning outside the corner tobacconist was chalked TRIUMPH AT EL ALAMEIN. Glancing at the front page, he saw that the Allies had continued their sweep around Rommel's forces. When he returned, Araminta had on makeup, a short-sleeved white blouse, and well-fitted slacks: her hair was tamed by a bright blue snood.

"I see you made breakfast," she said, chuckling at the sloppily set table.

"Lunch, you mean." He went to the kitchen for the jar of peanut butter. Of his gifts from the PX, peanut butter was the only one universally rejected by the British Kingsmiths.

On his return Araminta, too vain to wear her reading glasses with any member of the opposite sex, stood at the window, taking advantage of the June brilliance.

Suddenly she gave a breathy whimper. The *Times* rustled to the floor, but her elbows remained bent as though she continued to hold the pages. Brightly painted mouth curved down, eyes staring, she might have been the model for a Greek mask of tragedy.

" 'Minta, what is it?"

She stared blankly at him, then closed her eyes, swaying.

Wyatt took three rapid strides, gripping her round white arms, which were rough with gooseflesh.

Glancing down, he saw a photograph: even the blurred, grainy newsprint could not disguise the matinee-idol features. *Captain the Honorable Peter Reginald Gervase Shawcross-Mortimer, third son of the earl and countess of Mainwaring.*

It was the obituary page.

"Come on, 'Minta, you'd better lie down."

"I must talk to them. His parents."

" 'Minta dearest, it's in the paper, it's true."

"They lost their oldest son. And now Peter. Don't you see, I must tell them how most dreadfully sorry I am."

"That's not necessary."

She was going unsteadily to her room. She returned with a

little silk telephone book. Her hands were trembling and she couldn't open it. Wyatt fumbled to the page lettered *M*, finding two of the five residences, Mainwaring Court and Mortimer House near Marble Arch. He dialed the London number for Araminta.

A woman with a breathy upper-class accent answered. She was, she said, the countess of Mainwaring's secretary. "Whom might I say wishes to speak?"

"Miss Kingsmith."

Araminta breathed shallowly. Wyatt tried to put consoling arms around her, but she pushed him away.

"Miss Kingsmith," said the secretary, "the countess has requested that I explain. Her son was killed in action two days ago. Neither she nor the earl is taking calls."

"Two days . . ." Araminta responded dazedly. "Peter's been dead two whole days. . . . And I didn't even know. . . ."

Wyatt, who had heard both sides of the brief conversation, muttered "Bastards," and pressed down on the telephone. Leading Araminta to her room, he helped her onto the rumpled bed, coaxing her to take a sip of brandy.

She choked and turned her head away. "Leave me alone," she said in a grating whisper. "Let me have my weep."

He telephoned Kingsmith's, then succeeded in getting a trunk call through to Quarles. As an afterthought he flipped through Araminta's small silk telephone book for the number of the artillery school in Scotland. Before Euan and Porteous could arrive, a Major Downes, who spoke with a Canadian accent, was on the telephone. He said he was Aubrey's superior officer. Wyatt explained about Peter's death. "Please convey my sympathy to Miss Kingsmith," the Canadian said. "I'll arrange a leave. Lieutenant Kingsmith should be in London first thing tomorrow."

II

"Words seem idiotic and small," Aubrey said. "He was my friend, 'Minta."

"I do appreciate you coming down, darling," Araminta said

in a hollow, tired voice. Shoes off but otherwise fully dressed, propped by pillows, she lay staring at her ultramodern, pale-ash wardrobe.

"Of course I'm here. Come on, 'Minta, this is me. Practically your twin." Aubrey patted her hand, which was clenched around a handkerchief. "Let me help you."

She turned on the pillow, looking at him with puffy, reddened eyes. "Would you? Help me?"

"Anything."

"I need money. I can't ask Daddy. It's not certain yet, but I might need pots and pots of money."

"I won't ask why," he said softly.

"You can guess, though."

"Maybe there's a better answer to the problem."

"There isn't. I've done nothing but think about this." She blew her nose, sighing. "Aubrey, I'm not ethical like you. I never was. I'm too blindly self-centered. As long as I get my own way, I'm not too horrible, but basically I've never been a good person—"

"Stop it. You're brave, generous, and—"

"And astonishingly lacking in Christian morality. Yes, I know what you're thinking. She's doing away with Peter's baby. But it's also a bastard. And having people point their fingers at me and the child for the rest of our lives requires more stamina than I possess. Believe me, there's only one solution, a quick operation of the illegal type."

" 'Minta—"

"There's no point arguing. Nothing you say will change my mind."

"It can be dangerous unless you know a good man."

"I'll find one."

He stroked back her hair.

She shrugged off his hand. "Stop gentling me like a Shetland pony!" Her voice rose. "If you're too morally upright to give me the money, just come out and say so."

"I'll transfer all there is in my bank savings," he said. "The cash'll be in your account, waiting."

"Thank you. Oh, damn Peter, damn him! How dare he go and get himself killed?" Rolling over, she began to sob.

Aubrey sat by her bed. From his quiet empathy nobody would guess he was grieving for the old friend with whom, O supreme irony, he had signed the Oxford Pledge never to fight for crown and country. Certainly none of the long-faced visitors to the Mayfair flat had suspected Aubrey's stomach was twitching with nerves. Tomorrow night he would take the passenger plane that flew on a rough schedule between Scotland and Sweden. In Stockholm he would briefly contact the CI-4 agents (one was Käthe's "Ulla-Britt Onslager"), then make his way to German-occupied Denmark, and across the border to the Reich: in Kiel he would contact a naval officer in the Schwarze Kapelle, the espionage system buried deep within the Third Reich's military.

It was damn decent of Downes to let me come to London, he told himself. But the decency of his superior didn't make it any easier to leave his sister. In his entire life he had never seen her brought low like this. *I must find somebody to help her.*

III

That evening after dinner, while Elizabeth sat napping over her mending and Euan glared angrily at the evening paper, Aubrey edged Wyatt to the kitchen. Crockery had been piled in the sink for the charlady to wash up the following morning. Aubrey tried to speak, but as always when it came to asking a favor, he grew tongue tied.

Wyatt spoke first. "What gets me is the shitty way she found out. His parents knew how much they meant to each other. Why the hell couldn't they have had the decency to telephone her?"

"From what Peter told me up at Oxford, they were of the old-school aristocracy. Common folk have no feelings."

"Peter wasn't like that, not at all. A special kind of guy." Behind the blackout blinds there was a faraway buzz of RAF planes: recently the Allies had beefed up their raids over Germany, Americans by day, British by night. Both men listened, then Wyatt went on, "Aubrey, the thing is he was spooked. On that last leave I spent an evening with them. He got loaded to the gills and when 'Minta went to the head, he started in about grouse and hunters and no birds making it through the season. Fatalistic bullshit."

"Fatalistic maybe, but given the odds for a Spitfire pilot on his fourth tour of duty, fatalism is reality."

"He said he'd intended to marry Araminta this leave, then decided it wasn't fair to her."

"It would have been better if he had," Aubrey said.

"Come again?"

"He should have married her." The planes were overhead now, and the kitchen light vibrated, casting a flicker on Aubrey's moist high forehead.

"So that's how it is," Wyatt said softly.

"She says she's not positive yet, but knowing my sister, she's quite sure."

"Jesus, what a mess."

"I've had money transferred, but I have to be back in Scotland tomorrow. Would you keep an eye out for her?"

"Peter asked the same thing—"

He broke off as the door swung open.

"Ahh, here you two are," Euan said, glaring at his son. "What are you boys so secretive about?"

"We were talking about Peter," Aubrey responded.

"England owes him the greatest debt of all. He died a hero's death. At least Araminta has *that* to be proud of." Euan's voice reproached Aubrey. Yet in truth he felt only a profound relief that his irritating, bookish son had found himself a safe berth in Scotland.

IV

Wyatt was staying with Porteous.

That night he couldn't get to sleep. *Araminta,* he thought, and rolled over. As he considered her grief and intolerable situation, the repaired tendons of his hands seemed alive. He turned on his other side. *Aubrey asked me to help her.* After an hour of tossing and turning he reached for the bedside lamp and clumsily lit a cigarette. Switching off the light, he lay back in the pillows.

As he stared into the blackness at the glowing tip, a thought came to him. *I'll marry her.*

His mind jumped to the crazy rush of emotions that had surrounded Käthe, and a small knob of muscles showed at his jaw. The pain of her refusal to come to New York had abated very little. He was still haunted by the certainty that she had rejected him because of Myron Leventhal. *Oh, not on a conscious level,* he thought. *It was like a tumor in her brain, she didn't even know the Nazi beliefs were embedded there.*

All at once the night quiet was disturbed by a burst of deep-voiced Dutch song. Queen Wilhelmina had founded a club for the Free Dutch a few doors up the Bayswater Road, and servicemen came and went at all hours.

Pushing himself to a sitting position, Wyatt took a long drag on his cigarette. *Stop stewing over Käthe,* he told himself. *That's over and done with. Think about Araminta.*

Araminta had spent her days off from the Knightsbridge Fire Station traveling on crowded trains to visit him at the hospital. Her liveliness and high spirits had buoyed him through the post-op blues. Her delightful vanity and charming selfishness had amused him, but he had seen through to her warmth and loyalty. Though he had never doubted her love for Peter, she had a way of tossing her bright hair whenever she caught sight of him that made him suspect she liked him more than she'd let on.

And as for her baby, considering his own experience, he believed he could carry off being a good father. *Araminta's one terrific dame,* he thought. *We'll make a great team.* There was no tinge of self-sacrifice in his impulsive decision. Stubbing out his cigarette, he fell asleep almost immediately.

V

"You have only yourself to blame if this evening turns out to be a disaster," Araminta said as they left the flat.

"We both have to eat, so why not do it together?"

She made a bright rejoinder, but as he started the jeep her

attention wandered. How odd it felt, not having her mind firmly anchored. She had never been a woolgatherer. Until now she had been able to detect the feel of a crooked stocking seam, she knew the instant her lipstick needed replenishing. Though congenitally late, she could gauge the time accurately without glancing at her watch. Since she'd seen that blurred photograph in the *Times,* however, entire hours had disappeared as if down rabbit holes. She kept reliving Peter's last leave—the bruise-dark shadows under his eyes, his rapid recital of Victorian poetry, his triumphant shout whenever he came. Out of his poor, sweet difficulties had come this ruinous if banal problem.

Aubrey had been better than his word. Not only had he put the money in her bank account, but when he'd kissed her goodbye he'd slipped her a folded memo sheet with a name, a telephone number, a Harley Street address. A reputable specialist who did illegal operations? Hardly information a womanizing rake would have at his fingertips, much less her shy, sensitive brother. Yet although she remained intent on abortion, she still hadn't gathered up the energy—or was it the will? —to make the call.

"Here we are," Wyatt said.

She jerked to attention.

Ahead of them Buckingham Palace reared up against the twilit sky. They were in Green Park. Along the dusk-shadowed paths men in the uniforms of various countries either strolled or lounged on benches with their arms around English girls.

"Wasn't this a dinner invitation?" Araminta asked.

"First we need to talk."

"Darling, do I hear ominous rustling in the trees?" Her attempt at archness ended in a sharp little gasp.

"Promise me you won't say anything until I've finished."

"Don't you sound somber. This isn't like you."

His dusk-lit expression was stern. " 'Minta, I want you to be my wife."

"What?"

"I'm asking if you'll marry me."

Her eyes filled with tears. "Aubrey told you?"

"Look, you can say no or yes. But don't tie what I'm asking to anything else. Take it seriously."

"Wyatt, how very sweet of you."

"Sweet, hell. You'll notice that I haven't inquired whether the situation still exists—or whether it ever did."

"You must give up this obsession of yours about proposing to girls named Kingsmith."

A spasm contorted the muscles around his mouth. "I told you. That was kid stuff."

"The objections are the same. We're first cousins."

"We're not. Cousins."

She stared at him.

He raised his shoulders in a little shrug. "Mother also had a little problem, and Dad was in love with her. So here I am, no prize, but not your cousin either."

She leaned back in the car seat. "That's a closely guarded secret, Wyatt."

"You can say that again. Mother didn't tell *me* until a few years ago. Dad, well, he's been fabulous. He's totally forgotten there was ever anyone else in the picture. I'm his son and that's that."

"I knew you arrived a little too promptly. What did Aunt Rossie tell you about your father?"

"Dad's my father."

"Was he married?"

"He died," Wyatt said tersely. Why didn't he tell her the whole truth? He couldn't. His silence had nothing to do with trust, he trusted Araminta completely. His silence was caused by the old pain. Though far from a coward he was not a masochist either. He shrank from reactivating the pain. *I'll tell her later,* he thought. "This is for real."

"For real?"

"I'm crazy about you."

"Darling, you like me, I'm your chum," she said. "That's not love."

"Arrows through the heart," he said, clapping a hand on his chest. "Why do you think I've been hanging around? If Aubrey hadn't asked me to look out for you I'd have waited a decent interval before springing this on you. It's taking advantage of you in a bad moment."

"Give me some time to think," she said in a faraway voice. "Now do let's have dinner."

Facing one another in the narrow French restaurant in Soho, they both picked at the excellent rabbit stew.

When the plates of scarcely touched food were removed, Wyatt asked, "How long're you leaving me dangling?"

"Darling, it's *un peu* awkward. You see, I used to have the silliest little infatuation with you. I can't be cold blooded and say to myself, 'Here's Wyatt, what a godsend.' "

"If you're worried I'll be a good father, remember I've had a wonderful example all my life. Come on, say yes."

"Why're you doing this?" Araminta's eyes narrowed with Euan's hard shrewdness. "And please, no more of the moonlight-and-roses tosh."

"Okay, on a practical level. We make a terrific team. You'll fit in perfectly with my life in New York, be a big asset for my career, charming the socks off my clients. But, 'Minta, I don't take back a word of what I said about you. You're fun to be with, you brighten up my life, you're spectacular looking. And I intend to spend the rest of my days telling you so. I don't give up easily."

Araminta twisted Peter's diamond around her finger. She had lost weight and the ring was too loose. Abruptly she rose to her feet. "I won't be a minute," she said in a tight little voice, hurrying on her high heels to the rear. The beaded curtain jangled as she rushed through.

When she emerged five minutes later, her face was repowdered, her lipstick renewed. The rose-cut diamond was gone from her finger.

"You'll have to tell Daddy," she said.

VI

Euan, bewildered at Araminta's sudden reversal of allegiance, pursed his small, hard mouth. "What the devil's the matter with you, Wyatt? First poor Alfred's girl, now mine."

"Araminta's said yes."

"The girl's weeping her eyes out for Captain Shawcross-Mortimer."

"Uncle Euan, it's settled. We're getting married."

There was an expression of such determination in his good-looking American nephew's face that Euan shrank back. Much as he doted on his lively daughter, he wasn't blind to the traditional reason for a hasty marriage. The earl of Mainwaring's son, poor boy, had been home on leave a couple of months ago. . . . Still, on the other hand, she had been rushing down to the American hospital whenever she was free. Had she been carrying on an intrigue with her fiancé? Or her cousin? Or both? Distressing thoughts for a man who until a few minutes earlier had never considered his daughter anything other than a virgin.

"What about her duties with the Auxiliary Fire Service?"

"She's turning in her badge."

"I see," Euan said in a muted voice. "We'll have a small wedding at Quarles. Say at the end of the month?"

"Fine. Perfect."

The vicar of the old Saxon church married them in the side garden of Quarles. The warm south wind teased pink rose petals onto the bride's smart, big-brimmed hat and the groom's sandy hair. Wyatt had been unable to reach Aubrey at the gunnery school, so Porteous filled in as best man. Euan, his face working with bellicose regret, gave the bride away. Elizabeth wept noisily in her unbecoming salmon frock, bought the summer before the war for garden parties. The crotchety Irish cook, the only servant remaining at Quarles, shushed the giggles of the evacuees. It was the Irishwoman who took the wedding pictures. The ship bearing Wyatt's letter about the engagement was torpedoed and this package of badly focused snapshots would be the first herald to Rossie and Humphrey that they had a daughter-in-law.

VII

"Wait until you see the nightgown Mummy gave me. She splurged all of her coupons on it." Araminta was moving rapidly around the large, flowered Axminster carpet. "Should I change in the bathroom? It's very worrisome, being Mrs. Kingsmith, not Miss. Do you think I have wedding nerves?"

"The innkeeper's prepared the bridal suite with that eventuality in mind," Wyatt said, putting his feet up on the lumpy, flowered-chintz sofa. "I'll sack down here."

"Darling, would you mind awfully, waiting?"

"I expected it."

"Can't you sound a little less relieved?" she asked, smiling tearfully.

"Hey, hey." He went to put his arms around her.

He intended it to be a cousinly embrace, but she pressed closer. He hadn't been with a woman since before the commando raid. The spectacular body touched his everywhere. Their mouths opened, the kiss going deeper, the first kiss of passion that they had ever exchanged. The blue-shadowed light of the fading August day threw the room into soft shadows, a faraway nightingale called, the old walls creaked faintly, but neither of them noticed. His almost-healed hands were curved around her buttocks when she pulled back a little.

"I always knew you'd be divinely sexy," she murmured unevenly. "Does this sound sluttish? I've changed my mind about waiting."

They strewed their clothes on the carpet. Naked, Araminta stood absolutely still, her hands at her sides. He gazed through the soft light. Her breasts were opulent with pregnancy, the nipples a warm, toasty pink, her stomach slightly curved. Her hips flared from the still slender waist, the pubic curls a brassier, truer red than he had imagined, her toenails were polished with wine-dark lacquer. He knelt, kissing the toes, kissing his way up her legs.

"Come to bed," she whispered. "Come to bed, husband darling."

The room grew dark, and the tall, fruit-laden old pear tree outside the window whispered in the breeze. Wyatt made love to his bride as though they were on a journey of discovery, an odyssey that he desired above all else for them to share, and yes, he longed for them to reach the end and spiral down into climax together, he wanted this to be more than satiation, more than release, he wanted a complete fusion between them—he wanted sex the way it had been with only one woman. Yet as he reached the end of his endurance, pounding faster and faster, he accepted that even though Araminta's breathing quickened, the response was to please him.

Afterward, they smiled at each other, and in that scarcely visible smile, that sweet, sad glimmer of teeth and eyes, was the acknowledgment that four lovers lay entwined in the brass bed.

VIII

Aubrey darling,

I should have written earlier, but I'm not reliable about correspondence, am I?

First of all, we missed you horribly at the wedding.

Second of all—whatever possessed you to tell Wyatt to look after me?

It was inspired!

In the recent past I would have bet a million pounds that I'd never smile again, and yet here I am, beaming. He can be very sweet, my spouse. And, at the right times, not so sweet.

Yet the oddest part is that I still feel absolutely attached to Peter. How can I adore my husband, yet at the same time wish with all my heart I were married to Peter? In love with two men, one living, the other dead. (Oh, God, my fingers clenched as I wrote that.)

When I discussed this with Wyatt, he cupped my face in his hands and told me I am quite simply caught up in a syndrome of the war. Another aside. I can talk about everything with Wyatt. Anything, that is, except about Katy. When I mention her he gets a nasty smile and calls her "the enemy."

We have told the parents about impending grandparenthood. Since I'm absolutely huge, it seems hard to imagine they were surprised. Daddy got very red in the face and Mummy oozed her customary tears. "Oh, my little girl," she wept.

On the American front Aunt Rossie—ever practical—has promised New York maternity clothes and a layette while Uncle Humphrey has already sent this sweet, idiotic family tree to prove that there has never been a two-headed Kingsmith.

Aubrey, I adore you for sticking your nose in.

IX

Wyatt, attached to a regiment taking part in training exercises for the invasion of some unspecified beachhead, was stationed at a camp near Brighton. On the windy afternoon of February 12, 1943, he received a telegram. *Araminta delivered of a boy, 6 lbs 11 oz at 8:35 AM. Son healthy. Mother doing well.*

He wangled an immediate leave.

Arriving at Quarles before teatime, he found Araminta leaning back into a nest of pillows, her face exhausted but proud.

"Well done, Momma," he said, kissing the top of her sweat-odored hair.

She flung her arms around him, pulling him to her swollen breasts, smearing lipstick on his forehead. "Just like a man, turning up after all the hard work's done."

"Hey," he said, kissing her mouth.

She smelled of tiredness and toothpaste. "Hey."

"Was it very rough?"

"Devastatingly. But do take a look at Geoff." They had agreed if the baby were a boy to name him Geoffrey, spelled the English way. "See what you think."

As Wyatt moved to the cradle in the window ell his legs began to shake. Though he had assured himself often enough that Araminta's child would be as his own firstborn, something within him cried out that the baby in the lace-festooned cradle was not his. The few steps across the bedroom were the most difficult he had ever taken.

He closed his eyes and drew a breath before he looked. The

sleeping infant lay on its stomach. All he could see was a curve of cheek, neck creases, and a fuzz of hair that appeared pink.

"Red hair," Wyatt said.

"Exactly. Darling, bring him over here." Araminta said.

"Pick him up?"

"They're very sturdy." Araminta's laugh was forced. "Babies."

Gripped by paralysis, Wyatt understood that this moment was a test for the three of them, him, his wife, this new morsel of humanity. For a moment his hands again felt flayed. Outside, the evacuee girls were skipping rope. Onesie, twosie . . .

He lifted the infant, and the head bobbled backward. Wyatt braced the warm neck with three fingers, peering down. The skin of the baby's neck was loose, like a puppy's. The fine, pinkish brows were drawn fiercely inward, the lips pressed together. The Mainwarings' middle son, like their eldest, had been killed in Burma. If, on that last, despairing leave, Peter had not considered it a rotten trick to get married, this infant would one day have been a peer of the realm, taking his place in the House of Lords.

The baby opened his eyes, gazing up unfocusing, then yawned. There was something so disgruntled yet so trusting about the yawn that Wyatt chuckled. *We Americans, kid, we don't need titles,* he thought, nuzzling the sweet, milky-smelling folds under the baby's chin. "Yeah, yeah, yeah, Geoff old buddy," he said. "Welcome to the world, such as it is."

"Bring him over." Araminta patted the edge of the bed.

Wyatt sat on the counterpane, one arm around Araminta, the other cradling the baby. With a joy that was the more all-encompassing for being unanticipated, he thought, *We're a family.* They were a trinity, one of the links in the chain of humankind that reached back into the dimness before recorded time and stretched forward into the unseeable mists of the future.

"He looks the littlest like Daddy, doesn't he?"

"Don't worry about a thing, son," Wyatt said huskily. "We'll find you a top-notch plastic surgeon."

EIGHT
1942–1944

The V-2, as the second type of *vergeltungswaffe* rocket came to be called, rose sixty miles into the stratosphere, diving like a predatory bird at five times the speed of sound. Unlike their predecessors, the far slower V-1's, the rocket bombs could be neither seen nor heard and thus could not be intercepted.

—from *A History of the Second World War,*
Sir Aubrey Kingsmith

Thirty-six

I

When Käthe and Clothilde had decided to brave wartime travel for their traditional Christmas at Garmisch-Partenkirchen, Käthe had not anticipated anything more than a week of skiing. It had never entered her head she would be at a party of this sort.

Even by peacetime standards the Dietrich Eberhardts' 1942 Yule festivities sparkled with extravagance. Thick pine logs blazed in stone fireplaces, hundreds of candles glowed in the ten-foot tree, an army of liquor bottles flanked the gargantuan cut-glass bowl of mulled wine. The dining-room table, pushed into the main hall and extended with leaves, was continuously replenished with platters of sliced ham, pork, and veal, Bismarck herring, potato salad, pickles, and lingonberries. The silver tureen was kept filled with ivory-colored weisswurst—Munich's famed soufflé-light, mild sausage—while pretzel breads, the traditional weisswurst accompaniment, were heaped in baskets.

A round-faced foreign servant with a large pink *P* for Pole sewn on her loose smock pursed her lips in nervous concentration as she bore out a haunch of venison—because it wasn't rationed, venison had become extremely difficult to obtain. A trio of gray-haired accordionists were striking up the haunting chords of "Lili Marleen."

Käthe was the guest of Hannalore Eberhardt, the daughter of the house. Hannalore, with her buck teeth and very clear blue eyes, was a top-notch skier: the two had formed a tenuous friendship on the difficult runs. This was the first time, though, that Käthe had met the senior Eberhardts. Frau Eberhardt, from whom Hannalore had inherited her unfortunate bite, hovered near the kitchen. Herr Eberhardt, who had bought this imposing chalet a few months after the conquest of Poland, wore a gold Party badge on his outsize green Bavarian jacket. He was extremely stout and the bumps on his bald pate made it appear as if his skull were also padded with fat. Waddling about, he pressed food and drink on his guests. Most of the men wore uniforms expensively tailored of SS black adorned with the skull and crossbones insignia of the SS-Totenkopf, the Death's Head formations that administered the concentration camps. Käthe, on her own initiative, had risked photographing horrified reports from Wehrmacht officers about the bestial conditions in the camps and the SS-Totenkopf's massacres of entire Jewish populations. She wanted nothing more than to escape this jovial Nazi gathering. But on her arrival Hannalore had linked arms and since then had been taking her around with introductions that started, "May I present my dear friend, Fräulein Kingsmith, who won an Olympic gold medal for the Reich." Several couples had moved to the dining room, which, denuded of its table, formed an impromptu dance floor, and now they twirled beneath the carved beams.

". . . wir bei der Laterne stehn,
wie einst, Lili Marleen."

"Käthe?" called a familiar Bavarian voice. "Käthe Kingsmith, can that be you?"

Whirling around, she saw a stocky SS officer shrugging out of his ankle-length black leather coat.

It was Otto Groener.

Käthe hadn't seen Groener since Villa Haug. She had responded to his dozens of letters only once. When he had planned an elaborate tryst during his upcoming leave, she'd shot off a blatantly concocted excuse.

Yet here he was, stamping toward her, his coarsely handsome

features alight with pleasure. "Käthe! Imagine finding you here!" Ignoring Hannalore and the others, he said, "Come, let me fill your wine-cup."

She was too dizzy with loathing to argue.

II

". . . saw you from the back," Groener was saying, "and thought to myself, 'What a knockout shape that blonde has!' And then it hit me. Not that seeing you in Garmisch-Partenkirchen should be any surprise. Sigi often talked about your place up here. By the by, how is old Sigi? Haven't heard from him in ages. Still in Russia?"

"Sigi's with his uncle at . . . uh . . ." She wasn't meant to know they were safe in Zossen, the secret OKW nerve-center near Berlin. "They're not in Russia."

"That's good news. Anywhere's better than the Eastern front. Those Russians! Animals, all of them! Well, here's to Sigi." Groener lifted his glass in a toast, downing the Polish vodka in one gulp. "Vodka and ham, that's all the Polacks are good for. How wisely the Führer analyzed them. Filthy and lazy, liars every single one. Believe you me, the world will thank us for cleaning up that particular situation."

"So you're still stationed in Poland?" Despite her repugnance Käthe found herself gleaning information.

"No." He cut off her questions by stuffing herring in his mouth. Swallowing, he launched into a monologue of his achievements. The German Cross Order had been pinned on his tunic by the Führer's own hand. He had been promoted to *sturmbannführer*, the SS equivalent of major. The Görings often invited him to weekends at Karinhall, their country estate. "And the best news of all is that little Otto has a brother. Adolf. What a fine fat baby. Only six months old and already he can sit up by himself." Groener leaned forward. "No need to look so mournful, Käthe."

"What?"

"Forget your worries," he said softly. "You're brooding about *our* boy, aren't you?"

Never in all those letters had Groener referred to her son. Her legs went weak and she leaned against the wall.

"He's in the pink," Groener said.

"How do you know?"

"We gave a child to the Führer."

"You found him! Where is he?"

"No more questions." The accordions swirled into a waltz. "Let's dance."

Groener knew where her little boy was, and wouldn't tell her. Oh, how she loathed him.

"As a matter of fact," she said, "when you got here I was about to leave. A ferocious headache."

"Why didn't you say so? I'll drive you home."

"I don't live far," she lied. "A walk'll do me good."

"This cold air is hell on sinuses," he said.

III

The rear of his Horch had been equipped with one of the torpedo-shaped engines that burned charcoal. Käthe inhaled the smoky fumes and held a finger to her brow to ward off conversation. Flotillas of clouds blackened the Milky Way, but the unshadowed moon shone on St. Martin's, the old church where the two Nazis had jumped Wyatt after he tore down the anti-Semitic signs.

"As a matter of fact, I did see him," Groener said.

Startled from her recollections, she blurted, "Who?"

"Our kid, of course. It was pure chance. This summer I had some business with a civilian and he invited me for drinks. He kept bragging about his boy. After a few rounds he whispered that the child was living proof of selective breeding. He came from Villa Haug."

"A lot of babies," she said, "were born at Villa Haug."

"My thoughts exactly. So I dropped a few questions. The boy's birthday was April tenth. When he invited me to his place, I jumped at the chance. Käthe, I'd thought my little Otto was bright! This boy puts him to shame. The cleverest little tyke. He was barely two then, but he could throw a ball right at me, and he raced around on his tricycle. And talk? He talked a blue streak already." The raspy voice had softened with pride. "What a tough little guy he is—reminds me of myself when I was a kid. Fair hair like us, but otherwise there's no physical resemblance."

So he still looks like Wyatt, she thought, and realized how fatuous she was being. "Where is he?"

"Käthe, I've already told you too much."

"How do you know he's still all right?"

"Don't you think I've stayed in contact?"

"What's the man's name?"

"Käthe. A Lebensborn adoption is sacred."

"You know."

"I know too damn many things." They were passing the Kurhaus, and Groener stared at the bulky silhouette. "Having so much locked away is like carrying a hod of bricks. But believe me, Käthe, our boy's perfectly safe."

"Is he still called Erich?"

"Of course, and Erich he'll remain. A son of the Black Order. Put your mind at rest. These are fine, fine Nazis."

She shivered. "There's my house."

Groener insisted on walking her up the icy path. At the front door he said, "Take care of that headache. And tell Frau Kingsmith I'll drop by tomorrow afternoon to convey my Christmas wishes."

"That's not necessary—"

But he was stamping back to the car.

IV

"So you know Sturmbannführer Groener," Hannalore Eberhardt said the following afternoon as she plopped down at Käthe's table. A dense cloud had settled over the top of the Zugspitze and the veranda of the Schneefernerhaus was crowded with skiers waiting for the milky fog to lift.

"He's a friend of my brother's."

"He's very good looking—but did you ever see a man so positive he's God's gift to women? Still, I'm a sweetie-pie with him. Father's high up in the Special Office of Labor Allocation, and he's important to him." She leaned across the varnished wood, whispering, "He's in charge of the work force for the *vergeltungswaffe.*"

"The *vergeltungswaffe?*" Käthe peered into Hannalore's vividly blue eyes. Rumors of miracles swirled brightly in tandem with the whispers about the reprisal weapon, the *vergeltungswaffe.* Having never seen any mention of a new type of weapon in her filing, Käthe had assumed the stories were opiates circulated by the Ministry of Propaganda to make people forget the increasing Allied air raids, the shortages, the defeats in North Africa and Russia. "It actually exists?"

Hannalore glanced around.

"I've heard such crazy stories," Käthe murmured. "It's a gas that turns conquered people into robots, a germ that kills everyone except the Nordic race. A bomb that destroys the enemy population but not the buildings or the animals."

Hannalore's superior little laugh showed a fleck of brown wedged between her buck teeth. "All I can tell you is that it'll win the war."

V

The cloud didn't lift. Käthe rode down on the last jam-packed cable car. Long before she reached the chalet, darkness had fallen. Even so, Groener was still drinking tea in the whitewashed main room.

"Sturmbannführer Groener has offered to drive us back to Berlin," Clothilde said in the bland tone she would use in praising a hardworking servant.

"You'll have a far more pleasant trip than by rail," Groener said. An understatement. The trains coming here had been miserably crowded, the stops interminable.

Even so, the thought of spending ten to twelve hours in a car with him brought goose bumps to her arms. "We couldn't possibly put you to the trouble," she said.

"Now you're being ridiculous," Groener said. "I'll be by first thing tomorrow morning."

As Groener's car approached Berlin in the gathering dusk, they could see brownish smoke hovering above the flatness of the central city, reaching like tentacles into the outer areas. "Damn terror bombers," Groener muttered. Turning in at their driveway, he jammed on the brakes. A barrier with the red and black DANGER sign barred entrance. Käthe wrenched open the car door. Brick dust and the odor of burnt, wet-down wood filling her nostrils, she dodged around the barrier and raced toward the curve of unpruned yews. She came to an abrupt halt.

Though many of the windows on the left side of the house remained intact, every pane of glass to the right of the front door was gone—the windows casements were as vacant as an idiot's stare. Slowly climbing the front steps, Käthe edged around the front door, which had been axed down by the firefighters. In the twilight the staircase and cavernous drawing room appeared undamaged. Otherwise her childhood home was a shambles. The dining room, Alfred's *Herrenzimmer*, the kitchen, pantry, and laundry were ceilingless and heaped with rubble. The master suite and boxroom where they stored old clothes remained. But Sigi's room with the ancient von Graetz tapestry—"Loyalty to country, fidelity to oath"—was gone, as was her own room with the inlaid box that contained Wyatt's letters and the amethyst brooch. *Thank heavens Trudi went home to Saxony for Christmas.*

At a creaking overhead Käthe looked up. The reverberations of her footsteps must have dislodged the bathtub. It teetered back and forth on crossbeams. Then the blackened tub crashed down. She leapt backward. The fog of disturbed soot made her cough violently.

The other two had come to the entry.

"Those damn air pirates! I can't wait until I get my hands on them!" Groener said angrily. "I have a new flat in Charlottenburg, quite swank. I'll drive you over there."

Clothilde gazed up at the ruined mansion where she had spent most of her second marriage. "How thoughtful of you," she said calmly. "But we can manage quite comfortably in the chauffeur's quarters."

THIRTY-SEVEN

I

Käthe used her lunch hour from Hall Six to check on King-smith's. Unter den Linden had been hit. A fierce stench rose from the central lane, where members of the *Technische Nothilfe* —the auxiliary specializing in emergency air-raid assistance— hurried about, supervising the Russian prisoners who strug-gled to dig out a ruined sewer main. Many pedestrians, protect-ing themselves against odors, ashes, and masonry dust, had tied damp towels over their noses and mouths.

Kingsmith's had the CLOSED sign on the door. Käthe climbed on the sandbags to peek through a space in the boarded win-dows. What she could see of the shop appeared reasonably undisturbed. Getting down, she held her gloved hand over her nose. People were rushing by the sewer repair squad. One man, however, had halted near a fire-blackened linden tree. Beneath the shabby topcoat his shoulders were hunched in a way that thrust his head forward like a turtle's. A pocket hand-kerchief covering his lower face, his hat pulled down to the metal rims of his glasses, it was difficult to tell much about him, but Käthe decided from his strange posture that he was a veteran. Nowadays men with amputations or deforming wounds were sadly common.

She started back to Bendlerstrasse.

II

Near the Potsdamer *bahnhof* she spotted a small bakery with no line. The baker's wife clipped her ration book, handing over a dark loaf with a cheery "Heil Hitler."

Since Aubrey's surveillance tutorials Käthe had fallen into the habit of looking around. As she emerged, she glimpsed a man retying his shoe in the shadow of a pillar.

It was the hunched-over veteran from Unter den Linden.

He's following me!

Coldness prickled on her skin and her thoughts skittered. Had the military intelligence, the Abwehr, caught on to what she'd been up to? Had the Gestapo caught on to the errands she ran for Schultze?

Her impulse was to run. She forced herself to continue at a normal pace. Reaching a four-story, bombed-out building plastered with DANGER signs, she used her free hand to clamber up into the ruins of the first apartment, edging deeper inside to the dining room. The broken window overlooked the debris-heaped courtyard. She couldn't be seen from the street.

In the direction she had come, tiny bits of broken glass were being crushed, a small sound as terrifying as the thunder of high explosives. She moved on rubbery legs to the far side of the fallen table and stood absolutely still, scarcely breathing. The hunched veteran appeared in the arch of the dining room. The round table and a shaft of dusty light all that separated them, he peered through his glasses at her.

Unconsciously cradling the bread in front of her breasts, she attempted Clothilde's most arrogant tone. "Must you keep annoying me?"

"Ich dachte du bist tot," he said in a *Berlinische* accent. Pulling the handkerchief from his face, he said it again. "I thought you were dead."

III

"Aubrey?" she whispered. "Aubrey . . . How could I not recognize you?"

"Käthe. My Käthe."

"You've been sent back?" Relief and joy caught in her throat, and she laughed. "That's a ridiculous question. You're not on holiday in Berlin."

"I wasn't to contact you," he said. "But I snooped around the house and saw it had been bombed. Since then I've been circulating between Unter den Linden and the Bendlerblock, praying I'd spot you."

"We were in Garmisch-Partenkirchen over Christmas."

"Thank God."

"What about you? Your shoulders, I mean?"

"Tip-top shape. But Rutger Metz was wounded at Stalingrad." Aubrey continued to hold his turtle position while tilting his head. "Käthe, how could I have forgotten how beautiful you are?"

"There's an example of Kingsmith eyes. Or maybe it's those German spectacles you're wearing," she teased. *How strange,* she thought, *not being on guard. Is this what peace was like, being able to speak without constraint?* "Aub—Rutger, how are the family? How are they all?"

His smile faded. He shook his head, a warning he couldn't tell her what she shouldn't know.

"I'm alone, so alone!" she burst out. "And you know the most unbearable part? Not knowing whether they're alive or dead. Think how frantic you were about me."

After a long pause he came around the table, touching her cheek gently. "Alive. They're all alive. And your people?"

"Mother's the same as ever. And Sigi's . . ." Her voice faded. She had never given the British information tethered in any way to her half brother. "He's all right."

"Good."

Suddenly, without the routine advance warning of sirens, far to the west there was the excited rattle of ack-ack, and the distant sound rather like a tearing of cloth that she'd learned to recognize as approaching airplane engines.

Aubrey listened a moment longer. "B-17's," he muttered. "Again. The bastards."

"Bastards? They're Americans. On your side. You should be cheering."

"What, that women and children are being bombed out of their homes?"

"Once a pacifist, always a pacifist." She laughed softly, and because she was so at ease, she asked, "Is Wyatt in their air force?"

"Käthe," he warned with a pitying look.

She wanted to shout not to pity her, she wanted to shake him, her unrelentingly professional English cousin. She wanted to hug him. The sirens had started their howling, and there was a distant reverberation of bombs. A block warden shouted, but from the voices and sounds in the street nobody appeared to be making a dash for the shelters.

"Aubrey, have your people heard about the *vergeltungswaffe*?"

"We're fairly positive there's some top-secret weapon being developed." He spoke guardedly. "Why?"

"A . . . friend knows about it."

"Steer clear," he said.

"What sort of response is that?"

"Darling, do only what they ask."

"But this thing's brand new."

"Aren't you in enough danger?"

"It could be terrible for all of you."

"Go to the shelter!" The shout rang clearly over the thunderous cacophony of the raid. The block warden must be right outside. "Everybody to the U-Bahn shelter!"

"No use attracting attention," Aubrey said quietly. "Let's get a leg on."

As they emerged, a formation of Messerschmitt 109 fighters cut across the sky. In the direction of Lankwitz, American bombers were dipping between barrage balloons to drop what appeared to be giant eggs that burst into smoke and flames. Puffballs formed around the big American planes. One plummeted downward, trailing blackness.

"Forget the miracle weapon, Käthe," he said quietly.

"Will I see you again?"

"Not this time." He was staring at her as if to imprint her on his memory. Raising his arm in a salute, he said, "Heil Hitler, *gnädiges fräulein,* and thank you for the directions."

* * *

That evening at five-thirty a man with a peculiar wound that drew his head into an awkward position was walking along Bendlerstrasse as the civilian employees poured from the Bendlerblock. The girl with the slender legs and platinum hair spread like a white-gold shawl on her drab coat didn't see him. Aubrey, watching Käthe disappear, wished he could protect her from all manner of dangers, including her own integrity and goodness.

THIRTY-EIGHT

I

Käthe and Clothilde made their dinner of bread with some carrot jam, eating in the larger of the two garage rooms. (Trudi, who had returned that morning, had scrubbed and rearranged the chauffeur's quarters and then Clothilde had led her to an acquaintance's servantless mansion, where she was hired on the spot.)

Clothilde was making entries in her diary and Käthe was at the yellowed corner washbowl rinsing the thick pottery donated by Trudi's grateful new employer when cars rumbled into the driveway. The dish slipped in Käthe's hand. Her first thought was of Aubrey. *He's been captured and tortured into confessing. They've come for me. They'll take Mother, it won't matter to them that she knows nothing.*

A car door opened and slammed, footsteps crunched on the gravel drive. Groener's voice called out, "It's me, Otto. I've brought a few things to tide you over."

Käthe's jaw hardened. It was Clothilde who turned off the light and opened the door.

Groener planted his gleaming black boots proprietarially inside the threshold, flicking a gold cigarette lighter to provide minimal illumination in the blackout, bawling commands to a pair of SS men as they lugged in a small stove, two deep easy chairs upholstered in brocade, a luxurious floor-model radio, a round electric heater. After the duo had brought in several large, topless crates, Groener closed the door on them. Pulling the light chain, he took a lumpy object from the smaller crate, peeling away newspaper to reveal a delicate blue-flowered cup. "Herend from Hungary, the finest china available," he said. A second crate contained bedding. "Genuine goose-down." Beneath the coverlets were saucepans that gleamed like new—but there had been no new cooking utensils in the Third Reich since 1939. "Prewar aluminum."

His ultimate gifts were cans—Danish ham, sardines, and pineapple. "Sigi once told me his family liked pineapple."

"Imagine remembering all these years," Clothilde said, thanking him with the same gracious smile she had bestowed on the ragamuffin he once had been.

After the car and small truck had driven away, Clothilde picked up a cup, staring at it. "Even as a little boy Siegfried was good natured, but how could he have been friendly with such a coarse braggart?"

"Every bit must be stolen. Mother, we can't use it."

"Stop being ridiculous, Käthe. Our things are gone. And it's not as if we can return these to the proper owner." Clothilde plugged in the heater and radio. Warmth and a Mozart piano concerto.

Käthe sat on one of the brocade chairs. Her mother was right. In wartime one used what came along. Groener would ask her out, she knew he would, so why not make the most of the invitation? Despite Aubrey's misgivings she would try to discover the nature of the new miracle weapon. More important, she would find out more about Erich. Those fine, fine Nazis, his adoptive parents, had driven a car with a Frankfurt am Main license plate. Was her baby still in Frankfurt? What was his last name? Squeezing out information wouldn't be easy: Groener hadn't climbed the black peaks of Nazidom by swapping pillow talk. But one thing she had learned: Opportunities arose.

As Käthe and Clothilde were preparing for bed, a downy-faced Hitler Youth delivered a message for Käthe.

Would you join me at a party tomorrow evening? Otto.

II

The party, like the Yule festivities at Garmisch-Partenkirchen, was hosted by Dietrich Eberhardt. Another lavish display of unobtainable foods and drink, more Turkish cigar smoke hazing the rooms, similar anxiously docile foreign servants. The male guests were interchangeable, wearing black uniforms or dinner jackets adorned with gold Party badges. At tonight's gathering there was one vital difference: The women were universally young and shapely.

The bald host was nowhere in sight.

"Eberhardt must have wandered off with his little cream cake. He can't get enough of her," Groener said. "Käthe, you won't mention this evening to his daughter?"

"Of course I'd never say a word."

Groener snapped his fingers, calling an order in Polish. Two maids rushed over, one with champagne and glasses, the other carrying a silver tray with black caviar and its accoutrements. He barked another order. Caviar and chopped egg were mounded on toast, the servant curtseying as she handed the triangle to Käthe.

"Thank you," Käthe said. She forced herself to nibble, sipping the Mumm's. "Hannalore mentioned that you and Herr Eberhardt do business together. Is everyone here involved in the same project?"

"Yes. And it's highly sensitive."

Käthe pouted prettily. "As if anything could be more sensitive than my job. Otto, stop acting as if we met at some street corner." A reminder that she, too, had been a guest at Hitler's Eagle's Nest.

Groener's brows drew together thoughtfully. "Let's just say that the project will destroy the enemies of the Reich without shedding a drop of German blood."

"Exactly what Hannalore said." Käthe gripped her glass, nerving herself to whisper, "She told me it's the *vergeltungswaffe*."

"Hannalore should keep her mouth shut. And so should her father."

"I'm interested in what you do."

Groener thoughtfully passed a hand over his slick-combed hair. A flash of lightning penetrated the blackout blinds, thunder rumbled again, and the women sitting nearby chattered yet louder. "Christ, what a racket," he said finally. "Come on in the other room."

He led her to a small sitting room.

"When I sent the invitation," he said, "I wasn't sure you'd accept."

"After your generosity?" Her laughter trilled. "How silly men are."

"You never answered my letters. Sometimes you look at me with eyes like the winter sea."

"I'm still angry with you, Otto."

"Why won't you believe that day in my office was an accident? If anyone was at fault, it was you."

"Me?"

He assumed that boyishly pleading expression so at odds with his personality. "How could I not lose control? My ideal woman, honored by our Führer, a pure Nordic image, the most beautiful girl ever, stretched out on my couch."

"And now there's Erich," she said. "Can't you understand? When the planes come over, I panic for him."

"He's not in Berlin."

"That's cold comfort. There are rumors other cities—Essen, Dresden, Cologne—are getting the worst of it."

"He and his mother have left town."

"Which town?"

"I swear to you he's completely out of danger—"

"I don't even know his full name! Every time I hear about children being killed or hurt, I go crazy!" Tears, honest tears, sprang into her eyes.

Groener clucked sympathetically. How odd, this tender little sound. "Käthe, when I found out about your condition, nothing would have delighted me more than to have married you."

"You're evading telling me where he is, that's all."

"It's God's truth. You've cast a spell on me, Käthe. I want you and the clever little rascal with me always." He sighed. "It's impossible, though. Deserting little Otto and baby Adolf would be bad enough. But there's my work. The Führer's opposed to divorce. If I left my wife, I'd be shunted into backwater jobs. And what's the use of false modesty? Very few men have my energy, my intelligence, my dedication. The New Order needs me. How can I sacrifice the greater good for my personal happiness?" Conviction shook the rasping voice.

"You *have* your sons, but I don't even know where mine is." Her voice also shook.

"He's mine too."

"At every air-raid siren I'm in hell."

"The bombers never come near him."

"Nowhere's safe."

A wild expression distorted Groener's face. "He and the mother live in a fine large farmhouse thirty kilometers away from Frankfurt am Main."

III

When they returned to the living room, Herr Eberhardt was there. Laying a pudgy, manicured hand on Groener's sleeve, he said, "Excuse us a moment, fräulein. A little business." The two men moved into a corner and Eberhardt leaned his bald, lumpy head close to Groener's.

Käthe ordered a fresh glass of champagne, inching in their direction.

She heard Groener say, "The important thing is, how many *stücke* can we contract for."

Stücke. Units. Pieces.

"I just shipped you five hundred in October," the host rejoined with the same businesslike roughness.

"Some feeble lot. And we were behind schedule so sometimes I had to work them thirty-six-hour shifts."

Distant thunder growled.

"How many of the shipment are left?" Eberhardt asked.

"Less than a quarter. Having them drop like fleas is bad for the German workers' morale. To hear some of them, you'd think we ought to put the *stücke* up in hotel suites and feed them butter and eggs."

"You're taking that crap? Groener, it's not like you."

"How right you are." Groener chuckled. "I made an example of a few of the bleeding hearts, packed 'em off to Bergen-Belsen. Since then there's been a damn sight less softheartedness. If only I could do the same to those fucking rocket scientists! What prima donnas! To hear them, we're obligated to provide any machinery they ask for, and produce top-notch, technically skilled Yids. Which brings me to the next point. Eberhardt, I'm counting on you. Please, this time no weaklings and idiots."

"Now who's talking like a prima donna? What sort of specimens do you think we have?"

"Krupp gets healthy ones."

"Krupp pays well."

Groener smiled cynically. "I'll see to it that you're paid top mark."

"Let's go in the study and work out the numbers," Eberhardt said, ignoring his other guests as he ushered Groener from the room.

A tall, weedy *obersturmführer* in the Leibstandarte-SS came over and began asking her if it was true that she had won the two-hundred-meter race at the Olympics. Käthe stared blankly at him. With an apology he backed away. Her exultation at learning Erich's whereabouts had shattered into horror. *Pieces of labor . . . work them thirty-six straight hours . . . drop like fleas.* Was Heinrich Leventhal one of the desperately weary, starving workers? Was he still alive?

She stood holding the stem of her glass while voices and laughter rose and fell amid the rumble of thunder.

"Sorry about the interruption." Groener had returned. "The party seems to be breaking up. There's some hundred-year-old French brandy at my flat."

"Sounds marvelous, but I have to get to work tomorrow." It was difficult to speak, much less manage courtesy. "I must go home."

IV

As the driver started the car, Groener reached for her.

Until now Käthe had intended playing him along for more information. Her will proved far less powerful than her loathing. As he drew her to his thick body, nausea rose in her chest. She pulled away.

"Little Käthe, it's not the first time for you. I go back to duty tomorrow . . . take pity on me."

The car swerved around the corner and she shifted on the leather, her thigh inadvertently touching his.

"I understand," he said gently. "Seeing me has reminded you too much of our boy. And then there's being bombed out. No wonder you're all nerves." He put his arm around her firmly.

She pushed at the chest of his leather coat. "No!"

"You said I was generous."

She was going out of control and could do nothing about it. "Where did you steal those things?"

He released her. "I'm no thief. I'm proud of my war record."

"Murder record, you mean!"

"So you heard me and Eberhardt?" he said coldly. "I've killed enemies of the Reich. Like any other soldier."

"Soldier? You should see the letters I've filed protesting the SS slaughters, the concentration camps."

"That's the OKW for you. Riddled with hypocrites. They pretend the Führer is beneath them, but they support his ideology. Your army friends are delighted that the Yids're gone, but they refuse to dirty their lily-white hands on the job. And you, Käthe. You seemed *führertreu,* filled with faith in the leader. But you're like the other aristocrats. No understanding of the New Order, no stamina, no moral fiber. Well, I'm honest enough and strong enough to put the *untermenschen* to some useful purpose."

"No wonder you had a medal pinned on you by our Great Leader himself!" she burst out.

"For that I should see you hauled into the People's Court. But you're the mother of my son." Groener's voice was a low rumble in the darkness. Leaning forward, he tapped on the glass, calling, "Stop here."

Before the car had squealed to a complete halt, he had wrenched open the door. A palm against the small of her back, he thrust her out.

Her foot splashed into the gutter, and she almost fell. As she trudged through the rain, the red fury drained, and she assessed the evening. On the plus side she had learned Erich's whereabouts. On the minus side she had made a powerful enemy. And as for the *vergeltungswaffe,* she would watch carefully in Hall Six for any hint of information to be sent via Ulla-Britt Onslager to England.

V

The train was overcrowded and passengers braved the icy wind between the cars. The hunchbacked man swayed along, one hand gripping the handle of a small cardboard suitcase. The village station signs were all in German, for Alsace was once again part of the Reich. Aubrey, though, considered it France, and gulped at the blasts of frigid air as if to clear the grime deposited in his lungs by his months in the Reich. Whenever the isolation and fear had threatened to engulf him, he had conjured up those few minutes in the ruined apartment. Käthe —the pure oval of her face, the bright hair, the slender, graceful body, the glowing blue-green eyes.

Finally he reached the coast and the *Zone Interdit.* In Rouen, German civilians of an educated cut sipped wine at the cafés surrounding the Place du Vieux-Marché. He was stopped numerous times, and although he carried a German passport and excellent forgeries of passes from the local *feldkommandantur,* the Gestapo searched the small suitcase with its frayed shirts and cardboard snips of samples. At the small fabric shop off Rue de Crosne a man with nervous tic and straggly goatee introduced himself as the new proprietor. The former owner had turned out to be a terrorist, and was shot, he said, adding, "The widow's lucky to have found a buyer."

Aubrey, sickeningly aware that this new proprietor might be a collaborationist spy, schooled his expression as he gave his sales pitch for ersatz yardage. After he left, he doubled around to ensure he wasn't being followed. DuPont's Crémerie had a FERMÉ sign on the door, as did Pollit's Boulangerie. He was fearing that the entire CI-4 network in Rouen had been swept up when a thin prostitute approached him. After a shrill exchange about the price she took him to her cold slit of a room. They sat on her bed with its rankness of sweat, semen, and wartime cologne while she reported bleakly on the arrests and executions. Then she told what she had learned while pursuing her profession. The new Germans were engineers and scientists. Nobody was allowed near their encampment overlooking the sea.

Leaving her room, Aubrey, head still thrust forward but smiling like a satisfied client, strolled down to the harbor. The following dawn he was aboard a dory and sending messages on a shortwave radio. He floated in the choppy, cold water for two and a half hours until a British submarine surfaced.

The following afternoon Aubrey was in the isolated Devonshire house, sitting blessedly erect as he ladled illegal clotted cream on scones spread with black currant jam. Between mouthfuls he told Major Downes about the enormous rockets he was convinced were being manufactured by slave labor in the Baltic island of Peenemünde, the launching sites he believed were being set up along the Normandy coast.

Downes told him he had corroboration from various sources, including True Blue, the code name for Käthe.

The Allies launched massive bombing raids on Peenemünde and the French coastal installations. Manufacturing of the rockets was removed to the safety of the labyrinths of an old gypsum mine near Nordhausen. Here, below the mountains of central Germany, thousands of concentration camp inmates were worked to death.

The Normandy launching sites, though heavily hit, remained operational.

THIRTY-NINE

I

On September 8, 1943, the Italian government signed an unconditional surrender. The Germans, under tough, wily Field Marshal Kesselring, continued to fight for each inch of their former ally's soil. Wyatt's company battled their way up disputed hills to ancient tile-roofed towns. The icy Volturno River twisted through so many artillery-echoing gorges that Wyatt began to believe "Volturno" meant *river* in Italian. A pastoral valley erupted with land mines. A German tank with a black cross burned while inhumanly shrieking men emerged with their field-gray uniforms ablaze. Toppled churches, smashed antiquities, and smashed men, that was Italy. Cold food and the too solid taste of K rations, hungry children begging for K-ration chocolate, that was Italy.

And Italy was Captain Arnie Johnson, a big, placid twenty-five-year-old Wisconsin dairy farmer, faithful husband, father of three little girls, a virtuoso on the harmonica, Wyatt's friend Arnie with his brains scattered on the blood-red Italian soil.

Enter weeping, Captain Wyatt Kingsmith.

In July of 1944 Wyatt was given a furlough.

II

A postprandial somnolence hung over Quarles. The evacuees were helping a local farmer during their summer holidays, all except for Lucy. Refusing to attend school beyond the legal age limit of fourteen, Lucy had been elevated to nursemaid:

she was watching over Geoff. Elizabeth had retired to her room for a secret nip. Wyatt and Araminta were alone on the terrace, he lounging with his long legs stretched out in front of the bench, an arm around his wife. Robins chirped in huge oaks that had sheltered Cromwell's men, fat bees foraged in the wisteria that clung to the walls.

"Happy?" she asked.

"Miserable," he replied, squeezing her shoulder.

Wyatt might joke the same as ever, but he had suffered a sea change. The quality that Araminta inwardly thought of as boyish had vanished. This husband of hers was a man. A tough, lean man with his skin burned dark, his voice pitched unconsciously into a tone of command. A new, even more attractive Wyatt.

She turned, kissing him. He rubbed the nape of her neck. His caress had more than a hint of appetite. Another difference. In the past Wyatt had been a tenderly considerate lover, but now sex was urgent—almost impersonal in its urgency. Each time was the same as his homecoming, when he'd not wasted time to take off her clothes or his own. There was a kick to his roughness, and several times she had held her breath on the edge of the cliff. *Now, now let it happen,* she would think, and move with him. Yet never had she been transported over that precipice.

She and Wyatt moved hastily apart. The tall French doors were being jiggled open.

Geoff, thumb near his mouth, stared gravely at them.

"Damn that Lucy, she's meant to be looking after him," Araminta muttered. "Come here, Geoff, come to your daddy and mummy, darling."

The child didn't move. Though his hair had turned the vivid red of Araminta's and he had retained his early physical likeness to Euan, his personality in no way resembled either of theirs. In his own babyish way he kept aloof, playing quietly with his toy blocks, staring at his picture books. *Is this how Peter was?*

"Need wee-wee."

"Okay, Geoff old buddy," Wyatt said, rising to his feet. "Let's us guys head for the latrine."

"Darling, next thing he'll be calling the loo that."

"Big sweat."

Smiling, Araminta watched the pair, the tall man stooping to hold the toddler's upraised hand, as they disappeared into the velvety shadows of the library.

III

Saturday, another fine, cloudless day, Wyatt bought black-market gas so they could drive to the Faversham station and meet Euan and Porteous.

Euan stumped ahead to the Daimler with his daughter.

Wyatt and Porteous followed at a slower pace.

"Well, my boy, how was it in Italy?" Porteous asked, holding on to Wyatt's arm.

"Wouldn't miss it for all the world. One thing I'll say for the Krauts, they're damned good fighters. But so are we."

"How has the invasion affected you?" On June sixth the Allies had crossed the Channel, a mighty armada that had landed beneath Hitler's Atlantic Wall, capturing the supposedly invincible fortifications, then barreling into France. "Taken the pressure off?"

"Not so I notice. But don't worry, Grandfather, eventually we'll pound the bloody shit out of the bastards."

Porteous chuckled at the obscenities, which he never used himself, then tilted his head. His sensitive hearing had picked up a faraway hum. As the sound grew louder, Wyatt, too, heard, and sheltered his eyes against the sun. American Flying Fortresses and their fighter escorts, the new P-51's, swarmed like gnats in the blue sky.

"This bombing night and day." Porteous sighed. "I can't tell you how I worry about my poor little Kate."

Wyatt's mouth tightened. "Save your worries for the doodlebugs." A week after the invasion a new type of weapon, an unmanned rocket plane—the *vergeltungswaffe*—had begun hammering down on London. Later these rocket missiles would be called V-1's, but at the moment because of their peculiar throbbing roar they were nicknamed "doodlebugs."

"The flying bombs aren't getting through the coastal defenses too often." Porteous gazed sightlessly up at the roaring aircraft. "We're bombing Germany to bits. I can only hope she's not still in Berlin."

Gripping the insubstantial arm tighter, Wyatt firmly changed the subject. "Watch out for the step, Grandfather."

Araminta and Euan had reached the car.

"How much did you give for the petrol?" he demanded over the noise of airplanes.

"I haven't a clue, Daddy. Wyatt bought it."

"A pretty penny, I'll bet. You'll need to watch him. Humphrey never had any idea of the value of money, always enjoyed playing the big man. And like father like son."

Like father like son. . . .

Araminta's expression was thoughtful as she recalled Wyatt's confession in twilit Green Park. Since then he had never brought up the subject of his paternity. It had occurred to her that he'd told a white lie to set her mind at rest about their consanguinity and also that in her weird, dislocating grief for Peter she had somehow misinterpreted his words. Now she peered nearsightedly at the American captain towering above the old man. Nobody else in the Kingsmith family tanned darkly or had that satirical smile. She shrugged. Why peer in corners? There were so many lovely, exciting things to think about. After the war she would have smart new clothes, an American motorcar, a divinely warm New York flat, all sorts of delicacies to eat. A husband who slept in her bed every night.

IV

Monday morning dawned softly, with glowing pink clouds streaking the sky. Birds sang and the sweetness of wisteria and roses hung in the air. Wyatt and Araminta took their coffee out on the terrace.

"I'll come up to London and wave you good-bye."

"Didn't I already tell you no, woman?"

"But, darling, it's not the least bother. Tomorrow I go to the shop anyway." After Geoff was born, Araminta had weighed returning to the Auxiliary Fire Service, finally deciding she

couldn't leave her baby so much. Instead, she helped out at
Kingsmith's on Tuesday, Wednesday, and Thursday, sleeping
Tuesday and Wednesday at the flat and putting in the evenings
at the Rainbow Club, the big American Red Cross center on
Piccadilly.

"I want to remember you here with Geoff. No bombed-out
backgrounds, just you in this English countryside."

"Such romanticism."

"A romantic guy I."

She balanced her coffee cup on the clematis-covered ledge.
"All in all, darling, I rather fancy you."

"Keep feeling that way. Hey, and we've got one terrific kid."

"I noticed you think so."

"We Americans take paternity seriously."

She set her coffee cup down, putting her arms around his
waist, resting her cheek against his ribbons. "I live for you,"
she murmured. "Come back safe and sound."

V

That night Araminta couldn't sleep. Something nagged at her
like an unfinished task. The old house creaked, an owl hooted,
one of the children coughed. Finally she got up. Moving to her
dressing table, she bent to open the bottom drawer. Pushing
aside the delicate prewar silk underwear, she fished out a Scandinavian painted wood box. Inside were photographs and the
black velvet box that contained Peter's rose-cut diamond. Slipping the ring on next to her wedding band, she went into the
hall. The moon shone through the stained-glass skylight, casting faintly colored shadows on the walls. She tiptoed into the
nursery and turned on the nightlight, examining the matted
portrait photograph of Peter with his RAF cap at a jaunty angle,
the badly blurred newspaper obituary photograph, and several
small snapshots of him at Mainwaring Court. Then she peered
down at Geoff. After several minutes she replaced the ring and
the photographs in the wooden box. Going to a place between
the windows and the fireplace, she unerringly pressed a spot on
the dado. A hidden catch released a tiny door. When she and
Aubrey were adolescents they had discovered this hidey-hole.

The Scandinavian box was a fraction too wide to put inside, so she removed the ring box and photographs, carefully laying them in the secret cabinet before swinging the door shut.

She set the painted box at the foot of the cot. "Someday when you're old enough to understand," she said softly to the sleeping infant, "I'll explain about the other things."

FORTY

I

The *vergeltungswaffe zwei*, reprisal weapon number two, was far more advanced than the V-1, or doodlebug. The dreaded V-2's were forty-seven-foot-long rockets with a one-ton warhead. They traveled far faster than the speed of sound. No air-raid sirens announced their coming. They could not be heard. On September 8, 1944, the first silent predator rushed down on London, burying itself deep in the ground. The ensuing explosion reverberated like an earthquake and people for miles around were convinced that an ammunition factory had exploded. From then on Londoners lived with the fact there was no escape from the soundless death that could sweep down on them at any time.

Darling Aubrey,

I can't write any of this to Wyatt, it would be hard on his morale, but I can tell you. Here in London all anyone talks about is this new brand of pilotless airplane-bomb. The V-2's, as we call them, petrify a lot of people. Myself, I prefer them to our old chums the doodlebugs, which made such a racket, then cut off so you had a heart attack waiting to see if they'd land on top of you. With the V-2's there's no point whatsover in sleeping in a shelter. Daddy of course argues with this vehemently. On the nights I'm in London, he always says, "Better safe than sorry," and tries to drag me down to the basement. Poor sweetie, he's never caught on that with these new-type missiles one can be both safe and sorry.

Mother, whisper the words, has once again STOPPED DRINKING!

That's all from the home front. I must be off to the Rainbow Club. (In my opinion we could force the entire Axis to surrender if there were some way to broadcast continously and loudly the Bing Crosby version of "White Christmas.")

The truth is, I don't want to write any more. Aubrey, I've been feeling a bit mopey. Have you heard from Wyatt? He's been transferred, I suspect he's in the thick of this awful Belgian fighting. I couldn't bear losing a second man to the war.

You'll hear from me sooner this time, I swear it.

God bless, and, in the immortal words of the denizens of the Rainbow Club, "Hubba hubba."

II

"The thing that's driving me nuts," said the very young, chubby-faced Army Air Corps navigator with his left arm in a sling, "is that you English chicks are so gorgeous."

"We are a smashing lot, aren't we?" Araminta responded.

They were in the foyer of the American Red Cross's club for GIs, the Rainbow. It was the second week of December of 1944. Between the brightly decorated tables a stout fir tree was lavished with ornaments, tinsel, and multicolored lights. In the Back Room, floodlights beamed jeweled tones on the gyrating, bouncing GIs and their English partners.

"The problem is, the best numbers are hitched."

"That puts me right in the top flight. My husband's with Patton's Third Army."

"In Belgium? You're married to an American? Did you meet him here at the Rainbow?"

"I've known him all my life. He's my cousin."

"Now, that's luck. My cousins had to go be German."

"We have a German cousin too."

"No sh—no kidding?"

"She lives in Berlin."

"Not much left of her hometown." He leaned closer, taking a long gulp of his Christmas eggnog. "My grandfather came from Essen, and it sure gives me a creepy feeling to think soon I might be blowing the bejesus out of some Nazi pervert with my name and face. It's something I don't usually talk about."

"When we were children, Katy spent her summer holidays with us. And two summers before the war we went to New York together, to see our other cousin."

"The one you married?"

"Yes . . ." *But he was in love with her then, not with me.*

"Probably spying on us even in them days."

"Katy? She turns heliotrope every time she tells a lie. Not very good spy material."

"They showed us a training film about the Germans. From when they're little kids, they're indoctrinated to kill for Der Fewrer."

"Actually she's rather sweet and dreamy. Stubbornly honorable."

"Take it from me, they're all indoctrinated. My cousin, your cousin, the kit and caboodle of 'em, would just as soon slip a knife in our ribs as not."

Looking away from her, he raised his good hand to finger away the eggnog that curved over his lips like a child's milk mustache. Araminta peered nearsightedly at the arrow signs on the wall. BERLIN—600 MILES, NEW YORK—3,271 MILES. They were both embarrassed, he by his relationship to the enemy, she by his naively unshakable belief in propaganda. Above the roar of voices and clinking Coca-Cola bottles rose the brassy notes of a trio playing boogie-woogie in the Back Room.

"Care to dance?" the boy asked, then blushed. "I haven't tried cutting a rug one handed."

"No time like the present," said Araminta, who had danced with enough wounded and drunk GIs to accommodate herself to every variation.

III

The Monico and the adjacent Lyons had been commandeered for the Rainbow Club: Araminta emerged onto the bitter cold of Shaftesbury Avenue. With the pilotless rockets the blackout had been changed to a dim-out. The blue headlights showed mobs of servicemen, some of them drunk enough to stumble into the gutters. Curses rang in various languages and accents. As Araminta moved through the crowd, she caught a whiff of heavy scent, a glimpse of yellow light: a giggling whore was aiming a flashlight in the faces of a group of Free French sailors.

Araminta walked swiftly up Piccadilly. Here, slurred American voices sang:

> "This is number three
> And his hand is on my knee.
> Roll me over, lay me down
> And do it again."

White helmets, white belts, and white gaiters of a pair of American MPs jumped out like ectoplasm. Turning onto Sackville Street to wend her way to the flat, Araminta left the crowd behind her. The moon had risen but the skyscape was disappointing. The great silver barrage balloons that had floated so gracefully above the chimney tops were gone—with the advent of the V-1's and V-2's the balloons had been moved to Surrey and parts of Kent.

Katy, Araminta thought, hugging her coat tighter around her. *Why did I tell the boy about her? I suppose because he had a German cousin and I thought he could understand. Is he right? Is she a staunch Nazi now? Wyatt thinks so. For all I know she's dead.*

Araminta shivered. In wartime, thinking of death is an ill omen. Käthe, dead? Käthe with the tender smile and film-star hair, Käthe who had sailed home with her when Euan had his heart attack. Käthe, whom Wyatt had loved. Araminta stumbled down the curb, regaining her balance. *Serves me right,* she thought. Did Wyatt have these jealous flashes about Peter?

As she thought of Peter, she felt a great rushing in the air around her, as if a huge winged creature had swooped down. In that swift instant of explosion the electrical impulses of her brain had one final surge.

Out of the darkness stepped a shortish, exceedingly handsome man. "So there you are, darling," he said.

"Peter," she cried happily.

"I've been looking everywhere for you."

"They said you were killed in action."

"What matters is we're together," he said, squeezing her hand.

"It's so marvelous, darling."

"We won't be separated again," he said.

FORTY-ONE

I

The freezing predawn gale rushed down from the Arctic Circle to wrap around CI-4 headquarters, a vast, isolated Scottish hunting lodge that had been built by a coal baron. Drafts prowled through the stone dining hall that now served as a communal office. Aubrey, however, was as oblivious to the chill as to the ranks of empty desks beyond the sharp circle of light from his lamp. The tendons of his freckled hands stood out as his fingers danced across the typewriter keys. The previous day he had once again returned from Germany, and the small stack of sheets to his left dealt with the damage inflicted on industry by around-the-clock Allied bombings of the Ruhr. There were no carbons. Everything he wrote tonight was for the eyes of the Prime Minister alone. He pulled out his summation, glancing at the capitalized head—THE KRUPP FACTORIES CONTINUE TO TURN OUT ARMS, THOUGH AT A SLOWER RATE—before he inserted a fresh sheet.

His expression altered to one of unhappy determination. His mission did not include gathering information about Krupp's slave labor, but his scruples compelled him to add this to his report.

He condensed both what he had heard from a German agent within the Krupp plant and witnessed himself, briefly describing the workers' gaunt bodies, gray faces, and bleeding hands, the watery soup that supplied the day's calories, the muddy cellars where they were jammed to sleep, the exhaustion, the illness, the dogs.

Halting, he sighed. As always the Third Reich reserved its most unspeakable treatment for Jews. And how could he unemotionally describe what he had seen on his last day in Essen? Though Käthe, unasked, had photographed memos from outraged army officers about the concentration camp factories and sent an encoded letter saying that Jewish labor was worked to death with governmental sanction, nothing could have prepared him for the reality. That dawn he had seen SS guards waving their rifles to double-march a long line of women with stars on their thin, ragged burlap dresses—several of them were children who could not have been more than twelve. Terrified eyes had stared from skull faces, wooden clogs had been tied with rags to bleeding feet, emaciated bodies had been twisted out of shape by dropsy and starvation. As he had watched, one of the smallest girls had crumpled. A black boot had kicked her in the chest. The limp pile of rags had stirred on the rime-covered cobbles. The SS guard had casually aimed his rifle downward. The shaven head had exploded like a dropped melon. Two German workers hurrying on their way to the truck assembly plant had not stopped their conversation as they had separated to avoid the pool of blood and small twisted corpse. Yet from that agent within the plant Aubrey had heard of an occasional older Kruppianer who saved bread for the women—a generosity that could cost the man his own life.

Aubrey began to type again, describing the incident—the black-uniformed guard, the child's body—which to him personalized the landscape of the Third Reich. Despite his intensive training to be aware of his surroundings, he was too engrossed to hear the green-baize door at the far end of the dining hall open.

Over the roar of the wind, a nearby voice said, "Kingsmith."

Jumping to his feet, Aubrey said, "Major Downes. The report'll be ready by morning, sir. But they told me you were in London."

"I flew up."

"In this gale?"

The major's single hand gripped an alligator handbag. "I'm here as the bearer of bad news, I'm afraid," he said gruffly.

Aubrey flinched. "Käthe?"

"No, Mrs. Kingsmith—your sister."

" 'Minta?"

The major set the bag on Aubrey's desk. "By sheer fluke one of our people found this earlier tonight. Her identity card was was inside. There was a letter inside addressed to you, and thinking it might contain information, he brought it directly to my flat."

"Araminta?" Aubrey repeated in the same questioning tone.

"A V-bomb landed not far from Berkeley Square. The handbag was blown clear of the crater."

"But Araminta . . . ?"

"I'm sorry, Aubrey, terribly sorry. Your sister is dead."

Aubrey turned away, shivering violently. Araminta? How could she be dead? Araminta, always so full of vitality . . . Araminta leading him into mischief, Araminta with the tip of her nose wiggling when she told some joke, Araminta with her voluptuous body and her high, pretty laughter. Younger than he by a scant eleven months, the companion of his childhood, his ally against his father. Little Araminta stamping her foot and shaking her red hair. Suddenly his thoughts flashed to the splintered skull on the cobblestones of Essen. *That* was death.

He touched the alligator bag.

And so is this.

Araminta, oh, Araminta . . .

"I've arranged transport so you can break the news to your family."

"That's good of you, sir," Aubrey said, taking the sheet of paper from the roller. "The report's finished."

"Is there anything I can do?"

Aubrey carefully covered his typewriter. "If you could help me reach my brother-in-law by phone. He's with the U.S. First Army in Belgium."

II

The gaunt, leafless trees and swirling fog gave the Belgian farmhouse a surreal look. From the front the barns and gray stone house appeared deserted, but between the bare apple trees in the rear were nosed a pair of jeeps. Upstairs the windows of the larger bedroom had been shot out, and the big old bedstead and armoire had been shifted to cover the lower panes. The crushed cartridges on the floor were German, but the dozen or so bearded men wore mud-matted American uniforms. Some had their helmets tipped forward as they slept with heads on their chests, others sprawled with cigarettes. The smell of tobacco could not drown out the odor of unwashed bodies and fear.

They were lost.

The dense fog that had descended on the Ardennes sometimes thinned but never lifted. No matter how often Wyatt had checked his compass, he couldn't figure where the American line was meant to be. So when they'd found this farmhouse, previously shelter to Germans, he'd let the remnants of his men take a rest.

Reaching for his Camels, he felt paper. He fished out an unopened V-mail letter. It had been handed to him three days earlier—centuries earlier—at Regiment Headquarters. Because the writing was not Araminta's but Aubrey's, he had shoved it in his pocket and forgotten it. Scratching a match to his cigarette, he slit the thin blue paper.

> Dear Wyatt,
>
> First of all, I can't apologize enough for sending you the news by telegram. I did my best to put through a call, but you know better than I how impossible that is. Second, I'm most terribly sorry I didn't send a letter of explanation immediately. But this is the first time I've been able to collect myself enough to write.
>
> As far as I can piece together, she was doing her regular Tuesday-night stint at the Rainbow Club. The other hostesses said she left before eleven. She must have been winding her way home to the flat. Another street, a few minutes

earlier or later, and she would have been safe. The one consolation is that death came instantaneously. The flying bombs are merciful that way. She never knew she was hit. She didn't suffer. They found fragments of her coat, and very little else. Oddly enough, her handbag was thrown clear, and that was how we found out so quickly.

You know how Father doted on her. He has been completely dazed, and keeps referring to her as if she were still alive. The doctor assures me that this is his way of dealing with the shock, and he'll snap out of it. Mother hasn't stopped weeping, and Grandfather looks so tottery that I fear for him. But he keeps a stiff upper lip and has promised to manage Kingsmith's until Father's up to it.

I took Geoff on a walk, and tried to explain as much as one can to somebody not yet two that his Mummy wouldn't be coming home. He tilted his head in that quiet way of his, and then began to cry. I cried too. After a minute he patted my cheek, and said, "Hurt self, 'Ncle Aubwee?" I couldn't answer. Araminta was the light shining through my childhood, all the brightness and fun and happiness. I cannot believe she is gone.

Although there was no body, I decided a funeral would give us all a chance to vent our grief. So yesterday we put a seal, as it were, on her death.

Even with the crowded trains more than a hundred people came down to the services. Our neighbors saw to it that they had transport from the Faversham station. Do you remember the Frognall plot? It is just behind the fourteenth-century extension of the church, and fenced off from the rest of the graveyard. The older stones are mossy and grow out of the earth, but the last century produced marble angels and crosses that have stayed an astonishing white. Araminta's grave is next to the memorial obelisk for our uncles who were killed in the Great War.

It was a bitter morning, but afterward we did not disperse the way that mourners usually do. Instead, we took turns talking about her. Some stories I never knew. Maybe you don't either. The station officer told how she never turned a hair during the worst of the Blitz, speeding him along burning streets where the buildings might collapse at any moment. Once, while he was directing the engines, an old woman came to the car, crying for help for her grandson. Araminta rescued the little boy just before the house caved in.

The Rainbow Club contingent had stories of how she bucked up the wounded. Fellow debutantes told of her popularity with the opposite sex. Old school chums eulogized pillow fights she organized. The evacuees repeated her less respectable jokes, and though some of the stodgier folk glared, Araminta would have adored the laughter.

Telegrams arrived from all over, including one from the Prime Minister himself, which I read aloud.

Wyatt, the Knightsbridge Fire Station are banding together for a plaque that says, "Araminta Kingsmith, remembered by us all for her gallantry during the Battle of Britain." Gallant is the exact description of your wife, my sister.

> Sorry, but I cannot write any more.
> Keep safe, Wyatt, we need you.
> Your cousin and brother,
> Aubrey

III

It was almost dark. Wyatt didn't notice the waning light as he refolded the thin blue V-mail paper back into its creases.

"Sir, looks like the fog's lifting."

"What?" Wyatt looked up at the man standing over him. It was Pelissi, the burly sergeant with the silver star from Normandy.

"Maybe when it's dark, we should get out of here."

"What's that?"

Pelissi was squinting down at him, a peculiar look in his round, bloodshot eyes. "You okay, sir?"

Wyatt was on his feet. "The noise, dammit," he said in a low voice. "What's that fucking noise?"

Over the faraway rumbling of artillery came a rattling snort of engines.

"Jeeps," somebody said. "Thank God for giving us jeeps."

The lounging men had come alert. Wyatt was already at the window, peering through his binoculars into the brownish-gray soup of dusk.

Three jeeps emerged from the fog, swerving toward the farmhouse. The first halted behind what had been a pigeon coop.

The mud-covered helmets were the wrong shape. Wyatt raised a hand, signifying silence. There was a command in German. The four in the front jeep jumped out. The big corporal ran to the dovecote, the short, thin private following. The other two covered them, then in turn were covered, and the big corporal trotted forward again, a smoothly professional warriors' ballet.

Below, the front door was kicked open. A high-pitched voice said in German, "Place is empty."

Then the four men trotted back toward the jeep, two of them talking about having some goddamn shelter tonight.

Suddenly the twilit mist erupted with sound, and the Germans fell in turn. At first Wyatt didn't realize he was firing a M-1 rifle and screaming, "You lousy motherfuckers! You filthy shits, you filthy Kraut shits! Goddamn rocket bombs killing women! You rotten lousy Nazi motherfuckers!"

In less than a minute bodies in field gray were sprawling in the jeeps or on the road. The mist shifted, and he saw a prone German bellying his way toward the cover of a tree. Wyatt peered down the sight. The German jumped, then lay still, but Wyatt continued to spray the corpse with .30 caliber bullets.

NINE

Enjoy the war, the peace is going to be a lot less fun.
—Graffito on a bombed-out Berlin warehouse,
March 1945

FORTY-TWO

I

By March of 1945 Hitler's lunatic military decisions had cost the Third Reich the immense new empire that had been paid for dearly in Wehrmacht blood. The Russians had advanced to the Oder River. The Allies were crossing the Rhine. Saturation bombing was pulverizing German cities into heaped rubble. After eighty-five raids in less than eleven weeks, Berlin was missing so many landmarks that native Berliners continuously lost their way. (Kingsmith's was one of the gutted shells along the ruins of Unter den Linden.) The Führer refused to look upon his shrunken Reich. After the attempt on his life the previous July, he had grown yet more misanthropic and fearful, more dependent on the drug injections of his physician. A pasty-faced addict, he shuffled through the maze of cement bunkers far below the Chancellery gardens, issuing his martial manifestos and dictating proclamations that adjured every German man, woman, and child to fight to the death.

The remaining buses, S-Bahn and U-Bahn lines were unbearably crowded, and never on schedule. Käthe, like many other Germans, had taken out her old bicycle.

One cold, bright Saturday afternoon in early March as she pedaled along Bendlerstrasse, she spotted a shawled old woman sitting on the curb with a display of snowdrops. Buying a grass-tied bouquet, she stowed it carefully in her handlebar basket. Through soot and smoke from a raid earlier that afternoon gleamed the enormous gilt statue of Victory, marking the way to the Tiergarten. At the Siegessäule a policeman raised his palm to halt the stream of bicycles. A bundled-up pregnant woman called out asking where Käthe had found the snow-drops, and other cyclists turned, chorusing heartfelt delight at the white flowers. Käthe found it touching that weary people who lived in privation and constant danger should be capti-vated by these traditional harbingers of spring. The nostalgic sweetness remained with her as she followed detour signs. So many streets were blocked because of fires and burst water mains that it took her nearly two hours to reach Grunewald.

By the time she reached the pharmacy where they were regis-tered, there was no aspirin.

II

In the chilly garage bedroom she found Clothilde exactly as she had left her, red eyed, pale, huddled under blankets and over-coats.

"I'm sorry, Mother, Herr Edendorfer was out of aspirin." She brandished the flowers. "But I found these."

"How lovely," Clothilde said, and went into a spasm of hoarse coughing.

"Let me make you something to drink."

After two cups of hot, grassy tea Clothilde drowsed. She slept while Käthe prepared dinner, cabbage and potatoes sim-mered with two thin slices of long-life wurst.

"I'm not hungry tonight, dear," she said. "If you'd make another pot of tea. And turn on the news."

"Hier spricht Hans Fritzsche," intoned the famous newscaster who by some magical trick of delivery made Goebbels's most idiotic pronouncements believable, even palatable. Tonight Fritzsche's main story was of a Wehrmacht division booby-trapping the Ludendorff Bridge at Remagen, thus killing many Americans. Following the news there was an all-Brahms con-cert. Despite the round-the-clock bombing, the fires, the tight rationing, an eerie kind of normalcy laced the city together. Newspapers printed advertisements for sales at the Berliner and other department stores, postmen delivered mail,

milkmen delivered milk, and the Berlin Philharmonie under Wilhelm Furtwängler played out its season.

During the applause for the Academic Festival Overture Clothilde lifted her head. "I'm sorry, Käthe. It slipped my mind. You have a letter."

The envelope, postmarked Berlin, lacked a return address. The handwriting was unfamiliar.

Käthe slipped out a lined sheet wrapped around a crumpled, flimsy scrap of toilet paper. She read the covering message.

> Dear Fräulein Kingsmith,
> It is wiser for both of us if you do not know my name but I have the honor of being a friend to your brother, Colonel Siegfried von Hohenau. He has requested that I pass this on to you.

They had not heard from Sigi in months, not since his promotion to full colonel, but then, he'd always been a sloppy correspondent. As far as they knew he was with his uncle in Zossen. With shaking hands Käthe unfolded the toilet paper.

> Dearest little sister,
> I feel rotten that I haven't seen you and Mother in so many months. And now it's impossible. Käthe, last summer in my own dilatory way I served the Reich, services for which I am currently being rewarded by a billet in the safest quarters on Prinz-Albrechtstrasse. Please don't worry. The Gestapo are most intent on keeping matters quite legal.
> There is some sad news. My uncle died last week, a heart attack, and he—

She had reached the end of the flimsy little page. There was no other. Tears were rolling down her cheeks. The few sentences had told her everything.

Sigi had somehow been involved in what people were now calling the July Plot.

The plot, an attempt to overthrow the Nazi regime by killing

Hitler, had taken place on July twentieth of the previous year at Wolfsschanze, the Führer's headquarters in a gloomy East Prussian forest. Colonel Claus von Stauffenberg had detonated a small but powerful bomb beneath the conference table. The stout oak of the table had preserved the dictator's life. Since that hour Hitler had been wreaking a maniacal vengeance. The officers who had spearheaded the failed assassination were executed that same night. During the following months more and more of their cohorts as well as other suspected anti-Nazis were hauled in. Hitler had already reinstated *sippenhaft*, the ancient Germanic law that punished families of criminals, and thus the bloodbath spread.

Gestapo interrogators plied whips, prodded with electricity, maimed, and mutilated. The dungeons below Prinz-Albrecht-strasse rang with hoarse screams. Those whom the Gestapo considered culpable were sent to the People's Court, where they were further degraded by fanatical Nazi judges. Eventually the Ministry of Propaganda had determined that the huge number of "fiendish villains" cast a poor light on the Leader's popularity. The circus of public trials dwindled. Prisoners were reported to have succumbed from "natural causes" or in a few cases, to have "died a hero's death for the Führer at the front."

Käthe clutched at the flimsy paper. Sigi? How was it possible? Sweet-natured, indolent Sigi, with his spotted uniforms and overage mistress, bestirring himself to join the conspiracy? Had he merely followed the one-eyed general, his uncle? The Brahms flowing majestically over her, she recalled Christmas Eve at Garmisch-Partenkirchen and Sigi jumping—or rather, stumbling—into the fray at Wyatt's side.

"Is it bad news?" Clothilde was looking at her.

Käthe dashed a hand across her eyes. "No, a friend's been redeployed," she mumbled. Why was she lying? Clothilde would have to know.

III

Käthe muffled her tears until her mother slept. When the sirens wailed, Clothilde was snoring fitfully. Käthe didn't even consider waking her to go to the shelter. After the Christmas raid that had made the house and cellar unusable, the block warden had insisted they dig a shelter in the garden. Even in good health they seldom used the dank tunnel because of its unfortunate resemblance to a crypt.

Over the roar of planes and the rumble of faraway destruction, she heard a faint sound. It was as if a branch were tapping on the glass. But there were no trees near the window. Deciding her ears had deceived her, she rolled over. But no. There. Another slight riffing on the pane. *Maybe somebody's brought news about Sigi,* she thought. Tying her robe, she tiptoed hastily to the other room, opening the door. The garish clouds over Berlin shed a half-light. She could see nobody in the overgrown garden.

She jumped. As if by supernatural means a cadaverous figure had materialized a few feet from her.

"Who are you?" she asked shakenly.

"Fräulein Kingsmith?" The whisper was nearly inaudible.

"What do you want?"

"It's Heinrich Leventhal."

"Herr Leventhal! Come away from the garage." He followed her toward the lake, where a copse of firs grew. "But Herr Schultze told me you'd been relocated."

"Relocated," he echoed.

The quiet yet mordant intonation, so like Wyatt's, reminded Käthe of love and warmth. She touched Leventhal's arm, feeling the bone. "Weren't you?" she asked.

"I was smiling at the charming euphemism. Yes, I was relocated. Have you ever heard of Bergen-Belsen?"

Among the Most Secret files had been accusations of the obscenities committed at the Bergen-Belsen concentration camp, as well as accusations of murder on a scale that defied belief. "Oh, my God."

"Take it from me," Leventhal said, "the Almighty never shows His face at Belsen."

"But you escaped."

"A long story. Fräulein Kingsmith, I'd never put your neck so near a noose, but Berlin's really caught it! Should I clap my hands or weep? Schultze's apartment's not there anymore, nor any of the other safe houses I know. D'you have any idea where Schultze is?"

Käthe swallowed. "The building was hit last November, an incendiary. Everybody in the cellar suffocated."

The reddish light flickered on Leventhal's skull face. "Poor old Schultze. A good man, a decent man. I've known him all my life. His father worked for my grandfather. . . . Schultze was head of Leventhal's deliveries, did you know that?" After a sigh he asked, "What about the rest of the network?"

"I never even knew their names."

"Well, that's that," he said with a sigh.

"The Americans have crossed the Rhine near Cologne."

"Already?"

"At Remagen, Hans Fritzsche reported tonight. Could you make it that far?"

"If there's one thing I can thank the Führer for, it's resourcefulness."

There was enough murky light to see the wooden clogs worn without socks, the torn and filthy trousers, the uniform tunic with sleeves far above his wrists, the shaved head. "Some things of my father's are left," she said. She and Clothilde had given away most of Alfred's wardrobe to bombed-out friends, or exchanged warm garments for a chicken, a half pound of butter. "I'm sorry, they're very old."

"Sorry? Fräulein Kingsmith, you're offering me the world."

"The first door you come to upstairs, they're in the wardrobe. Be careful, some of the steps are rotted."

"That's an epitaph! 'Here lies Heinrich Leventhal, Bergen-Belsen escapee who broke his neck climbing a flight of stairs.' "

They made chuckling sounds that fell short of laughter. Then she went back into the chauffeur's quarters, searching in the darkness for bread, the long-life sausage, margarine, the small piece of strudel she'd been saving for Sunday.

She was wrapping the food in a worn towel when Clothilde mumbled sleepily, "What are you doing?"

"On my way to the lavatory," Käthe responded, wondering why she was lying again. Her mother would approve.

Shivering in the icy, fir-scented air, she waited.

Alfred had been a stout man, and the antiquated dark suit billowed around Heinrich Leventhal's skeletal frame. Still, the waistcoat, tie, shoes, and socks branded him with acceptability. Many a bombed-out Aryan went around looking more of a clown.

"In case you're hungry," she said, her face growing hot as she extended the wrapped-up food.

He was silent.

"I'm sorry, but it's all we have."

"Fräulein Kingsmith," he said in a choked whisper, "I have no faith left in German humanity, so you must be an angel. Promise me one thing. If I come out of this intact, don't let anyone else do favors for you. Leave that to me."

IV

The following morning as Käthe wheeled her bicycle to the street, she found the gate blocked by a stubby Volkswagen. Two SS noncoms sat in front. Seeing her, a corporal jumped out. The left side of his face was slickly red, as if from a healed burn.

"Fräulein Käthe Kingsmith?" he asked politely.

Gripping the handlebars, she nodded.

"If you'll be so good as to get in the car."

"I'm due at the Bendlerblock," she said, raising her chin in a try for arrogance. "Can't you find anything better to do than arrest essential workers?"

"Arrest? Who said anything about arresting you? The *untersturmführer* wants to talk to you."

"Me? Why?"

"Officers!" The unscarred side of his face loosened in a smile. "Your guess is as good as mine." He put his hands below hers on the handlebars. "Like me to wheel this back up to your house, fräulein?"

His geniality had no menace in it, but the black uniform did. Thinking of her mother coughing in bed, Käthe said, "It's safe behind the hedge here."

* * *

As they skirted through bomb-damaged suburbs the two
men exchanged quaint sayings of their children, who had been
evacuated to an SS hostel in southern Austria. Käthe, alone in
the narrow backseat, heard the commonplace conversation as
the babbling of madmen. They turned onto the Potsdam road.
Houses gave way to vegetable patches, vegetable patches
stretched into fields. Glossy black crows cawed and swooped at
the furrowed earth.

The Volkswagen swerved onto a rutted lane, bouncing down
an incline to a large new farmhouse and outbuildings that had
been invisible from the road. The high barbed-wire fence that
enclosed the yard proved this no ordinary farm. At a beep a
sentry, his black tunic unbuttoned, emerged from what appeared to be a barn to open the gate. Dobermans sprang across
the yard, snarling.

The scarred corporal whistled. "Down, Hansi, Ensi. Good
boy, Bodo, good boy."

The guard dogs jumped playfully around them as she was
escorted to the house. Evidently the animals had been trained
to go no farther than the door. Inside, all pretense at camouflage ended. The long wall was adorned with a mural of muscular, golden-haired gods in SS uniforms. As she was hurried
along, Käthe glimpsed an office with a huge map, men smoking
in a mess hall. They went up three steps and along a dimly lit,
narrow corridor.

Using a key, the corporal said affably, "In you go."

The cell was small, but the ceiling was high. The glass was
gone from the barred clerestory window, and the air seemed
far colder than outside, maybe because of the dampness. The
furnishings consisted of a coverless plank bed, a washbowl with
a light skin of ice, a latrine bucket whose cover didn't fit so that
a foul odor escaped.

"How long will it be?"

Rubbing his scarred cheek, the corporal winked jovially.
"Don't you worry, fraulein. You'll be eating lunch with your
friends at the Bendlerblock."

The heavy door banged shut. A chain jangled, a bolt was
shot, a key turned. She was triple-locked inside the cell. She

sank down on the plank bed. After a few minutes she was shivering uncontrollably. She began pacing the cell's length, four steps up, four steps back, swinging her arms and stamping. Although she felt no warmer, activity jarred her brain. Why had she been brought here? Whatever the corporal said, it wasn't likely, was it, that she would have been driven this distance to be returned to Berlin after a few questions? What did the Gestapo want with her? The possibilities were numerous. First, she had committed the undeniable crime of being Sigi's sister. Or then again, maybe they had picked up Heinrich Leventhal with clothes and food donated by her. Or had the grouchy ticket seller at the Grunewald station spilled the beans about the strips of filmed secrets? Or was she triple-locked in here because of her letters to Ulla-Britt Onslager? Her rebuff of Groener?

As a crook of substance she began fabricating excuses.

She kept glancing at her wristwatch, which ticked slowly, impervious to her chafing dread. Outside the dogs snapped and barked. In the corridor occasional footsteps and voices. By two o'clock her mind was rubbed raw. *Is this what they mean, softened up?*

V

There was no electricity in the cell, so she couldn't see her watch, but she estimated it to be around eight when the air-raid alert howled. Footsteps were pounding in the corridor. In the yard commands were shouted to get to the shelter. Nobody came to move her. The roar grew louder until the deafening throb against her eardrums told her a formation of bombers was passing directly overhead.

Suddenly the darkness beyond the window turned bright. From her cot she could see Christmas trees, the nickname for those weirdly beautiful red and green phosphorus markers that delineated the area to be bombed.

This fake farmhouse was the target!

Käthe had never been one of those people who went to pieces during a raid, but then again she had never been locked

up during one. At a deafening roar the cell shook. She darted
to the inner wall.

The chorus of yelping dogs grew yet more frantic. Something, either a tree or an outbuilding, burst into flames, and
burning scraps of debris showered between the bars onto the
wooden floor. Käthe jumped about, stamping on the embers.
When they were all extinguished, she realized that two of the
window bars had been jarred loose, leaving a space.

Her mind suddenly went cold and clear.

Get out of here. Get out!

The dogs had reached pandemonium level. There were no
human shouts. She dragged the plank cot to the window.
Adrenaline strength flooded through her and she used her
arms to haul herself onto the embrasure. Clutching the rusty,
insecure bars, she breathed shallowly because of the smoke.
Fire was everywhere. Flames shot up from the barn. Several
trees blazed, their branches etched with fire. She could see no
sentry. *Go,* she told herself. *Go!*

She jumped.

A terrified doberman lunged toward her, pointed teeth
bared and eyes gleaming red in the flames.

"Ensi, Hansi—Bodo," she screamed, remembering the
names by a miracle. "It's all right, boy, all right."

The dog whirled away to rejoin the frenzied pack.

The roar of engines was drowned out by the thunder of
flames. Coughing, eyes streaming, she ran toward the smoke-
shrouded entry. The heat forced her a step backward.

But there was no going back.

The air was sucked from her as she edged around the burning gate. Then she was sprinting along the unpaved lane that
led to the Potsdam road. The fire blew a tropical gale. At a
deafening crash she whirled around. The barn had collapsed.
Tongues of fire spat white sparks. She ran yet faster. Miles
away, to the north, the sky was ablaze. Thoughts swerved past
her brain. *Poor old Berlin, getting it again. Mother, alone and ill, she
must be frantic. Has the house been bombed?* How she loathed the
smell of fire, once the war was over, she'd never have a fire.
There weren't any German fighter planes. The bombers could

dump their loads wherever they chose. *Damn them, damn them,* she thought, sprinting at full speed onto the main road.

Suddenly she was hit in the back.

The blow caught her by surprise. As she went down, she thought, *Is it a bomb? Wyatt, is this death?*

TEN
1945–1946

GERMANS SURRENDER
> —headline of *The New York Times*,
> Monday, May 7, 1945

TODAY IS V-DAY
CHURCHILL SPEAKS AT 3 PM, THE KING AT 9;
TODAY AND TOMORROW ARE NATIONAL HOLIDAYS

—headline of *News Chronicle*, Tuesday, May 8, 1945

The task of holding Germany will not be a hard one
—it will be much harder to hold her up.

> —Winston Churchill in postwar speech
> to Parliament

FORTY-THREE

I

The bells of London's churches and cathedrals boomed their exultation through the open windows of Major Downes's flat. From Morpeth Terrace came laughter and off-key voices singing "There'll Be Bluebirds Over the White Cliffs of Dover." Horns honked in joyous discord on Victoria Street.

It was Tuesday, May 8, 1945, officially designated by His Majesty's government as Victory in Europe Day. After almost six years of war, tens of millions dead, a continent laid waste, the Third Reich was no more.

Aubrey, slumping in the major's sagging horsehair sofa while his superior poured two large Scotches, was thinking of those who hadn't made it through—of Araminta, of Peter. *Käthe,* he thought. For months now the Swedish agent had received nothing from her, and no matter how often he told himself that wartime mail at best was uncertain, that the saturation bombing surely had disrupted if not destroyed the German postal system, that numerous post offices had gone up in flames along with tons of letters, he could not stem the fear that she was among his dead. He had been summoned here to be given his next assignment. His mind was made up. If ordered to Germany he would search for her: if ordered to stay in England, he would request a leave and find his way over there to search for her.

"To peace," the major said, raising his glass.

"To peace," Aubrey echoed in a subdued tone.

Downes sat behind his desk. "We're going to have a bad time of it with the Russians," he said.

"The Russians, sir? Not the Germans?"

"What's the matter with you, Aubrey? You know better than I that all Germany's crawling in the mud. Whatever Nazi brass are left will be taken care of by the War Crimes Commission. Stalin's another story. This is top secret, but we've managed to obtain the Soviet plans to take over all four sectors of Germany." The previous February, at a conference in the Russian city of Yalta, Churchill, the dying Roosevelt, and Stalin had hammered out the fate of their not wholly defeated enemy: the Reich would be divided into four zones of occupation, British, American, Russian, and French.

"The Russians aren't in any condition to start another goround," Aubrey said.

"Those plans outline Stalin's strategy to communize all of Europe—and Germany's their beachhead. The Prime Minister has stressed that we must keep our CI-4 network intact—and secure. The day after tomorrow you're to fly to Hamburg. You'll see who's left in our own sector."

"What about Berlin, sir?" Berlin, deep in the heart of the Soviet zone, would be administered by the four occupying armies.

"Later. Even in our own sector it's going to be a bit dicey, finding who's left of our people."

Aubrey winced and thought, *Please God, let me find Käthe.*

"Millions of Germans're already on the move getting out of the way of the Soviet armies," the major said. "And now the war's over, there'll be millions of conscripted laborers and DPs finding their way back to their own countries. Jews trying to discover if they have any of their families left. Our estimation is that this'll be the greatest mass migration in human history."

"Chaos."

"Yes, but that's to our advantage. It will be easier for our agents to remain submerged and operational."

"Operational, sir? The war's over. Don't they deserve some peace?"

"It's up to you to assess who has communist leanings." The

level Canadian voice held a warning that Aubrey's last remark was out of line. "Approach only those who remain unimpeachably loyal to us. Now about Fräulein Kingsmith—"

At her name Aubrey's hand jerked and his drink splashed. "Have you heard from her?"

"Not since that January message about evacuating German farmers from Poland. You decoded it."

Aubrey slumped back in the horsehair.

"She's not strictly one of your network," the major continued. "If you find her—*when* you find her, you're not to ask her to do anything further. However, you *are* to issue a stern reminder that she signed the Official Secrets Act."

"She won't break her oath."

"No, of course not. But she should be aware that she can't expect the least recognition from us."

Aubrey's eyes narrowed. "Are you saying, sir, that if she needs help, we won't give her any?"

"Nothing would please us more than to pin on the medals she deserves. But unfortunately that's impossible."

"So we'll leave her high, dry, and nailed to the wall?" Aubrey asked in low, clipped anger.

"Kingsmith!"

"Sorry, sir."

"The same goes for every one of our people. Exposing CI-4 is a luxury we can't afford." The major set down his glass and it vibrated with the force of the Catholic Cathedral's bells. "Go on home, Aubrey. Spend the rest of the day celebrating with your family."

II

Captain Wyatt Kingsmith now was part of G-5, the United States Military Government. He went about his tasks with an angry-eyed vigor that was buttressed by two proper nouns: Araminta, Buchenwald. Araminta had been robbed of her life and he of their shared future by a Nazi rocket. And as for Buchenwald . . . He had arrived at the concentration camp the day after its liberation, and at that hour for him the clear German sunshine had turned forever black.

He was in the Legal Division. According to Military Government Law #1, all Nazi laws were to be abrogated. Some of the thousands of pieces of legislation enacted since 1933 were harmless enough. Others were connected either openly or deviously to the racial laws and to maintaining Hitler's absolute dictatorship. Every law shadowed with the swastika must be wiped from the books, a staggeringly complex task that Wyatt realized would take many people many years to complete.

In early August, just after the atom bombs were dropped on Japan, he was transferred to Berlin.

The fallen Quadriga atop the battered Brandenburg Gate looked down on macabre destruction. The Tiergarten with its shady trees and magnificent flower beds had vanished into the mud of battle, with burned tanks and army vehicles rusting where they had been abandoned. Weeds grew rankly in the ruins of the Hotel Adlon and the Pariserplatz. The government buildings of the Wilhelmstrasse, including Hitler's beige marble Chancellery, were toppled. Along the Unter den Linden the famed trees had burned to stumps while the magnificent museums, the palace, the opera house, the Lutheran Cathedral, the fine hotels and shops—including the Berlin branch of Kingsmith's—were either shells or craters. Decaying corpses reeked corruptly beneath fallen buildings, broken sewer lines spread hideous odors. Berliners whispered and scurried like ghosts.

The Grunewald was in the American Sector. Several days after his arrival Wyatt drove out there. The small lakes must have acted as bull's-eyes for Allied bombardiers: every house that edged the water was destroyed.

He turned off the ignition at his uncle's home, pushing open the gate and walking slowly along the drive, halting. Hands in his pockets, shoulders slumped, he gazed at the shambles of the gingerbread mansion where he had been welcomed first as a kinsman, then as a suitor. One side had collapsed into a mound of rubble while the other was a facade with chimneys pointing up at the clear blue sky. As he stared, a flight of starlings burst from the gaping bay window of what had been the drawing room.

The ruins depressed him utterly. Then into his mind popped the memory of the toothless, skeletal ancient with a star on his striped uniform who had shuffled painfully to greet him, an ancient who had turned out to be twenty-five years old, a former student at the Sorbonne who had collapsed while telling him his background, dying a few hours later. *They deserve whatever they got, the Germans,* he thought. *I'll steer clear of them all, and that goes for the Kraut Kingsmiths too.*

He kept his resolution slightly over a month.

III

Wyatt and thirteen other officers were billeted in the formerly fashionable district of Dahlem, not far from the *kommandatur* building. The roof and attics of the big yellow stucco house had been damaged, but the two other floors had miraculously survived intact, even to the windowpanes. On this balmy afternoon in mid September, as he drove up, the door was flung open by a scrawny, jug-eared old butler, who smoothed his patched green apron and bowed obsequiously. The housekeeper, Frau Lowe, welcomed him with equal deference. (Though the servants were paid by the local German authorities, they would have worked for nothing: the house was heated and they were fed one meal a day for which they didn't have to surrender food coupons, a meal that represented two days' calories in German terms.) Wyatt responded with brusque nods, trotting up the stairs.

His airy room, papered with pink flowers as if for an adolescent girl, had windows that overlooked the front garden. At shrill cries he went to look out.

The two little boys who lived in the basement of the ruins opposite were at it again. The taller child pulling at the other's ear, they danced around. The frailer boy screeched with pain but refused to unclench his fist—obviously he had found a treasure, maybe a scrap of potato peeling, maybe even a cigarette butt that could be traded for a thumb-size potato. With German adults Wyatt never failed to conjure up Araminta or

Buchenwald. But what did Nazi war crimes have to do with these hungry six-year-olds? He trotted downstairs to the dining room, where the long table was already set, spreading butter thickly on a couple of white rolls. Outside, the combatants rewarded him with smiles and polite Nazi salutes.

When he got back to his room, Lieutenant Joe Hedpeth was sprawling on the pink chaise longue. Hedpeth, a good-natured goldbrick in the Counterintelligence Corps who shared the big blue-tiled bathroom, often dropped by to shoot the breeze.

"Got any Jerry relatives, Kingsmith?"

"Why?"

"Bunch of papers came in from the Public Safety guys. One for a Frowline Kingsmith. It's not your regular German name."

Wyatt occupied himself with lighting a cigarette. "What sort of papers? A *fragebogen?*" Every German was compelled to fill out a *fragebogen*—a six-page single-spaced questionnaire that included questions about Nazi affiliations.

"Nope. Just this." Hedpeth extended a smeared white-on-black photocopy.

> Kingsmith, Käthe
>
> Age 26, birthplace Berlin. Father Alfred Kingsmith, British subject at time of her birth. Deceased. Mother Clothilde von Graetz Kingsmith. Deceased. Half brother, Colonel Siegfried von Hohenau, aide to uncle, General Baron Klaus von Hohenau of the OKW, both deceased.
>
> Worked in Secret Files of the OKW 1940–1945. Admits to having Top Security Clearance. Admits to knowing Hitler so well as to be invited to Berchtesgaden. Denies being Party member. This checks out with Party register. Held at Ober Tappenburg for further questioning.

"Just as well she's not related," Hedpeth was saying. "Okay, she wasn't on the Big List"—he meant the Party register: the entire Nazi party membership rolls had been discovered awaiting pulping at a Munich paper mill—"but everything else about her spells N-A-Z-I." He got to his feet. "See you at chow," he said, leaving through the connecting bathroom.

Wyatt still held the photocopy. The chemical smell acrid in his nostrils, he told himself, *She spells Nazi. Leave her alone, leave her the hell alone.*

IV

He hitched a ride on a Flying Fortress to Frankfurt, headquarters of U.S. Force, European Theater. Borrowing a jeep, he wound through farmland and destroyed villages of half-timbered medieval houses. Beyond Aschaffenburg, with its square palace, he drove up the Odenwald—Odin's Wood. Mythical home of the king of the Norse gods, the great rolling hills were clad in evergreen. He turned into a deep forest posted with warnings that trespassing was strictly forbidden—STRENG VERBOTEN. He came to great barbed-wire walls. He showed his pass. Sentries admitted the jeep through the stone gates with OBER TAPPENBURG carved into the overhead arch. He moved slowly among thousands of Germans clad in oddly assorted civilian clothes and ragged uniforms who milled between the barracks. He parked in the designated area, walking briskly. But as he neared the hoops of barbed wire that set apart the women's detention center, his footsteps lagged. What was he doing here? Why couldn't he dig a moat between the past and the present? Why couldn't he lock Fräulein Käthe Kingsmith in the *streng verboten* dungeon of his memory?

A Wac corporal with pillar legs and a plain, pleasant red face led him up an echoing wood staircase. Women's voices ebbed and flowed around them on the long corridor.

"You'll have no problems talking to her, Captain," the Wac said tentatively.

Wyatt didn't respond.

"She speaks terrific English, just like she was born in jolly old London town. I hope this isn't out of line, sir. But she's been locked up for two months and she's not in tip-top health."

"Have you suggested she should ask for a medic?"

"Yes, sir, I have. But all she wants to know is when she'll be questioned so she can get out of here."

"A whiner, then?"

"No, no, I'm putting it all wrong. The way I figure it, she's sort of desperate to find somebody. So many of them are. But she's different from the others. Most of them either crawl or act like they're still the master race. She's quiet and sort of sweet— basically a fine person. It's hard to believe she had any connection with the Nazis."

"That's why she's in Ober Tappenburg." A muscle worked at Wyatt's jawline. "So we can figure out her loyalties."

The Wac's face grew yet redder. "Yes, sir."

"Does she know she has a visitor?"

"Negative, sir."

"Let's keep it that way, then."

Saluting crisply, she opened a newly painted door with black lettering: INTERROGATION OFFICER.

The Ober Tappenburg facility had been built as an SS barracks. Either the contractor for the SS had done shoddy work or the earth below the building had subsided. The floorboards of the small room slanted downward so that the two straight chairs that faced each other across a pine table were at different levels. Instead of sitting down, Wyatt went to the window, putting a cigarette between his lips but not using his lighter.

He was standing there when the door opened quietly behind him.

No blowing off steam, he commanded himself. *No judgments, no accusations. Don't let her talk about the old days. The important thing is to keep it impersonal.*

FORTY-FOUR

I

He ground the unlit cigarette to shreds in the ashtray before he permitted himself to turn. For several heartbeats he gazed across a dozen feet of badly joined floorboard and six years of warfare.

The neckline of her gray pullover was discolored to an ugly brown, the elbows patched in black wool. It hung loosely over a bagging ersatz wool monstrosity that passed as a skirt. Even this bulk of unseasonal winter clothing could not disguise how thin she was. Waif thin. The delicate bones of her jaw showed, her eyes were shadowed and huge. With her pale hair parted on the right and drawn neatly to the left, she looked younger than when he'd met her at Hitler's big extravaganza, the Olympics.

The red-scrubbed Wac corporal had obeyed his orders.

Käthe had no inkling of who awaited her. As she stared at him, she raised her hand to the blue, throbbing vein at her throat and her eyes seemed to grow yet more immense. Worried that she might faint, he took a step forward.

Then she smiled.

Nobody past infancy should smile like this. Her joy was completely undisguised. She couldn't have been more naked than if she had abruptly stripped off those hideous clothes. He felt a stirring that hovered between the erotic romanticism of the past and a blunt urge toward rape.

"Yes, it's me," he said sharply. "Come in."

The smile faded a little and she crossed the threshold.

"I'll be out here, sir," said the Wac.

The door closed and they were alone in the shoddily constructed office.

Not trusting himself to speak again, he nodded at the chair that faced the window, the lower chair. She sat, folding her hands awkwardly. Since he didn't know himself why he was here, in lieu of an explanation he held out a crumpled pack of cigarettes.

She shook her head. "I don't smoke," she said.

He had forgotten her voice. The low, soft timbre was a reminder of endearments whispered in twilit beds.

"Nowadays they're the medium of exchange in your country," he said. "Take one—take a couple."

Coloring, she stared down at her clenched, thin hands. The men's voices rose outside, an indecipherable command was shouted, and then there was a rustling quiet.

"Are you going to write down what I say?" she asked.

"What kind of question is that?"

"I thought . . . Haven't you come to interrogate me?"

"I'm here on a visitor's pass."

"You are?" She pushed up her sleeve, but it dropped below her wrist again. "Please, is there some way you could get me paroled?"

She spoke so rapidly and quietly that at first he didn't understand. "Paroled?"

"Leave the camp for a little while."

"Why?"

"I need to . . . find somebody." Her voice wavered on the *somebody*.

"Come to think of it, the corporal mentioned you were hot to get out."

"Just for a couple of days. Would it be possible for you to arrange it?" She pressed down on the table, disturbing the precarious balance of the legs. The ashtray slid several inches. The old dreaminess, the tender vulnerability, were peeled from her, and her gaze was direct and fierce. All at once he was positive that the somebody she needed to find was a man. Her lover. Her Nazi lover.

"Sorry," he said in a tone that indicated the opposite. "Against regulations."

"Wyatt, please, couldn't you try? Just one day. I swear I'd come back. There's somebody I need to find."

"A fact of life here in the American zone. You Germans're looking for each other. We're looking for Nazis. Oh, don't get me wrong, I wouldn't dare suggest you were in the Party. We've already discovered there weren't any more than a dozen Nazis. The rest of you were only following orders."

She raised her chin for a moment, then she bent her head and reached in her sleeve for a tattered, unironed scrap of cloth to blow her nose. "How is Grandpa? Is he still . . . is he all right?"

"Fine and dandy," Wyatt snapped. The situation, him the victor facing the thin, defeated, yet still beautiful woman whom he had once loved to desperation, was as corrosive as battery acid. Despite his resolve he could not control his rage.

"And Aubrey."

"He served out the war in Scotland."

Her fingers tightened on the handkerchief. "Could I write to him?"

"Do you have mail privileges?"

She shook her head.

"Araminta's dead."

At this she looked up. " 'Minta?" Tears clung to her lower lashes.

"We were married," he said.

"Married?" Her lips were parted, trembling. "How did she die?"

The anguish came as sharply as it had in that Belgian farmhouse. "She didn't die. She was murdered. In London. On her way home from working at the Red Cross. One of your V-2 rockets pulverized a couple of blocks."

"Oh, poor 'Minta. . . ."

"We have a little boy."

Käthe's eyes widened, and again he had the feeling she might pass out. "A baby," she whispered. "A boy?"

"Geoff is his name. Geoffrey. Spelled the English way. Uncle Euan and Aunt Elizabeth have him at Quarles." How could this information ring so vindictively?

"Wyatt, once we meant something to each other," she said rapidly. "Can't you at least try to get them to release me for a few hours—"

"Jesus Christ, is that all you have to say! Don't you give a damn that she's dead?" The clump of many feet wearing wood-soled clogs filled the hall. The women internees were on the way to their exercise hour. After a few beats he said, "I was at Buchenwald right after it was liberated." Even taking the clatter into consideration he spoke too loudly.

"Ah."

"When you're questioned, I suppose you'll give the usual answer. You had no idea what was going on."

"No, I'll tell the truth," she said. "I knew about everything."

"Tell 'em in that same fine, cheery tone and you'll go before a military tribunal and get the death sentence."

"We both knew about the camps from the beginning. Aubrey told us." Rising, she started for the door.

He darted around the table, blocking her way. "How could you have stood being with me?"

"What do you mean?"

"Exactly what I said. How could you have gone to bed with me?"

"I loved you." Her lips were very white.

"Knowing what you knew about Myron Leventhal?"

"What do you want to hear? That I'm guilty? Of course I am. Everybody in Germany is guilty. And there's nothing worse that you can say to me than I've already said myself. There is no absolution." Moving around him, she tapped on the door.

After the Wac corporal led her away, he sat down, burying his face in his hands. He kept seeing that first nakedly joyous smile, seeing the unrepentant pride of those thin, erectly held shoulders as she had left the room.

Damn all Germans to hell. Damn her.

II

Käthe had the upper bunk at the far end of the dormitory. She walked between the rows of neatly folded khaki U.S. Army blankets, grateful in a dulled way that she was alone.

Climbing onto her bunk, she sat with her legs dangling.

That first sight of him had filled her with such joy—no, call it by its rightful name, ecstasy—that there was no room for breath in her lungs, no place for rational impressions. He was taller than she remembered. It had taken her several minutes to realize that his quizzical half smile was gone, and that the years had left a certain hardness along his jawline. There were deep lines scored at the corners of the eyes gazing at her with undisguised hostility and repugnance. A few white hairs sprinkled his tawny crew cut. He was hopelessly handsome, this well-fed American officer in his pinks, but he wasn't the Wyatt she had known.

Of course not, he's Araminta's widower.

She wanted to mourn for Araminta, playmate of her girlhood whom she had loved, but she couldn't. It was even impossible to feel the normal jealousy. Her relief that Aubrey and the rest of the Kingsmiths had survived was benumbed. Stretching on the bunk, she stared at the whitewashed wall.

Why didn't I explain that I needed to find our child, his and mine? What a waste of time! Fat chance he would have believed Erich, born in a Lebensborn home, was his. Besides, he has his own son. All right, what if I had broken the Official Secrets Act? Told him I had worked with British intelligence, and seen Aubrey twice during the war. I couldn't break my sworn oath. I should have told him what he'd always believed. That I idolized Hitler. Yes, why didn't I lie about being a Nazi, then fall to the floor and lick his shoes, begging forgiveness? Anything, I should have done or said anything so he would have helped me to leave here for a few days to find Erich.

I'd already begged him, and I couldn't beg more.

Oh, God, it's the same old story. Käthe Kingsmith has her pride.

"Pride!" she murmured aloud, a humorless laugh escaping her. "What do I have left to be proud about?"

She closed her eyes.

FORTY-FIVE

I

The women detainees would be out in the air for another hour. Käthe lay on her bunk with her arms wrapped around herself, eyes closed. The few minutes with Wyatt in the interrogation officer's room had hurt too deeply for tears. After a few minutes she forced herself to stop thinking about it. Rolling onto her side, she stared through the window at the sky and attempted to make some sort of logic from the chaotic, disconnected events of the past months.

She had bolted from the burning SS farmhouse during the air raid, an unplanned breakout, and been felled by a blow in the back: by some quirk of malignant fate she had come to in the same cell from which she had escaped. The reek of smoke still clung heavily in the air. The windows had been boarded over. She knew it must be hours later, though, because daylight streaked between the boards. She tried to sit. Dizzy, she sank back onto the hard cot. Lifting an exploratory hand to her forehead, she felt a hard, egg-size bruise. *Concussion?* she questioned woozily. She was bruised everywhere. Each involuntary movement made her whimper, but remaining in the same position on the hard bed was equally painful. She drowsed and woke with a violent thirst. There was no water in the cell. After a while she drowsed again.

* * *

She wasn't sure if it was that same day or the next that she was taken to the SS-*untersturmführer*. He sat behind the desk, silently stroking his bony jaw as he stared at her. It was difficult to look away from him. His eyes glittered, the eyes of an invalid or a fanatic.

"Luckily you were hit by a police car," he said. "They searched you for your papers, and when they found nothing, you were brought back here for questioning."

The giddiness had returned. "May I have some water?"

"If your answers satisfy me."

"Can I contact my mother?"

The lieutenant stopped caressing his chin and leaned toward her. "I ask the questions."

"She must be worried sick."

"As far as Frau Kingsmith—and everybody else—is concerned, you've vanished."

"Vanished. . . ." she quavered. In 1941 Hitler issued a decree poetically named *nacht und nebel,* night and fog. Prisoners could disappear without a trace, as it were into the dark fog.

"He's dead," said the *untersturmführer*.

"Who?" She began to tremble. "Erich?"

"Is that what you call him? The uncle's kaput, too, so there's no point trying to keep their secrets."

"You're talking about my brother . . . ?"

"Who else? Officially, he died defending the Fatherland on the Ukrainian front, but just between us, he croaked during an interrogation. Prinz-Albrechtstrasse is enthusiastic about ferreting out traitors." The eyes shone yet brighter, as if lit by inner rays. "He and the one-eyed uncle were both in on that cowardly attempt to take the Führer's life last July. Oh, don't look so innocent. This isn't coming as any surprise."

Croaked during interrogation . . . Sigi, oh, Sigi. From the note on flimsy toilet paper she expected her brother's death, yet foreknowledge couldn't stem her involuntary outburst of grief. Standing before the gimlet-eyed SS interrogator, she bent her head into her hands, gasping and sobbing.

"Control yourself," the *untersturmführer* said coldly. "I want the names of other traitors. You will give me names."

Suddenly the air-raid alarm blared. The guard prodded her hastily back to her cell, handcuffing her to the iron ring in the wall, locking the door. His footsteps raced swiftly down the hall.

She never again saw the fanatic-eyed SS *untersturmführer,* nor was she interrogated. The fourteen-year-old SS guard whispered that many of the officers had been transferred to defend Danzig against the Russians.

II

After a couple of weeks she was shoved into a van and driven to a village train station. Here, an unhitched boxcar was pushed onto a siding. Inside, twenty men and three women were locked into individual cages like those used for transporting pet animals, cages too small for even a child to stand in. When the other prisoners learned she was Siegfried von Hohenau's sister, they welcomed her—everyone here had either conspired to usurp Hitler in the July Plot or was related to a conspirator. They were en route to a concentration camp, whichever camp remained in the shrunken Third Reich. Military trains and hospital trains chugged by in both directions, but the prison car remained on the siding. The guards, Hungarians wearing faded blue jackets like the railroad workers, spoke no German. Mornings and evenings they unlocked the prisoners in turn for "exercise," first the men, then the women: when it was Käthe's turn to squat, they stared at her. The guards, like the thunder of artillery, became a condition of life. Then from faraway in the east came a weird, howling screech.

"Katyushas," pronounced a bald Wehrmacht major. "The men call them Stalin's pipe organs. The Russians fire their rockets from multibarreled launchers."

Despite the persistent pain of being cramped in her cage, Käthe felt transformed by being with others in similar circumstances. Talking to them, she sometimes for long minutes forgot her impending fate, forgot her grief for Sigi, her anxieties about her mother—and Erich. Each captive supplied scraps of information; it was as though they were making a potluck stew. From the simmering kettle emerged the significant news that the Ruhr had collapsed, that the Russians were at the Oder River. Germany had been compressed into a small hourglass.

The oldest woman, a deeply religious titled octogenarian, summed it up in her own way. "The Lord is marking an end to the war."

"Not soon enough for us, Gräfin," sighed a narrow-faced colonel who wore the maroon stripe of the general staff. "The war won't end soon enough to save us."

On their fourth day a closed cattle train rumbled by. Atop the roof of each car two SS troopers knelt with machine guns. A hideously foul odor spread and above the sound of wheels could be heard a thin, wailing hum.

Long after the train had passed nobody spoke, then a Luftwaffe major said quietly, "Jews. Being evacuated to other camps. Can you make any sense of it? The Reich's shriveled to nothing, the war's over any day now, and still those swine keep shipping away the poor bastards."

"We Germans have a lot to answer for," said the *gräfin.*

"*They*'re doing it," voices clamored. "*Them.* Hitler's pigs."

"We allowed it," Käthe said.

And the *gräfin* added in a quavery tone that rang through the boxcar, "In the hour of judgment each of us will have to answer for it to God."

On the fifth day Käthe and the other female prisoners were taken into the small station house. With gestures the Hungarian guards indicated they should strip, all of them, even the aged *gräfin.* None of the women made a move. The guards jerked Käthe to the table, yanking off her clothes. Thrusting her face down and naked on the varnished oak of the table, they took turns beating her with their truncheons. She tried not to give them the satisfaction of hearing her scream, but when the blows landed on open wounds she could no longer stifle her grunting whimpers. She was jerked to her feet. Torn clothes were thrust at her and she was shoved from the station house.

Stamping into her shoes, she pulled on her coat. She bled copiously into the lining as she raced along the narrow street.

The nervy beat of machine guns rattled behind her. She

clapped a hand to her heart. Her companions of the past few days were being massacred.

Why had she been let go?

Was it because she was young and blond?

Or was it haphazard chance? She ran faster.

III

At the brink of exhaustion she reached the farmhouse. Her tentative tap was answered by an old woman with a face as wrinkled as an apple left over from the previous year. "Don't tell me where you came from, I don't want to know," she said.

The old woman drew water from the well to fill the bath—cold, of course; there was no fuel for heating bath water. Käthe started to take off her coat, then swayed at the agony. The farmwife eased fabric from the coagulating blood and purple-black bruises, and helped Käthe into the wooden tub. "There'll be scars," she mumbled sympathetically. The water turned rusty. Afterward the old woman daubed Käthe's back with a soothing concoction that smelled of mint and exchanged the coat for a clean if hideous outfit.

"Get to the Americans quick," she advised.

"My little boy is near Frankfurt. Erich." How wonderful to say the name aloud. "Erich's not far from Frankfurt am Main."

"That's good. The Amis are in Frankfurt."

"First I must get my mother."

"Where is she?"

"Berlin."

"Berlin! Are you out of your mind? Maybe the Russians are already in Berlin. They tear the pants off anything female—a pretty, skinny little thing like you with the Ivans going at her?" She made a coarse pumping gesture with her freckled, veined fist. "Pah! You'll never survive. Forget Berlin."

IV

The bombers no longer wove above Berlin. Now barrage after barrage of Russian artillery shells keened and shrieked down, spreading terror and death impartially across the capital's three hundred and fifty square miles. Katyushas added their otherworldly howl to the destruction.

On Potsdamerstrasse Käthe was ordered into the public shelter. Wavery candlelight illuminated hell. People sprawled everywhere, not an inch of space left. There was no food. There were no ventilators. Running water was a luxury of the past. To reach the foul, nonfunctioning toilets Käthe had to climb over dead and living bodies. Hungry children wailed. Women clutched their comatose babies. A group of nuns prayed softly but Käthe, dizzy with starvation and half crazed by the crash of Russian mortars and the shriek of rockets, doubted that God could hear them. Badges, Volkssturm armbands, and uniforms were being burned. Two men discussed with loud frankness that now was the time to get rid of Hitler. A madman wearing a black uniform silenced the conversation by firing a pistol into the air and screaming that if all the *volk* remained loyal, the Führer would work a miracle and bring victory to the Reich. Astonishingly there were nods of agreement.

I can't stay here, I must find Mother.

It was dark when Käthe left the shelter, winding her way toward the Grunewald. Fires blazed everywhere. A mob was crowding into a grocery shop. Käthe, ravenous, joined them. There was nothing on the shelves. As they left, shells raked the street and within seconds razor-sharp shrapnel had decimated the looters. Again, randomly, she escaped.

When she reached the Grunewald, a weird half-quiet prevailed. The long line of Katyusha launching sites in the forest had fallen silent, as had the mortars, but capricious rifle fire rattled from the direction of Dahlem. Fires set by phosphorous shells smoldered along her street.

Her house was not burning, but had been bombed again. Nothing was left except the walls of the living room, the chimneys rising like tall tombstones. Moving down to the garage, which appeared undamaged, Käthe slowed. Affixed to the door was the Gestapo seal. Her heart made a strange lub-lub sound as she forced the lock. The odor of corruption rushed out.

Sleek rats scurried, one halting to rise up and stare insolently. She moved slowly inside, and a thin, involuntary cry escaped her as she saw what remained of her mother.

Her chest a cold bar of pain, she wrapped a quilt around the gnawed skeleton.

A bomb had landed near the two small oaks, and the earth was soft, so she decided on it as a gravesite, but weak from fatigue and hunger, she took until midafternoon to dig properly deep.

Clothilde von Graetz Kingsmith, descendant of Teutonic knights, a woman who rigidly adhered to her own code of honor, became one more of the millions consigned to the uncaring earth during the twelve-year Nazi night.

I am the resurrection and the life, Käthe thought as she shoveled back the dirt. *And whosoever believeth in Me shall never die.*

She was cutting pale, aphid-eaten roses, early blossoms, from her father's derelict garden, when the car racketed along the street. Only then did she realize that for hours there had been no rifle fire.

Instinctively she used animal camouflage, standing absolutely still, scissors in her right hand, thorns biting into her left palm. But someone in the car must have spotted her. Tires screeched and after a few seconds two men strolled along the drive with rifles held casually under their arms. Ammunition belts were slung around their shoulders and they wore filthy brown uniforms with the pants gathered like bloomers into their mud-caked low boots. Their caps were affixed with red stars. Russians. Catching sight of her, they laughed, poking each other and calling out something to the car. Two more comrades appeared.

The one with the bottle—inconsequentially she noticed it was Leibfraumilch—held it out, then brought it toward his body, an unmistakable gesture for her to approach. *"Komm Frau,"* he called. A phrase that would become familiar to her the next few days.

There was no way to escape, yet flight was as automatic as her earlier stillness. She had reached the untended, leaf-strewn terrace when the Russians caught up. The tallest one was young, maybe seventeen, with pimples along his jaw and a scraggly reddish mustache. As he reached out for her, she stabbed the closed scissors at his chest pocket. He dodged the point. The others laughed, and he grabbed Käthe's arm, squeezing the wrist until the scissors clattered on stone, then aimed a casual boot at her stomach. The roses scattered as she toppled backward onto the stone terrace. Her head hit so hard that lightning streaked behind her eyelids.

The red-mustached boy was already unbuttoning his trousers. She tried to get up, but the other soldiers spread-eagled her on the cold stone. She continued to twist feebly. The Russians laughed, obviously amused by her struggles, yet without malice. It was as if after battling their way into the heart of Berlin, they perceived the city as a giant circus of women, liquor, booty, spread out for their enjoyment. Käthe's skirt was pulled up, and with a sharp tearing sound her pants were torn.

At the pain she gritted her back teeth.

It was dark before they had finished with her. Battered, her eyes swollen to slits, she heard another Russian phrase that would become familiar. *"Voyna kaput."*

It meant "The war is ended."

Now I can go to Frankfurt, she thought.

V

Uprooted families, wounded soldiers, emaciated concentration-camp survivors, and ragged conscripted laborers trudged in every direction through farmland and woods, all nationalities attempting to avoid the Russian road barriers and sentries that blocked the route to the American zone. Käthe smeared mud on her face and into her hair to appear as ugly as possible. Weaving along light-headedly, she traded possessions from the garage for food. Once she stole currants from a kitchen garden, wolfing down the unripe berries, then vomiting. She wept at unexpected times for Sigi and Clothilde. All that kept her moving those terrible first weeks of peace was the hope of finding her son.

Among the refugees were SS who had shucked their uniforms. Accustomed to giving orders, trained to be intimidating and unscrupulous, they were resourceful survivors.

VI

It was raining when she reached the road that marked the boundary of the American zone. While she waited under an oak tree for the shower to pass, a canvas-covered U.S. Army truck pulled up. At first, fearing another rape, she shrank back. But the corporal with the heavy eyebrows had a warm smile. He indicated that she should climb in back.

Now she assumed she was being offered a lift. "Are you going in the direction of Frankfurt?"

"Hey, you a Limey?"

"No, German."

"Do you got your denazification?"

"Denazification?"

"Well, no big deal, frowline. You just gotta answer a bunch of questions, then you're home free."

They stopped to pick up other border jumpers and soon the truck was filled with anxious people. They came to a station where the platform was crowded with a snaking, slow line of Germans waiting to board a passenger train.

On the track ahead of her she saw a short, thick-shouldered man in shabby civilian clothes talking earnestly to an American officer. Though the German's back was to her, she saw the sleek blond hair. Was it Groener?

She passed through the Pullman cars where U.S. Public Safety officers and their interpreters were at work on the denazification. Unnerved by the sight of Groener—or his doppelgänger—Käthe blurted her answers without premeditation. Where had she worked? (The top-secret files of the OKW.) Had she personally known any top Nazis? (Once she had visited Hitler's Eagle's Nest.) At the caboose end of the train the majority of the Germans, those deemed without Nazi leanings, had their legs painted with a stripe of washable white paint.

Käthe was transferred to the detention camp at Ober Tappenburg to await further questioning.

FORTY-SIX

I

In the middle of September, two weeks after Wyatt had visited Ober Tappenburg, he received a note from the British Sector. Aubrey would be in Berlin on an ordnance survey the following Tuesday.

Wyatt stood at one of the Dahlem drawing-room windows, watching his brother-in-law get out of a khaki-painted sedan. The receding hairline, glasses, abstracted expression, and slight stoop as he came up the path typecast Aubrey as an Oxford don rather than an officer in His Majesty's spit-and-polish army. *Poor Araminta,* Wyatt thought with a rueful smile. *Could anything be more off the mark than those deep, dark suspicions of hers that Aubrey was one of the SOE glory boys?* Before the bell could ring to summon the obsequious jug-eared old butler, he ran to fling open the front door. "Hey, Aubrey, hey, old buddy," he said, pulling his reticent brother-in-law into a clumsy male bear hug that was heartfelt on both sides. They hadn't seen each other since 1942, when Aubrey had come down to London after Peter's death. When they pulled away, their eyes were moist. Going upstairs to Wyatt's frivolously pink bedroom, they had predinner drinks.

Wyatt saw that Aubrey, though as self-deprecating as ever, shrugging off compliments on his captain's pips, had an air of confidence lacking in the prewar years.

Aubrey saw the near invisible line of a scar in Wyatt's sandy, close-cropped hair, saw the lines cut deep in his suntanned face. That clear-eyed American naïveté had vanished, replaced by a quizzical toughness. It wasn't in Wyatt to be unjust, but Aubrey could tell that any German who came in contact with Captain Wyatt Kingsmith, U.S. Army of Occupation, must find him exceedingly tough. Sighing, Aubrey wished it were otherwise. *Easy does it,* he told himself, and decided to wait for the propitious moment to ask whether Wyatt knew anything of Käthe. He took out his new snapshots of Geoff.

Wyatt, laughing, fingered through the gray-wrapped package. "Run that by me again. Uncle Euan's been teaching *my* kid to play cricket?"

"Well, he bowls one of those big plush balls at Geoff's little bat."

"Cricket my ass!"

"Geoff means everything to both of them, Wyatt, and Grandfather too," Aubrey said quietly. "They haven't recovered from losing Araminta."

Wyatt's grin faded. "Who has?" He glanced at his thin gold watch. "Twenty after seven. In precisely ten minutes you'll hear the dinner gong. Frau Lowe, our housekeeper, runs the joint like a Waffen-SS training camp. Germans!"

"They're going through terrible times."

"It couldn't happen to better people."

"Isn't that rather a blanket indictment?"

"Damn right. Aubrey, you're talking to a guy who toured Buchenwald right after it was liberated. Newsreels and photographs don't do the place justice. That stink—I'll never get it out of my system. The shower rooms with holes for the poison Zyklon B. The ovens. The poor, sad corpses that insisted on moving around! A toothless old man told me he had been a student at the Sorbonne and was twenty-five. He collapsed at my feet. Twenty-five fucking years old when he died, and he looked a hundred! How one group of humans could inflict such misery on another is beyond me."

"Up the street I saw three little girls, they couldn't have been much older than Geoff, burrowing through a barrel with a sign, EDIBLE GARBAGE."

Wyatt sighed and refilled his glass. "Okay, I feel for the kids, I wish we could ship in enough eggs, milk, and Hershey bars so they wouldn't keel over in the streets. But as for the rest of the country—" His hand pantomimed a cutting slash across his throat.

"How do you imagine they feel about us and our bombing raids?"

"Buddy, they asked for it! Wait and see what a big humanist you are after some Kraut tells you in a conversational tone, soldier to soldier, that he was only following orders when he marched a hundred or so Russian Jews through the snow. No matter how bad he felt about shooting the three quarters of them who fell by the wayside, the army is the army and no soldier tells his superior what he will and won't do. Then later on he forgets himself and blurts out that the Yids only got what was coming to them."

"You can't judge all Germans by the SS. They were Hitler's elite."

"Never fool yourself, Aubrey. Maybe the Fritzes didn't all put on a black uniform, but it was the love affair of the millennium, the Third Reich and old Schicklgruber. Remember the Olympics? Those huge crowds oozing adoration. When the Führer delivered the goods, they were nuts for him."

Aubrey sipped his drink. From his own top-secret observation he was forced to agree. While panzer divisions racked in country after country, all Germany (with the exception of a few courageous souls like Schultze and Käthe) delighted in playing follow-the-Leader. And Teutonic necks were crooked from looking in the opposite direction when neighbors, Jew and gentile alike, were whisked onto trucks.

Wyatt cocked a knowing eyebrow. "No arguments, huh? Well, you're the one who quit Oxford to alert the world to the camps."

Aubrey, who had never confessed authorship of *Tarnhelm*, made a noncommittal shrug.

Wyatt's expression turned bleak. "The thing is, Aubrey, those early camps were vacation paradises compared to what came later and—" He stopped at the sound of the downstairs gong. Glancing at his watch again, he said, "Seven-thirty, right on the dime."

II

"So what think you of the Neue Femina, glittering apex of our famed Berlin nightlife?" Wyatt asked, raising his foaming glass of beer.

After the elaborately served dinner of GI staples in Dahlem, Wyatt had bounced his brother-in-law between the wrecked facades of the Kurfürstendamm to the Neue Femina. The nightclubs' male clientele for the most part wore American officers' pinks while the German distaff side wore short, tightly belted dresses and complaisant smiles. "Fraternization" with German women was as much against regulations as thievery and black-marketeering, but there was no way to keep young men far from home separated from hungry women desperately willing to sell themselves for a meal.

"Livelier than our clubs in the British sector," Aubrey responded. Glancing at the blackened stone wall, he added, "The ambiance reminds one of the Führer Bunker."

"That's postwar Germany."

Aubrey, who had observed very little softening of Wyatt's kill-every-German line, drew a breath. "Wyatt, I need your help."

"Hey, what are brothers-in-law for?"

"Have you been out to the Grunewald?"

Abruptly Wyatt turned to stare at the next table. The contralto was now singing a medley from *Oklahoma!*, and the two boisterous Army Air Corps pilots, with their arms around a pair of vividly made-up adolescent fräuleins, had joined in, bawling, "Oh what a bee-yoo-tee-ful mo-o-orning . . ."

"Have you?" Aubrey prodded.

Wyatt, who was drinking a boilermaker, chugalugged his beer, then caught the eye of an overage waiter in shabby lederhosen, pointing down at his shot glass and the cracked stein to indicate he wished a refill. Only then did he look at Aubrey. "If you're asking whether I dropped by the house, yeah, I was there."

"Did you see any sign of Aunt Clothilde or Käthe?"

"The place is bombed out, old buddy. Uninhabitable." The flesh of Wyatt's jaw was pulled taut. "Aunt Clothilde's dead, and so's Sigi."

"God . . . How?"

"Sigi probably gave his life for the *Vaterland.* Clothilde, who knows? Maybe a raid, maybe natural causes."

"Käthe?"

"Matter of fact, I saw that li'l ole gal this month."

Aubrey jerked and his iceless gin and tonic sloshed onto the planked table. "You saw her? All these hours and you never mentioned that you saw her? Where is she? Here in Berlin?"

"Ober Tappenburg."

"Isn't that one of your detention camps?"

"You bet your ass."

"Why in God's name is she being held?"

"The usual. Further questioning regarding war crimes and Nazi leanings."

"Käthe? I never heard such rubbish! She's no Nazi."

"She didn't join the Party, but she did everything else. A wartime stint with the OKW—"

"You know as well as I do that Sigi was his uncle's aide."

"She was such a good buddy of the late lamented Adolf that he invited her to his Eagle's Nest hideaway." Wyatt ground out his cigarette viciously. "Aubrey, she admitted knowing about the camps. Not even a stabbing gesture at remorse. We were discussing Araminta's death and the only thing on her mind was me getting her sprung."

"Could you have helped her?"

"Nope."

"Did you put in a good word?"

"Nope."

Aubrey thought, *Why don't I tell him? Why don't I simply say, "She worked for us—she risked her life for us"?* But telling the truth was treason. "I don't know what happened between you, Wyatt," he said in a clipped voice. "The fact remains. She's still our cousin."

"Denazification means getting rid of Nazis just like delousing means getting rid of lice. And cousin or not, this broad is a louse."

"You bastard!" Aubrey was on his feet. "You bloody, idiotic bastard!"

At the next table the young flyers had stopped singing. The thick-necked, muscular young lieutenant pushed back his chair. Taking a step toward Aubrey, he asked, "What's that you just said to my fellow officer, you Limey prick?"

"I told this arsehole here that he's a bloody stupid bastard, and if you're too drunk to understand bloody English, then ask him to explain it."

"Take off those fucking glasses!" The pilot outweighed Aubrey by a good thirty pounds.

Without hesitation Aubrey slid his horn-rims onto the table, standing. The pilot swung a boxer's upward blow. The strong, whitened knuckles never connected with Aubrey's chin. Aubrey, moving so swiftly his actions were near invisible, stuck out his long, thin leg, tripping his assailant, jamming him into the wooden seat he himself had just vacated. Replacing his glasses, he strode around tables filled with noisy Americans and hectically gay German girls. Wyatt scratched his forehead as he watched the tall, slightly round-shouldered British officer disappear into the smoky shadows of the cellar stairwell. It was entirely possible that his late wife had been a better judge of her brother's character and wartime activities than he.

III

The thunder had faded behind the Odenwald mountains and the rain was a drizzle when Aubrey was led to the interrogation room on the second floor of the Ober Tappenburg's women's barracks. It was regulations, the short, nervous-eyed PFC said as he stationed himself inside the door, for detainees to be kept under surveillance during visits. Aubrey knew the surveillance was as much for him as for Käthe. Suspicion reigned supreme in the four occupying powers' intelligence communities, for each maintained a well-hidden covey of German agents that the others would kill to uncover. Aubrey took out a bottle of aspirin, fumbling. White tablets spilled across the floor. As he knelt to gather them, he glimpsed microphones hidden under the table.

He was swallowing a second aspirin, dry, when he heard women's footsteps.

Käthe halted at the doorway, tilting her head as if in disbelief. "Aubrey," she whispered.

He saw only her tearful smile, nothing else. Crossing the room in two swift strides, he put both arms around her. He could feel how thin she was, he could feel the beating of her heart. He was swept by a tumult of emotions—righteous anger that she was imprisoned, relief that she was alive, irrepressible joy to be holding her.

"Sorry, sir, but you and the prisoner aren't allowed to touch."

Käthe pulled him closer. "Aubrey, I heard about 'Minta, and I wanted so to write but they're strict about letters here. I'm sorry . . . sorry."

"And I'm sorry about Aunt Clothilde and Sigi," he said.

"Sir."

Worried that prolonging the embrace might go against Käthe with her captors, he pushed her gently away.

"Sir, will you take the far chair? The prisoner will face you."

After they were seated, she said in German, "How I missed you! Aubrey, all during the war, I kept hoping that you would—" She stopped as he shook his head slightly. She bit her lip for a moment, then caught on. "I kept longing to see you. And now the war's over and here you are."

"You look like a good breeze could blow you away. I don't like how thin you are."

"That's not flattering," she said with a smile. Then her face grew haggard. "Aubrey, I must get out of here. Is there any way you can arrange it?"

"It was difficult enough for me to get a pass."

"But you must know somebody who knows somebody."

"I have no influence in the American zone. Käthe, I wish I did, but I don't."

"Just for a few days? There's a little boy I need to find."

Aubrey had been schooled to maintain his facial expressions, yet for a brief instant he goggled. "A child?"

"He's five." Her voice shook. "Aubrey, I must find him."

Hers, hers, hers, he thought. *Käthe has a child. A son.* "Wyatt's the one to help you," he blurted.

"I couldn't beg him." Misery contorted her face. "Aubrey, he hates me."

"It's not you." Regaining his poise, Aubrey lied soothingly. "He's bitter. Araminta, the atrocities."

She nodded, her mouth working as she made an effort to control tears.

"What's the child's name?"

"Erich. He was adopted by a couple who live near Frankfurt."

"Let me see if there's any way I can track the adoption—"

"You can't! It's impossible. Only I can find him! I don't know his surname, but I saw the couple. *I saw them!* Please, please, it'll only take me a little while. I haven't said anything about—" She stopped. "It's so rotten being here. It has the quality of movies one sees nowadays." *Quality of movies one sees nowadays* was code for CI-4 spying activities.

"Yes, I understand."

"The weather's been calm." This meant secret. She was looking at him with tear-filled eyes, and he understood that she was trying to tell him her work would remain secret.

"It generally is at this time of year."

Then she burst out, "But, Aubrey, does everything have to be taken from me, even hope?" She bent her head and her sobs shook her thin body. He started around the table.

The guard stepped forward. "Sorry, sir, but your time's up."

His ten minutes were not up, but arguing for three extra minutes would not get Käthe released. A Wac whom he had not seen earlier came into the room to put a comforting hand on the thin, quaking shoulders.

At the door Käthe turned her tear-streaked face. "Just a couple of days, that's all," she said in English.

"I'll move heaven and earth."

FORTY-SEVEN

I

A baby?

His Käthe?

Frowning at the windshield, Aubrey didn't see the dark, dripping Odenwald forest but instead clearly visualized Käthe's early letters to the Swedish agent—the letters topped with dates between the autumn of 1939 and the spring of 1940, that freezing first winter of the war. While she had been away from Berlin acting as a translator her mail had been brief, and she had seldom mentioned anyone but female friends. He let out a sigh. She might well have been in a home for unwed mothers. Questions about the father crowded into his mind with an oppressive jealousy, yet swerving down a steep turn he accepted one irrevocable truth. Nothing could alter his trust in Käthe's essential goodness, nothing could alter his trust or his love.

II

"She must have lost over a stone, I've never seen her look so ill," Aubrey said to Major Downes. "And she's trapped in that drafty barracks."

"Couldn't be colder than here," responded the major with a rare smile. It was two evenings after Aubrey's visit to Ober Tappenburg. Having telegraphed his Mayday emergency code, he had been recalled to London. Austerity continued to rule

Britannia: the two men's breath streamed in the icy air of the Morpeth Terrace flat; they both had on coats and mufflers. "Why are they holding her?"

"Further interrogation."

"That sounds suspiciously like a ploy to force us to act."

"Ploy, sir? The Americans are completely bollixed up in their denazification program. Millions of Germans in the camps—it'll take years to question them all, much less sort out the criminals." Aubrey sneezed vehemently.

"Bless you," the major said.

"Caught a bit of a cold."

"Take care of yourself. A lot of strange germs going around over there. Our Public Health people predict the German civilian death toll this winter will be higher than during the war— and that includes the air-raid casualties."

"Precisely my point. Käthe's in a weakened state."

"We can't simply tell them to release her."

"Why not? She risked everything for us. Her family are dead, she's at the end of her tether. The least we owe her is her freedom."

"Aubrey, be reasonable."

"What's so unreasonable about trusting the Americans? All we'd need do is drop a hint to their intelligence that she worked for us."

"You know as well as I do that the OSS leaks like a sieve."

"You're turning down my request, sir?"

"What choice do I have, Aubrey?"

Aubrey's jaw set in what Araminta had called the Kingsmith clench. "Then I'll have to go to the Americans myself—to General Clay, even Eisenhower."

Major Downes stood, his good arm and neatly pinned stump pulled tightly to his sides. "You're walking the road to a court-martial."

Aubrey started to respond, then his mouth opened, his face grew red, and he went into a violent paroxysm of sneezing.

The major fished out a fresh handkerchief. When the sneezing fit ended, he said, "Aubrey, you're leading with your heart, not your head. Think for a minute. What would our move be if Washington came to us with a request to release a German agent we hadn't known existed? We'd make every effort to find out if she were part of an ultrasecret network. We'd keep her tucked away. No trial, mind you. Never a trial. On the surface she'd just be one more interned German. But we'd have our top people interrogating her. Don't you see? If we go to the Americans she'll be stuck in Ober Tappenburg for years."

Aubrey's reddened eyes were fixed on the window. Finally he said, "What if I came to you with an acceptable excuse to get her out?"

"We'd give it every consideration."

III

Aubrey had arranged to stay with Porteous. He went to Victoria station to get a taxi, but the queue was long and he decided to walk the three or so miles. A cold autumn night. The chill wind cut through his uniform coat. He was shivering so savagely by the time he reached the Bayswater Road house that he had difficulty inserting his key. Hoping a drink would thaw him, he went to the drawing room tantalus for a Scotch. His teeth clattered against the Waterford tumbler. Before he finished, he was sneezing again.

"Aubrey?" Porteous's thin old voice drifted down the staircase. "Is that you, lad?"

"Be right up, Grandfather," he called.

Maybe it was Aubrey's condition and his mood of melancholy pessimism, but Porteous—a paisley shawl around his shoulders, silvery head resting on the pillows, thick-lensed glasses neatly folded on the bedside table—appeared far frailer than when he had last seen him on V-E Day.

"Come over here near the bed," Porteous said. "Well, did you find her? Did you find my little Kate?"

"I found Käthe, yes."

"You sound a bit queer. Isn't she all right?"

"She's well."

"Thank God, thank God." Tears glimmered in the sightless

old eyes. "Mark you, in my heart I knew she was. But where is she? Why hasn't she written? How are Clothilde and Sigi?"

Aubrey was saved from relaying the plethora of bad news by another sneezing fit.

"Run along, lad, hop into bed." Porteous said. "It's enough knowing all's well with my Kate. The rest will keep until morning."

IV

Aubrey drifted between truncated nightmares. When he woke, dawn was brightening the sky beyond the curtains. As he lifted up to see the time, pains stabbed his head and chest. He fell back into the pillow.

"It's not me who's ill," he mumbled. "It's the chap in the next bed."

Neither of the maids was back in service, so Mrs. Plum, the housekeeper, lumbered up with the early-morning cups of tea. Taking one horrified glance at Aubrey's bluish lips and livid, sweating skin, she hurried downstairs as fast as her rheumatism permitted and telephoned Porteous's doctor.

Having come through six drops into Nazi territory unscathed, Aubrey had been felled by a German bug.

The diagnosis was bacterial pneumonia. Before the new wonder drug, penicillin, the odds would have been against surviving this severe a case. Even now moving the patient was a risk, so the doctor ordered an oxygen tent and sent around a nurse. After three days of shots Aubrey's temperature was down and he was coherent.

By now the nurse had two patients on her stubby, capable hands. Porteous had a bad cold. Listening to his grandfather's surprisingly robust sneezes, Aubrey lay very still, his eyes thoughtful. After the nurse went belowstairs for a chat and a cup of tea with Mrs. Plum, he disobeyed the medical injunction to remain in bed. Edging slowly down the stairs, he tottered to the telephone chair, his breath coming in a peculiar, chesty rumble as he dialed the major's number.

"Aubrey?" Major Downes said. "Is that you? Your doctor told me you wouldn't be out of bed until the end of the week."

"Sir, I've thought of a way to get her out, at least for a holiday."

V

"Wyatt, Aubrey here."

"We have a rotten connection." Wyatt had to shout, and the echo reverberated in his ear. "You sound like hell."

"I've had pneumonia. . . . Grandfather's caught it."

"Jesus. At his age? That's a rough go."

"The doctor's not giving out much hope."

"I'll arrange for a leave."

"Wyatt, he wants to see Käthe."

The humming on the long-distance wires sounded like a swarm of bees.

"Our people have talked to your people. It's been agreed that if she has a suitable escort she'll be permitted a compassionate parole."

"Grandfather . . ." Incomprehensible words.

Aubrey ignored the faraway rumbling. "She always was his favorite. He's longing to see her one last time. You're in charge of bringing her over and taking her back."

FORTY-EIGHT

I

The Army Air Corps maintained an abbreviated and slovenly transport schedule around the American Sector.

At the temporary buildings of much-bombed Tempelhof airport, the Red Cross served doughnuts and coffee, but Wyatt, awaiting the plane from Frankfurt, decided he needed something stronger. In the bleak Quonset hut that served as a bar, he ordered a double Scotch on the rocks, his expression brooding, his thoughts on the time Käthe had picked him up at the Lehrte station, so proud of her ability to drive that old Austrian heap. In those days her face had been as mysteriously pure as Botticelli's Venus. God, how crazy he had been about her! It hadn't mattered that swastikas were stamped all over her slim, graceful body, he'd been out of his mind crazy for her. The night in Garmisch-Partenkirchen after he'd first made love to her he'd felt exalted, as if he had participated in some holy rite.

One of the young GIs fed the jukebox and "Dig You Later" blared. Gulping his drink, Wyatt went outside to scan the overcast sky. Eventually the battered Flying Fortress landed and military passengers stepped down the aluminum ladder. He was wondering whether she'd missed the flight when a pair of burly military police emerged. Käthe followed. Immediately after her came another hefty MP. Surrounded by her guards, holding back strands of pale hair whipped by the propellors' wind, she looked entirely too fragile—breakable, even. *It's those godawful clothes,* Wyatt decided.

He was handed an outsize official envelope with the detainee's papers, and the trio of MPs hurried across the airfield in the direction of the Quonset bar.

"How is Grandpa?" she asked. Her eyes were reddened: obviously she had been crying some on the flight from Frankfurt. He wished she hadn't wept; those reddened eyes smudged his official portrait of the family Nazi.

"He can't be in great shape if they've sprung a dangerous war criminal." He could hear the flatness of his attempt at humor. "Since Aubrey lined all this up I haven't had any bulletins, so I guess the sweet old guy's holding his own."

"That's good," she murmured.

The fatigue-clad ground crew, unloading freight from what had been the bomb bays, darted stares, then bent their heads together, yakking and snickering, doubtless about the officer and his illegal fraternazi.

"Listen," Wyatt said. "There's a minimum of three and a half hours before we take off. What say we head over to the Tiergarten and get you something new to wear?"

She gave him an odd, hopefully appraising glance. After a lengthy pause she said, "Wyatt, I do appreciate all you're doing."

II

The Tiergarten's bustling black market, the center of commerce in Berlin, was located between the burned-out husk of the Reichstag and the lambasted Brandenburg Gate. The pitiless final battle had been fought here in the once beautiful park. Tacked to the burned tree stumps were warnings printed in English, Russian, and French that it was a criminal offense to sell or buy PX or NAAFI goods.

As soon as Wyatt and Käthe left the jeep, they were besieged by cries of *"Zigaretten!"* Some people bartered goods for goods, a few counted out Occupation marks or foreign currencies, but for the most part the bargaining was done in Germany's new medium of exchange, cigarettes. The victors held out packs of Lucky Strikes, Camels, Craven "A" 's, Gauloises, even the terrible-odored Russian cigarettes. The defeated stood bundled with layers of clothing or sat beside a variety of merchandise that ranged from eighteenth-century landscapes, bits of antique Meissen that somehow had survived a thousand air raids, and heirloom jewelry to Leica cameras and battered household objects. A blind veteran held open his Wehrmacht tunic to display a Knight's Cross with Oak Leaves. Two shrewd-eyed little girls—they couldn't have been more than eight—haggled over the price of a diamond ring with a Russian colonel. The frenzied commerce was not slowed by a cruising jeep with its four military police, French, American, British, and Russian.

A shivering woman held up a baby's christening dress. "Handmade lace," she said to Käthe. *"Zweihundert Mark."*

"No, thank you," Käthe murmured.

The woman followed them a few steps. "The silk's excellent quality. *Bitte?"*

Käthe fished in her pocket, coming up with a pack of Camels. "I'm sorry, but this is all I have. Will it do?"

The woman gave a sigh of relief, nodding. As they moved on, Käthe folded the infant's dress into her purse.

Wyatt cocked an eyebrow. "A bit small for you."

"One of the Wacs in Ober Tappenburg gave me the cigarettes. As far as I can tell, the rate of exchange is five dollars a pack. That woman was well brought up, she never would have taken so valuable a gift."

"It won't work," he said.

"What?"

"Putting me on the defensive."

"Wyatt, don't ever think I'm ungrateful. You're being very generous, taking me to see Grandpa, buying me clothes. I'm just not very good at kowtowing."

"Hey, there you go again."

"Oh, my God!" she cried. "Can't you see what this park is now? They should put photographs of before and after in every school primer with the caption *This Is What War Does."*

"Doubtless you've forgotten," he said, "but the Tiergarten was not such a fantastically happy place for some of us."

Her downcast eyes and what he perceived as her flicker of

shame gave him no satisfaction. Turning, he craned his neck. Taller than most of the four thousand or so bargainers, he spotted a blonde holding open her fur coat to display a beige suit. The outfit was far too large for Käthe and he should have let her decide if it could be belted to fit. He was incapable, though, of transacting the deal under her humiliated, reddened gaze.

"Wait here," he said, pointing to the plinth of a fallen statue.

"Wyatt . . ." She hesitated, apparently searching for words.

"For once don't argue, okay?" he said. "Just sit."

She perched on the marble.

"Don't move. Be back in a jiffy."

He moved around swirling knots of buyers and sellers to the blonde, a hard-faced Valkyrie who shed her fur and the jacket. Below her suit she wore a pretty pink sweater and skirt which were far smaller. He bought the outfit and when the blonde took them off, he bought the dark silk afternoon dress she had on underneath. He paid her what she asked in American dollars. Without bargaining the transaction didn't take long.

But when he returned to the ruined statue, Käthe no longer sat there. She wasn't in any of the nearby groups.

Climbing on the broken plinth, he had a view of the crowd. With a grunt of relief he spotted her in the direction of the Landwehr Canal. He shoved his way through the crowd.

It wasn't Käthe but a plain teenager with the same beautiful hair. He thrust the clothes at the startled girl.

III

". . . and then the bitch disappears!" Wyatt shouted over the long-distance line. "Just takes off!"

Aubrey, wearing a too-short dressing gown from his school days, leaned against the wall, gripping the receiver.

"Gone?"

"Vanished."

Why didn't it occur to me? Aubrey asked himself. The deal he'd struck with Major Downes had been intended to give Käthe a holiday, a little time to recuperate. The penicillin must have dulled his mind. He had seen the desperation in her eyes. How could he not have considered she would make a run for it? Even drugged, he should have known that she would search across the tormented German landscape for a five-year-old called Erich, surname unknown.

"When?"

"Three fucking hours ago. Since then I've been scouring the Tiergarten with a couple of MPs. The miserable cunt! Not a care about Grandfather!"

"She's heading toward Frankfurt am Main."

"Frankfurt? What sort of bullshit is that? She just came from fucking Frankfurt."

"She's looking for . . . somebody."

"Yeah, some hotshot Nazi bastard she's been shacked up with all during the war."

"Wyatt, don't waste your time looking for her with a man, she's not with a man."

"For once open your goddamn eyes about her. She's in Berlin with him. They have a grapevine, these Nazis. Christ, I could shoot myself, letting you talk me into playing her patsy!"

"You've got to find her."

"Damn right! It's my ass that's in a sling."

"She's on her way to Frankfurt. She's going through the Russian sector. You know how they treat German women—"

The line had gone dead.

FORTY-NINE

I

A noise like the beating wings of a great formation of snow geese woke Aubrey. During the night the tyrannical north wind had torn the curtain nailed across the glassless window and the brocade was twisting and flapping. Three Russian officers snored with undisturbed gusto in the big double bed. Aubrey had been dealt the hard pallet on the floor—and was lucky to have it. Eighty-five percent of the buildings in the outlying Potsdam suburb had been destroyed and this was the only surviving hotel. Beyond the swooping fabric a hint of light showed. He peered at his watch. Seven thirty-five!

Käthe had been missing nearly three days. She was without papers in a country where ration books and IDs determined one's right to survive.

Pushing aside the tabletop that served as a door, he picked his way around the Soviet noncoms, men and women, who sprawled in the corridor. The desk clerk explained that because the Russian guests slept late, the dining room did not open until eight-thirty; however, if the captain went into the kitchen the cooks would prepare him breakfast. Impatience rode Aubrey but he decided to take the time. Food alleviated the spells of light-headedness that plagued him. Gulping down what was set before him, he used the hotel's only functioning telephone. It took an hour to get through to Frankfurt and the headquarters of USFET—United States Forces, European Theater. Second Lieutenant Robby Lear, his American liaison, told him that the American Captain Kingsmith had just called in. So far, nothing. Though Aubrey hadn't spoken to Wyatt since that furious long-distance conversation, he knew that by now his brother-in-law, having blown off steam, would be giving the search his all. But in Berlin. And Käthe was trying to get to Frankfurt.

Putting up the collar of his uniform topcoat against the wind, Aubrey left the hotel. A loud clinking rang in the street. A line of rubble women, *trümmerfrauen,* were lugging bricks to other *trümmerfrauen* who sat with small mallets pounding away the mortar to make the bricks reusable. Aubrey directed his keen but undetectable observation to the women, then to the bundled-up female passengers bumping along on the horse-drawn flatbed truck that served as a tram. None remotely resembled Käthe.

An elderly man pedaling a bicycle rickshaw called out, "Take you anyplace in Potsdam for three cigarettes." Being propelled by another human being went against Aubrey's grain. He was ready to say no when he saw that the man wasn't so old, about his own age, and there was a desperate gleam in the deep-sunk eyes. Before Aubrey climbed into the makeshift vehicle, he held out his snapshots of Käthe, taken in the summer of 1939.

The German whistled. "What a stunner! No, I haven't seen her. But if it's a blonde you want, I know beautiful, clean girls—"

"She's my cousin."

The old-young face pulled into cynical lines of disbelief, but he nodded politely. "Why not try the *bahnhof*? At all hours there's a mob trying to get a train."

Since no German in any zone was permitted to move more than six kilometers without a travel permit, Käthe wouldn't be attempting the journey by rail, but would be trekking by shank's mare.

"Take me to the Schönebeck road." Schönebeck was on the most obvious route for anyone traveling to Frankfurt.

"You haven't been in the Soviet zone long, have you? There's no buses anymore."

"I'll get a ride," Aubrey said.

"You'll walk, Captain, you'll walk."

A ragged sentry wearing a Mongolian dog-fur hat demanded to see the British officer's travel pass. Aubrey produced an excellent forgery made by a survivor of his Berlin network and was let through. He had passed another barrier and was well into open country when it began to sprinkle. Just then a Mercedes with fresh-painted red stars on its punished khaki frame pulled up beside him, and a round-faced lieutenant smiled out the window, gesturing that he'd give Aubrey a lift. The lieutenant communicated in broken German that he was Sergei Vasilievich Novikov, engineer, from the city of Minsk. Aubrey, using his halting Russian, introduced himself, then showed his photographs of the old sweetheart for whom he was searching. Novikov dug out a bottle of vodka, insisting they toast Aubrey's old love, his own wife in Minsk, his girlfriend, Fräulein Brigid. They drank to Aubrey's excellent grasp of Russian, to Stalin, Churchill, Tolstoy, Shakespeare, Lenin, and Queen Victoria, toasting until Aubrey's head was spinning and the round Slavic face had turned crimson.

II

Käthe had avoided a road barrier by detouring through a small wood and was back on the highway to Schönebeck when the fine rain started. Plodding through the drizzle, she brooded about Porteous, praying that he was recovering. She also arraigned herself for betraying Wyatt's trusting custodianship. But what choice had there been? An opening to find Erich had been given to her and she'd snatched it.

The clouds had darkened to a mottled brown and she realized that for some time she had seen no horse carts piled with belongings or families shoving possessions and young children in a wheelbarrow. Soon it would be curfew. At all costs she must avoid being picked up by the police: with no travel pass or identification papers, she'd land in jail. Peering ahead for a barn or outbuilding to spend the night, she didn't hear the engine. A dented Mercedes was barreling from one side of the road to the other as if the driver were drunk. She dodged out of the way, sliding into the ditch. Ankle deep in the chill mud, she used her remaining strength to silently curse all drivers, particularly Russians.

The Mercedes had squealed to a halt and was erratically backing up. Anticipating the call that haunted her nightmares, *Komm Frau,* she was too wearily desolate to care.

"Käthe, is it really you?"

I'm hallucinating, she thought. The twilit gloom prevented her from seeing into the car, but wasn't it flatly impossible that the British voice could belong to Aubrey? Still, hadn't he appeared at other impossible times?

"Oh, God, what a marvelous people the Russians!" Käthe had just returned to the bedroom with her hair turbaned in a towel, her throat rosy from the bath, swathed in a bright green dressing gown that belonged to the lieutenant's housekeeper-mistress. "I'd forgotten the sheer heaven of hot water—that's the first real soak I've had in years—since the house was bombed. No, since before the war. During the war we weren't allowed more than two inches of tepid water. Maybe I'll go downstairs and kiss darling Lieutenant Novikov."

"He and Brigid are otherwise occupied until dinner."

"Then I'll kiss you." Humming a waltz from *Der Rosenkavalier,* she whirled around the room, planting a kiss in the air above his forehead. Candles flickered as she continued to sing and swoop. When the turban came loose, she bent to comb the long, wet strands. After a minute she asked soberly, "You're positive Grandpa's all right?"

"Käthe, I've told you ten times. He only had a cold. I came up with pneumonia to get you a holiday from Ober Tappenburg. Who dreamed you'd make a dash for it?"

"You're too honorable for such suspicions." She paused. "What are the chances that Brigid would loan me something to wear?"

"She hung the things inside the wardrobe. Novikov's orders."

"He's a king—no, a czar."

There was the sound of water running in the bathroom, then loud singing, "Volga, Volga, you're my mother. . . ."

"Didn't you say he was otherwise occupied? Damn, I was just going back in there to dress."

"I'll close my eyes and look the other way."

Going to the window, he took off his glasses, blowing to clean the lenses. When he turned, Käthe had her back to him and was wearing the flannel petticoat. Between its straps he saw an intricate pattern of shiny white tissue.

He couldn't control his sharp, horrified gasp. "Oh, Jesus Christ. . . . Darling, what happened to you?"

"My back, you mean?" She yanked on the woolen blouse, hastily buttoning it. "Those lovely scars saved my life."

"How?"

"Instead of killing me, they beat me."

"Käthe, did the Gestapo or the Abwehr discover you were working for us?"

"No." She sighed. "I was hauled in for being Sigi's sister."

"Sigi?"

"He and his uncle were in the July Plot."

"But I got hold of your American Military Government report. You didn't say a word about it when you were being denazified. A brother in on the July Plot would do wonders in your favor."

"Favor?" She stared bleakly down at her gap-toothed comb. "Sigi was tortured to death in the Gestapo basement."

"Those monsters!"

"Just before he died he somehow managed to sneak out a letter on toilet paper. The next day they came for me. They killed Mother, I don't know when, but they left her body, and the rats . . ." Käthe shuddered. "I buried her on the day of the cease-fire."

"Where were you until then?" he asked gently.

In a purposefully matter-of-fact tone she sketched in the camouflaged SS center, her escape, her meetings with the gimlet-eyed SS *untersturmführer,* her sentence to vanish into *nacht und nebel.* The prison train. The beating that saved her life, the sound of machine gunning. "Aubrey, please, no more questions." She pulled the comb savagely through her wet, tangled hair. "I can't talk about it."

III

At supper Novikov made numerous toasts. Russian-style courtesy obligated Aubrey to reciprocate. After the two men had drained the brandy bottle, the host noisily bussed Aubrey's cheeks, roaring, "Comrade, take your sweetheart back to bed."

Upstairs, Aubrey closed the door. It had been a long day, he was having one of his spells of light-headedness—and besides, he was quite squiffed. The Jesus above the bed seemed to be writhing on His crucifix. Stretching out below Him, Aubrey closed his eyes.

He felt Käthe unknotting his tie.

"Tell me about the child," he said.

She stopped tugging on the tie and went to the window.

"Käthe?" he prompted.

"He's mine," she said. "Born in a Lebensborn home."

"You telling me you had an affair with—?"

"An SS officer," she said. "Yes."

"Rot." The liquor had vanquished Aubrey's reserve. "You're telling me utter rot."

"He was an old school friend of Sigi's. Otto Groener."

"Käthe, I've spent endless hours thinking about this. The child was born while you were on that so-called translating job, sometime in spring of 1940. He's Wyatt's, isn't he?"

There was an outburst of "Volga, Volga," accompanied by feminine giggles, then the door across the corridor slammed shut. Käthe, at the window with her back to Aubrey, hadn't stirred. So still was she that her silhouette might have been carved from the same oak as the crucifix.

"Why in God's name didn't you tell him?" Aubrey asked.

After a long pause she said in a dead voice, "By the time I realized, he was already involved with other girls."

"He'd have taken you to the States. Married you."

"He's never trusted me."

"What are you saying? That he wouldn't have accepted the

child as his? Käthe, you don't realize this, but you're the most wonderful woman there is. I've loved you forever." *God, how drunk am I, blabbing this?* "Nothing could make me stop adoring you or believing in you."

"Oh, Aubrey, there's so much about Wyatt you don't know."

"I know one thing. He was insane about you."

"When he showed up at Ober Tappenburg, I was happy. Beyond happy. For a few moments the whole rotten war was wiped out. But then I saw his face. Aubrey, the other side of love is hate."

"He's bitter. 'Minta. The camps."

"I'm never going to tell him."

"About the boy? That's not reasonable."

"He'd believe I was lying. Lying about my baby. And I couldn't bear that." She took a ragged breath. "Aubrey, I'm not like I was. It's as if I've been crowded to the edge of a steep cliff. One little push and I'll fall. Fall forever."

"Maybe someday he'll accept—"

"I'll *never* tell him." Her voice rose. "Never!"

"Hush, it's all right. We'll find your little boy."

"You'll help me?"

"Need you ask?"

"You will?"

"I'm not leaving your side until you're together with him."

"Thank you," she said, and came to sit on the edge of the bed. "You won't tell Wyatt?"

"Not if you don't want me to."

"Promise?" She touched his sleeve.

"Käthe, I want you, darling, want you with me for the rest of my life. Now, why on God's destroyed earth would I give Wyatt any sort of information that might bring him back to you?"

"Say it."

"I promise, darling." He pressed his own cheek to her wet cheek, inhaling the scent of her tears and fresh-washed, silky hair. She had said she wasn't the same, but he didn't need to be told. For her the six years of warfare had been years of danger, of painful attrition and excruciating loneliness, of loss. He thought of her desperate, single-handed crusade to regain her child, her pride, her courage, the code of honor that had prevented her from saving herself by telling the Americans about CI-4. As he put his arms around the fragile body an unendurable tenderness spread through him.

He brushed his mouth lightly on hers.

Her lips parted softly, and she allowed the kiss to continue. Emboldened by brandy, his heart galloping, he drew her down onto the deep indent of the bed. He pressed both palms between her shoulders, where the woolen blouse covered the scars, running his hands tenderly down the delicate curves of her back. How often had he dreamed of holding her like this, of physically manifesting his love?

Then she tensed, pulling away. Though the sagging mattress made it difficult, she was no longer touching him anywhere.

"Käthe?" he whispered with such transparent supplication that additional words were unnecessary.

"Dearest Aubrey," she responded with the saddest smile. "My very dearest cousin."

He turned so she couldn't see the tears that had sprung to his eyes. "Sorry," he muttered. "Too much brandy."

He slept on the floor a second night.

IV

They were wakened before five. Novikov, walloping on the door, bawled that he had just received orders from a Party bigwig to send a staff car to Frankfurt am Main.

As the ungainly Russian-made limousine bounced through the dark countryside, Käthe leaned in her corner and fell back asleep. Aubrey, his expression abstracted, stared out the window as the first faint silver spread and redness tinted the clouds. The sun had risen when Käthe awoke. They opened the food basket Novikov's girlfriend had supplied, taking out thickly buttered bread, salted sprats, and a thermos of jam-sweetened tea.

"I've been planning this out," he said softly, with a significant glance at the driver's back. Even taking into consideration the unlikely possibility that the good-natured, hard-drinking

Novikov had arranged for a driver who was an NKVD agent fluent in English, the racketing engine would have precluded eavesdropping. Nevertheless CI-4 had engraved caution in Aubrey's brain cells. "I'm in the American zone surveying what's salvageable of German ordnance. You're Miss Catherine Osmond, one of our civilian staff, my secretary."

"I won't ask how you'll get the required papers." She smiled at him over the thermos cup. The harsh early-morning light showed the earth-colored shadows beneath his glasses and the way that his uniform collar stood away from his neck as if he had dropped a lot of weight quickly. "Aubrey, you're the one who had pneumonia, aren't you?"

He shrugged deprecatingly. "A few hypodermics of penicillin and hey presto. Fit as a fiddle."

"You look positively dreadful. You ought to be taking it easy. Not having me inveigle you into going AWOL to tramp around Germany."

With another meaningful glance at the blocklike back of their driver's head, he whispered, "My orders *are* to tramp around looking for my people under whatever cover I can invent. And as for inveiglers, you're the one who needs to watch out. Käthe, I wasn't all that drunk last night. I meant what I said."

Flushing, she was filled with self-recriminations for letting that embrace continue—but, oh, it had been so very long since anyone had held her with love. "That's why dragging you into this is rotten."

"Wild horses wouldn't keep me away. Now tell me why you're so positive the boy's in Frankfurt."

"Not actually in Frankfurt. The parents had a large country house, Groener said."

"Groener? Oh, Sigi's charming friend. You never mentioned you'd kept up with him."

She gave a shudder. "The Christmas the house was bombed, when you were here, I ran into him again, a party up at Garmisch-Partenkirchen. Remember? I told you I knew someone involved in the *vergeltungswaffe*. Groener was in charge of the slave labor."

Aubrey looked out the window. A shawled woman guided a

plow. How had Käthe come to choose this blood-handed SS officer as stand-in father? "Righto," he said. "Let's assume he's still in the vicinity. How'll we find him?"

"Everybody has a ration card."

"I already discarded that," Aubrey murmured gently. "You said you didn't know his surname."

"I'll sieve through the records for Erichs born on April tenth, 1940!"

"Käthe, even if the Americans let us do that, and it's a large if, searching through all their files is impossible."

"What do you think *I* did all during the war?"

Aubrey stared out at the bleak Brandenburg farmland. Her shrill voice warned him to argue no more. He didn't consider inquiring into her plans if in this maelstrom—the greatest mass migration in human history, as Downes had put it—by some miracle they found a five-and-a-half-year-old adopted boy named Erich. From personal experience he knew that, in order not to crack during a mission, the single-minded focus must be on accomplishment, and not what lay beyond.

He, however, had already determined that they must kidnap the boy and spirit him out of Germany. As for Käthe, either she could disappear with her child into the Latin American countries that asked no questions of Germans on the run, or she could send her son to England while she waited to be sorted out by the Military Government. A woman befriended by Hitler and cleared to see the top military secrets of the Third Reich would draw a long prison term.

Over my dead body, Aubrey thought, his eyes narrowed.

V

Set on high ground above the Main River and the ruins of Frankfurt, the massive, seven-story I. G. Farbenindustrie building had regularly spaced, jutting wings that contained over a thousand rooms. The odds against such a vast structure surviving intact were so astronomical that jokes centered around supposed orders from Eisenhower to all bombardiers to steer clear because he had an eye on it for USFET Headquarters. Aubrey was one of the stream of uniformed men hurrying up the cement path that bisected the broad slope of lawn where German gardeners knelt clipping the yellow autumn grass. Paratroopers stood guard, thin sunlight catching sparks on the nickel plate of their bayonets, highlighting their parachute-silk scarves and the white shoelaces that crisscrossed their boots. Aubrey's papers were unquestioningly accepted. He asked directions for the office of Second Lieutenant Robby Lear, with whom he'd been communicating about Käthe.

Lear, with his pink cheeks and plushy brown crew cut, might just have graduated from high school. "Jesus, what a night!" He grinned, propping his shoes on the gray metal desk that nearly filled the cubicle. "So you made it through the Russki zone. Find the German cousin?"

"Not a trace."

"The other Captain Kingsmith, our guy that is, called in yesterday with the same sad song—my nose tells me he's been heavily reamed out. When he heard you were on the way to check in, he suggested I get photos from you so the local MPs could be on the lookout."

"Sorry, but I don't have a picture of her," Aubrey lied.

"No sweat. The way I see it, what are the odds she'd stick her nose anywhere near Ober Tappenburg?"

"Right you are. Actually I'm not here about her." Aubrey opened his briefcase for papers with Supreme Commander-in-Chief's letterheads. "These are my orders."

The young lieutenant thumbed through the sheaf, touching the signature: *Dwight D. Eisenhower.* "Fact-finding mission, huh, sir?" he said in an awed tone. "I'll have my sergeant give a jingle to the motor pool and make the arrangements for a car." Then he relaxed, winking. "A sedan with a big backseat for you and Miss Osmond."

"I'd be most grateful for the largest seat you can spare. The lady's a dragon with terrible breath." Aubrey paused while Lear guffawed, then went on casually, "If it's all right with you, I'd like to scour about a bit for this German girl I knew up at Oxford. Married a doctor from around here, but damned if I can remember the bloke's name. If you would arrange for me to have a glance at the ration card registrations . . . ?"

"No problem, no problem at all. But talk about needles in a haystack! Millions of Krauts have crammed into Württemberg-Baden and Greater Hesse, our Western District."

"She was a good sort and, well, you know how it is. We had a little fling. Maybe she needs help."

"You bet your life she does. Jesus! No food, no medical supplies, no fuel, not a damn building intact for housing. What a fucking jolly winter this is going to be." The lieutenant's boyish brow creased briefly, then the white smile showed again. "My sergeant'll type up a request."

FIFTY

I

A week later Käthe and Aubrey were eating lunch in Offenbach, a leather-manufacturing town up the Main River some ten miles from Frankfurt. The cavernous, arched restaurant was almost empty—Americans could get far better food in their clubs, and the locals couldn't afford to eat out. It was, of course, unheated. Käthe wore her overcoat draped over her shoulders. She had returned Novikov's girlfriend's clothes on their arrival in Frankfurt, when Aubrey had miraculously produced this prewar three-piece costume with Harrods labels. In the gray tweeds, a sweater of a meltingly pretty shade of powder blue, and pearl beads, Käthe looked county English. The table of British officers kept darting her glances of homesick appreciation while the pair of French civilians in the corner ogled her with straightforward, admiring lust.

The *Rippchen mit Sauerkraut* was tasty enough despite the Argentine canned corned-beef that stood in for smoked pork chops, yet after a few listless mouthfuls, Käthe handed her plate to Aubrey. After demurring that she ought to eat, he fell to with all the hunger of a recovering convalescent. Käthe gazed out at the rain-dappled river. On the opposite bank a cape-swathed fisherwoman was reeling in her line to display a long strand of water weeds. Käthe sighed.

During the past week she herself had been fishing up useless weeds at the local Military Government headquarters within the circle of towns they had drawn around Frankfurt. They had found ration files for three Erichs born on April 10, 1940. The father of the first was a Lutheran minister executed for anti-Nazi activities, the next was a twin, and the third's mother had told them that her husband gave his life in France before the boy was born—*Poor Willi never saw his only son.* This morning in Offenbach, the last remaining town, they had combed the filing cabinets. Unsuccessfully.

"I didn't realize how much I was counting on finding him here," Käthe said, as if they had been carrying on a conversation.

Aubrey placed his knife and fork neatly across the top of his empty plate. "Everybody in Germany has shifted around," he consoled.

Käthe, who until now had refused to discuss the possibility that Erich might not be in the area, clutched at the straw. "You're right! Naturally they've moved. What Party bigwig would stay in a village where anybody who carried a grudge might turn him in? I'll bet they're back in Frankfurt."

"They could be anywhere," he said, mentally kicking himself for raising her hopes. He himself had become more and more convinced that the little boy had been killed in a bombing raid or fallen prey to one of the routine childhood diseases that malnutrition made fatal.

"The Frankfurt files are the obvious place to begin."

"Käthe, you can't go back. By now every MP in the city will have a mimeographed picture of you."

"Any photo'll be from England and positively creaking with age." She was on her feet. "Aubrey, do hurry up and pay. We can get going this afternoon."

Still protesting, Aubrey followed her to the motor-pool Mercedes. He was inserting the ignition key as a black-painted Kübelwagen—the German equivalent of a jeep—swerved into the wet courtyard.

Käthe made a sound halfway between a gasp and a grunt of pain. She was gaping at the potbellied American colonel and the short, well-built German with smooth blond hair as they left the car and trotted across the rainswept cobbles.

"What's wrong?" Aubrey asked.

In a strangled tone, she whispered, "It's him. . . . Groener." She reached for the Mercedes door handle.

II

Aubrey leaned across the seat to grip her wrist. "Stay where you are!"

Struggling to free herself, she hissed, "He knows the parents' surname!"

Sheltered by the peaked entry, Groener took his hands from the pockets of his well-tailored topcoat, spreading them in a gesture to indicate size. Aubrey hadn't visualized him as vigorously handsome. The two men disappeared into the restaurant.

Käthe turned on Aubrey. "Can't you see? *I must confront him.*" Her eyes seemed flattened. "He's my only real chance to find my baby."

"I couldn't agree more. But think, Käthe. What's the obvious reason for an American officer to be fraternizing in this outpost?"

After a moment she said, "A black-market deal."

"Exactly. Groener'll say anything to get rid of you. What we'll do is sit tight until they come out, then follow until he's alone."

Her eyelids fluttered, then she nodded reluctantly.

He released her arm. "I'll park behind that hedge so we can't be seen," he said. "Käthe, if I'm to be of any help, you'll need to tell me all about the gentleman."

Under his questioning she dredged up her memories of Groener. The other lunchers left, then the staff. Aubrey neither flinched nor commiserated, and this enabled her to speak about the rape and those misleading spots of blood on the leather couch. The rain fell more softly. Finally Groener and the colonel came out, thrusting their heads forward as they hurried through the fine, penetrating drizzle to the Kübelwagen.

Aubrey stayed well behind the Kübelwagen as Groener drove toward Frankfurt. Headquarters had its own generator.

Because of the gray weather the rows of windows blazed with lights so that the vast building seemed a celestial beacon floating above the wet ruins. In places the city's destruction was so complete that there were no streets and they bounced on depressions between hills of rubble. The road along the Main had been cleared, and here the Kübelwagen sped along, halting briefly on the Mainkai near the pontoon bridge so the potbellied colonel could get out. Alone, Groener followed detour signs. The surviving hotels around the *hauptbahnhof*—the main railroad station—were used as billets and the square in front of the terminal's battered, grandiose arches swarmed with American uniforms and khaki-painted vehicles. Käthe held her breath, expecting Groener to stop and conduct further business. Instead, he continued.

The cram of traffic swallowed up the jeeplike vehicle.

"We've lost him." She sighed.

Aubrey ignored her. Leaning forward, squinting beyond the windshield wipers, he remained in the twin lines that bumped over mortar holes toward the Main River. The two large trucks immediately ahead of them turned. Once again she saw the Kübelwagen. Weak with relief, she gazed out the window. The rain had ceased and the river seemed covered with a slick, dark-gray varnish. Road signs, all in English, informed them that they were en route to Höchst, which was a manufacturing town. The highway carried a good deal of traffic, lessening the chances that Groener would be aware they were tailing him. In Höchst, Groener turned left at a pair of medieval half-timbered houses standing amid the devastation. In the empty ruins of the side street Aubrey fell farther back.

"Look out!" he cried, jamming on the brakes.

The Kübelwagen had stopped. The headlights went out. They were too far away to see more than Groener's outline in the dusk as he moved into the shadows of a large flat-roofed building.

Aubrey unbuttoned his khaki overcoat to display a webbing belt and shoulder holster. The planes of his thin face showing prominently in the dusk, he checked his Webley service revolver. Käthe watched somberly. At Ober Tappenburg she had heard boasts of husbands, sweethearts, brothers, who were with the Werewolves, that underground organization of Nazis on the ready for an opportunity to bring back the New Order.

III

Allied Control Authority posters of concentration-camp scenes were pasted across the cracked, fire-blackened brick walls. Every window was boarded up. In peacetime Käthe would have considered the warehouse abandoned. Nowadays any premises still standing, no matter what the structural damage, was utilized.

Aubrey vaulted onto the dock, squatting to lend her a hand. They hurried past gargantuan doors used for unloading trucks. Aubrey knocked on a normal-sized door. There was no response.

Käthe hammered her fist on the splintering wood.

Finally a man's voice shouted, "We're closed. Come back Monday."

"I have *geschäfte mit* your boss," Aubrey called in pidgin German.

The door creaked open. A tough-faced man with a growth of stubble peered through the gloom at them.

"What's the trouble, Loock?" Groener's voice inquired from within.

"Herr Direktor, it's an *Engländer,* and he's got a blonde with him."

Rapid footsteps sounded. It was impossible to see him but he could see them. "Käthe!" he said in a shocked tone. "Käthe?" His voice took on a speculative note with his third repetition. "Käthe."

Facing her enemy at long last exhilarated her. Uncertainties dropped away. She felt immortal, strong. "Yes, I've found you," she said.

"Loock," Groener said, "get yourself a beer."

"What if you need help, Herr Schwägermann? I'm not thirsty."

"Take a piss, then. Do whatever you want. Just get out of here."

Darting a sullen glance at the interlopers, the man jumped from the dock with the practiced agility of a well-trained soldier. Aubrey took Käthe's arm, and they went inside toward Groener's voice.

IV

Within the cavernous warehouse a faintly lit open door showed a small room had been constructed of raw plyboard. Other than this cube nothing could be seen. However, the heavy sweetness of dried figs that mingled with a tainted odor like spoiled meat indicated the storage of black-market food. Groener led the way to the makeshift office. Two candles stood on the cluttered worktable beside a telephone—civilian telephones were an unheard-of luxury in postwar Germany. In the shadows Käthe glimpsed a stack of flattish boxes red-printed PENICILLIN.

Groener immediately threw the past into the open. "Nothing like my swank quarters in Prinz-Albrechtstrasse, eh, Käthe?" he asked. "Sit down, both of you, sit down."

Aubrey pulled out a chair for Käthe but remained standing, his hands clasped loosely behind him, his thin legs apart, a military at-ease position.

Groener sat at the desk, showing uneven teeth in his cocky grin. "So, Captain? You told Loock you had business?"

"Groener—" Aubrey started.

"It's Schwägermann now. Let me guess why you're here. You've heard about my game and you want a bit of what Amis call 'the action,' isn't that it? So you've brought your trump card. Käthe. Well, Captain, don't expect too large a cut. This isn't your zone. And my connections at headquarters go all the way to the top."

"Your black-market operation doesn't interest me. A little information is all I want."

Groener's smile faded. "One rule goes with me. I never deal against the Amis."

"Nothing to do with them. My cousin wants to know about—"

"Cousin, pah!" Groener interrupted. "You've got yourself a pretty blond *schatzi*—Käthe warms your bed."

"You're well aware that Fräulein Kingsmith's father was English, Groener, so why should an English cousin be such a strange pill to swallow?"

Groener eyed Aubrey thoughtfully. "Forgive me, Captain Kingsmith," he said after a pause. "I'm not normally forgetful or stupid. But Käthe has that effect on a man."

"Fräulein Kingsmith wishes to know what happened to the child born at Villa Haug in April of 1940."

Groener's sharp inhalation sucked at the candle flames and enormous shadows danced across the plywood walls. "So you told him about our boy, Käthe," he reproached.

"Where is he?" Aubrey asked.

Groener shifted the candlesticks toward them so that his face was obscured. "One of your brave bombardiers dumped his load on a Bavarian farm. My wife, my little Otto, my Adolf, were killed." The heavy shoulders were slumped. "I have only this child. To be absolutely frank, I've been mulling in my mind whether I should find him and get him back."

"It's as you say." Aubrey used a conversational tone. "There are certain Americans who have a vested interest in not seeing you exposed as a war criminal—"

"I served my country, and just as honorably as you served yours, Captain Kingsmith."

"At that party in Berlin," Käthe said hoarsely, "I heard you and Hannalore's father talking about slave labor. You'd end up in the dock at Nuremburg."

"On what evidence? The word of a woman involved with the OKW against the word of a decent, denazified German?"

Aubrey had taken out a small leather memo pad. "They wouldn't believe Käthe. But from where I sit I can see a great many questions about Herr Schwägermann and Sturmbannführer Groener. We're talking about an investigation, a full-scale CIC investigation."

"Is this blackmail?"

"Just give us the child's surname, and where he is."

"That's all?" Unhappiness etched Groener's voice. "You're asking me to give up my son."

"He's Käthe's son."

Groener sat, his head slumped onto his thick chest. After a few seconds he muttered, "Reinhard and Fulda Detten."

"Detten." Aubrey jotted the names. "Where do they live?"

"After the surrender they moved to Darmstadt."

"Are they still in Darmstadt?"

"I haven't contacted them."

"Has Detten changed his name?"

"My guess is he's still there and still Reinhard Detten." Groener looked up at Käthe. "I've prayed for the boy."

Through her haze of joy Käthe felt an irrational flicker of sympathy for her enemy.

FIFTY-ONE

I

On the road out of Höchst they were pulled over by a pair of young MPs, politely informed that it wasn't safe to travel by night, and directed to a former Hitler Youth hostel where there was a small dormitory set aside for women. Käthe, burning with impatience, hadn't believed she could sleep, yet as soon as she stretched on the wood bunk, she was out. She awoke to another gloomy day. In her excitement the layers of clouds had a wild beauty.

She chafed while they crawled along ruined stretches of road. They didn't reach Darmstadt until midafternoon. The year's first snow was falling. The fat, lazy flakes turned to slush as they hit the narrow cleared trail that meandered through the heaped rubble.

Near what remained of the Darmstadt town hall, the few standing structures bustled with Military Government personnel. A chubby Wac bounced ahead of them along narrow corridors, jumping up creaking staircases. She left them alone in a dank attic room filled with tall American-made filing cabinets.

Käthe pulled open the *De* drawer, then her hand dropped nervelessly. "Would you look, Aubrey?"

Drawing a breath, Aubrey rapidly flipped the manila folders. "Thank God," he whispered, removing three.

The Dettens, Reinhard and Fulda, both holders of Card 6, the so-called "death card" that entitled the bearer to eight hundred calories a day, lived on Sohnerstrasse with their five-year-old-son, Erich. Since Reinhard had responded to Question #41 on his *fragebogen* in the affirmative—yes, he had been a member of the Nazi party—according to Military Government Public Law 8 he could be employed only for ordinary labor. He worked on a farm a few kilometers outside of town. Fulda cleared rubble—a *trümmerfrau*.

Their son, born on April 10, 1940, had been recommended for additional milk ration. His name was Erich.

The typing blurred before Käthe's eyes, and she leaned against the cabinet for support. Until this moment she had not realized how desperately she had been keeping at bay the armies of uncertainty.

Clutching the form to her tweed coat, she gave a joyous, laughing whoop. "Eureka!"

II

The pudgy Wac gave them the directions to Sohnerstrasse. "I'd better warn you, sir, this friend of yours"—Aubrey had given the routine excuse of looking for his old sweetheart—"isn't living in the Ritz. In fact, that side of town gives me the heebie-jeebies."

"How could anything be worse than this?" Käthe murmured as they drove past the children—many of them wearing rags around their feet instead of shoes—who searched for American cigarette butts in the slushy cobbles of the otherwise empty marketplace. "We shouldn't have any difficulty convincing the Dettens that Erich will be better off with us."

"They consider themselves his parents, Käthe."

"You have your revolver, then."

He smiled. "What, kidnap him at pistol point?"

"If we have to!"

Negotiating around the shell of a church, Aubrey asked quietly, "Given any consideration to what you'll do when we get him?"

"A little. I'll have to go back to Ober Tappenburg. But Erich. . . . Could you—would you take him to Grandpa's?"

"And then?"

"You said you . . ." She swallowed, flushing. "Last week in

Novikov's house, you said you'd like me with you always. My little boy's part of me."

"And I want both of you, what do you think?"

"As far as the family's concerned, then, we'll invent a story, maybe, about jumping the gun by adopting a war orphan before the wedding."

"Käthe, are you positive about marrying me? I'd take your little boy to England anyway."

She turned to him with the same joyous laugh she'd given in the attic. "You're the best, bravest, finest man I ever knew. You're talented, you're clever, you're kind. You care already about my son. Why is it so incredible that I'd promise to marry you?"

Steering one handed, he reached for her fingers, raising her arm to press his lips on the blue veins between her cuff and her glove. "Darling," he said, and his voice shook.

III

Sohnerstrasse could be reached only by climbing a footpath over the ruins. As they left the car, the snow was falling harder, veiling the worst of the devastation, but somebody had chalked GRUESOME in block letters, and this single word said it all. The dung-colored apartments, ugly before the war, now were either pyramids of masonry or facades behind which families had hammered together flimsy shacks. Here and there thin wisps of smoke curled above grotesquely repaired chimneys. Scrawny, coughing children waited to fill containers at an old-fashioned street pump. A desperate-faced woman emerged from a bakery, raising her empty shopping bag like a white flag of defeat, and the queued women plodded off hopelessly. A snow-covered mound looked suspiciously like a body.

"I don't care what it takes," Käthe said. "I'm getting him out of here. This afternoon."

"There's no choice," Aubrey agreed grimly.

They needed to ask directions three times before they reached the board painted SOHNERSTRASSE. They gave the Dettens' number to a squint-eyed little girl listlessly scratching in the snow for twigs.

"Does anybody live there since the bombings?" the child asked. "It's behind the fortune-teller's."

Next to a crude sign, COUNTESS ROMANY, PALMIST, an alley of sorts had been cleared between a great slagheap of bricks and a building with its upper stories gone. Aubrey held Käthe's arm, cautiously eyeing the DANGER warnings plastered over the singed stucco. In the few square feet that once possibly had been an airshaft they saw a propped ladder that seemingly led to nowhere.

"We must have copied the wrong numbers." Käthe sighed, her optimism plummeting. "We'll have to go back."

"Somebody put the stepladder here. It's worth a look. I'll trot on up."

Käthe was already scaling the rungs.

A ledge that protruded a few inches had hidden a wall and an interior door. Leaning forward on the ladder, Käthe tapped on the lower panel. There was no response. Climbing the final rungs, she used her left hand to balance herself on the jamb as she turned the yellowing china knob.

The tiny windowless slit must have been a storeroom. The draft stirred newspapers heaped atop a stained mattress. An upended U.S. Army packing crate held dishes, a battered tin jug, and a handleless chamber pot. There were no other furnishings or possessions. But what chilled Käthe's blood was the odor. This was the unforgettable stench of the Berlin air-raid shelter that last week of the war, when the living had been wedged among the dead.

Legs shaking, she stumbled into the lair—she couldn't think of it as a room.

Aubrey followed her. "Oh, my God," he whispered. To deaden his horror he reminded himself of what he had seen in the camps: to the skeletal inmates crammed in their tiered bunks this eight-by-eight hole would have seemed an earthly paradise.

Käthe wet her pale lips. "They've moved. They don't live here anymore."

"Herr Detten's working at the farm, Frau Detten's chipping

away at bricks, and Erich's with her." Aubrey forced reassurance into his voice. "They'll be along soon."

They waited below, stamping their feet on the fresh-fallen snow as the tiny courtyard filled with winter twilight.

IV

A small clatter of falling debris sounded on the path and a woman shambled into sight.

Käthe gripped her purse strap, unable to move or speak. This crone bore no resemblance to the plump, thirtyish hausfrau who had so proudly carried Erich down the steps of Villa Haug.

"Frau Detten?" Aubrey asked.

"Yes, I'm Fulda Detten," the woman said defiantly. Clutching at her ragged coat, she stood more erect. "And it's too late. I'm alone now."

"What do you mean?" Aubrey asked. "Alone?"

"The funeral was last week."

"Whose funeral?" Aubrey rasped.

"My husband and my little boy."

"Erich?" Käthe coughed to loosen her throat muscles. "Erich?"

"Of course you know the name!" The words came spitting out on breath-clouds. "Why wouldn't you know? The Americans have sent you for their ration cards, isn't that it? But why did you bring the Tommi?"

"Tell me about Erich?" Käthe whispered.

"You sound like a German. May you rot in hell for swooping down on a poor woman in her hour of grief!"

Käthe made a high, breathy sound.

"Are you laughing because my Reinhard caught the mumps? Oh, it's very funny. A grown man dying of mumps. Go ahead and split your sides, you collaborating whore! Aren't you happy your friends won? Isn't it marvelous that the British and the Americans have destroyed our cities so we have to live like animals? And that my Reinhard, God rest his soul, was pushed into shoveling manure?" The shrill, belligerent voice rushed on. "My husband was an important man! Let me tell you, a very big man. He was commended by Reichsführer Himmler for his efficiency. The Führer himself invited us to the Chancellery—the proudest day of my life. And you know why?"

"Frau Detten," Aubrey soothed. "We aren't here to—"

"Oh, Reinhard put on his *fragebogen* that he worked on railroad schedules, and they were too stupid, the Amis, to ask exactly what he did." She sucked in a breath. "He was in charge of routing every one of the trains that rid the Reich of Jewish vermin."

"God," Käthe whispered.

"He did his duty as a good German! Not like some of these concentration camp scum who run things today. And believe you me, Reinhard gave us a fine life. Big house. Fine car. Three servants to help me. Lithuanian girls. Ach, how our little Erich teased them, wild little rascal that he was!" The sentences streamed from the moving white scar that was Frau Detten's mouth. "Reinhard and I had to hide from the scamp how proud we were, but the minute he was out of the way, we would laugh until the tears came. Some of the clever pranks he played on those Lithuanians!"

"I'm sorry for your loss," Aubrey said stiffly. He reached in his pocket for Occupation marks.

Frau Detten snatched the bills, hurling them onto the snow, spitting. "You aren't going to pay me off for my husband and my baby! May God in heaven damn you forever, murderer! And your whore too! I lay my Reinhard and my Erich's death at your feet!"

The woman's expression was unrelenting and hard as she watched the Tommi officer tighten his grasp on the blonde and draw her into the blackness of the path. Waiting a minute, she retrieved the bills, wiping them against her coat before folding them into her handbag with the four packs of American Chesterfields, which were worth far more than the money.

FIFTY-TWO

I

Their breath clouding the inside of the windows, rime forming on the outside, and darkness surrounding them, they were encapsulated in the car. Käthe slumped as if a huge fist had mashed her. Aubrey, respecting the initial blow of her grief, had maintained a tactful silence, but she was shivering.

"Käthe, we'll need to put up here in Darmstadt," he said. "There's a hotel near the Luisenplatz."

When she said nothing, he started the engine.

American officers clamored impatiently around the desk and Aubrey had ample opportunity to memorize the typed sign: *We regret that due to lack of sufficient quarters of any nature in Darmstadt we have orders not to billet transients more than one night. The Commanding General of this area forbids the use of this hotel for immoral purposes.* When it was finally Aubrey's turn, the clerk, a technical sergeant whose heavy jaw showed a blue gleam of five o'clock shadow, inspected their papers and in a Brooklyn accent so undiluted that it might have been a parody explained that there was only one room left.

"My secretary's just received word of a loss in the family," Aubrey responded. "I prefer not leaving her."

One glance at the dazed ashen face convinced the sergeant that although Miss Osmond was a knockout, the Limey couple wasn't registering for immoral purposes.

"Kingsmith?" he asked. "Any relation to the big store on Fifth Avenue?"

"It belongs to my grandfather."

"Me and the wife, we exchanged a wedding present there. You'd have thought we was Rockefellers buying up the joint, the way we was treated. They got real class, Kingsmith's. Tell you what, Captain, the lady ain't exactly in shape to face the crowd in the dining room. We don't got room service, but I'll arrange for room service."

Bless you, Aunt Rossie, Aubrey thought, and drew Käthe through the kaleidoscope of American uniforms.

II

The small, high-ceilinged room with the narrow twin beds was by postwar German standards tropically hot. Käthe stood by the door until Aubrey helped her off with her coat and jacket, undoing the buttons as he had when she was a toddler on her first holiday at Quarles. Dinner arrived promptly.

"Do eat something," he coaxed.

Obediently Käthe took a nibble of butter-drenched baked potato, then set down her knife and fork. "I can't, Aubrey. I just can't."

Encouraged by this, her first remark, he said, "What about the sweet? You always loved ice cream."

She shook her head, sighing.

"Would it help to talk?" he asked.

Käthe shook her head again.

After Aubrey had finished and put the tray in the corridor, Käthe slid off her shoes and stretched on one of the neatly turned-down beds. Her face was lax, her eyes closed. Assuming her to be dozing, Aubrey took a notepad from his valise—he had returned to his prewar habit of keeping a journal each evening.

"She was awful, wasn't she?"

Aubrey looked up from his description of Darmstadt. "Frau Detten, you mean? God, rather!"

"You'd be surprised how many there are like her at Ober Tappenburg. The women who talk about Hitler as if he were the Second Coming. He built the concentration camps, they say, to reeducate the criminals and the sex offenders and the usurers and the black-market profiteers. They're positive nobody was harmed—the photographs and newsreels, they say, are cleverly doctored propaganda put out by the American Jews. It's another article of faith with them that Poland attacked us, then England and France joined in. The Führer, they say, never wanted the war and did everything in his power to avoid it. All he wanted was to reunite the *volk*. What we need to put us back on our feet, they say, is another strong leader."

"People never learn, do they?"

"Did you see how her mouth puckered when she spat at your money? Like a venomous snake."

Aubrey slipped his notepad back in the valise, letting Käthe ramble on about Frau Detten, the Lithuanian servants, Reinhard Detten's career of dispatching the death trains. She never mentioned Erich. Although she talked for several hours, she never once mentioned Erich. Her voice grew hoarse. In the middle of a sentence she fell asleep.

Aubrey pulled the quilt over her, and turned out the light. He didn't change to his nightclothes but stretched out with his coat over him.

III

He awoke to the sound of muffled sobbing.

Moving to the other bed, he put his arms around the fragile, quivering body and murmured wordless consolation. Käthe turned to face him, pressing her hot, wet cheek against his.

"Ah, Aubrey, Aubrey . . . Why do I hurt so much?"

"Darling, it's just happened."

"But I haven't seen him since he was a day old."

"You're having a perfectly natural reaction."

"I only held him once."

"He was yours."

"Yes, mine. What kept me going was knowing I'd find him."

"You've been through so much."

"And to miss by a few days. If only I'd been cleverer, quicker . . ."

"Don't blame yourself, darling. Blame me. I should have insisted on your release, no matter what. Hush, hush." He traced the fragile knobs of her spine.

Käthe pushed aside the quilt that separated them, putting her arms around his waist, clinging to him. Thinking of the kiss at Novikov's billet, and the mournful tenderness of her rejection, Aubrey made no move to tighten his grasp, but contented himself with resting his chin on her hair. He had no idea how long the embrace lasted: in the darkness time could be measured only by the rough beating of his heart.

It was she who took his hand, molding the fingers around the firm warmth of her breast. When he kissed her mouth, it was her lips that parted first, her tongue that first touched his. He understood that for Käthe this wasn't desire or even affection —although certainly she cared for him a great deal—but a complex need to escape, however briefly, from the cataclysm that had blotted out her family and now her son. She had lost her past and her future, she was frantically scrabbling for some connection to life.

As she caressed his erection, a magnetic charge traveled along the neurological paths of his body. *This isn't Oxford, stop intellectualizing,* he told himself. He had always loved Käthe, he always would love her, and if she wanted him, why should he analyze the chemistry of her bereavement? He wasn't taking advantage of her susceptibility, he was responding to her wordless request for solace in its most elemental form.

A church bell tolled high on the dark hill of ruins that once had been Darmstadt. He pushed up the soft wool sweater, caressing the tracery of slick tissue on her back with the same tender homage that he paid to her breasts. Her flesh was softer, warmer, smoother, than the flesh of the other women with whom he'd had minimal affairs. Except for the striations her skin was like warm chiffon. She murmured an erotic plea, and he moved on top of her. For an anxious, jealous beat of his heart he wondered, *How will I measure up to Wyatt?* Then he thought no more, heard nothing of the outside world—heard only Käthe's gasping and small, wordless cries. Because of her ethereal quality he had imagined she would be a delicately compliant partner; he had never considered that she might be passionate. Yet her caresses were explicit, her responses ardent, and her murmured suggestions of nuances, variations, and positions drove him berserk. He held back as long as he could, and when he came, gasping, sweating, shaking, he imagined himself utterly hollowed out. As her kisses trailed down his throat, he was ready again.

In a life not unrewarded with love and worldly applause, Aubrey Kingsmith cherished above his other earthly hours this night with his cousin Käthe in a ruined German town.

IV

A rumbling convoy of military trucks shattered his sleep. It was after eight, and a streak of gray morning light showed between the curtains. The arm under Käthe's neck felt numb.

"Käthe?" he whispered. "Awake?"

"I never dropped off."

He drew her closer. "About last night. Unless you want, it needn't count."

"Are you jilting me?" Her attempt at archness failed.

"Never, darling, never." Reaching for his glasses, he sat up.

Käthe didn't move from the tangle of bedclothes. It seemed impossible to Aubrey that this could be the passionate maenad of the darkness. With her pale blue jumper ruckled up, her eyes rimmed with shadows, her complexion haggard, the delicate features twisted, she was the embodiment of grief.

He smoothed back her moist, tangled hair. "I can't send you back to that place," he said in a low, humble voice.

"There's no choice."

"We could go somewhere like Switzerland or South America."

"Desert? You?"

"The war's over. I'm sick to death of sneaking about in this underhanded game. We'll make a new life."

"Yes, but later."

"Why should you wait for an interrogation? They've got millions of other Germans in detention to interrogate."

"I never meant to get Wyatt in hot water," she said. "What's the difference where I am?"

"It matters to me. And though you can't believe it now, once the pain numbs a bit you won't enjoy being locked up either."

"All through the war I've been planning how I'd find him and snatch him away from those awful people—I knew they'd be like the Dettens." She closed her eyes. "You have no idea the silly details I dreamed up. The way he'd drum on the kitchen table while I cooked us both cocoa. As if anybody but black marketeers have cocoa! I would buy him a tricycle and hold the saddle while he learned to ride it. We'd play snakes-and-ladders. Isn't this ridiculous? I had the idea that once we were together the sadness and horrors would be over. All those millions had died in the camps, Sigi had been tortured to death, Mother left to rot, but having Erich with me would somehow wipe the slate clean, and I'd be the same as before the war. As though anything could ever wipe away these terrible guilt pangs."

"You of all people shouldn't feel guilty."

Her grimace repudiated his remark. She was right, of course. Only Käthe could absolve herself. He sensed that she never would.

"My daydreams are even more humiliating," he said, hoping to distract her. "Straight from a Dorothy Lamour film. You and I are on some tropical island living in a lean-to artistically draped with palm fronds. I'm typing away on some great masterpiece that will make the entire world sit up and take notice. And whenever I look out the window, I can see you sunning yourself on the sand or bathing in azure water. Sometimes you bring me a pineapple."

She was staring up at the cracked ceiling.

Kissing her forehead, he got up. As he adjusted his uniform, he said, "I'll call Lear and tell him you found me and turned yourself in—that should count for something."

She nodded absently.

"You'll be released from Ober Tappenburg soon," he said.

The hesitancy that had afflicted his voice during the earlier conversation had vanished, and he spoke in a hard, level tone. "I promise you it'll be soon."

V

After Lear hung up on the British Captain Kingsmith, he scratched his head. The Limey had promised to bring her in before lunchtime. Then what? Would there be a heap of awkward forms for him to fill out? And what was the protocol? Was he, personally, meant to deliver her to Ober Tappenburg? What if she gave *him* the slip?

He put in a call to Berlin.

Wyatt said very little as Lear ebulliently blurted out that Aubrey would be bringing Käthe to USFET Headquarters before lunch. "Much as I'd love to take the kudos," Lear said, "it seems to me you should be the one to put a cap on this foul-up and take her back."

"If there's a plane, I'll be there."

Hanging up, Wyatt leaned back in his swivel chair and stared out the window at the American flag whipping in front of the handsome two-story building across the courtyard: he was in his office in the Legal Division's section of the former Luft Gau complex. After he had wasted nearly a week chasing his tail through the horror that was central Berlin, Colonel Behr had irascibly ordered him back to his desk.

Wyatt swung a little in the chair. His angular face looked morose, but in actuality he was experiencing a great surge of relief. No more visualizing Käthe being raped by Russians or making love to some guy with SS lightning zigzags tattooed under his arm. He could stop waking with his heart pounding and his fists clenched as if around her throat. He could put the whole miserable business behind him. Not that he didn't have good grounds for bitterness. She had exploited his momentary weakness by taking off. Furthermore, by now he knew that Porteous had been laid up with a head cold rather than fatal pneumonia. Aubrey—his best friend, his brother-in-law—had engineered the "compassionate visit" to England. It was entirely probable that Aubrey had found her immediately and had been with her ever since. Why not? Before the war, in that other, innocent life, in a wooden mansion whose ruins lay not far from here, Aubrey had confessed how much he loved Käthe.

And Käthe?

The two times he had seen Käthe since the Occupation, he'd had a weird glimmer that she was bound to Aubrey. Not in the same romantic sense that Aubrey was tied to her. Nevertheless, in some enigmatic way, she was bound to Aubrey.

Wyatt walked slowly to the window. Ignoring the unpleasantly hot steam from the radiator, he drummed his knuckles on the window ledge. How could such a tie have developed? Hadn't six years of warfare kept them forcibly apart?

He shrugged and went down the hall to Colonel Behr's office. He explained that his cousin had been found, requesting leave to return her to Ober Tappenburg. At Tempelhof a Flying Fortress by some miracle was taking off immediately for Frankfurt. Wyatt bounced in the canvas seat, his mind chasing after the conundrum of Aubrey and Käthe's attachment.

VI

It was almost two before Aubrey reached the USFET Headquarters building. With an unpleasant tingle he saw a familiar tall figure pacing in the slush between the smart-looking paratrooper guards.

Staff cars and jeeps were angled in toward the barbed wire. Aubrey parked as close as possible to the footpath that led up to the main entry. "Wyatt's here, darling," he said, lightly kissing Käthe's forehead before he leaned across her to open the car door.

As she got out, he noted an alien docility in her posture, as if her unique spine of courage and will had crumbled. His vibrant, graceful Käthe had become another of the vast and vanquished army of DPs.

He jogged toward Wyatt.

"Lear called," Wyatt said. "Told me you'd be here before lunch. I was figuring you'd given me the shaft. Again."

"I'm truly sorry about the hoax, but at the time getting her a holiday in England was the only thing on my mind." He paused. "Wyatt, she's had a bad shock."

"If this is leading up to what I think it is, the answer's no. No more time. You've used up more than your allotment of time."

"Käthe *wants* to go back to Ober Tappenburg. But, well, things have gone badly for her."

"She didn't find the Nazi she was looking for?" Wyatt felt a burst of shame at his mean tone. "Okay, okay, I won't give her a tough time about ditching me."

"Would you put in a good word for her?"

"A good word? Look, Aubrey, she was being held in a detention camp and that's strike one. She was allowed out and she took off. Strike two. She's been tooting around the countryside for well over a week. That's strike three. Now, what sort of good word would you suggest?"

Aubrey ignored the hostile, mocking tone—Wyatt had every reason to be incensed. "There's a Wac she's friendly with."

"The corporal with thick legs." Wyatt shrugged. "Sure, I'll ask her to keep an eye out."

Käthe stood absolutely straight near the Mercedes. Uniformed men were eyeing the pale, charming blonde, but she looked too English and too aristocratically remote for any of them to flout the nonfraternization laws and try a pass. To Aubrey, Käthe's gathering together of pride was yet more touching than her earlier posture of defeat. He held her loosely, kissing her forehead. "It won't be for long," he promised against her ear as he helped her into Wyatt's covered jeep.

FIFTY-THREE

I

As Wyatt drove, the heavy overcast cleared, swatches of blue sky showed, and the temperature dropped. In Aschaffenburg the slanting, cobbled marketplace was empty and the inhabitants, bundled in ragtag clothing, hurried along the narrow, winding streets. The jeep was passing the town's Renaissance castle when the sun came out: lit by late afternoon brilliance, the massive red sandstone walls and four great towers glistened ruby-red, as though they had risen wet from the Main River, which sluiced below.

Wyatt broke the wall of silence that had separated them since Frankfurt. "Pretty damn impressive, isn't it?"

Käthe, not responding, stared ahead with her chin lifted haughtily. Wyatt's hands tightened on the steering wheel. *Screw you, lady,* he thought. He drove more swiftly, swerving up the mountain curves of the Odenwald. Along the side of the road the patches of snow resembled broken marble stepping-stones.

Finally he could no longer take the silence. "A freak early snow," he said with a trace of awkwardness.

Again she didn't speak.

He glanced at her. The head was as arrogantly held, but in the long shadows the delicate profile appeared ashen. *She's had a bad shock,* Aubrey had said. Wyatt's annoyance and anger faded. "Rough time?" he asked quietly. This time when she didn't respond, he tapped her shoulder.

She jumped. "Did you say something?"

"A remark about the weather, a safe if boring subject."

"It's a lovely morning." The soft, melodious voice that once had filled him with joy was projected, as if she were an actress reciting to him across a proscenium.

"Afternoon," he corrected, and saw that she was shivering. "It's cold. There's a rug in the backseat."

"I'm perfect," she said.

"Käthe, look, it's no big deal if I just turn around and let you out at Aschaffenburg." The words didn't surprise him. In the face of the compassion he felt for her, why shouldn't his impulsiveness manifest itself?

"I don't mind going back," she said, adding formally, "But it's most kind of you."

"Chances are you'd never be caught," he persisted. "We sure as hell aren't able to keep up with the swarms of refugees and DPs. What sort of papers do you have?"

"None. I left Aubrey my travel pass and British passport. He got them for me."

They had reached the NO TRESPASSING signs of the Ober Tappenburg turnoff. Käthe's remark about Aubrey and the fake papers had crystallized Wyatt's thoughts. He made the turn, stopping the car on the narrow lane through the woods.

"I know you're not in the mood for conversation," he said. "But you just turned down my offer of escape, so all you've got ahead of you is time."

"There's nothing to talk about."

"You owe me a week." He smiled to show he was joking. "A couple of minutes is all I ask."

"Please don't talk like that."

"Like how?"

"As though I'm a Meissen figurine about to break."

"Okay," he said crisply. "I'm putting forward a hypothetical case. 'Minta always said Aubrey was with the SOE or one of the dashing intelligence branches. I used to tease her that she couldn't bear to have a brother stationed anywhere so drab as a gunnery school. But a few months back old Aubrey got into a bit of a brawl in a Kurfürstendamm dive. Taking off his glasses, he calmly decked this big gorilla of a pilot who outweighed him by thirty pounds and could have been a Golden Gloves contender. Then I began to notice other things. Take his German. Before the war it was your typical Anglo-Deutsch, but now he sounds like a native Berliner. He knows his way around—look at how he dug up your phony papers. The thing is, was Araminta on target?"

Käthe continued staring at a fir tree. Snow covered the lower branches to the protection of the branch above, and in the dusk the inner green appeared black.

"Well?" Wyatt asked. "Was she right?"

"Aubrey told me," Käthe said, "that he was stationed in Scotland."

"You two're very cozy."

"We're going to be married."

Wyatt felt his facial muscles loosen. "And here I figured you'd taken up with some SS *gruppenführer.* So big congratulations are in order?" He could not control a note of adolescent snideness.

"You're right," she said softly. "Aubrey deserves better."

"That hadn't entered my mind. You took me by surprise is all. Look, I'm happy for you both."

"Thank you."

"So back to my hypothesis. Did your fiancé contact a group of Germans willing to risk their lives against the Gestapo? Did he have an underground cadre?"

"Wyatt, I'm not in the mood for sparring."

"Then tell me the truth. Was he dropped into the Third Reich? Did he have agents here? Did you help him—were you part of his underground?"

She turned to him, her eyes glittering as if she had a high fever. "If I'd made up a cock-and-bull story like that when you visited the camp this summer," she asked, "would you have tried to get me out?"

He recalled her nakedly joyous smile, his own melee of conflicting emotions. "I was pretty bitter. But you know me, Käthe. First the explosion, then the debris settles down." He shrugged. "As soon as I got back to Berlin I'd have been on the horn to Aubrey. Not that it would have been any major deal.

Nature would have taken its course and he'd have dreamed up an excuse to get you out a few weeks earlier, that's all."

She bent her head and pressed her finger pads to her browline.

"Käthe," he said gently, "tell me, am I smoking on some crazy pipe?"

She looked up. Her eyes no longer glittered, but seemed dead and sunken. "Aubrey was in Scotland," she said. "I was filing documents for the OKW."

He was pretty sure she wasn't leveling, but then again the wavering note in her voice might be shame for the OKW job. What did it matter that she had been on the other side? Her home was gone, her family had vanished. She was left with nothing, not even her freedom. And now, according to Aubrey, she had borne yet further diminishment.

"Take me back," she said. "Take me back."

He realized she was shaking all over. "It's all right, Käthe, no more badgering." As he spoke, he reached out to drape his arm solacingly around her shoulders. She shrank back against the side of the jeep. And with her gesture she reactivated memories of that prewar rejection, when he'd thought he'd surely die of the pain. He raised his arms as if stretching, then started the jeep.

"You won't be inside long." His voice was kind yet impersonal, the tone he'd use with one of his witnesses after a cross-examination. "Aubrey knows the top strings to pull."

II

It was unseasonably fine weather and Aubrey breathed the fresh Kentish air deeply as the tall butler led him under Chartwell's autumnal oaks and beeches and around a pond where black swans glided. After knocking on the open door of a high, bright studio, the servant departed. Waiting at the threshold, Aubrey took in details—the odors of turpentine, paint, and cigars, the strew of brushes and jars, the shelves lined with hundreds of brightly colored oil paintings—landscapes, scenes of cathedrals and ruins—that were the work of a gifted amateur.

Winston Churchill sat on a low stool in front of his easel, his spine hunched in a half circle, a shawl over his shoulders. Aubrey, finding it impossible to believe that this enfeebled ancient could be the vigorous Prime Minister who had led the country until a few months earlier, couldn't stem a poetic thought: Churchill, like the legendary Arthur, had appeared to rally Britons in their hour of greatest need and then, having served his purpose, had vanished once more into the fabled mists, leaving behind this frail old husk.

For a few seconds longer Aubrey watched the brush, held by a liver-spotted hand, hover above the canvas, then he coughed. "Sir?"

Churchill turned. "Why are you standing there? Come over here, Mr. Osmond."

Aubrey crossed the sunlit space, thinking that maybe Churchill had sprung from mythical Avalon. What, short of wizardry, could explain how this old man, after the hectic workpace, the monumental decisions, the endless political maneuvers of a six-year global war, could conjure up a minor underling's literary pseudonym?

"I'm honored that you remember, sir."

Churchill gave a wheezing chuckle. "You must try another novel."

"I plan to, sir."

The old man swabbed his brush on the palette, throwing a streak of azure across his rendering of a romantically tumble-down Greek temple. "Well, what is so urgent that you needed to drive down here?"

"It's about my cousin."

"Fräulein Kingsmith?"

"She's been in an American detention camp for months."

Churchill's bushy white eyebrows drew together. "It's necessary to cast out the Nazi villains."

"Sir, you know that Käthe wasn't a Nazi."

"Do I?"

"You yourself convinced her to work for us. We have an obligation to her."

"I am aware of my obligations!" Massive pink head bent to

his rounded chest, Churchill was exhibiting one of his celebrated temper tantrums.

Aubrey's guts turned to jelly, yet his voice remained calmly stern. "Sir, if you refuse to help her, I will have to tell the Americans precisely how she helped us."

"You are in His Majesty's service!" Churchill growled.

"I'm aware the penalty will be severe."

Setting down his palette, Churchill opened a humidor. He sniffed a Romeo y Julieta cigar, his mood changing from anger to reason. "Surely by now," he said, "you understand that we must retain our few hidden warriors. Without them, where is the hope of stemming the tide of Stalinism?"

Aubrey in the past months had seen enough of the eternal Soviet maneuvering to impose puppet communist regimes in all four zones of the conquered country; he accepted that Stalin not only intended to swallow up Germany but also the countries of Eastern Europe, and possibly Western Europe too. Churchill was right. They needed an ultrasecret German network as much as ever. Yet he went on doggedly. "I won't be endangering our secrecy, sir. Käthe was never part of CI-4 proper. I'll use any means available to get her free."

"Kingsmith, that's treason you're talking!"

"I'll face the firing squad, then."

Churchill continued to glare from under those tangled white brows for a few more seconds, then he gave a laugh that shook his belly. "Downes said you were a good man. Decent and honorable to a fault, Downes always said."

"About getting Käthe released, sir?"

"A rather delicate spot you're putting us into, Kingsmith. Let me think what can be done." Chewing ruminatively on the unlit cigar for nearly a minute, he said, "The best answer is a swift interrogation."

Aubrey's fists clenched. "Have her questioned? Now? When the world's in an uproar?" The horror stories trickling out of Nuremberg had cast every German as a moral leper: once the War Crimes Trials started, there would be a greater deluge of loathing. "Käthe will be drowned."

"The Americans want to be fair. Fräulein Kingsmith isn't guilty of anything, is she?"

"Only of being stupid. She wouldn't be in the detention camp if she'd broken her oath of secrecy and told our ally's Public Safety people that she'd spied for us."

Churchill's jowls quivered, but he spoke mildly enough. "Yes, yes. Some excellent information, including advance notice for those damnable rockets."

"We lost my sister to one, sir." *Forgive me, Araminta, for using your death so shamelessly.*

"I recall, my boy, and it saddened me." Churchill squinted appraisingly at his painting. "But can't you see how vital it is, Kingsmith, that the American intelligence community never gets wind of CI-4? Should they hear of our depleted little band, then it must follow as night to day that Mr. Stalin will hear too. Fräulein Kingsmith will need to go through the motions of a trial."

"The motions, sir? You yourself ordered me to ask her for information about Barbarossa. She managed to get clearance for top-secret files—and that makes her guilty."

"If need be we'll let you pick a battery of barristers. The girl's father was an Englishman, after all, so a cousin helping won't be amiss. In the meanwhile it would be best for her to start out with one of their lawyer chaps."

III

"Today in medieval Nuremberg, a city that once resounded with millions ecstatically cheering Adolf Hitler, there opened the trial of twenty-two top Nazis. Martin Bormann will be tried in absentia, but the twenty-one other defendants were transferred under heavy guard from the connecting prison to the Justizpalast, that same gray sandstone building where the Nazis enacted their heinous racial laws. The defendants spent this entire day hearing the list of charges against them: crimes against peace, crimes against humanity, and crimes against defenseless minorities. Specially constructed earphones with channels for translation into four languages were used. Afterward many in the jammed courtroom discussed the impact of

seeing the accused Nazis listening impassively, even with boredom, to the stream of their hideous and grisly crimes. This
correspondent spoke to—"

At a tap on the door Wyatt switched off the American Armed
Forces Network. He was in his Dahlem billet and he crossed the
cabbage-rose carpet of his spacious, over-pink bedroom to let
in his guest. Aubrey.

After the greetings Aubrey said, "Käthe's going to be interrogated next week."

"So quickly? Who told you?"

Ignoring the second question, Aubrey said, "The timing
couldn't be worse."

"Yep, rotten," Wyatt agreed with a depressed glance at the
dome-topped radio. "She'll be hauled before a tribunal for
sure, and then—" He raised his palms. "God knows. Apropos,
word is out that General Clay's decided to hand over the job of
denazification to the Germans next April."

"She'll certainly be tried before April," Aubrey said. "Tell
me a bit about your tribunals."

"They vary. The legalities of denazification are murky. The
definitions of who is a war criminal and who isn't are pretty
cloudy too. But in the light of what's going on in Nuremberg,
none of our guys will be weak sisters. For the time being there'll
be twenty or thirty-year terms. Capital sentences."

"She'll be allowed counsel, won't she?"

"That's for sure."

"Do you know any top-rank trial lawyers?"

"In civilian life there were those who considered me deviously warped enough to be a good litigator."

"You?" Aubrey stared at Wyatt.

After a long pause Wyatt said, "You can be quite a prick,
know that? I *am* good. If you don't believe me, cable old man
Uzbend. He keeps writing piteous letters to find out when I'm
being discharged. Look, I'll work my tail off to get her acquit-
ted." Wyatt went to the maidenly dressing table, pouring two
stiff drinks. He handed a tumbler to Aubrey. "If our former
entanglement's got you hot under the collar, forget it. 'Minta is
still my wife."

"And you blame the Germans for her death," Aubrey said. "I can still remember a night in New York when you swore Käthe was a Nazi. You told me so at the Neue Femina."

"Guilty on all counts. But Jesus Christ, Aubrey, you can't honestly believe I'm conniving to shove my future sister-in-law into jail for the next twenty years."

"There's certain evidence she won't divulge."

Wyatt peered at Aubrey. "I put a hypothetical case before Käthe the day I returned her to Ober Tappenburg," he said. "I postulated that you were in the SOE or some other intelligence group. That you were dropped into Germany. That she helped you."

"What did she say?"

"That I was nuts."

A cat howled—there weren't many cats left in this starving city. Aubrey said without inflection, "There's never been any insanity in the family, has there?"

Wyatt stared a moment longer into the bespectacled eyes. He had a partial answer. Aubrey, bound by secrecy, was telling him as much as possible of his wartime activities. But what about Käthe? Couldn't the strong hint that she'd been a British agent also be a ploy on Aubrey's part to make him more sympathetic to her case? After all, granted she might not have babbled English official secrets to the denazification team, but surely when he had visited her in Ober Tappenburg, when she had been so desperate to get out, she would have said *something*. As he'd told her later, one little clue that she'd worked for Aubrey and he would have contacted Aubrey pronto. *There's certain evidence she won't divulge.* The cynic in Wyatt pointed out that this evidence could well be incriminating.

Nevertheless he said with absolute sincerity, "I'll give the case my damnedest. And consider the impression we'll make. A gallant American cousin defending her. A gallant British cousin as star character witness."

"I've been ordered back to our zone."

"That's a lousy break for her." The dinner gong sounded. "So if—when—Käthe goes before a tribunal, I'm her counsel?"

"That's up to her."

FIFTY-FOUR

I

Two American Public Safety officers interrogated Käthe. On the windswept morning of January 2, 1946, she was transferred from the Ober Tappenburg detention facility to the König-strasse Prison in Frankfurt, where she would await trial before an American tribunal.

Seen from the street, the high-walled prison complex appeared to have sustained no damage; however, a high-explosive bomb had destroyed the row of warders' housing in the rear and dangerously weakened the roof of the women's wing. The roof had been replaced with corrugated tin that intensified the cold weather and amplified every sound. As a guard led Wyatt along the tier, their footsteps resounded like masculine drumrolls beneath the shrill voices of the inmates. The narrow slits of cells gave off a strong odor of carbolic.

As Wyatt was admitted, Käthe rose. The English tailored clothes she'd acquired on that escapee week with Aubrey were now as rumpled as her earlier German rags had been. She appeared yet thinner. But her hair was neatly drawn into a thick single braid and her skin no longer was underlaid with the waxen pallor of the afternoon he'd delivered her back to Ober Tappenburg.

"As a family member I'm allowed to visit," he explained without prelude. He was only permitted ten minutes. "Treatment here okay?"

"When it comes to prisons"—she forced vivacity—"the Amis win hands down over us Jerries."

Was the visit being monitored? Wyatt glanced at the open door. His GI escort chewed at a hangnail while tilting his head toward the guardroom, where a radio was playing the Armed Forces Network's record of the Jack Benny show, very little of which could be heard through the surrounding din.

"You were locked up?" Wyatt asked in a low voice.

"Toward the end of the war."

"Any particular reason?"

She shrugged. "How's Aubrey? Could you get them to let me write to him?"

"The officer in charge of Königstrasse Prison is a hard-nosed bastard. It took a lot of fast talking to get him to authorize this visit."

"After what happened in the Tiergarten, it was nice of you to take the trouble." She gestured that he should sit at the foot of the cot as she sank down on the pillow at the top.

Since she was making an effort at normalcy in this noisy zoo, Wyatt sat. "This isn't a social call. I'm here to offer my services as your counsel."

"That's very kind, but not necessary. The charges are all true."

"During the interrogation did you mention being in prison during the war?"

"I don't need a lawyer."

He gripped her wrist. "Wrong, Käthe, wrong. You need one in the worst way. You could get a life sentence. Hell, right now there's tribunals who'd hang you!"

She looked down at the large hand clenched around her fragile wrist, then directly at him. He saw that although she might have more color, her eyes had that same drabbed suffering as earlier. He let go of her wrist.

"How's your little boy?" she asked.

"Geoff?" He frowned. His brutal if honest appraisal of her situation couldn't have sunk in yet. Otherwise why would she be inquiring about a child she'd never met? "Didn't I make it clear? No light sentences right now."

"Yes, I know. They let us see the newspaper. Have you a photo?"

Taking out his wallet he extracted the latest snapshot.

She examined it. "He looks like 'Minta," she pronounced. "Not you."

"How did you get the job at OKW?" he asked.

She continued to stare at the picture. "Is his hair red too?"

"Will you quit playing games!"

The guard cracked his gum and poked his head in the cell. "Sorry, sir, but time's up."

Wyatt jumped to his feet, extracting his fountain pen and a paper that he'd typed up before leaving Berlin. "No time to argue. Just sign this."

Without reading the request to have Wyatt Kingsmith, Captain, U.S. Army Legal Division, act as her counsel, she signed her name.

II

"Your case is on the docket," Wyatt said on his first official visit.

"When?" she asked without interest.

"The second of February. Which means I have to get a defense together in less in three weeks." He took out a yellow legal pad. "Why were you at Berchtesgaden?"

"Eagle's Nest," she corrected.

"Oh, for Christ's sake, quit the nit-picking! Berchtesgaden's the generic name. Answer the question."

"Hitler called a meeting of the High Command. Sigi went with his uncle. The lunch was a social event, women were included, so he invited me along."

"Was it a Nazi function?"

"*Hitler* was there."

"Goddammit!"

"You knew Sigi," she said reproachfully. "He wasn't in the Party. Neither was General von Hohenau."

"I'll check."

Wyatt received a written deposition that neither Sigi nor the general was listed in the Nazi register. But so what? They were

Prussians with a *von* in front of their name. The army had been their career. They were part of the OKW. Wasn't Field Marshal Keitel, chief of the OKW, one of the defendants at Nuremberg?

"What about conspiracies against Hitler?" Wyatt asked as a matter of routine on his next visit.

"Sigi and General von Hohenau took part in the assassination attempt at Wolfsschanze in 1944."

"The July Plot?" His spine had straightened. "Why the hell didn't you throw that on the floor my last visit?"

"You didn't ask."

"Käthe, for Christ's sake! I'm *your* counsel, not the prosecution. Don't you realize that this is the only line of defense we've got?

"Defense?" she asked. "I keep dreaming about those pictures taken in the concentration camps."

"Right now our people are having the same nightmares." He spoke impatiently. "Tell me about Sigi."

Rain had begun drumming on the roof and several of the women were tapping on the bars, a primitive, improvised form of dissonance. Käthe said something.

"I didn't quite catch that," he said.

"Could you bring me a chocolate bar the next time? Magda —the woman in the next cell—is pregnant."

"I'll bring the whole goddamn PX if you'd come a single step in my direction!"

"She's having a bad time."

Suddenly, without understanding why, he yanked Käthe to her feet. Forcing her chin up, he kissed her.

For a moment her lips parted softly.

He put his arms around her, splaying one hand above her waist, the other below, drawing the slender body tight against his. With the embrace it seemed as if his life had come a full circle. He was back in the flower-decked Tiergarten on that summer evening when he'd first held her. Almost a decade had passed, yet he remained as powerfully attracted—and as ambivalent about her Nazi beliefs. His fingers sought the roots of her breasts.

She struggled to pull away, then slammed her palm at his shoulder.

He released her. Turning to hide his erection, he muttered, "Finally got your attention, didn't I?"

After that she reported the little she knew of Sigi's and General von Hohenau's involvement in the plot against Hitler.

III

After leaving the prison he drove by the red limestone cathedral. With the tower and spire gone Frankfurt's *dom* squatted in its nave. Near the sacristy a woman sauntered along under an umbrella. Her skirt was short, her heels high. Because of the rubble, women wore flat shoes—except those who were soliciting.

Since October first, when the unenforceable nonfraternization regulation had ceased to be official Occupation policy, whores were everywhere. Most weren't professionals but what the GIs called fraternazis or furlines, women seeking to support a family, a child, or merely to stay alive themselves, exchanging their bodies for cigarettes, a meal, a Hershey bar. Since Araminta's death Wyatt had paid for joyless sex, a release during which he invariably thought of the starvation that had forced his partner into his arms, and of the fact that she probably had cheered herself hoarse at the Führer's anti-Semitic howls.

This particular furline spoke excellent if heavily accented English, and there was a hint of derision in her tone as she directed him along Niddastrasse, a reasonably intact street that radiated from the main station. The traffic was heavy. Americans cruising in their cars eyed doorways where shivering women loitered—and sometimes a brightly painted young boy.

His woman led him up the dark staircase of a rooming house that smelled of rancid food and cabbage. Unlocking her door, she turned to him. Her face was too strong featured and arrogant to be pretty, but under her shabby, well-cut raincoat, she was all slender curves, like Käthe.

She helped him off with his overcoat, draping it on a hanger. Standing by the high-legged bed, she slowly, provocatively, unbuttoned her dress, revealing her naked breasts. The nipples were brown, with large aureoles. Käthe's were pale rose and delicately shaped.

"I've changed my mind," he said abruptly.

"What is the matter, Captain? Do you crave something exotic? Oh, we can invent such pleasures, you and I. Shall I get another girl? Yes, a trio. Or would you prefer a boy for our third?"

"I'll pay you anyway," he said, reaching for his wallet, handing her a five-dollar bill, a fortune in Germany.

He drove the few hundred yards to the station, parking in front of the Excelsior Hotel, where he had a room. He didn't get out. He stared at the rain beating on the windshield.

ELEVEN
1946

Though at the outset many questions were raised about the legality of the Nuremberg Trials, the leaders of the western Allies, torn on many issues, remained united in their decision: Those responsible for crimes against humanity would be brought to justice. The voices against the trial grew silent as one after another witness testified to the monstrous aberrations within the Third Reich.

The marble-and-mahogany courtroom in Nuremberg's Justizpalast cast a long and dark shadow over the unpublicized tribunals being conducted across the divided land.

—from *In the Wake of Hitler,*
Sir Aubrey Kingsmith

FIFTY-FIVE

1

Wyatt could find no evidence in the captured records that Sigi or his uncle had been connected to the July Plot. Sigi's death was listed "In the Service of the Führer on the Ukrainian Front."

"That was the official reason," Käthe told him. She had emerged from her torpor to keep a wary distance in the minuscule cell. "So many people were involved that it began to reflect badly on Hitler."

"Poor old Sigi." Wyatt's voice was a low rumble. "So they shot him without a trial?"

"Leave my brother out of this!"

"We have to get some sympathy going here, Käthe, and it's not like there's a lot else to grab on to. Sigi arranged for your job at the OKW, that makes him crucial. What we need is a witness that he was in on the plot. Didn't he have a secret lady friend, a dentist's widow?"

"Frau Salzwebel? He never would have talked politics with Frau Salzwebel."

"Were you under the bed?"

"I won't have Sigi used, or his friends—"

"Hold it right there! You're the client, I'm the lawyer. How did she spell her name? Is that a *d* or a *b*?"

"I haven't a clue," Käthe said coldly.

Wyatt, controlling his temper, didn't say good-bye.

II

It was a clear, breezy afternoon—warm for winter. In the An Der Hauptwache rubble women were clinking away at the pyramids of ruins while their children played tag around the twisted girders. Adolescent boys chased Wyatt's car in hopes of a tossed cigarette butt. Turning into Grosse Bockenheimerstrasse, which in prewar days had been nicknamed Fressgass, guzzling street, for its numerous cafés, pastry makers, and delicatessens, he halted at a shop with a restored window. Here, the International Red Cross was setting up cross-references in an attempt to help the millions of displaced people find each other. Every wall was covered with snapshots and photographs of missing relatives. The three long tables were crowded with people poring over files.

Wyatt took his place in the queue at the desk, well aware that everybody was darting curious glances at the American officer. Him. The clerk with the deep twin furrows between her eyes insisted on helping him ahead of the others. "My colleagues and I will seek to find a Frau Salzwebel or Salzwedel—we will try every possible spelling in both Berlin and the surrounding area," she said officiously. "If you would be so kind as to take a seat, Herr Captain Kingsmith."

An elderly hollow-cheeked man looked up, staring openly, then pushed to his feet. Wyatt, dreading being offered a chair, turned to light a cigarette.

"Pardon the intrusion, Captain." The hollow-faced man had come over and was speaking in English. "But I believe that the lady called you Kingsmith?"

Anticipating a question about the Unter den Linden shop, Wyatt nodded.

"Are you by any chance related to Fräulein Käthe Kingsmith?"

"She's my cousin." Wyatt scrutinized the older man. His English was cultivated and he lacked the obsequiousness currently endemic in Germany—in fact, the lines around his mouth would have indicated sardonic humor if it weren't for the brooding, deep-set eyes. Because of his age Wyatt dropped him into Alfred and Clothilde's circle of friends. "Were you acquainted with my uncle?"

"I met Herr Kingsmith on a business matter. A highly generous gentleman. But it's marvelous to hear you speak of Fräulein Kingsmith in the present tense. That means she's in good health?"

"Yes." Wyatt stared at his cigarette.

"Thank God for that. Would it be possible to have an address? You see, she saved my life." With a slight bow he said, "Heinrich Leventhal at your service."

The small muscles around Wyatt's eyes tensed. He was remembering a dim, stiffly formal room, Judge Leventhal and Mrs. Leventhal not admitting any relationship to him while the judge obliquely worded a request to Käthe for information about Heinrich Leventhal, his cousin. That blazing-hot Manhattan afternoon he had told Käthe to steer clear of the Leventhals' affairs—and later proposed to her. Stunned, he didn't take the proffered hand.

Leventhal quirked an eyebrow, as if inwardly acknowledging an expected reaction. "I'm sorry to have disturbed you," he said dryly.

Wyatt reached to grab the bony fingers. "Weren't you in a camp?" he blurted.

"Twice. It was after my first release in 1937 that I met Fräulein Kingsmith—but possibly she's told you?"

"Nothing . . . When you said she'd saved your life, that was a figure of speech, wasn't it?"

"Hardly. It's quite a story. Perhaps when you're finished with your business, we can talk?"

"I'm finished," Wyatt said.

Heinrich Leventhal glanced at the clerks bent over filing drawers, then smiled at the younger man. "I can see that, Captain."

III

"You owned the Leventhal department store, didn't you?"

"It was Aryanized with a more appropriate name, the Berliner."

"Aryanized! They stole your business."

"A perfectly legal sale. Not top mark, mind you, but a legal sale according to the laws of the time. The new owners were happy, the government was happy. As for me, after the deductions I had enough left to help thirty-seven people with their immigration taxes, so I was happy too."

They were sitting in the parked car. "You have a cousin in New York," Wyatt said. "Judge Abraham Leventhal."

"Yes. As a matter of fact that's how Fräulein Kingsmith heard I was in a camp." He hit the side of his head. "How dense of me. She must have been visiting your branch of the family when she met him."

"He had a son," Wyatt said, and clenched his hands on his knees. "They had a son who died."

"Yes, Myron. My second cousin," Leventhal said. "We were good friends."

"He was my father."

"Myron?" Leventhal jumped. Then his jaundiced, deep-sunk eyes flickered over Wyatt's face. "My God, I *knew* you reminded me of somebody! Yes, except for the fair hair almost a mirror image. He married a gentile girl—"

"Mother. He died a few months after the wedding. Before I was born my mother married Dad—the man who *is* my father. Nobody in the Kingsmith family knows about the first marriage, except Dad, and he's forgotten."

"What about Fräulein Kingsmith?"

"Yes, Käthe knows." Wyatt turned the ignition. "Let's go someplace to talk."

IV

German guests were not permitted in the Casino, but Wyatt, truthfully, informed the guard that Heinrich Leventhal was his long-lost cousin. The smell of roasting beef was strong, but lunch wasn't yet being served. The two men sat in the near-empty bar, Wyatt sipping his drink as Leventhal described meeting Käthe—through Schultze—in the New Museum.

"Was that when she saved your life?" Wyatt asked.

"No, later." Leventhal stared down at his drink so that Wyatt couldn't see his face properly. "Even now I can't talk about Bergen-Belsen—just let's say that by comparison the first camp seems like the Hotel Adlon." He paused. "It's a year ago since I managed to escape. The war was almost over then, yet still they kept on killing us. Eight men on my work detail planned to break out and tell the Allies what was going on. I was the only one who survived." His voice faded. "Forgive the blanks. The journey's not easy to talk about either. You can imagine how I fit in, a skeleton in stolen rags with my head shaven. I had planned to go to Schultze's so he could pass on a report to your people. But poor old Schultze's building was gone, an incendiary bomb. So were the other safe houses I'd known. I was starving—"

"Nobody helped you?"

"It was a capital crime. Why would they risk their lives and their families' lives? Fräulein Kingsmith gave me food, she gave me clothes that had belonged to her father." The sunken eyes were wet.

Wyatt gestured to the waiter for more drinks. "Käthe's declared a moratorium on the war," he said. "She seems bogged down by shame."

Leventhal had regained his composure. "We survivors do carry heavy burdens."

"She's not Jewish."

"Is there something wrong with my hearing? Or my English? Didn't you tell me her father, mother, and stepbrother are dead? That makes her a survivor, and eligible for the benefits. Guilt, and more guilt." The drinks appeared. Leventhal downed his. "Wyatt. Such an American name."

"The Wyatts are my mother's family."

"Myron was named after our great-grandfather, the Leventhal who founded the business. Mendel. Did you know that?"

"Mother only talked about him once, when she told me."

"Still, you went to meet the judge with a poker up his ass?"

Wyatt gave a brief smile and shrugged. It was twelve, and the bar was filling up with officers having prelunch drinks. "Heinrich, would it be too painful for you to repeat what you just told me? Would you testify for Käthe?"

"Testify?"

"I'm defending her. She's being tried as a Nazi."

"Fräulein Kingsmith? I can't believe it! You Americans are crazy."

"We do our best with the cards dealt us."

"But why her?"

"Among other things she admitted to having top clearance at the OKW and being friendly with the late lamented Führer."

"I'll not only testify, I'll see if I can trace any of the others she helped."

V

The following afternoon Wyatt set his briefcase on the board table. Because this was his last pretrial visit to his client, he was permitted to meet with her away from the cell, in this bare little room that had been used for similar anxiety-laden conferences since before Kaiser Wilhelm's coronation.

A guard with a rifle led her in.

"Good afternoon," Käthe said.

Wyatt didn't respond. The encounter with Heinrich Leventhal had shaken him in so many areas that at times his thoughts got derailed.

"Thank you for the chocolate bars. Magda enjoyed them." After another silence she asked, "What's wrong?"

"You baffle me. You always have," Wyatt said. "Will you answer one simple question honestly?"

"If I can."

"Are you trying to kill yourself and make both me and the Military Government accessories?"

She lowered her eyelids, hesitating. "It's difficult to care about anything."

"Don't you owe Aubrey a bit more than that?"

"Aubrey?"

"Remember him? The man you're meant to marry. You realize, don't you, that he won't let you serve a sentence. He'll go to our top brass and explain that you were spying for the British—"

"He told you *that*?" she whispered through white lips.

Until now Wyatt had not been positive whether Aubrey's hint had been on the level. Warning himself not to soften up on her, he went on, "The story will be officially denied. And as for Aubrey—have you ever met anybody better qualified to play Sydney Carton? He'll face a court-martial."

"Please, Wyatt."

"I'd also like you to consider that these trials are not frivolous. We Americans are revolted by what a bunch of sadists did in Germany. We want to punish those who gave the orders and those who carried out the horrors. If that's simplistic and naive, well, we are both of those. But, Käthe, we are trying to reach the world with a message that some evils are too monstrous to be borne. And if our military tribunals convict the wrong people, why, then our efforts become a laughingstock. Is that what you want? It sure as hell is what the Nazis want. Germany will heal eventually, and the same old bunch'll be right back in power. Hitler will have won. Do I sound as if I'm on a soapbox? Well, I am. But I mean every word. I'm telling you exactly what I believe."

The sun had gone behind a cloud, and the light coming through the barred window was gray.

"I've never heard you like this before," she said in a low voice.

"Normally I hide behind my brilliant wit. But now I'm laying myself on the line." He leaned so close that he felt the warmth of her breath. "Fräulein Kingsmith, I'm going to lose this case if you keep playing your nihilistic little game with me."

"You've twisted everything around."

"The tribunal's decision might be no big deal to you, but it's important to me. And to Aubrey." He paused. "And to Heinrich Leventhal."

"Herr Leventhal?"

"I met him yesterday."

Sudden pleasure blazed on her face. "So he made it to the American line!"

"Because of you, or so he says."

"Thank God! But how did you find him?"

"One of those coincidences that make me believe in the

Sledgehammer of Fate. Or a Higher Power. I went to the International Red Cross to get a bead on Sigi's lady friend, and who should be there at the exact moment? Who should be sitting near enough to hear my name? A great way to learn there's a star witness, right?"

"Could I see him? Can a witness visit the prison?"

Wyatt relaxed, perceiving that he had blasted through some sort of barrier. For the time being at least, he had hauled Käthe out of her enigmatic, grieving inertia. "He'll be at the tribunal."

FIFTY-SIX

I

Zeppelinalee, a long, narrow parkway where old trees exposed their wintry limbs, was surrounded by Belle Époque homes built by a happier generation of Frankfurt bankers and industrialists. A few of these mansions had survived, and Käthe's trial would take place in one of them, in a third-story ballroom.

Reddish scars showed in the ebony paneling, and much of the lacelike ceiling molding was gone. The stained-glass oriel windows had been repaired with ordinary glass so that glaring sunlight mottled the jewel colors falling on the huge American flag stretched across the musician's dais behind the judges' empty table. A hundred or so of the uncomfortable gilt chairs once used by Frankfurt chaperones and wallflowers had been neatly ranked, but only the front rows were taken. Those present were relatives of or witnesses for the two other defendants who would be tried this morning.

As the MPs led Käthe in, she peered searchingly at the worried-looking women, the men in shabby, brushed suits or Wehrmacht uniforms. A legless veteran perched on a little wheeled cart. Herr Leventhal wasn't in the courtroom. She sighed. She had been looking forward to seeing him.

Wyatt already sat at one of the pair of tables facing the bench. "Don't look so worried," he said. "Heinrich's not playing hookey. He's at the airport meeting a witness who stayed at your house. He'll be along in a few minutes."

Käthe put on a look of interest. She hadn't given a thought to how Herr Leventhal's absence might affect her case. Other than her concern about Aubrey's reaction, she had no interest in the outcome. Since that snowy evening in Darmstadt depression had clamped her like an iron maiden, constricting her arms and legs, compressing her lungs so that on occasion she imagined her breathing needed to be monitored. *Inhale, exhale.* She slept lightly and awoke weeping.

In the paneling to the right of the flag a nearly invisible door opened. A stout, ruddy-faced major strode out, followed by two far younger lieutenants. When they were seated behind their triangular brass nameplates, the marshal, a bemedaled sergeant, clicked his polished heels. "The Honorable judges of Military Tribunal One-B!" he bawled. "Military Tribunal One-B is now in session. God save the United States of America and this honorable tribunal."

The white-haired woman who sat at the end of the judges' table translated the words rapidly into German.

"The two looies were traffic cops. Major Fitzpatrick in the middle is a lawyer, he's the one who counts," Wyatt said in Käthe's ear.

Occupation courts mixed U.S. and German legal customs. She, the accused, went to stand at the table in the lonely space below the bench.

The prosecuter, Lieutenant LeFar, stood to read the indictment. The muscles around his left eye jumped as he droned that the accused had been cleared by the Gestapo to work with military secrets, she had been a guest at Hitler's Chancellery and been invited to his ultimate hideaway in the mountains above Berchtesgaden. Though not a member of the Nazi party, she was one of the Third Reich's inner circle. The white-haired woman repeated the charges in German.

Major Fitzpatrick leaned forward. "So you knew Hitler, Fräulein"—he consulted his papers—"Kingsmith?"

Before the white-haired interpreter could say anything, Käthe responded in English, "I met him three times."

The mustached lieutenant to Fitzpatrick's left inquired suspiciously, "Where'd you learn to speak like that?"

"My father came from England."

Fitzpatrick did not so much as glance at either of his fellow judges. "The court feels it'll speed things up if we proceed in English," he said. "Tell us how you came to be in such close contact with Hitler."

When she said the dictator had congratulated her on winning a gold medal at the Olympic Games, the young lieutenants sat up straighter. Fitzpatrick skipped to her work, inquiring what she had done at the OKW.

"I filed documents in the Most Secret Hall."

"In our country," he said, "for a job like that you'd have needed some mighty heavy clearance. There must have been even tighter security here. Or did the Führer put in a word for you?"

Wyatt responded, "My client obtained the job through her half brother, Colonel Siegfried von Hohenau, adjutant to General von Hohenau, of the German general staff. Both were involved in anti-Nazi activity. And so, as we intend to prove, was Miss Kingsmith." He emphasized the *Miss*.

"The accused will answer for herself, counselor," Fitzpatrick said, turning back to Käthe. "You were cleared by the Gestapo, then?"

"Before 1943 the OKW used its own intelligence, the Abwehr."

"Are you trying to tell us," said the lieutenant with the curly hair, "that a gal entrusted with filing the biggest secrets in the Axis wasn't given the once-over by the Gestapo?"

"I'd assumed only the Abwehr," Käthe said uncertainly. "But I understand what you're saying. Possibly they did clear me, the Gestapo."

As the tribunal exchanged glances, she heard Wyatt's fingers tapping on the wood. A warning.

"In your work," the major asked, "did you spot any evidence of the camps?"

Anger briefly clenched Käthe's throat. *Yes, and I sent on the information to a branch of Allied intelligence.* "Several times," she said.

Fitzpatrick's face mottled a darker red. "What?" he asked excitedly. "Army orders for the exterminations?"

"Nothing like that. The camps were administered by the SS. I filed letters and memos from Wehrmacht officers expressing disapproval of the brutal mistreatment."

"Did you tell your superiors about these papers?"

Her superiors? The *Blitzmädchen*? The chief filing clerk with her Nazi party badge? "No," she said.

"Did you tell General von Hohenau?"

She couldn't remember seeing the one-eyed general at more than a distance after the journey home from the Bavarian Alps. "No."

"You never spoke out to anyone?"

She shook her head. "I didn't, no."

The three faces hardened to intransigent antipathy. Käthe agreed wholeheartedly with their opinion of her.

II

The tribunal, once again following German custom, permitted a far more liberal admission of evidence than an American court. An MP flown in from Berlin was called. He testified that Käthe had escaped when granted a compassionate parole to visit her ailing grandfather in London.

"May it please the tribunal," Wyatt said. "I was Miss Kingsmith's escort. She didn't escape. I permitted her to leave."

"According to Berlin military police records"—Fitzpatrick's ruddiness increased as he consulted the papers placed in evidence—"your report used the word *escape.*"

"I was worried about her safety, and needed help finding her. Anyway, I fail to see the connection between this and whether or not she was loyal to the Nazi party."

Käthe's head was throbbing, her legs felt rubbery. They seemed to be haggling over a third person. At a stirring behind her in the ballroom she turned.

Heinrich Leventhal was coming down the aisle between gilded chairs. Though thin, he wasn't the skeletal wraith of the previous year. She smiled and he smiled back—that quirkily caustic expression that she had seen often on Wyatt's face. (Had Erich done his childish mischief with that same familial smile?) At Herr Leventhal's side marched a short young brunette in an ATS uniform. Käthe couldn't recall seeing the girl before, much less giving her shelter. Wyatt requested an Old Testament so that his witnesses could be sworn in, a bit of courtroom theatrics that went right past Käthe.

"Herr Leventhal, could you tell me when you first met Miss Kingsmith?"

"In the latter part of 1937."

"Can you recall the whereabouts of that meeting?"

"The Berlin New Museum's Tel el Amarna hall. We were in front of the head of the Pharaoh Akhenaton's mother."

"Was it a chance introduction?"

"Not chance at all. Miss Kingsmith had heard I was in a camp —it was Esterwegen—and had contacted a mutual friend to see if she could be of assistance to me. Believe me, that sort of solicitude was rarer than diamonds. By then I'd been released, so I showed up to thank her."

"Was your imprisonment common knowledge?"

"No. The story came to her attention in New York. She is a friend of my cousin there, Judge Abraham Leventhal." He paused to give weight to Käthe's friendship with an American Jewish judge. "He was concerned about me."

"What was the upshot of your meeting?"

"She offered her help to anyone who needed it. Though the persecutions weren't so intense in 1937, we were already in the soup. I gave her a paper to take to a friend of mine in the underground, he was what they called an Aryan."

"What was his name?"

"Christian Schultze."

Fitzpatrick leaned forward. "Where can the court contact Herr Schultze?"

"Alas, the next world." Leventhal sighed.

"Did the Gestapo get him?"

"They visited him five times to my knowledge, but he was clever as well as brave. They never found any evidence. Poor old Schultze, he was killed during an air raid. But you're right about the Gestapo keeping an eye on anyone who helped us. When Miss Kingsmith took the papers from me at the museum, she was well aware that she was risking a three-year sentence."

"A girl friendly with Hitler imprisoned for running an errand?"

"Running an errand for a Jew, Your Honor."

Wyatt asked, "Can you tell the tribunal when you last saw the defendant?"

"Almost exactly a year ago. I had been in Bergen-Belsen, but I'd managed to escape and make my way to Berlin." Leventhal's face had taken on an unnatural pallor, but his voice remained level. "Fräulein Kingsmith gave me a loaf of bread and some other food. An outfit of her late father's clothes. It doesn't sound like much, does it? But by then helping us was a capital crime. And at the risk of offending the tribunal, I doubt if anyone else in this courtroom, German or American, would put his or her life on the line to help a near-stranger."

The next witness, Ursula Kohn—the round-faced young corporal in the ATS—was sworn in.

"Corporal Kohn," Wyatt asked, "can you give an approximate date when you met Miss Kingsmith?"

"I can jolly well give you the exact date," retorted the corporal. "November ninth, 1938. Kristallnacht."

Käthe frowned, and then her mind's eye flicked on a remembrance of the narrow courtyard behind Kingsmith's, a little girl shrinking back into the red-tinged darkness. The corporal's neat features had dissolved into misery, and she took out a handkerchief.

"If you'd like to wait," Wyatt said sympathetically.

Corporal Kohn blew her nose. "I'd rather go ahead and tell your court what your Nazi prisoner did for me. It was called Kristallnacht because everywhere in Germany that night gangs were breaking our windows. They also burned our houses and our synagogues. The police held back anybody who tried to help. I tell you, that night was worse than the Blitz. There was no place to hide. Big bullies came into our flat and threw my father out the window—we were on the fourth floor." The corporal blew her nose again. "My mother pushed me out the back door. I ran miles, then hid behind a shop. Miss Kingsmith and Mr. Kingsmith, her father that is, came out and saw me.

They drove me to their house. On the way we picked up two old ladies, Brandsteiner they were called."

"Good old Uncle Alfred," Wyatt muttered to himself.

Corporal Kohn overheard. "It wasn't only Mr. Kingsmith and Miss Kingsmith. Frau Kingsmith entertained the three of us, I'll never forget what a lady she was. A real German lady. She served us tea with rum from a tiny crystal jug like we were visiting royalty."

"How long did you stay?"

"Only that night. But the next morning Miss Kingsmith drove us to another house, where we'd be safe. Herr Leventhal found out about my mother—she'd been arrested for 'assaulting an Aryan.' Then he arranged for me to get on one of the children's boats to England. Off I went, no luggage, no papers, only a placard around my neck with my name and a number. I thought a lot about going in to Kingsmith's on Bond Street, saying thank you to the family. But it's not my sort of shop, if you know what I mean. Very, very posh. So I let it slide. When Herr Leventhal contacted Aunt Dorrie—that's Mrs. Gibbs, the lady who took me in—she called me at the base and said, 'You always wanted to thank Miss Kingsmith, so hop to it.' If the Kingsmiths are your idea of Nazis, you've got another think coming."

During this emotionally delivered recital Käthe was swamped by memories of her mother. She had indeed served the little girl and the frightened spinsters as if they were royalty, for it had never occurred to Clothilde von Graetz Kingsmith that there was another way to treat a guest. *Mother, how I miss your irritating schedules and your annoying certainty, that gracious generosity.*

Corporal Kohn paused on her way to the seats to kiss Käthe's cheek.

III

Lieutenant LeFar, his eye twitching, rose. "If it please the tribunal, I will read a letter into evidence."

Wyatt groaned. Grudges were settled by mailing anonymous

letters of denunciation to the U.S. Military Government, but the information also had led to a number of top-ranking Nazis.

"The envelope is postmarked November twenty-first, two months ago. It was mailed in Frankfurt."

"Unsigned?" asked Fitzpatrick.

"Yes."

"Objection," Wyatt said. "It could have come from anyone."

"As you are aware, Counsel," Fitzpatrick said, "we follow the German law, giving far more latitude to admission of evidence than our own courts. Go ahead, Lieutenant."

The prosecutor began to read.

" 'To whom it may concern. Fräulein Käthe Kingsmith, currently in detention at the facility of Ober Tappenburg, was a Nazi sympathizer deeply committed to the Lebensborn program—' "

At the word *Lebensborn* a peculiar rustle went through the ballroom. This winter virtually the entire German population stuffed newspaper under their clothing to keep warm, and the spectators were all leaning forward to peer at Käthe. Swaying, she pressed her hands on the table.

"Lebensborn?" Major Fitzpatrick was looking at the secretary/interpreter.

"It means the fountain or well of life," the white-haired woman responded with prim disapproval.

"May it please the tribunal," said LeFar. "Lebensborn was a Nazi program, but it wasn't talked about openly even then. And now it's completely squashed into the woodwork. To find out what went on I had to dig hard. It seems that Hitler wanted more Germans, so homes were set up for unmarried girls to have babies." He paused. "The SS men serviced them."

"My God!" the major expostulated. "Human stud farms?"

Käthe concentrated on breathing. It was the most appalling sensation to be standing alone in her rumpled Harrods suit with everyone staring at her while a monotone voice displayed the unhealable scar across her life. She tried not to imagine the shock and revulsion on Wyatt's face. *His baby.* But of course he would never, never know that Erich had been his. *Dead, dead, dead.*

" '. . . Only girls who could prove their racial purity back to the year 1750 and were dedicated Nazis were accepted in a Lebensborn home. Evidently Fräulein Käthe Kingsmith fulfilled both of these requirements. She bore a son in the Villa Haug house in 1940.' " The prosecutor's flat voice grew chatty. "These places had their own secret registry offices and the babies were given to top Nazis." He returned to his drone. " 'It is possible that afterward she recruited other girls to the program.' "

Listening, Wyatt had balled his hands into fists until the knuckles stood out like ivory knobs. The manner in which Käthe had swayed, then grabbed the table, had convinced him that the letter was faithful to the truth. He attempted to distance himself. Wouldn't he have been as jolted if any client withheld such incriminating evidence? But it was a purely intellectual exercise. Emotionally he felt as if he'd been drenched by a bucket of human waste.

He jerked to attention as Major Fitzpatrick said, "Continue."

"That's the end of the letter," the prosecutor said.

"Mark the letter for identification," the major said. "The envelope should be marked too."

A courtroom attendant uniformed in the gray green of the local police stepped forward to take the evidence.

Major Fitzpatrick stared down at Käthe. "Have you anything to tell this tribunal?"

She shook her head.

"You were part of this breeding operation?"

"Yes," she whispered.

"The tribunal can't hear you," Fitzpatrick said.

"Yes." Käthe's voice worked like a mechanical device. "I was at a Lebensborn home."

For the first time Major Fitzpatrick consulted his fellow judges, the three of them whispering.

"This is a complicated case," he said at last. "The tribunal will have to take it under consideration."

FIFTY-SEVEN

I

"You're looking better," Wyatt said in a strained voice. It was early the following morning, before the exercise period in the yard, and he had been brought to Käthe's cell. Then he burst out, "Jesus! Couldn't you have warned me?"

"I'm sorry," she said.

"Listen, as far as I'm concerned, who you hop into the sack with is your own damn business! But I'm meant to be your lawyer. So tell me right now if the tribunal's liable to get word you were jerking off Adolf."

She raised her chin. It was the same look of pride covering misery she had worn on the long drive back to Ober Tappenburg.

Drawing a sharp breath, he said in a quieter voice, "The decision'll be handed down a week from Monday. My orders are to head back to Berlin. I'll come here then. I can't promise anything, but they did seem to be listening to my closing argument."

"I suppose I should thank you, but . . ." She shook her head.

"Is that why you ditched me, to look for this child?"

"It was my only chance."

He was silent a moment before he asked, "He's dead, isn't he?"

"A few days before . . . He died a few days before we traced him down."

Could I have gotten her out of Ober Tappenburg when I visited? It seemed unlikely, yet he felt awkward and guilty. He sat next to her. "Käthe, you aren't contemplating anything more drastic than trying for a prison term, are you?"

"So many killed in the war, millions still dying from illness and starvation—what difference would it make?"

"There're religious and ethical answers to that one, but as of the moment they escape me."

"You don't need to worry." She sighed. "The authorities at Königstrasse Prison are strict about everything, including the confiscation of self-destructive items."

"That's good," he said. "Käthe, listen, I'm sorry about your boy."

She rubbed a fingernail on her tweed skirt. "After Araminta did you try to . . . ?"

"In a big way. Eight dead Germans and a Distinguished Service Cross, that's what happened while I was trying. I won't con you and say you'll get over it. The wound closes, the bleeding stops, but the pain's always going to be there."

"But what if all that's left is pain?"

"The first thing is to get through today. Then you get through tomorrow. Then the next day."

Down on the ground floor, doors were clanging open and shut, women chattered, a guard's bass voice bawled for silence.

"Thank you," she said.

"I promised Aubrey I'd do my damnedest."

"Not for defending me," she said under the cover of the din. "For not staying angry. For being kind."

II

As sentries passed Wyatt through the locked grate to the locked courtyard, he spotted Leventhal in a sheltered corner, writing on a pad of paper.

"I'd hoped to see Fräulein Kingsmith," Leventhal explained. "She's not allowed visitors, so I'm dropping her a note."

"No mail either. But I'll give her the message that you were here."

At the thick-walled, old-fashioned gatehouse Leventhal retrieved his papers. They emerged onto the street. He pulled his shoulders back. "That's the first time since Bergen-Belsen that I've let a key be turned behind me. So tell me, how is Fräulein Kingsmith?"

"Not real great. But she looks more human than yesterday." Though the sun was out, the morning was cold and Wyatt buttoned his overcoat. "Jesus! That damn letter! How could she?"

"Wyatt, have you noticed that Germans don't look directly at me? They're overly friendly, most of them, but their eyes never connect with mine. I'm the living reminder of what this country wants to forget. Fräulein Kingsmith looks me in the eye."

"Don't tell *me* it doesn't give you the dry heaves to know she was in bed with some guy who maybe sent thousands of people to the ovens."

"Forget what she did between the sheets, Wyatt. She saved my life, she helped save a lot of other lives. She could teach those martyrs and saints of yours lessons in unblemished altruism."

"The jeep's over there," Wyatt said. "Come on, give you a lift."

At a gust of wind Leventhal clamped a hand on his shabby homburg. "You *are* doing everything that's possible to get her off?"

"That's a hell of a question."

"You've never explained your past relationship, but I can tell it wasn't on a cousinly basis. Yesterday there was murder on your face."

"You noticed it didn't interfere with my closing argument!"

"My God, you're like Myron. That same quick temper." Leventhal chuckled. "I'm sorry I asked, it was insulting—and unnecessary. You have that same streak of obstinate decency as he had." They climbed into the jeep. "I've got one last name to look up at the Red Cross, so if you'll be so good as to drop me off there. Tomorrow morning I'm leaving for Switzerland. Fräulein Kingsmith means a great deal to me. If I give you an address, will you let me know the outcome?"

"It goes without saying." As Wyatt detoured along the passable streets to Grosse-Bockenheimerstrasse, he asked, "What's the straight dope on Lebensborn?"

"It was Himmler's pet project. You'll have an easier time understanding if you keep in mind that he was a chicken farmer. When he came to power with the Nazis, he set out to breed the new Aryan superrace. But alas for Himmler, humans aren't as docile as chickens. Not enough German girls were willing to do their share, so during the war he initiated another Lebensborn program in the Occupied Territories. Mostly Scandinavia. He kidnapped racially and physically acceptable babies, thousands upon thousands of them."

"Jesus!"

"They were placed for adoption with SS families and other loyal Nazis. Now the real parents are here, searching through all four sectors. What a nightmare. I've met a few of the poor people. They follow the wildest leads. They drive themselves crazy—several of the women, the mothers, have gone insane. The Norwegians set up an agency to help. A couple of days ago I had lunch with the person who runs it. She was very down in the mouth. To her knowledge not a single kidnapped child has ever been returned to its own family."

"Not one? That's hard to believe."

"Think of it. The children were infants when they were taken. They have no memories, different names. Blue-eyed blondes in a land of blue-eyed blondes."

"Still, you said there were thousands. Never to have found even one child?"

"She's convinced the SS run a network capable of falsifying birth registrations, baptismal papers, death certificates."

"Wouldn't that have come to light?"

"How? Your denazification program isn't working very well. The Germans know you won't stay here forever. They're a beaten people. They worry, quite reasonably, that the same group will be back in power soon. So even the ones who despised the Nazis keep their mouths shut."

"We call it closing the ranks."

"Exactly. The SS are able to do what they must to keep the children for the Master Race."

III

Arriving at his office in the Berlin Luft Gau complex, Wyatt called London.

"What happened?" Aubrey's voice came thin and metallic over the buzzing long-distance line. "Is she free?"

"The decision won't be handed down until Monday week."

"With so many cases I shouldn't have believed they'd take time to deliberate," Aubrey said. "How did it go?"

"Pretty well." *Badly, very.* "I dug up a Jewish man she sheltered." *My cousin Heinrich found me.* "He brought along one of your ATS, Berlin born. She testified that Käthe and her family helped her and others on Kristallnacht."

"I should have thought the tribunal would have given her three cheers and carried her out on their shoulders."

They would have, if my client hadn't been fucking her way through the SS officer corps. "She doesn't give me much to work with. It's like pulling teeth."

"Did she tell you that Sigi and his uncle were in the conspiracy to get rid of Hitler?"

"I pried it out of her. But according to captured OKW records Sigi died for the Führer in the Ukraine."

"Do you know what *sippenhaft* is?"

"One of the sweetest laws on their books. Retaliatory measures against the families of Hitler's opponents. Käthe only told me she was in jail. So Sigi was the reason?"

"Precisely. Wyatt, if it goes against her, tell them about the beating."

"What beating?"

"Just before the surrender. She has scars from it."

"She's never let out one peep about any damn Nazi whipping her."

"Over her entire back."

The operator cut in. "Sorry. All calls must be limited to three minutes."

Wyatt sat back in his swivel chair. His eyes were narrow and brooding, his cheeks drawn in. His mind was giving off warning signals. Aubrey had never lied to him and was the most high-minded, ethical person he knew. Yet if he'd learned one thing in his legal career, it was not to have any illusions about the use of perjury when it came to saving a loved one. Furthermore, Aubrey's wartime activities, though God knows courageous, had called for massive dosages of fabrication.

Had there been a beating?

FIFTY-EIGHT

I

On the Monday when the tribunal would hand down its decision, Wyatt arrived in Frankfurt at lunchtime. In the Buick assigned to him at the Rebstock airport motor pool, he headed for the Casino Officer's Club. Both dining rooms were full. He spotted Major Fitzpatrick alone at a small table. Normally at such a time he would have avoided a judge, but he was far from sanguine about the verdict so he weighed eating in the snack bar against the possibility of a little out-of-court finagling. After a momentary hesitation he jostled around the noisy tables.

"The joint's packed," he said when he had shaken hands with Fitzpatrick. "Mind if I join you?"

"If you're not out to suborn me," Fitzpatrick said with a braying, good-natured laugh. "Sit you down, sit you down. Eating alone puts a crimp in my appetite. Not that I couldn't stand to lose a few pounds." He patted his substantial belly. "Hahaha."

While Fitzpatrick eagerly spooned the Heinz cream of tomato soup, Wyatt toyed with his bowl, talking about his task of weeding out Nazi legislation.

"They enacted some lulus," he said. "Take *sippenhaft,* for example."

"*Sippen* what? That's a new one on me."

"Kith-and-kin detention. The Nazis legalized the punishment of families of anyone they considered a traitor." Wyatt aligned his spoon. "I'm not meant to discuss the case but, hell, strictly off the record, you surely must realize my client is my cousin."

"It's an unusual name, I figured you had to be related."

"Well, Katy," Wyatt said, pausing purposefully as he anglicized her name, "had a half brother from an old Junker family. He's the one who got her the job at the OKW. Incidentally, one hell of nice guy. As far from a Nazi as you can get, Sigi. Back before the war, we were up in Garmisch-Partenkirchen—"

"Fabulous spot. Went skiing there over the holidays."

"How about that Zugspitze? In those days, though, parts of the scenery could get pretty obnoxious. I tore down a couple of their Jews-*verboten* signs. Some Party plug-uglies jumped me, and Sigi plowed right in at my side. That was Sigi all over. It came as no surprise to hear he was in on the July Plot."

"The July Plot? With von Stauffenberg?"

"Right, right. There were so damn many defendants that it began to reflect badly on old Adolf, so Goebbels swept some of them under the rug. They put out that Sigi was killed in action. Then turned to *sippenhaft*. My aunt was shot. And Katy." He paused. "Katy has scars covering her back."

"Those sadistic Heinie sons of bitches!" Fitzpatrick burst out. "A gorgeous gal like that! But, Kingsmith, you know we follow European procedure when it comes to admissible evidence. Why didn't you tell the court that she'd been beaten by the Nazis?"

"To level with you, the story was news to me. There's a lot Katy refuses to talk about. I only found out by accident that she helped Herr Leventhal and the others."

"Doesn't like blowing her own horn, eh? Must be the British side. Say, how did you Kingsmiths get to be a United Nations anyway?" The newly formed U.N. was the subject of many jokes—and much hopeful conversation.

"My grandfather has a silver and fine arts shop on Bond Street. Before the first war he opened branches in Berlin and New York, sending Dad and my uncle to manage them." Wyatt tore off the end of his roll, buttering it. "I've often wondered what would have happened if Dad had been the pick for Berlin.

Probably we'd all be dead like my uncle, aunt, and poor old Sigi. Or have scars like Katy."

On that pensive note he stopped. The German waiter with the threadbare white cotton gloves was setting down their porterhouses.

II

The helmeted MP who escorted Käthe from prison to the de facto courtroom on Zeppelinalee stepped away to give her and Wyatt privacy. But after the initial muted greetings neither counsel nor client spoke. The tribunal filed onto the dais. Käthe went to stand in the lonely space below them.

Fitzpatrick turned toward Wyatt with a long glance before he spoke to her. "The court has given much careful consideration to your case," he said. "According to your own testimony you supported certain of the Nazi party's most odious principles. However, the evidence given by Herr Leventhal and Corporal Kohn has swayed the tribunal to be lenient. The sentence we must pass is mandatory under Public Law Number Eight. You may not hold any position higher than ordinary labor."

Käthe returned to Wyatt. "What did he mean?" she whispered.

"You can't get a good job," he said. "But you didn't draw a jail term."

"I'm free?"

"You've been sprung." He was laughing. "Get your coat and I'll walk you out of here."

III

Great wads of threatening clouds scudded below the blanket-like overcast. In Zeppelinalee the ancient beeches that grew in a hallowed circle were waving their branches menacingly. The only people about were the driver of a staff car and two old women shuffling after twigs to use for kindling. As Wyatt and Käthe paused at the entry, he asked, "Now that you're a free woman, what's on your agenda?"

"I haven't had time to think."

"Aubrey'll take you to England."

"Not in the near future, not with my record." Her soft voice wavered. "Oh, how I'd love to see Grandpa! And the family. And your little boy."

"He'll get you there, believe me, at least on a visit."

"I need a job," she said. "What I'd really prefer is working with small children, but probably that would be considered higher than ordinary labor."

"Nobody familiar with little kids would agree."

She made a smile. "First things first. I'd better register right away at the *Rathaus*. Get identification papers, a ration card. Wyatt, you've been marvelous, and it wasn't easy. I'm sorry about . . . well, the letter."

"Water under the bridge," he lied.

"You're quite a lawyer."

"I played a little dirty pool is all."

This time her smile was impish and natural, then she said gravely, "There are no words to thank you, but it's in my heart." Raising her hand in lieu of a good-bye, she pushed open the glass-and-ironwork outer door.

Squaring her slight shoulders, holding on to her English beret, then pulling it off, she ran across the street, walking rapidly around puddles, slowing to trudge through the desolate circle of trees. Wyatt watched the wind flap at her tweed coat and tear pale strands from the smoothly combed hair while descriptions tolled through his mind: lonely, fragile, doomed, lost . . .

"Käthe!" he shouted, jogging after her. "Hey, Käthe, hold on there!" She waited beneath the bare, whipping branches. Reaching her, he said, "A celebration's the next order of business."

"Don't you need to get back to Berlin?"

"Not yet. And no arguments. A victory brawl is an integral part of American jurisprudence. I saw Rumpelmayer's on the way here."

Across the broken stucco of the renowned café's facade a sign had been painted: BATTLIN' B COUNTRY CLUB. One of the infantry regiments of the 70th Division had requisitioned Rumpelmayer's: the floor shows, the jazz band, the excellent liquor, had proved such a hit that the GIs had opened their doors to all ranks of Allied troops. In the afternoon, when business was slow, a pianist performed. The chords of "I'll Be Seeing You" rippled as a German waiter popped open the Piper Heidsieck.

Käthe watched.

"Those look like long thoughts," Wyatt said.

"Trying to remember my last champagne."

"The past is behind you." He raised his glass. "To the future."

Käthe gulped, sneezing. "I'd forgotten how the bubbles go up your nose."

The pianist switched to a haunting rendition of "In the Still of the Night," a song that had been among the records Wyatt had brought to Germany that long-ago Christmas. They glanced at each other, then looked away.

Wyatt refilled their wide-bowled glasses to the brim.

"To the pride of the Columbia Law School," Käthe toasted too vivaciously. "When are you being discharged?"

"I have more than enough points, and the folks are panting to see Geoff."

"Yes, your little boy." She smiled, then tears began to ooze.

He poured more champagne. So what if they got blotto? He knew he needed to escape his red-haired phantasm, and she had so many more ghosts to lay to rest than he did.

"Käthe," he was saying, "they kidnapped the babies."

Her querying eyes fixed on him, eyes the blue-green of the huge, drowning sea.

"They?"

"The SS. They took the blondest little kids in the occupied countries. It was part of the Lebensborn program."

"I know," she whispered.

"The real parents have come searching. They never track down a living child."

"You mean the SS killed the babies?"

"Not at all. They get people to phony up the records. They fake death certificates." Jesus, how crocked was he? If he weren't loaded, why would he be gazing into these beautiful, wet aquamarine eyes and uttering words of hope about a child whose brief existence on this earth sickened him? "They go to any lengths to keep their adopted kids."

"My Erich . . . he's dead."

"What makes you so certain?"

"She told us, the woman who adopted him."

"So how did you find this Nazi bitch?"

"Through Groener."

"Groener? Who's Groener?"

"He thinks he's—" she said, and stopped abruptly. She had been about to tell Wyatt the truth—she had the perfect opening. She had drunk more than enough champagne to say anything. Yet a sober part of her mind told her that Wyatt would question her—and she knew she would break down completely under his cross-examination. She knew also that even though he might appear convinced, he would always retain his doubts. *What difference does it make who fathered Erich? My baby's dead. He's dead.* The unaccustomed alcohol, rather than dulling her grief, compartmentalized it, making the anguish sharper. Resting her elbows on the table, she propped her face in her hands.

"Is Groener the SS boyfriend?" he asked.

"Wyatt, I'm all woozy."

Wyatt drove her to the Excelsior, where he took two single rooms.

IV

In London late that same Monday afternoon Aubrey sat at his typing table. The telephone, stretched to the cord's limit, stood on the rug five feet away. His fingers tapped out a sentence, then he glared reproachfully at the silent instrument. He had come home to his bed-sitting-room early to await word from Wyatt, using the pretext of transcribing his notes about the scattered, sadly depleted German network, information too sensitive, or so he said, to be entrusted even to Miss Cockle, the secretary assigned him by CI-4. Thus far he had typed only two pages.

The telephone sounded. Jumping to get it, he tripped on the cord and fell to his knees.

"Aubrey?" asked Porteous. "Is that you?"

"Grandfather," Aubrey groaned.

"Will you be going down to Quarles this coming Sunday?"

"Sorry. Can't talk now. Ring you later."

Getting up, he returned to his typewriter chair and sat staring at the telephone, symbol of his chafing impotence. What was bloody wrong? Didn't Wyatt realize he'd be on pins and needles to hear? Had the ruling gone against her? Was his brother-in-law trying to spare him? Aubrey's orders were to remain in London. Yet he gathered his notes and the typed pages, opening a drawer and pressing a catch to reveal a secret compartment. The papers safely stowed, he packed his small valise.

TWELVE
1946

In the vast incoherence following the Second World War, life was cheap. It was not unheard of for war criminals to escape retribution by murdering those who might give them away.

—from *Maelstrom,* a 1987 PBS documentary

FIFTY-NINE

I

The rooms in the Excelsior adjoined. Käthe didn't bother shutting the connecting door. She pulled off her overcoat and kicked away her brogans, which were lined with cardboard because of the holes worn in both soles, stretching on the bedspread. She fell into a heavy slumber.

Wyatt stood at his window gazing at the monumental curve of the nineteenth-century railroad terminus against the curdled sky. The way Käthe had slid from questions about her SS lover had revitalized his original skepticism about the beating. Had Aubrey invented it to insure a more spirited defense? A few drops of rain splattered on the glass. With slow footsteps Wyatt moved to the door. As if sensing his presence Käthe turned on her side, facing away from him. Waiting a few breaths, he went to the bed. Carefully he drew the pale blue sweater away from her neck.

The scar tissue on the luminous flesh between her shoulder blades resembled embroidery.

His eyes squeezed shut and he winced as if forcing back tears. Gently covering her with her coat, he returned to his own room, sinking into the easy chair.

II

He slept as if the impulses of his brain had been short-circuited, awaking to darkness. His mouth tasted foul. Closing the door between the rooms, he went to the built-in washbowl, brushing his teeth and splashing cold water on his face. *I'd better find out if the kid's really dead.* Lifting his head, he stared at his dripping reflection. The idea was preposterous. He had never wanted food less, but from experience he knew that after drinking he must eat in order to think straight. He pressed the room-service buzzer. Finishing the regulation hotel cuisine, American canned goods abetted by fish from the Main, he lit a cigarette. His decision to discover the facts about the child held.

Pouring coffee from the nickel-silver pot, he carried the cup into the other room.

"Käthe?"

Opening her eyes to see him, she jerked up. "My head," she groaned.

"Too much celebration." Wyatt held out the cup. "Java'll help."

Sniffing, she said, "It's real." She took the cup reverently in both hands, as if holding a chalice.

He waited until she had finished. "Up to talking?"

"What about?" she asked warily.

"Remember anything I said at Rumpelmayer's?"

Her eyes widened, and she clasped her hands together. "The SS alter the death records," she said softly.

"Sometimes. But don't get your hopes too far up. The odds that he's alive are—" Holding his forefinger and thumb almost together, he left a minuscule space.

"I know." But the eagerness that shone in the big, slightly bloodshot eyes proved otherwise.

"First, you need to tell me a little about this Groener, or whatever his name is." Wyatt couldn't control a hint of sarcasm. "Think he might be your poison pen pal?"

"Nobody else *could* have written the letter. He was Sturmbannführer Groener. Now he's Herr Schwägermann. A *grosschieber,* a big operator in the black market. He told us he had high-up friends at headquarters."

"What did he do under the swastika?"

Her eyelids lowered. "First the Gestapo. When the war

started he transferred to the SS in Poland. Later he worked on the rocket bombs, controlling the slave labor."

The food Wyatt had just eaten rose sour in his throat and he spoke thickly. "A sweetheart, your fella."

"He raped me," she mumbled.

"If you say so."

"He did," she said, nearly inaudibly.

Wyatt shrugged. "How did you know he was in Frankfurt?"

"I didn't." She explained that she and Aubrey had been searching the records of nearby towns and she had spotted Groener at the restaurant in Offenbach. "We followed him to a warehouse in Höchst. At first he refused to tell us the name of the adopted parents, where they lived or anything."

"But eventually he did."

"We blackmailed him." Excitedly Käthe held out her arms with her hands curved and moving as if jiggling a huge ball. "I'll bet anything *he* has Erich! Of course he does! Both his little boys were killed in an air raid, and he even told us he'd been thinking of getting Erich. That awful creature who said Erich had just died, Groener must have put her up to it. She wasn't the mother—I *saw* the people who adopted him. The mother was far younger."

"And that brings us to one final salient detail. How old is the kid?"

"Five," she murmured.

Five. She had saved lives, she had possibly risked her life working with Aubrey, she had those scars. Wyatt had every intention to be forebearing. But he was inundated with memories of that last summer of peace when he had begged her to marry him and she, oh, so virtuously, had persisted she must keep her covenant with her parents, then had rushed home to get raped (?) by her friend, this Aryan prince.

"You're a mystery to me, Käthe. Maybe Aubrey understands what makes you tick, but I sure as hell don't," he said bitingly. "First thing tomorrow I'll get over to headquarters and uncover what I can about your buddy." He kicked the connecting door shut behind him.

III

Wyatt spent the next morning tangled in red tape.

The squeaky-voiced top sergeant in charge of records insisted on a signature from the colonel before he would release the files for Kurt Schwägermann. The colonel was on a three-day inspection trip. Wyatt tried several of the colonel's subordinate officers: none would take the responsibility of releasing the dossier. Finally he ran into a guy he'd known at Columbia, now an adjutant to General Clay, who cut through the snafus. It was after one when Wyatt carried the accordion file to the window and scanned the typed interrogations. Kurt Schwägermann, born in Munich in 1908—there was a copy of the birth certificate—had served a three-month prison term in 1938 for his anti-Nazi statements. Immediately after his release he had married Jolenta Mohr, age seventeen. No children. In 1939 he had been drafted into the Wehrmacht. There was a mimeographed Gestapo form stamped POLITICALLY UNSUITABLE FOR OFFICER TRAINING. He had been wounded in the left shoulder at El Alamein, and in the chest by Italian guerrillas. This second wound had caused such extensive lung damage that he had been given a medical discharge, the record of which had been destroyed during an air raid. Eminently qualified to rise to the top of the Occupation barrel, he now headed a plant in Höchst that manufactured photoelectric cells for the PX. He and his wife had taken four invalids into their home. None of these invalids were children.

Wyatt weighed the papers in both hands. The guy was as far from an SS officer as a German could be. But it was not unknown for war criminals to shroud themselves in the identities of the dead.

He jotted down the address.

IV

And a very fine address it was, on the outskirts of the Stadtwald. As they drove there, Käthe recalled from history lessons, that Frankfurt had been the first city in Europe to sow a forest. Many of the ancient trees still stood. At the outskirts of the forest they knit their branches with the branches of their descendants to shelter a few well-set-back mansions.

The Schwägermanns' residence, although built of a particularly ugly brown brick, was commodious with the look of solid comfort. Tacked onto the left side was a conservatory. Tropically green ferns pressed against the outsize panes, none of which was cracked or boarded over, a mass of unbroken glass that was near-mythological in postwar Frankfurt. Wyatt, idling briefly at the cross-hatched gate, continued past several houses and made a U-turn, parking. A huge pine fairly well hid the car.

Käthe's attention remained riveted on the Schwägermanns' property. Not a soul went in or came out. The haze of coal smoke evaporating above the main chimney was the sole sign of habitation.

For nearly an hour she stared, fidgeting, while Wyatt calmly read his pocket book—of all things, *Anna Karenina.*

The front door was opening.

Käthe leaned as far forward as the dash permitted. Trees impeded her view, so she caught only a fleeting glimpse of a young woman wearing a red felt hat with the brim pulled smartly down on one side.

Wyatt hadn't been so intent on Tolstoy after all. He whistled softly. "Must be Frau Groener-Schwägermann."

After a minute the brunette swung open the big gate, halting to call in thin, sharp sounds like ack-ack. "Stop dawdling. Hurry up!"

A child in a heavy coat, short pants, and gray knitted stockings burst into sight.

Arms outspread, he raced along the pavement, dipping and swaying to simulate an airplane in flight. His shining platinum bangs swung and flapped. Color suffused his cheeks. His glowing skin shone a robust, sun-kissed brown rather than the milky white that normally accompanies such pale hair. His legs pistoned. He seemed to vibrate with dynamic energy.

"Erich . . ." Käthe breathed.

"Kid's pretty big for five," Wyatt said doubtfully.

"It's Erich!"

"You said Groener had two other boys—"

"This is my baby!"

"Shhh!"

The child slowed, actively interested in the American car, then he stared into her face. His soft, babyish mouth curled in a saucy half smile that brought an ache to Käthe's frantically pumping heart. Then he swerved, racing under the trees in his pretend airplane.

"Erich!" the woman shrilled. "Erich! Come back here this minute." With a put-upon, long-suffering grimace in their direction, she trotted after the child, who was already a hundred feet ahead of her.

Käthe rested her head back on the car seat and breathed deeply. Perspiration beaded her forehead. The joy that was sweeping through her in great waves was so powerful, the reverberations of her heart so precipitate, that she understood the expression *die from happiness.*

V

For the next hour the external world passed like a shadow show. She barely heard Wyatt reiterate that she didn't have a thread of evidence that the boy was hers. How could he not have seen himself in Erich? Had he never glanced at a reflection of his own smile?

The duo returned, the woman dragging the child's arm. "Erich, you hurry up!"

Watching the woman hustle the child inside the gate, Käthe said, "Did you hear that?"

"Okay, okay, I grant that in a few seconds and without a word you established a mystic oedipal bond—"

"She called him Erich!"

"It's not the secret name of God. Aubrey might like more positive proof than a first name that the boy he's about to rear is at least half a Kingsmith." As he said this, his cheeks splotched with red.

"Aubrey trusts me."

"Listen to yourself, Käthe. Trust? There's only one way to trust that this kid is yours and that's to have a talk with your wartime buddy."

Suddenly she laughed. "Why're we snapping at each other? I've waited this long. I can wait until Groener gets home."

Wyatt had brought his service pistol and was inspecting it.

"Aubrey took his to the warehouse," she said, eyeing the weapon nervously. "We never needed it."

"And Groener didn't exactly level with you either." Wyatt slid a clip into the Colt. "Käthe, there're no second chances. Once we confront your old friend, he'll be gone—vanished. Maybe he won't even take the boy with him but will send him to another sector. One thing's for sure. We'll never find the kid. So if he is yours, he's got to leave with us."

VI

A cold waning moon lit the way as their footsteps crunched on the gravel path that curved around the trees. Since Groener had parked the Kübelwagen on the street thirty minutes earlier, Käthe's hands had been shaking and she'd had difficulty catching her breath. Wild with impatience as she was, she'd nevertheless agreed Wyatt was right: they should give Groener time to settle down.

Seen up close by moonlight, the house appeared yet more imposing than it had that afternoon. Electricity was not available for German housing after nine: an old-fashioned oil carriage lamp diffused its glow around the arched entry.

They went up the three broad steps.

"Ready?" Wyatt asked.

"All nerved up, like before a race, except multiplied by a thousand—a million." Without forethought she raised up on tiptoes, kissing his cold cheek. "Thank you, Wyatt."

The door opened. A manservant stood holding a chamberstick. The draft wavered the candle flame, but even in the uncertain shadows it was possible to see that he wore his green livery jacket with the same air of martial fitness as the watchman at the Höchst warehouse.

Apparently the household was accustomed to American officers arriving late at night. "Herr Schwägermann expects you?"

"Yes," Wyatt said.

The servant marched through the hall to the rear of the house. A few seconds later Groener's stocky outline came striding toward them.

Nearing the door, he halted. "Käthe?" His shadowed face displayed a consternation similar to when she'd arrived at the Höchst warehouse. "But what are you doing here?"

"We need to talk," she said, adding, "This is Captain Kingsmith."

"Ah, the American 'cousin,'" Groener said, and she could tell the hint of derisive amusement was forced. The brunette had come into the hall. With a brusque jerk of his head Groener dismissed her. The woman moved toward the staircase, puckering her lips to blow a coy kiss at him as she took the candle from the servant.

Groener said, "Come this way."

SIXTY

I

The small study was dominated by its fireplace. A pair of life-size wooden caryatids supported a mantelpiece adorned with a mass of carved dwarfs, the great heap of blazing logs threw off more heat than was necessary, and the reddish firelight competed with the glow cast by the spirit lamp on the table. Käthe perched as far as possible from Groener, clasping the handle of her purse to conceal the nerve spasms that swept through her.

"There are no children listed at this address," Wyatt said in his fluent, badly accented German. "But a boy lives here. Tell us about him."

Groener, apparently recuperated from his shock at seeing Käthe on his doorstep, picked up his snifter, warming the glass between his palms. "First, Käthe, what about you? I heard you had a bit of a problem with your denazification."

"That letter you wrote didn't cut the mustard with our tribunal, Groener," Wyatt said. "Now, let's forget the crap. Who's the kid?"

"My son."

"You told Aubrey and me," Käthe said, "that your sons were killed in a bombing raid."

"They were." Sorrow flickered across Groener's brutally good-looking features, and he took a sip of brandy. "But I had this other boy out of wedlock. What a scamp! A real handful. And my Jolenta's not used to children."

"She's not the mother, then?" Wyatt asked.

"I met Jolenta last August. It was easier to list her as my wife, but to use an American term, she's a shack-up."

"He's mine, isn't he?" Käthe asked in a strangled whisper.

"You could have asked that in the first place." Groener smiled. "Of course he is."

"And you sent me on that wild goose chase! I've been in every kind of hell. Who was that creature?"

"Wasn't her performance convincing? After thirty years acting with the Schauspielhaus in Berlin she ought to be able to play a bereaved hausfrau. And in case you're worrying about the real Dettens, they didn't want to give Erich up, but Reinhard was about to be arrested because of his war work—she told you the truth about dispatching the trains to the East. They needed me to sneak them out of the country and arrange passage. They've been in Montevideo since September."

"And you had the Darmstadt records altered?"

"Käthe, Käthe, by now you should know it's a favor here, a favor there." Groener shifted in his chair, looking at Wyatt. "Did you know Käthe as a flaxen-haired little girl, Captain? I did. When she grew into a Nordic princess, I fell in love. And in time I had her."

"Against my will," Käthe muttered.

A log broke, sending up sparks as the halves fell with a small crash. Käthe jumped. Neither of the men stirred.

"We were quite good friends at Villa Haug and later," Groener said. "And as for not taking pleasure in bed, why would you? Decent women don't."

"We're not here to talk over old times," Wyatt said coldly.

"This is between her and me, Captain. Käthe, call me a sentimentalist, but I still feel exactly the same. What about it? As my wife you'll have a fine home, servants, this son—and other eugenically sound children."

"You're a murderer," Käthe said.

"In a war all men have red hands."

"We didn't gas people—or work them to death," Wyatt said hoarsely. "You'll swing."

"So that's it, eh?" Groener's small eyes narrowed. "My son in exchange for your silence? Well, there's no deal, Captain."

"He's my baby!" Käthe cried.

"Uncle Kurt he calls me, but soon I'll ask him to call me Father. And when he's old enough to understand, he'll learn that I *am* his father."

"Käthe wants her son," Wyatt said.

"And I explained the terms by which she'll have him," Groener said, pausing. "The only terms."

"Like hell," Wyatt said and in a swift motion reached under his topcoat for his pistol. His arm steady, he aimed at Groener.

"A gun? You're kidnapping him?"

"Getting him back for Käthe."

Groener turned to her. "Steal my Erich and you'll never be safe in your own country." Sweat was trickling down his face. "This I swear, Käthe. As long as I live, you'll never be safe anywhere in the Reich."

"Too bad you Nazis lost the fucking war, Groener," Wyatt said. "Now, where's his room?"

Tears shone in the keen, little eyes. "Käthe, I love the boy, he loves me."

Wyatt's finger tensed on the trigger. "Move!"

Groener picked up the oil lamp.

He led the way up the broad, shadow-haunted staircase, Wyatt following a step behind, Käthe trailing. Again she was having difficulty catching her breath. Her legs refused to function properly and she needed to clutch the banister. Her mind, too, was performing oddly. She worried about ludicrous details, like whether she would have time enough to put on Erich's dressing gown and slippers.

They went down the bedroom corridor. Groener opened a door.

II

An insignificant drift under the down quilt. A soundlessly sleeping child.

At long last, her son. . . .

"Okay, Käthe," Wyatt said. "Get him."

She passed between the men. She could smell the odor of their sweat, hear the rasp of their breathing. Memories of them both jumbled inside her head. Wyatt's somber voice in the London hotel room telling her to decide whether she would return to Germany or marry him. . . . The streak of blood on Groener's brown leather couch. . . . Groener's fatuously proud smile above her bed in the tower room at Villa Haug. Groener's thick, careful hand on the knife as Erich howled on a swastika-pillowed altar. Wyatt's tense pallor last night when he'd stunned her by saying he would find out whether Erich was alive.

She bent over the bed, lifting her son.

He stirred sleepily and she pressed her cheek against his soft hair, hugging his limp, warm weight. In this instant, after nearly six years of privation and danger, of terrible doubts, of crippling grief, it seemed to her that there was, after all, a God.

Suddenly everything went black.

Groener had extinguished the lamp. She poised by the bed, clutching Erich. The fine hairs rose on the back of her neck as the floorboards reverberated with an invisible, gasping struggle. Her hands spread across Erich's back and she hugged him protectively to her body. He whimpered, pushing sleepily at her face.

There was the flat, almost hollow sound of a fist connecting with well-muscled flesh. "Käthe, get the hell out of here!" Wyatt panted.

"Put me down." Erich was more awake now. "Put me down!"

"Hans!" Groener bawled. *"Hans, she has Erich!"*

Small, moist fingers were tugging at her hair, pushing at the small bones of her nose, poking at her eyes. It didn't seem possible that she could hold Erich and run. Yet her feet were sure in the darkness. The child struggled in her arms, wild and slippery as a landed fish. The sounds faded as she trotted down the staircase. She heard only Erich's cries and the blood drumming against her ears. Balanced to take another step, she found she had reached the landing. Erich's struggles had loosened the quilt. The feather-puffed fabric caught her foot. She tripped. Clutching the flailing boy closer, she thumped onto the drugget. She struggled to her feet with what seemed night-mare slowness.

Above, in the bedroom corridor, a door opened and the wedge of light cast dim, brown shadows. By this marginal illumination Käthe sped down a half dozen more steps. She clattered across the front hall's marble floor. Erich was screaming now.

"It's all right, Erich, it's all right," she panted.

A sudden beam of brightness blinded her. Unable to see who held the flashlight, she guessed it must be Hans, whoever he was, probably the muscular servant in the green jacket.

"Halt!" The man's footsteps pounded toward her. "Put down that boy!"

"Hansi . . ." Erich wailed.

A sharp noise exploded above them. The woman screamed. Hans swerved away. His flashlight casting a mobile, brilliant circle on the staircase, he took the steps two at a time.

Wyatt, shoving his service pistol back into the holster, was barreling downward. The two men collided. The flashlight clattered onto the marble, breaking. Now the woman's screams issued in a high-pitched monotone like an all-clear siren. Hans's steps resounded upward.

"Is Groener dead?" Käthe asked.

"No such luck. We were fighting for the gun and it went off. I grabbed it and conked him over the head. Here, let me take him." He reached for the struggling child. "You open the door."

Käthe fumbled with the bolt in the darkness. The chain clattered. Then they were outside, racing along the gravel path between moonlit shrubbery and trees. Into her mind popped a memory of the last time they had run side by side, that soft summer dawn in Hyde Park. Probably she had been pregnant then. They curved toward the gate.

"Achtung!" shouted a voice behind them.

A shot rang.

Then another shot.

Wyatt staggered. Crouched over Erich, he called, "Run like hell!"

But she waited until he and Erich were through the gate. Bullets whined around them. *Hans must have been in the SS. A crack shot. Why can't he hit us at this range?* It didn't occur to her until later that he was firing through trees at swift-moving shadows.

Wyatt flung open the back door of the car, diving inside with the boy.

He tossed her the keys. "Stop at the first MP you see. Go. *Go!*"

Erich was crying more softly now, and she could hear Wyatt's wheezing gasps as she frantically tried to find the ignition in the darkness.

Her foot pressed down to the floorboards. As the gears ground and the car jolted forward, Wyatt gave a grunt. She felt Erich's light body hit the back of her seat. The motor-pool Buick's headlights bored between the ancient trees of the Stadtwald. She didn't slow.

Erich sobbed tonelessly.

Wyatt was silent.

SIXTY-ONE

I

Krankenhaus Frankfurt, on Klarastrasse, built at the turn of the century in the neoclassical style, had a grandiose gallery intended to serve as a visitors' waiting room, but after the hospital had been requisitioned by the Military Government the rare visitor was shunted down to a windowless basement room.

Erich lay weeping on the old-fashioned horsehair sofa while Käthe sprawled in the shabby armchair watching him. She had just finished the struggle to change the uncooperative child from pajamas soaked with Wyatt's blood to the government-issue, man's khaki undershirt that a kind-voiced, bespectacled nurse had given her. Sensing Käthe's gaze, Erich gave a bellicose kick. The army blanket slithered onto the linoleum. Turning his back to her, sobbing wearily, he sucked on the Hershey bar that the nurse had unwrapped for him.

Käthe leaned forward, once again attempting to reassure him. "You'll be safe here," she said.

He averted his face, his body convulsing with an effort to halt his sobs. He hadn't spoken a word since they'd left Groener's house. But why should a bright child, almost six, already uprooted from one home and one set of parents, put any trust in a stranger who had snatched him from his bed, then rushed him into the bullet-streaked moonlight? What sort of reassurances could go over after that wild drive? With a sigh he finished the last square and clutched the T-shirt to his mouth. After a few minutes his fingers fell away. He had cried himself to sleep.

Käthe tiptoed to cautiously wipe the ooze of chocolate from his chin and replace the blanket. "Sleep tight," she whispered, kissing his forehead. "Sleep tight, my baby."

Returning to her chair, she wore an expression of dread. She had no watch, there was no clock. How long had it been since the medics had rushed Wyatt away on the gurney? Plasma had already been dripping into his arm, an oxygen mask had covered his nose and garishly white lips. A swift-moving scene of terror. *Maybe he's already dead,* she thought. At a tap on the heavy door she gave a little gasp and jumped to her feet. She was aware of an icy chill as though the warm little underground room had suddenly frozen. This must be the doctor. Come to tell her—what?

But it was Aubrey who opened the door.

II

Too distracted to question either what he was doing in Frankfurt or how he had found her in a military hospital, she flung herself at him, weeping into his rough uniform as desperately as Erich had wept earlier.

"Shh, shh," he said, stroking her hair. "Käthe, it's all right."

Käthe pulled away, wiping her knuckles across her eyes, taking his handkerchief.

"So Wyatt got you off," he said after she had blown her nose.

"Oh, my God, we never told you. Yes, he did a masterful job."

Aubrey took a step toward the couch. "And this is Erich? But—"

"Groener took him from the Dettens." Telling what had transpired the previous two days, Käthe repeated herself or left out chunks of time, yet Aubrey nodded as if her story were fully coherent. "I blame myself," she finished. "I knew what Groener was. How could I have let Wyatt go there?"

"Käthe, this is Wyatt's son."

"He has no idea."

"Not even now?"

She shook her head, and began to cry again.

"Don't, Käthe, don't." Holding the slender, shuddering

body that he loved, he wondered at the paradoxes of human nature. How could Käthe, surely by any definition of courage a heroine, be so abjectly terrified of Wyatt's disbelief? And how could Wyatt, susceptible to every doubt about Käthe, put his life on the line to regain her child, ostensibly by a man guilty of crimes against humanity? And what about Aubrey Kingsmith? Why, when he desired only joy for Käthe, was he snared in this murky web of rivalry?

"If you'd seen him when they took him away. . . ." She wiped her eyes. "His tan looked like makeup, there was blood everywhere, and his breath rattled."

"He's strong, Käthe." Aubrey didn't add that Wyatt would need superhuman resilience to overcome the negative prognosis he'd heard at the desk.

Without a tap the door burst open. A narrow-shouldered officer with sleep grains in the corner of his eyes introduced himself as Lieutenant Rockwell. Although Rockwell's high-pitched tenor voice was loud and penetrating, Erich didn't stir.

"I'm here to investigate what happened to Captain Kingsmith—"

"How is he?" Käthe interrupted.

"Still on the table, and in damn grim shape, or so they tell me. Fräulein, there's a lot of questions before we get to the shooting of an American officer in the back." Rockwell's precision indicated a certainty that she had aimed the gun. "First off, both sergeants I talked to said you had no papers. That's a criminal offense. And why do you call yourself Kingsmith? And what about the kid? Is he yours? How's he involved in this mess? Straight answers, understand? No tricks."

On hearing Wyatt's condition Käthe had sunk into the chair. With a light touch on her hair Aubrey introduced himself. "It's an involved story, Lieutenant, and I for one can't blame you if you're dubious. But this lady's name *is* Kingsmith. You see, we're all three cousins." After several minutes Aubrey had convinced Rockwell that it might, just might, be plausible that Wyatt had been shot while rescuing Käthe's son from the home of a high-ranking SS officer who had falsified his *fragebogen.*

"If that's true it'll be a case for a Military Government prosecutor," Rockwell said, turning to Käthe. "I'll need you to take me to the house and identify this SS criminal."

She began to shiver. Her nervous system was tethered to Krankenhaus Frankfurt. Physically as well as mentally she was incapable of leaving either Erich or Wyatt.

"My cousin's had enough for one night," Aubrey said firmly. "I'll go with you."

III

"We had two jeeploads of men following us to the Stadtwald," Aubrey reported two hours later. "No need to tell you the house was deserted. Still, it gave me a chance to fetch those things for Erich." On the small table lay a tangle of boy's clothing, a board game, a battered toy truck with scratches where the swastikas would have been. "We left a sentry, and I led the parade to Höchst. Groener's watchman had decamped from the warehouse. But the crates of American food, the medical supplies, and cigarette cartons proved to Rockwell that whatever else, he was in the lair of an enterprising black marketeer. He stationed four guards around the place. On the way back he relaxed, thanking me profusely on behalf of USFET. I gave him full credit."

"That's you all over."

"I could scarcely request a medal, Käthe. I'm meant to be in London, and besides I've been given direct orders to stay clear of the American zone."

"What if you're caught?"

"Why should I be? Touring Germany with forged papers is child's play nowadays."

"They'll miss you in London."

"In my branch one can always concoct an excuse to have rushed off."

She managed a smile. "Aubrey, I feel so awful, not letting you know the verdict right away."

"No need to keep apologizing, darling," he said. "I'll trot upstairs and see if that nice old nurse with the glasses has heard anything about Wyatt."

He returned almost immediately. There was no news.

IV

At a little before six, when Erich began shifting and making wordless sounds, Lieutenant Harrison, the bespectacled, warmhearted nurse, came to tell them that the captain was out of surgery.

The operation had been complicated by the second bullet, which had grazed close to his heart, the nurse said. He had lost a worrying amount of blood. He remained in acutely critical condition.

As the door closed behind Lieutenant Harrison, Käthe slumped down, twisting her handkerchief. It was Aubrey who noticed that Erich was awake. The child had a strong boyish face with Wyatt's high cheekbones. The eyes were Käthe's blue-green, but far less dreamy than hers at the same age—or so Aubrey remembered. Intelligent, wary eyes watching them both.

The boy didn't respond to Käthe's introduction, but at Aubrey's offer to show the way to the lavatory, he nodded. Aubrey, recalling that at Erich's age he would have been mortified had a strange woman been in the room while he dressed, picked up trousers, pullover, and underwear.

After the door had closed on them, Käthe looked up at the ceiling.

When I see Wyatt will he be alive or dead?

SIXTY-TWO

I

". . . Frowline Kingsmith?"

The two words spoken in a questioning tone wavered through the sinister ruins where decomposing German corpses sat up to aim rifles, machine guns, and howitzers at him. But the voice was a woman's, American, and therefore had no place in this devastation.

He opened his eyes. Ocher colors wavered and tarnished. Blinking, he concentrated. The olive shades coalesced into walls and a screen at the foot of his painted metal bed. His mind sullenly refused to make connections. He sensed he was drugged, but the pain encompassing his chest and abdominal cavity was real, and so was the sweaty smell of the sheets and pillowcase, the cut of coarse cotton under one armpit, the foul taste in his mouth. The rack with the bottle was mistily out of focus, but he knew an IV when he saw one. And the woman standing over him wore a nurse's uniform.

He was in a hospital.

"Captain Kingsmith, are you up to a bit of company?"

He tried to say, "Sure," but to his befuddled surprise his larynx and tongue refused to cooperate. In his nightmares he couldn't move or function and now, with proof of further physical dereliction, he was no longer quite so positive that he had reentered the real, substantial world.

"Hello, Wyatt." Käthe's soft, disembodied voice.

His memory returned in random segments. Racing from

Groener's house. Odd punching sensations in his back. Throwing the boy into the car. The brilliantly lit surgery with green-masked figures. Pain. A hypodermic needle. Nurses and orderlies prodding him. Pain. Thirst. The delicious refreshment of cracked ice. Thrashing pain. Another hypodermic needle.

"How are you feeling?" she asked.

"Groggy. . . ." This time his voice worked, but in a strange croak. "How long . . . ?"

"Three days."

I've been out of it that long?

He peered toward the foot of the bed. A beclouded image of pale blue and the silvery shine of loose hair, the style he liked best on her.

"You've had us all worried," she said. "But you're on the mend." She moved a step closer. "Wyatt, you were marvelous."

"The boy?"

"Erich's fine. At first he wouldn't talk, but now he's chattering away. He beats us regularly at checkers."

"Us?"

"Aubrey's here. He's cabled your parents and the rest of the family. They all send good wishes."

"Sit down," he said. His voice was stronger.

The chair scraped as she sat at the head of the bed. Near him. Her face looked weary. "Erich's very quick for his age," she said. "He's got quite a sense of humor."

He didn't want her talking about the boy. He didn't want her talking about Aubrey. "The bottom sheet's twisted," he said.

"I'll get the nurse."

"Stay." He shifted a bit on his elbow. The rubberized tube twisted the long needle in his flesh. He winced.

"Does it hurt?"

"Me, I'm here for the waters."

"What?"

"Just a line from a movie."

She bent over and kissed his hand. Her lips were cool and soft, and he felt the moisture of her tears. He closed his eyes, sighing with an emotion that felt suspiciously like relief.

On this tough hospital mattress, glucose seeping through his veins, her lips on his hand, he dimly perceived that he had ratified an armistice. It was ended, his personal war, a war that had lasted almost a decade and been fought on terrain that he had never fully understood, love, hate, rejection, and fear of rejection. At the opening ceremonies of the 1936 Olympics he had fallen for a girl who in his mind embodied the Third Reich's physical ideal, and this image of the Nazi propaganda machine's flawless blond *mädchen* had been superimposed on his every thought of Käthe. Now at long last that obscuring double image was gone. He saw only a vulnerably beautiful woman with skin blotched and eyes red veined from weeping. Why his vision should have cleared at this particular moment was a vagary that scarcely brushed his mind.

His fingers rubbed weakly at her chin. "Hi," he said.

She raised her head and gave him a misty smile. "Hi."

The pain pills they were giving him seemed to be working better.

II

Aubrey had bartered cigarettes for two new dresses, a cardigan and skirt, a trim blue coat, and smart cocked hat. Aubrey had procured books, a soccer ball, crayons, and coloring paper for Erich. Aubrey had arranged with Lieutenant Rockwell to get Käthe and Erich identification papers and ration cards. Aubrey insisted she never leave either the Krankenhaus Frankfurt or the Excelsior Hotel without him.

"It's Groener, isn't it?" she asked a few evenings after his arrival, while they were finishing their after-dinner coffee. She spoke quietly in English. The door was open to the single room where Erich slept. "You're worried about Groener."

"You should have the wind up a bit too. After all, he warned you that you're not safe in Germany. And even if it weren't for Erich, you know entirely too much about his past."

"So does Wyatt," she said.

Aubrey took off his glasses, rubbing the heavy lenses with his handkerchief. "The hospital's well guarded."

"There's no reason to worry about Erich and me. Groener'll stay well clear of Frankfurt."

Aubrey glanced significantly toward the bedroom. "He's most attached."

"Yes, but he's too shrewd to come back—"

There was a whimpering sob. Erich must be having another nightmare. Käthe ran to waken the little boy, then sat comfortingly close on the bed.

Erich was not an easy child. Extremely bright and volatile, as she imagined Wyatt must have been, subjected to the ceaseless bombings and then uprooted, he swung on an altogether logical pendulum between a childishly resentful silence and rowdy obstreperousness. He often spoke admiringly of Uncle Kurt, quoting him as the ultimate authority. He seldom alluded to his adopted parents—Käthe and Aubrey conjectured that the Dettens' abrupt departure had cut the psychological ground from under the little boy's feet.

Within a few minutes his eyes closed and his jaw relaxed. Käthe tiptoed back into the other room.

III

Aubrey pulled his chair closer to hers, saying quietly, "I can't stay in this sector much longer."

She had known he couldn't but had put off thinking of his departure. "It'll be terrible without you," she murmured. "I don't know how I'll manage."

"I'll miss you, too, darling." He paused. "I've reserved these two rooms for you."

"Aubrey, how can I keep on taking from you?"

"There's no reason I should handle the bill. You're not in the least short. In fact, you're very nicely off indeed. There's your six years of back pay from His Majesty—that will need to be transferred secretly, of course. Through me. But the big balance is from Kingsmith's. As Uncle Alfred's heir you own a ten-percent share. Even with wartime taxes Father's branch has done handsomely. And thanks to Aunt Rossie the Fifth Avenue branch has boomed."

"I had no idea."

"I'm arranging a visit to London for Erich and you."

"Aubrey, you know how restricted travel is, especially for Germans. With the trial and my not being properly cleared, they'll hardly let me into England, even for a holiday."

"You still show remarkably little confidence in my abilities," Aubrey said with a rueful smile.

"I don't much care to be married to a man in the stockade for life."

The newly cleaned lenses magnified his eyes. "So you're still planning to marry me?"

"Any woman who passed you up would be an idiot."

"Are you saying that because you gave me your promise?"

Of course it was true that her promise bound her. But it was equally true that the emotional savaging of the war had torn her apart. In her exhaustion she perceived Aubrey's quiet, unassuming love and steadfast faith as the only sanctuary in a ruined world. She had always cared deeply for Aubrey. Although she had never ceased to love Wyatt and he evidently was involved again, too, she could not believe that he would ever give her his complete trust. And she could not bear any more suspicion. Any mistrust about Erich would topple her. Her future belonged to Aubrey, didn't it?

"Oh, Aubrey, Aubrey," she said, sighing. "Don't you see that you're getting the rotten end of the bargain?"

"Me? Darling, you're unique," he said.

She lowered her gaze. "I can't think about a wedding yet, though," she said.

"What will you do?"

"Aubrey, I've been searching my head for ways to turn the Garmisch-Partenkirchen chalet into a home for some of the orphans."

"German children?"

"DPs, Jewish, German. You know how many hundreds of thousands there are, scavenging, stealing, living like animals. I'd like to help as many as I can. The attic's huge, the bedrooms will make dormitories. Do I have enough to buy food, clothes, medicine, maybe pay an assistant?"

"Several assistants. This is hard English currency."

"And you? After you're demobbed, will you go back to King-smith's?"

Aubrey gave a little shudder. "Thank God I don't need to. No recurrences of Father's heart trouble—he's doing brilliantly without me. I'm going back to writing."

"Could you at Garmisch-Partenkirchen, with the children's hurly-burly?"

"Wherever you are is heaven for me." He put his arms around her.

"You're the finest, most decent man I've ever known," she murmured. Unhooking his glasses, she kissed him. She did not, however, respond in kind to his whispered avowals of love, and pulled away gently when he suggested they move to the bed.

IV

Aubrey had taken the room across the corridor. Leaving the door ajar, he sat at the desk. From here he could see Käthe and Erich's rooms. Setting the Webley in front of him, he opened his valise to remove six sharpened pencils and a spiral-bound notebook marked:

TROSPER'S PEOPLE
Section Three

At first his pencil moved across the page slowly, but after a few minutes the lead point raced. He had reentered the world of his spy novel. Though he could reveal nothing about CI-4, he inserted enough interbureau politics, murky loyalties, forgeries, agents, counteragents, incompetence, cold dread, valor, blind luck, and physical details to make his world real. He walked among the throng of characters who were more vivid to him than anyone he knew, with the exception of Käthe. He breathed this world's atmosphere, he responded to the world's specific gravity. Yet he dropped the pencil, his hand immediately on the weapon in front of him as footsteps came down the corridor.

It was the floor porter with his cart gathering shoes.

Aubrey returned to his fictive reality.

Trosper had long ago accepted that Analiese would never love him. It was ridiculous, and he knew it, to believe that the untamed passion she had nursed for Methuen before the war and all during the war would fade, or even lessen. His jealousy was equally ridiculous. His friend Roger Methuen, whom he had always envied for that spontaneous courage, that heedless generosity, that skin which tanned a rich chestnut instead of splotching red. What was the point for him, Trosper, to keep listing to himself the childhood memories and adult pleasures that he and Analiese shared—good music and books? He inwardly admitted an unromantic type like himself didn't deserve her. She was exquisite, she was brave, her character was the purest essence of gold, and like gold, her actions were never tarnished. He might not comprehend certain of her motives, but she invariably deserved the great reservoir of trust that he'd placed in her—a trust that Methuen lacked. Analiese knew Methuen had never banked on her, she knew that he often considered her the enemy. But love, as Carmen had sung, is a wild, free bird.

A bit sticky, Aubrey decided, but emotionally accurate, and therefore suitable for the pen of C. Osmond. He replaced the notebook, turning the small key in the lock of his valise.

SIXTY-THREE

I

Snow fell on Frankfurt that day and the next. On Sunday the sky was a hard Prussian blue and sunlight bounced off the whiteness, dazzling the eye.

Aubrey, taking off his wet gloves and brushing them against his coat, stepped back to watch the large and small bundled-up figures put the finishing touches on the snowman. Käthe's long hair had tumbled from its upsweep, and as she knelt on the path next to her son, the strands fell onto the boy's more buttery platinum thatch. Her face blazed with the same rosy-cheeked pleasure as his. The two were searching the slush for bits of gravel. With an exultant cry Käthe found three matching-sized stones and handed them to Erich. He pressed them like buttons down the snowman's rounded front.

"Splendid!" Aubrey exclaimed. "Now all he needs is a hat." He took off his cap, crowning the snowman's head.

"Captain Tommi," Erich said with a salute.

The adults smiled over his head.

"It's three o'clock," Aubrey said. Visiting hour. In his unobtrusive way he was examining the barbed wire strung above the privet hedge of the hospital's slit of a garden, the burly sentry pounding the cleared pavement, the armed staff sergeant in the metal security shed.

"Captain Snowman needs a private to order around," Aubrey said. "Why don't you and Erich start while I run on up?"

Käthe and Erich moved a few feet, scrabbling up snow with

sweeping movements of their hands, the two of them enclosed in a bubble of shared laughter. *He seems to be coming around,* Aubrey thought, yet he knew any obscure impetus could transform the child to anger or sustained silence.

The sun's warmth was melting the snow. The marble steps were slippery. Aubrey, in leather soles, ascended with mincing caution, hoping like some ridiculous adolescent schoolboy that Käthe wouldn't look up to see him.

II

Wyatt had shaved off the heavy fair stubble. Healthy color showed in his face. Instead of the hospital gown he wore blue-checked flannel pajamas whose unbuttoned top showed crisp beige chest hairs and a broad swath of bandaging.

"You're looking fit," said Aubrey.

"The fever's down."

"Been chasing the nurses?"

"According to the Geneva Convention a prisoner need reveal only name, rank, and serial number." They laughed, and Wyatt asked, "Did I hear Käthe and the kid outside?" He had not yet called Erich by his name, and, since children weren't permitted to visit, had not seen him since the shooting.

"They're building snowmen. She'll be in later." Aubrey sat on the white-painted chair. "Tonight I'm flying to Hamburg."

"Big doings in the British sector?"

"As far as my superiors are concerned, I've been in our zone the entire time." Aubrey paused. "I've asked for an MP to keep an eye on the two of them."

Wyatt was no longer smiling. His cheeks were gaunt, his jawbones showed, and it was possible to see how much weight he'd dropped in the past week. "Will they protect Germans?"

"In this case, yes. I suggested to Lieutenant Rockwell that Groener might contact Käthe."

"Must have been a good strong suggestion," Wyatt said. "When Rockwell dropped by yesterday, he told me there wasn't a ghost of a chance we'd see the Nazi bastard again."

Aubrey looked at the window, his eyes narrowing in the

brilliant winter sunlight. "In Hamburg I'll be making arrangements to take them home for a visit."

"Visit?" Wyatt's smile was rubber lipped. "Won't you be tying the knot?"

"Not yet." Aubrey turned to his brother-in-law. "When we do, you could be the best man."

It was a seemingly innocuous, even gratifying, request, yet something hot and wary flashed between them. Erich's childish laughter could be heard, a remote, merry sound out of place in a hospital—out of place in this ruined city.

Wyatt looked away first. "The thing that gets me, really gets me, Aubrey, is her and Groener. Do you understand it?" The twin furrows between his eyebrows showed the question was not rhetorical. "How could she have let that arrogant thug near her?"

Aubrey held his breath. The quiet room with the old-fashioned German hospital furniture, the chipped enamel bedpan and urinal, the linen screen, seemed poised. Everything in absolute stasis like the instant before a cracked dam breaks, before a delayed-action bomb explodes.

She ordered me never to tell him.

Yet . . . was it the right thing to let Wyatt remain in the dark? Was it fair to the boy, or to Wyatt—or, for that matter, to Käthe? *Be unfair, then,* Aubrey commanded himself. *I've always loved her, I've always trusted her. We're far more alike. She'll be happy with me. I'll spend my life making her happy.*

Unfortunately for Aubrey he was highly susceptible to acting against his own self-interest. "Aunt Clothilde wasn't the sort of mother a girl in trouble could go to," he said.

"But how did she get involved with him in the first place?"

"A Lebensborn home was secret."

"Will you quit going around in circles?"

"Erich's birthday," Aubrey said with clipped precision, "is April tenth."

The words seemed to be printed between them in the stuffy, medicinal air.

"What?"

"April tenth, 1940."

Wyatt's eyes narrowed and he was silent for over a minute. "Are you saying," he finally asked in a clogged voice, "that he's mine?"

"You know that better than I do."

"Why didn't she tell me?"

Aubrey might have too much integrity for his own good, but he was far from sainthood. "In New York you told me yourself that you'd sent a letter breaking it off."

"I sure as hell didn't know she was pregnant."

"And now you're going to say you'd have 'done the right thing'?"

"I'd have sold my soul to marry her."

"Unfortunately Käthe wasn't there to gauge the availability of your soul. And you can't honestly believe she'd let you marry her as a commitment. Let her child be your burden?"

"What about now? She's had a hundred opportunities to tell me."

"Just answer one question honestly." Aubrey spoke without heat. "Would you have accepted Erich as your son?"

"I just told you—"

"Or would you have put her through a cross-examination about dates and proofs?"

"Probably." Wyatt lay back in the pillow. "Yeah, I would have. But eventually I'd have believed her."

"Believed her completely? Never had the least feather of doubt?"

Wyatt covered his eyes with his hand, muttering hoarsely, "Get out of my room, Aubrey. Get the hell out!"

After Aubrey closed the door, Wyatt felt the pain stabbing his head and torso in the way that told him the fever had shot up. He pressed the buzzer.

The nurse came, then the doctor.

Sweating, filled with the bitterest of self-reproaches, Wyatt heard whispering: he could have no visitors.

He was grateful.

SIXTY-FOUR

I

Käthe and Erich's guard, Corporal Cosway, a recently drafted nineteen-year-old ranch hand with big ears that stood out, was waiting at the Excelsior. Before Aubrey left the following morning, the corporal had developed a crush on Käthe—his ears turned crimson when she spoke to him—and a rapport with Erich. A mercy. The child, viewing Aubrey's departure as yet one more in a chain of desertions, had become even more of a handful. He alternated between noisily charging along the hotel corridors and clinging silently to Käthe's hands or legs. The corporal, without any German and very little English, taught Erich to play the harmonica.

To the squeaky sounds of "Shenandoah" and "Red River Valley," Käthe worried about her son and Wyatt.

All week the NO VISITORS sign continued to dangle from Wyatt's doorknob. Were the nurses lying? Had Wyatt's sudden fever pushed him back onto the critical list? The new drugs didn't knock out all infections. Was he dying? When she succeeded in quashing these morbid fears, she would brood that Wyatt himself had ordered the sign to bar his only possible visitor. Her.

She could hardly burden Aubrey with her hair shirt of worries when he called from Hamburg on Friday.

Hamburg was the capital of the British sector, and he was billeted in ambassadorial splendor at a suite in the Atlantic

Hotel. "I'm flying home next week," he said. "It's all set for you and Erich to visit. The transport people couldn't give me an exact date when there'll be a pair of seats on a plane, but they're booked up for another fortnight or so."

There was a long hesitation, then the soft voice blurted, "Aubrey, you did understand, didn't you? I'm not ready to get married yet."

Aubrey gripped tighter on the old-fashioned German instrument. "We were discussing your travel plans. Or have you had other proposals?" He intended the remark as humor but was overly aware of Wyatt. His voice went clipped.

"If you're thinking of Wyatt," she said in a clear, formal tone, "I haven't seen him. Since his setback he hasn't had visitors."

"That's odd. A few minutes ago I spoke to his doctor, a nice chap called Wertheim. He told me the patient's doing better than expected."

The line had cleared suddenly, and he heard Käthe's sigh. Then she launched rapidly into Erich's virtuosity on the harmonica.

II

The cloud-mottled sky cast gloom on the orderly queue inching along Schillerstrasse. Ahead of Käthe a pair of preadolescent girls chattered about the parental injustice of dispatching them here every Wednesday and Saturday for a paper, opening their darned gloves every once in a while to ensure they still clutched the twenty pfennigs, the price of the *Frankfurter Rundschau,* the city's only German newspaper.

Erich, trailed by Corporal Cosway, had wandered over to join the urchins fascinated by the contortions of workmen jostling a great segment of metal water pipe into place. Erich said something to a taller, older boy; they both laughed, shoving each other playfully. As Käthe watched, the conversations around her came to an abrupt halt.

A large hand extended the four-page, ink-smeared newspaper with the heavy Gothic headline: PRESIDENT TRUMAN'S NINE STEPS TO FEED EUROPE.

"Here's your paper, lady," Wyatt said.

His khaki coat hung loose from his wide shoulders, the planes of his face showed, the tan had faded, yet his eyes were clear and quizzical. "Stop gaping," he said with a grin. "You haven't lost your marbles, it's me all right. The desk clerk at the Excelsior said you'd be buying a newspaper."

"But why aren't you in hospital? How long have you been out?"

He glanced at his watch. "Forty-five minutes. Have to check back in tonight. Come on, let's go sit over there."

Käthe, slowing her pace to his, moved at his side to the bus-stop shelter that by some miracle had remained intact amid the ruins. Several other children had joined in Erich's game, and he cheerfully shouted orders at them. Corporal Cosway was looking toward Wyatt and Käthe. When she caught his eye, his ears reddened. She pointed at the swirling, noisy group of children. The corporal plowed in to get Erich.

As they approached, Wyatt thrust his hands into his pockets, peering at the child with an expression of pain, as if his wound had reopened. Yet when he spoke to Käthe he used an offhand tone. "So that was your little rowdy bossing the gang?"

"Erich's a leader, yes." She bristled.

The boy shook clear of Cosway's grasp and moved toward them. He glanced at Wyatt with curiosity but no sign of recognition. It had been too dark to see his abductor.

Wyatt cleared his throat with a grating cough before he extended his hand. "Good morning," he said in his badly accented German. "I'm Captain Kingsmith."

The child lifted his cap politely, permitting his right hand to be briefly engulfed. "Delighted to meet you, sir." For all his mischievous wildness his manners never deserted him. "Kingsmith? Like Käthe and Aubrey?"

"The three of us're cousins," Wyatt said. "Is your name a secret?"

"I'm Erich Detten—no, Schwägermann."

"Bit of confusion there. What's the matter? Just get married?"

Erich laughed. Attempting to pay back humor with humor, he said, "Girls change their names when they get married!"

"Anyone can see that you're no girl, buddy."

Erich gave an upended grin so resembling the one on Wyatt's face that Käthe's hands loosened on the *Frankfurter Rundschau* and it fluttered to the cracked pavement.

To prevent the folded sheets from blowing away, Wyatt put down his shoe. "Corporal, you and my buddy here hike back to the hotel. We'll be along in a few minutes."

The corporal saluted. "Yes, sir."

Erich had picked up enough English to understand. "Käthe promised I could watch them put down the pipe."

"But I'm taking you to lunch. So march!" Wyatt emphasized his German with a swatting motion.

Erich stood with his hands on hips for a long moment to prove he wasn't intimidated, then, with a merry smile, brought out his new American phrase. "So long, pardner."

III

Watching the boy turn at the shell of a shop, Wyatt sank back down on the bus bench. With the lengthy, undisturbed hours of self-recrimination and dismal soul-searching, he had imagined himself altogether prepared for the elemental shock of coming face-to-face with Erich. In biblical terms his seed, the fruit of his loins. Yet looking into the rounded face, marking the resemblances, he had been battered by the accretion of many years, a ton of emotional garbage. There was no space at all for the unstudied tenderness he'd felt at Quarles when he'd first held Geoff.

"Erich's very outgoing." Käthe spoke with pride. "He's quite remarkable for a five-year-old, especially when you consider the war and all the catastrophes and turnabouts he's had. He can read, he can add. He's learning English as fast as anybody could. And he plays Corporal Cosway's harmonica."

Wyatt bent, stiff and dizzy, to gather her four-page newspaper. Pointing to the hospital jeep, he said, "I borrowed transport."

After they got in, he stared at the large red cross painted on the hood.

"What is it?" she asked.

"Maybe you've wondered why I stopped having visitors." He shook his head, falling silent again. He had argued Captain Wertheim, his doctor, into permitting him to leave the hospital for one purpose. To tell Käthe that he knew about Erich. He had planned apologies, planned the words to tell her of his shame.

"It doesn't matter," she said softly. "There's no way I can ever repay you."

She's given you the perfect opening, he told himself. *Say it! Tell her when a kid's yours, gratitude's not in order.* But his tongue had gone rigid. The speeches formulated in his hospital bed suddenly proved unsayable. But why? For one reason. Anything he said would be grossly unfair to his brother-in-law. Aubrey had always loved Käthe. Unlike himself Aubrey had always trusted Käthe. Aubrey was engaged to Käthe. Maybe out beyond the last, most distant galaxy there was an implacable, universal Judge who handed out equitable sentences, but in the meantime it was up to those involved in the case to do the right thing. What greater injustice than to give himself an edge because Aubrey had been decent enough to set him straight about Erich?

Starting the hospital jeep, he asked, "You and Aubrey set the date?"

"Not yet. Erich and I are visiting England. When we get back we're going south to Garmisch-Partenkirchen. There's money from Father's share of Kingsmith's and—" She stopped abruptly. "Well, there's money. The chalet'll be perfect for Erich and a few other children."

"Orphanage?"

"A home. For all of us. After Aubrey's demobbed, he'll come over. Then we'll have the wedding."

Wyatt curved around a jammed horse-drawn tram. "You're getting by far the better Kingsmith—by far the better man."

"It all seems so long ago, doesn't it? Before the war everything seemed so, well, rosy and innocent, so hopeful." Her sigh wavered.

He would have given everything he owned to reach for her hand. Instead, he gripped the gearshift. "That's how the past always seems, innocent and hopeful."

"The war was monstrous—all the unspeakable things that happened, the millions killed. I can't tell you how I miss Mother and Father and Sigi. Araminta. I think of them all the time. Yet . . . well, without the past there wouldn't have been my Erich. Or your Geoff."

The path narrowed between two great pyramids of rubble. Wyatt didn't see the bomb hole. Jolting over it, he stifled a groan. "Don't get me wrong." His voice was so low that it mingled with the vibrations of the jeep's engine. "I'm grateful with my whole heart that 'Minta and I were married and had time together—God knows I'm grateful. Geoff's my son, I'm crazy about that kid. But the thing is, now I know exactly how Dad felt about the biological lapses."

"You're saying . . . ?"

"Remember Peter? The Honorable Peter Shawcross-Mortimer? He was shot down over the Mediterranean."

"Geoff's Peter's child?"

"Genetically speaking, yeah. But he's mine. And I'm going to be just as good a father as Dad. Only one thing I'll do differently, and that's tell him as soon as he's old enough. Then it won't come as such a big shock to his system."

"Poor 'Minta. . . . But it was very dear of you—"

"Nothing like that," he interrupted. "Araminta was terrific, she made the world jump and hop. I loved her. Not the way I felt about you. That went farther than love. The right term's insanity."

Out of the corner of his eye he saw the giveaway tremor of her eyelids, her blush. It was as if he had pressed his naked body to hers. He looked away quickly.

Käthe was biting her lip. Now, if ever, was the moment to tell him the truth about Erich. Yet she couldn't say the words. Only in part because she feared his incredulity. To a far greater extent she kept her silence for the same reason Wyatt had. Aubrey—loyalty to Aubrey, abiding affection for Aubrey.

Braking outside the Excelsior, Wyatt mopped at his sweating forehead.

"You'd better go back to hospital and rest," Käthe said.

"I need some lunch is all."

IV

He took Erich and Käthe to the snack bar at the Casino. Erich ordered a cheeseburger, french fries, and a chocolate malted, finishing a surprising amount of the enormous portions. When they left, thick cumulous clouds hunkered over the tumbled city, and raindrops were splattering against the canvas top of the jeep. This time the detour signs led them through the *Messe,* Frankfurt's famed exhibition halls. Despite the weather the grounds were crowded. In and around the massive disemboweled buildings black-market dealers furtively exposed stolen army goods, impoverished men and women hawked their possessions, and pathetically underdressed *schatzis* solicited the American soldiers.

Erich, kneeling in the backseat next to Käthe, stared through the isinglass window. "Look, there's—" He stopped abruptly.

Wyatt slowed the jeep. "Who?"

The child's mouth snapped shut, and he sat back in the seat.

"You saw somebody," Wyatt said.

"I see hundreds and hundreds and hundreds of people."

Wyatt made a U-turn, returning slowly through the pedestrians and bicycles. An old man balancing a huge box on his handlebars swerved, his wheels skidding. The box toppled. A thin matron raised her umbrella with a vitriolic glare at the jeep.

Wyatt turned to look questioningly at Käthe.

She shook her head.

At the Excelsior, Wyatt laboriously climbed the staircase to their rooms. Taking a furled comic book from his pocket, he flattened it to show Superman streaking across the cover. "Bought you a present, Erich. It's in English, but you can figure out the pictures."

The boy opened the magazine. Captured by the vivid squares, he drifted into his room.

"Where's your corporal?"

"It's Sunday and raining, he knows we won't be going anywhere."

"The kid saw somebody back there at the *Messe.*"

"He grew up around here. It could have been anyone. Even if Groener were crazy enough to be in Frankfurt, he'd hardly come to a hotel swarming with Americans. Besides, Aubrey gave the desk clerks cigarettes not to let up any visitors."

"The one with the red scar along his jaw told me where you'd be this morning."

"You stayed here, he knows you. Wyatt, there's no need to worry. This is your first day out, you're overdoing it."

"Ever use a pistol?"

"When Sigi practiced, I pestered him to teach me."

"Then take this." Wyatt was leaning against the doorjamb.

Käthe decided it was the lesser of two evils to carefully store his Colt service pistol in her capacious pocketbook and risk having Erich find it rather than to argue. "You gave us a wonderful afternoon," she said. "Now go back to bed."

SIXTY-FIVE

I

"My father's a black-market grocer,
My mother makes illegal gin,
My sister makes love for a quarter,
My God how the money rolls in."

The farewell parties in the upstairs dining room followed the same sequence. Drinks before the meal, endless toasts to the lucky bastard on his way home during dinner, and afterward much wetting of the whistle as voices rose in songs that—according to the age and background of the celebrators—varied from Stephen Foster to the obscene. Fortunately Erich was a sound sleeper.

Käthe sat at the table by the window, a letter pad on her knee.

Dear Aubrey, she wrote. Her nib rose from the paper.

Tonight anything she set on paper would be inadequate. Even had she been capable of the brutality of candor, words would be feeble distortions of her state of mind. There were no phrases eloquent enough for her euphoria at seeing Wyatt, no exoneration for her mean, buttery delight when she'd heard Geoff was Peter's son. Sighing, she crumpled the stationery and replaced the pen in the hotel desk set. How strange, she mused, that Wyatt, at least to her admittedly hypersensitive eyes, had not fallen for Erich—his son—while Aubrey lavished unstinting affection on the child. *Marrying Aubrey's the best thing,* she thought. *The very best.*

She and Erich would visit England. At long last she would embrace her grandfather, smell his bay rum and cigar odor, feel his sensitive fingers transcribe her face. Then she would introduce him to his great-grandson. Porteous would not question the irregularities of the child's birth: he never permitted the iron of conventions to jam the compass point of love. It wouldn't be the same at Quarles. Euan and Elizabeth were far too laden down with proprieties to accept that most visible fall from grace, an illegitimate child. Also, or so she had gleaned from Aubrey, since Araminta's death they had become yet firmer patriots and therefore would view her as the enemy. As she thought of a stay with her future in-laws, a hint of nausea brushed her, but then she was comforted by the thought of Araminta's son. Closing her eyes, she envisioned Erich and Geoff—or rather the little boy in the snapshots—merrily chasing each other around the ancient oaks of the lovely, careless Kentish garden.

At a tap on the door she looked up.

"My sister makes love for a quarter . . ."

The good-natured roar almost drowned out the "Room service for the tray, *bitte.*"

II

The tray had already been removed. Had she not been sunk in woolgathering about the trip to England, she would never have opened the door. And having answered, she would have slammed it shut immediately—hadn't Aubrey used the same protective camouflage of a uniform? As it was, she blinked at the stocky American major with the combed-back blond hair.

The momentary hesitation was all Groener needed. With a palm on her shoulder, he sent her spinning backward toward the dressing table. The raucous singing covered the slam of the door.

"So, Käthe, good evening." He planted his polished shoes apart, guarding the exit. "We meet again. And this time without either of your captains."

Fear dried her mouth, but she knew Groener well enough to accept she must hide this fear. "The MPs are looking for you," she said.

"If they didn't find me in civvies, they certainly won't find me in this." He glanced down with distaste at the American uniform. "What rotten intelligence the Yanks have. But that's them all over. No organization, no discipline."

"Unlike us in the Third Reich. Still, they won." *Don't antagonize him. It's as big a mistake as showing fear, isn't it?*

"Say what you will, Käthe, the Führer worked a miracle. In six short years he gave us back all we lost in the Versailles Treaty. Bloodlessly. And after the war started he led us in conquering the largest empire the world has ever known."

Käthe wasn't listening. She was staring at the goosedown quilt at the foot of the bed, where she had dropped the handbag. During her months at Ober Tappenburg and her time in the Königstrasse Prison every detail of the bag had become as familiar as her own palm, yet she gazed at the scuffed brown English leather with the deep scar gouged up the side as though the shabby object had just been magically delivered by a genie. Inside lay Wyatt's service revolver.

Groener had followed her gaze to the bed. "You don't have a worry in the world," he said with a smirk. "I'm not half so ardent with my son in the next room."

She hastily turned away.

Tilting his head toward the battering voices, he said, "Soon they'll all pack up and go home. You're right, they won the war, but we'll win the peace."

"In the meantime you'll have been hanged." The words burst out.

To her surprise he chuckled. "Spirit! I've always admired that in you, Käthe. It's the proof of Aryan blood. Even that so-called cousin of yours, Leventhal or whatever he calls himself, seems to respect that. He didn't let you visit him at the hospital, did he? But what were you doing with him today?"

A barrage of voices rose in "The Wiffenpoof Song." *Baa, baa, baa.*

Her mouth was yet more parched and sour, as though the

liquid in her body had been evaporated by her terror. Groener could acquire a uniform that fit him perfectly. Groener had access to the hospital. Didn't that mean his SS cronies had infiltrated everywhere in occupied Germany? There was no escape. "So it *was* you in the *Messe* grounds," she said.

"Erich didn't tell you?"

"No."

Groener smiled. "That clever little rascal! My son has inherited the true Aryan spirit. Yes, I was there. You know me, always a bit mushy and sentimental. I was picking up a few souvenirs for when we're in Zurich."

"We?"

"I'm taking Erich with me to Switzerland. There's a tidy fortune in my account at the Credit Suisse. We'll be very comfortable."

"No!" she cried, protesting his taking Erich anywhere.

Groener, however, heard her denial from the depths of his own disappointed vision of himself. "You're right," he said dejectedly. "I deserve all the rotten names you're thinking. I believed in the Führer, Käthe, I completely believed in him. For years I was scrupulous. While the go-getters feathered their nests, I refused. But you have to remember that I had a wife and my little Otto and Adolf to consider. I knew by then that the generals weren't loyal to the Führer and that even those close to him were hoodwinking him." Groener's voice took on an automatic note, as if he had often mentally covered this ground. "The evening at Eberhardt's Berlin flat, the night we had our little quarrel? Later I discovered that Eberhardt had arranged the festivities for one reason: to have a chance for a private talk with me. I was in charge of labor for the rockets, and he was high up in the Special Office of Labor Allocation. He offered me a deal. I'd pay government funds for Auschwitz Yids, but he wouldn't get them from the camp. Instead, he'd send me shipments he'd ferreted out of hiding. We'd split the profit. I went in with him. Often we'd pick up a little bonus, one of them would try to bargain with a concealed diamond or two. We both put fortunes in those numbered Swiss accounts. Nobody really lost on the arrangement. Still, you're right. I sold the Führer out."

One man's idealist is another man's monster, she thought. *I can't risk Erich taking a step alone with him. I must stay with my baby.* "Should you be telling me this? Nowadays it's dangerous to say anything about the *untermenschen* . . . . Otto."

His dejection faded and he took two steps toward her. "Käthe, I meant every word I said the other night. Have you thought about it?"

She nodded.

"But what you just learned has put you off?"

"I have to be honest, yes. But, well, it also does prove you're a man who considers his family first."

Something, she wasn't sure what, reverberated against the window, and she turned. In the same instant Groener strode to her, clenching her arm. A finger rubbed her sweater sleeve, half a caress, half a warning to remain still. At his touch she flinched and knew that he must feel her involuntary reflex. "Probably a bit of falling stucco," he said after a few seconds. "Well. How do you feel about Switzerland?"

"I . . . it's my only real choice."

"Then you'll come?"

"Yes."

"Because of the boy?"

"He means everything to both of us."

Groener's hand dropped. "I prefer honesty to sweet talk," he said. "Get him ready."

"Shall I pack his clothes?"

"We'll buy new in Switzerland. Just get him dressed."

Sixty-six

I

Erich complained sleepily as she sat him up.

He saw Groener standing in the connecting doorway. "Uncle Kurt," he mumbled. "An Ami uniform?"

"It's the right thing to wear at the Excelsior. The three of us are taking a drive."

"Käthe never goes out in the dark."

"Tonight she is. Now get dressed."

Erich nudged closer to her.

Impossible to guess what was going on in his child's mind, but she sensed he was afraid. Afraid of Groener? But "Uncle Kurt" was his much-quoted pundit. Afraid of leaving her? Wishful thinking. Still, the last few days he had watched for her approval while puffing out tunes on the corporal's harmonica, and when something fazed him he had moved near enough to touch her.

"Are you coming?" he asked.

"Yes." She hugged his sleep-warm body, inhaling the milky smell on his cheek and the American shampoo on his hair. Kissing his brow, she murmured against his ear, "Do exactly what I say. Don't listen to anybody else—don't listen to Uncle Kurt. Understand?"

"Like a game?" he whispered.

"Nothing that babyish. *This is real.*"

He insisted on dressing himself.

II

The singing had stopped as they emerged into the corridor. Picking up Erich, Groener gave her a significant look to inform her that should she be considering any monkey business, forget it. Erich squirmed.

"Keep still!" Groener snapped, jerking the boy onto his shoulders.

The sleep-rosiness faded from Erich's cheeks and he allowed himself to be jounced along piggyback.

"Stay here next to me," Groener commanded Käthe.

She hurried down the hall at his side, grasping the worn purse strap with both hands so that the weight of the Colt didn't bang against her body.

Laughter boomed as if somebody had told a dirty joke.

"Lots of liquor flowing," Groener said. Now that she and Erich knew he was boss, he was again affable. "Reminds me of the old days. Those victory brawls of ours! We drank until dawn."

That Groener, striding along in his purloined uniform, was so sure of himself that he could feel a camaraderie with the boozed-up American officers made her physically ill. Well fed, smoothly shaven, comb marks showing in the brilliantined hair, no rags tied around his bare feet, no stinking uniform, no sleeping with his family crammed into one icy room with only the *Frankfurter Rundschau* to cover them, no fears about death-card rations, not for Groener. He was headed to a country with warm, intact houses, new clothing in the well-stocked shops, fat beefsteaks, fat chocolate bars, and fat secret bank accounts. She loathed him not only on behalf of the slaves he had worked to death, but also on behalf of her weary, defeated countrymen.

They had reached the staircase.

As she took the first step down, her fear and her outrage dwindled away. Her mind was spewing out decisions rapidly, fluidly. She would get behind Groener. How? It didn't matter: she must be behind him so he couldn't see her take Wyatt's pistol from her purse. Then she would order him to put Erich down. What if he refused? She would shoot him in the leg. What if she hit Erich? It had been twelve years since she prac-

ticed with Sigi's pistol. Could she risk it? She must. Did Wyatt's
Colt work the same as the Lüger?

She had forgotten the worn strip of carpeting on the staircase. Her heel caught. With a cry, she flung out her hand to
grab the banister.

"Steady there," Groener said, not slowing.

Her chance had come by accident.

She unsnapped her bag. The sound of the clasp opening
seemed to soar like an artillery volley above the background
roar of voices. The weapon dragged down her wrist. She let her
purse fall. Taking three rapid steps downward, she raised the
pistol, left hand supporting the right wrist, as Sigi had taught
her.

"Stop!" she shouted.

Groener had reached the floor with the private dining room.
For a moment she was positive he hadn't heard her. Then he
turned.

Seeing the Colt in her hands, his eyes narrowed and he
cautiously shifted Erich from his shoulders to the front of his
body. A shield. *So much for paternal love,* she thought
humorlessly. Erich was facing her and the muzzle of the pistol.
His blue-green eyes were wide, but there was no dullness of
fear, rather an odd glint as if he had somehow anticipated this
adult melodrama. Maybe he saw it as a replaying of his kidnap,
but more likely he had witnessed soldiers on both sides aiming
at their captives.

Arms outstretched, moving cautiously down the stairs, she
passed the landing, stopping so close to Groener that she could
see his sweat beading like a mustache.

"Put Erich down," she ordered.

"Käthe, stop acting the American gangster's moll." Groener
bared his uneven teeth in a parody of an indulgent smile.
"You're not going to fire that, you don't know how."

Her feet were slightly apart, her knees flexed. Her finger
moved. She heard the small click. Independent of her physical
activity thoughts were inquiring how she could release the
safety mechanism while aiming at her son. And another part of
her mind responded: *Your von Graetz ancestors were warriors.*

"Lower him slowly," she said.

There was a loud burst of laughter and applause from the dining room. She blocked out the sounds. Groener slowly set the child on his feet.

"Erich, get downstairs," she said calmly.

Groener roared, "Stay!"

"Tell the manager to bring the MPs."

As Erich moved a step away, Groener shouted, "Erich! A true German stands by his comrade!"

Käthe kept her gaze on Groener's eyes, but in the fringes of her vision she could see the child hesitate.

"Go!" she said.

The low intensity of her voice, the blazing whiteness of her face, galvanized the child. Turning, he skidded down to the hotel lobby.

Groener moved backward a step. "You're not going to shoot the boy's father."

A gavel pounded. During the lull in the roar Käthe was clearly audible.

"You're not his father," she said. "You have no son."

"I know what you're up to. It's a trick. Reminding me of my boys. But it makes no difference to me whether or not Erich's a bastard. He's a son of the Black Order. His naming ceremony is as clear as yesterday to me."

"To me too," she said coldly. "April eleventh, the day after he was born. Do you remember the date you raped me?"

"He came early."

"Wyatt is Erich's father."

"You lying bitch! You were a virgin. I saw the blood."

"Your fingernails were long. I struggled. You were rough." Her throat felt bruised, her mouth aridly sour, so how was it possible that these precise and impartial intonations could come from her? "But this can't honestly surprise you. You knew I'd seen Wyatt in London."

Groener's shoulders hunched and his head thrust forward. "The boy's mine!" he bellowed.

"Wyatt is Erich's father."

The small, clever eyes glittered. "Then by God, I'll beat his little Jew brains out against a wall!"

He wheeled about. As he took the first step down, she squeezed the trigger. She was aiming at his back just below his left shoulder. There was no hesitation in the movement. She didn't order him to halt.

The blast reverberated through every molecule of her body. The recoil thrust her backward.

She kept her arm straight, firing again—the insurance shot, Sigi had called it. In this fraction of time she thought of her brother, tortured to death in a cell below the Prinz-Albrecht-strasse Gestapo building, she thought of their mother's decaying corpse. She thought of Heinrich Leventhal, bone thin and hiding outside the door of the garage room, she thought of the smudged photographs of skeletal corpses stacked as neatly as cords of wood. She thought of the word *stücke.* Breathing in the acrid odor, she peered through the smoke.

III

Groener had somehow rotated so that he sprawled with his thick torso on the steps above his head. Still holding the service pistol, she edged down the steps to him. Mouth agape, eyes wide, he stared up at her in astonished horror.

There was no movement except the spreading redness on his uniform blouse.

Dead, she thought.

She had killed him.

For the first time she had killed.

A hot pleasure filled her, an atavistic elation that actually tasted like sweet liquid in her mouth. *You shadows and ghosts, all of you out there, know that at least SS Sturmbannführer Otto Groener suffered a little at the end.*

"Holy fucking Christ!" An American voice behind her.

Her arm was twisted, the pistol taken from her limp hand. She wanted to explain, but she sagged against her captor, abruptly too weak to talk.

IV

The ensuing tumult on the staircase disrupted the party. Men in various stages of inebriation jostled through the folded-back doors. The still smoking pistol, the dead American major with his blood dripping onto the step below, told the story.

"Jesus, it's the frowline who's under guard."

"Isn't she somehow connected to that Legal Department guy?"

"Kingsmith. Didn't she shoot him too?"

"Is he still in the hospital?" barked the lieutenant from Special Service who had an unnecessary hammerlock hold on her. "If he's ambulatory, get him over here!"

Käthe was shunted into the manager's windowless office. Erich huddled outside the locked door, his head bent into his upraised, scabbed knees. Festivities having come to an abrupt halt, the suddenly sober guests hung around the lobby describing their thoughts and emotions when they'd heard the two shots. Nobody could identify the corpse. So what? This was a hotel.

But the slain major had no papers. No dogtags. Further examination showed the lightning SS insignia tatooed on the underside of the left bicep.

Wyatt arrived just as Käthe was about to be interrogated. He identified the corpse as Sturmbannführer Otto Groener. No, this wasn't the man who had wounded him, but he was responsible for the shooting. A black marketeer. A war criminal.

The manager's office was unlocked. Erich rushed at Käthe. Lifting the child, she swayed, then sank into a tapestry-covered chair.

Erich buried his face against her shoulder, locking his legs around her waist. "Käthe, why did Uncle Kurt want to hurt us?" His voice was shrill. "Did the Amis hurt you?"

Wyatt answered, "We're proud of her. She's very, very brave."

Erich didn't hear. He had burst into wild sobs. He sobbed while Käthe carried him upstairs, he sobbed while she helped him back on with his pajamas. At last managing to stifle his sobs, he gripped her hand. She lay down, curving around him and stroking his moist forehead until he slept. Wyatt, who had waited in the other room, came to stand over the bed. Staring through the dim slant of light at the boy, he touched a knuckle lightly on the soft cheek.

"I'll let Aubrey know," he whispered.

He demanded his call to Hamburg be put through immediately.

"Until I can get them to England, they'll be safest in our zone," Aubrey said.

Two Military Government translators were bumped, and just after dawn Käthe and Erich, rambunctious and nervously excited about his first time aloft, were airborne in adjoining wooden seats of a converted Sterling bomber. Aubrey installed them in the Atlantic Hotel and then, according to a direct order from Major Downes, flew to London.

SIXTY-SEVEN

I

Käthe descended from the train at Victoria station, turning to help Erich: he had already scrambled down the high steps. Aubrey had arranged their transportation from the RAF air base where they had landed, promising to meet their train—they were to stay at Porteous's house. Looking around for Aubrey, Käthe rested one hand lightly but reassuringly on her son's shoulder. She could feel the rapid rise and fall of his breath. In the crowded first-class compartment the little boy had been silent, gazing through the drizzle-streaked window at the wintry countryside, and she had known that the thought *enemy territory* filled his consciousness because the train wheels were rumbling the same words to her. She also had kept mute.

Standing on tiptoe, she again scanned the crowd. A tall, slight British army officer stood at the far end of the platform. He turned and she saw he didn't in the least resemble Aubrey.

"Aubrey must have been delayed somewhere," she said after the platform had cleared. "We'll take a taxicab."

Hearing the German, a man in a bowler gave her a sharp, hostile glance, and the porter pointedly wheeled his cart by her. She picked up the light, battered suitcase that held their earthly possessions, transferring her purse to under that arm, extending her free hand to Erich.

He clutched her tightly. It wasn't only being in England. He had been subdued—for him, anyway—since the shooting. Käthe, still depleted and tense, had often reassured him that he'd acted like a hero, that Groener had been a bad man and wasn't really his uncle. The child invariably had turned away.

In the taxi queue he stood docile at her side, and after she gave her grandfather's address, he shifted close to her on the black leather seat.

II

How battered the British capital was! Despite the gloating newsreels of the Blitz she had never fully expected that she would see the same yellow weeds growing inside the facades of buildings, the same craters as in the Reich. The pedestrians, too, bore a striking resemblance to their German counterparts. Though none of the men and women slanting their umbrellas against the drizzle wore rags, the English coats were shabby, the children's clothes showed patches, the faces of the elderly had the grayish cast that comes from an overly starchy diet. Victor and vanquished alike had suffered. What madness inside the human heart could bring about such misery? The devastation couldn't all be laid at Hitler's feet—he was, after all, only one man. Was there a lemminglike recessive gene that made the human race susceptible to being led over the precipice to war? Did all of us await that martial beat? Yes, even her own tongue had tasted the sweetness of blood vengeance.

She realized that Erich was looking up at her, his expression oddly tragic for a child.

Stroking his hair, she said, "It's a funny feeling being here in England, isn't it?"

"I'm not worried." His voice wavered.

"You're braver than I am," Käthe said. "It's hard being in the middle of all the Tommis. But I don't feel so bad when I remember my father was English."

"Is that true?"

"Absolutely true. He was born here in London." She added softly, "He's dead now, but he's still part of me."

"I wish you were my mother."

Her eyes filled with tears, and she hugged him closer to her side. "But I am, darling. I am your mother."

He wrenched away. "My mother was from Düsseldorf."

"She wasn't your real mother. She took care of you during the war, when I couldn't. But as soon as the fighting stopped, I looked for you and looked for you. I looked everywhere until I found you."

He wiggled across the seat to press his nose against the taxi window. As they curved around Hyde Park he attempted to make sense of this new information. Turning, he asked hopefully, "So I'm part Tommi too?"

"Yes, you're a quarter English. And in a minute you'll meet a very old Englishman who's your great-grandfather."

III

The taxi pulled up on the Bayswater Road. The tall house was far shabbier than in her memory. The handsome ironwork railing was gone, the attic windows were boarded, cream-colored paint flaked on the entry pillars. Mrs. Plum, grayer and more shapeless, opened the door. As she surveyed Käthe and Erich her mouth drew into a thin line. Without a word the housekeeper flung open the doors to the drawing room. Here at least all was as Käthe remembered. The smell of beeswax and metal, the pampas grass feathering from tall China Export vases, the Victorian balled fringe on the pulled-back velvet drapes, the predatory flocks of silver birds.

Porteous stood in front of the fireplace. The last time she had seen him, that crisis-wracked summer of thirty-nine, he had been an erect old man. Now, at ninety, he crouched over a gold-topped cane, his feet encased in matted sheepskin bedroom slippers. Otherwise he was formally clad. The wing collar stood out from his wrinkled throat, his frock coat appeared a hand-me-down from a giant. The pink skull showed clearly beneath his brushed silver hair. The skin of his face and jaw sagged in translucent folds, like the smocking of a very fine white christening gown.

Käthe trembled with the effort of holding back her tears.

The sightless eyes were fixed on her. "Welcome home, my Kate," he said. Even his voice had withered and shrunk.

"Oh, Grandpa." She ran across the room to hug him. His body seemed nothing more than a collection of loose bones encased in camphor-odored cloth. "Grandpa, how I've missed you."

Lifting a hand, he felt her face. "No, none of that nonsense, my girl. No tears. Ah, how sweet it is to have you here with me."

They stood hugging each other, then Porteous pulled away. "But where's Wyatt?"

"Wyatt? You mean Aubrey."

"I'm not in my dotage yet," he said, smiling. "I know my grandsons apart. But if he's not with you, where is that young American rascal? He left two hours ago to pick you up."

"Käthe?"

Porteous's head turned toward the child's voice. "Eh? What's all this?"

She had briefly forgotten her son. "Grandpa, this is Erich."

"Yes, yes, I've been hearing about Erich. Come over here, lad."

Erich, feet lagging, came toward them. Porteous rested a hand on the boy's shoulder. Most children, Käthe thought, would shrink from so ancient a man. Erich stood straight and unflinching.

"Can you speak English?"

"Ein— a bit," retorted Erich. Then blurted out, "Käthe's my *mutter."*

"Yes, Aubrey said something to that effect."

"So you is *mein grossvater."*

"Great-grandfather," Käthe corrected softly.

"My eyes are a bit on the bad side, so I touch faces." The thin, veined hand touched Erich's features. "A Kingsmith," he pronounced. "A bit like you and a bit like poor Alfred, but there's someone else . . ." The fingers caressed the child's shoulder. "So it seems I have two great-grandsons."

Erich couldn't have fully understood, yet he scowled.

"You have a cousin, a boy," Käthe said in German. "But he's younger."

"How old?"

"About three."

"Ha! A baby."

"There's Wyatt," Porteous said before Käthe heard the

sound of a car pulling up. "In weather like this Mrs. Plum's rheumatism acts up and she can't dash about. Answer the door, Kate, will you? Erich, do you understand *present?*"

"*Ein geschenk*—a gift?"

"Exactly. Come along with me. I shouldn't be surprised if we find something or other for my older great-grandson."

IV

As she opened the door, Wyatt was locking the car—good heavens, it was Uncle Euan's treasured Daimler! But why not? Wyatt was Uncle Euan's son-in-law.

Looking up, Wyatt gazed at her, raising a hand as if the wintry grayness dazzled him. Clearing his throat, he said in a husky voice, "Sorry I missed you."

"I was looking for Aubrey."

"They announced the wrong platform. Did Erich meet Grandfather?"

"It went better than I hoped. He's feeling very swank about being an older cousin."

Wyatt came up the steps to stand next to her. A gust of wet wind tore around them, yet he stood at the open front door scrutinizing her.

"There ought to be some brilliant way to put this, Käthe," he said. "But if there is, it escapes me. Aubrey told me about Erich."

"He promised—"

"In the hospital he told me. All I could think of was that damned letter arrived when you needed me so much. . . . And after the war I put on such a dumb, stupid, holier-than-thou act." He shook his head. "There's no way to apologize, so I won't try."

"But you got Erich back for me," she said softly.

"He's mine too." They gazed at each other for another moment, then Wyatt said, "Aubrey suggested I meet you. Käthe, he's given me every opening. I told you, he's the better man."

She colored. "He's always trusted me."

"Yes, I know. And loved you." He bit his lip. "I've loved you too. Even when love showed its other side, I loved you."

A clock tolled the quarter hour, a bus hooted, and the fine rain drifted down. Neither of them moved. Another church bell tolled.

"Soot," Wyatt said hoarsely. Lifting his hand, he touched her cheek with trembling fingers.

EPILOGUE
1988

The Summer Olympics of 1988 in Seoul, the first since 1972 not beset by a major boycott, promise intense competition and stirring moments.

> —*Sports Illustrated*, Special Preview Edition, the Summer Olympics.

> Olympic Stadium
> 13:15　　Women/200m　　Round 2
> —*The Seoul Olympian*, September 28, 1988

SIXTY-EIGHT

I

Above the broad, lazy Han River the blue of the sky is as vivid as any of the colors in the national flags—Afghanistan to Zimbabwe—that flutter around the swooping perimeter of the Olympic Stadium. At one end of the arena a Russian heaves her javelin, while nearby a barrel-bodied Finnish hammer thrower whirls in his cage. Korean volunteers in yellow-and-white uniforms are emerging from a tunnel, followed by a single file of easy-striding young athletes in warm-up suits, the contestants in the second qualifying round for the women's two-hundred-meter race.

Marlys Kingsmith, tall and blond, is in the heat. Most of the family raise binoculars, smiling and pointing her out, but the two adolescent boys are exchanging their flags for the Stars and Stripes: Erich's son is lowering the black, red and gold stripes of the Federal Republic of Germany while his auburn-haired cousin and closest friend, Sir Aubrey Kingsmith's only child, carefully furls his Union Jack.

Lady Diana Kingsmith, a startlingly attractive, fortyish blonde, touches Aubrey's arm and says something, inaudible in the cheering. Possibly a reminder about the sun on his bald pate, for he puts on his Olympic cap. She is highly protective of her distinguished husband.

Geoffrey Kingsmith, who heads Kingsmith International, the worldwide chain of luxury-goods shops, has resumed his business-centered conversation with his older brother, Erich. Geoffrey lives in a Manhattan brownstone, but five years earlier Erich moved from New York to West Berlin, headquarters of the department-store empire whose flagship is Leventhal's. In 1963 Wyatt and Käthe had jointly inherited, out of the wind or so it seemed to outsiders, the long-respected Berlin emporium.

Käthe smiles ruefully at the two middle-aged businessmen below her. The years have enhanced Erich's original resemblance to Wyatt, while Geoffrey has grown to look almost exactly like Euan. The only hint that Geoffrey gives of his illustrious paternal ancestry is the dubious one of purchasing Mainwaring Court for the corporation, and transforming the history-laden mansion into an opulent country hotel. The brothers have been expanding into real estate now that Wyatt has stepped down from the presidency of Kay-Ell, the holding company that controls the Kingsmith and Leventhal chains. Wyatt himself is more active than ever in the Children's Foundation, Käthe's life's work.

II

Aubrey is also watching the two men ruefully. Impossible to discern the circumstances of their birth in opposing war zones: these two hardheaded entrepreneurs are closer than most birth brothers.

Sir Aubrey is by far the most illustrious of the clan. Rumors of a Nobel swirled around him long before he was summoned to Stockholm. The queen tapped on both his shoulders, a knighthood for his ten-volume *History of the British Isles* and for his histories of the Second World War. He has earned a fortune from the elegant spy stories written under his pseudonym, C. Osmond. The Trosper Novels, as they have come to be called, in their own way also chronicle European history from the rise of Hitler through the Cold War and Iron Curtain to this recent thaw.

He turns around to look at Käthe and Wyatt, who both have their field glasses focused on Marlys, the daughter of their youngest son, Timothy. They have aged well, as happily married couples do. Wyatt still has his thick shock of hair, white now, a handsome contrast to the tan, and he retains that look of strength. And as for Käthe, well, Aubrey cannot be impartial. To his eyes she has changed very little. She is as slender and shapely as she was in her girlhood, and the few wrinkles, the gentler flesh of her jawline, have softened that almost religious oval purity of her face, making her yet more beautiful.

Käthe lowers her binoculars, catching his glance.

"Poor Marlys," she says. "What competition."

"As I recall, you had that Stella Walsh, Helen Stephens, and a horde of other speed demons to beat," Aubrey retorts. "Apropos, I drove out to the Grunewald last week, when I was in Berlin. I can report those two oak trees of yours are flourishing."

"Don't I know it!" Wyatt laughs. "Käthe always drags me by."

"Aubrey, don't you swallow one word of that dragging nonsense. Ask who insists we go inside, ask who disturbs Dr. Bruch to take our snapshots every time."

"I always do what you want, don't I?" Wyatt drapes his arm around Käthe's shoulders.

Considering Aubrey's age and most fortunate of marital circumstances, why should it hurt to see Wyatt affectionately embrace a woman with near-adult grandchildren? Yet he swallows sharply and looks away. His most vivid memories are the ones shared with Käthe, the most treasured night in his life the night he comforted her with his body in the ruins of Darmstadt.

She would have been as happy with me. There is no shading of doubt in the thought.

Since his ascension to fame enough women have thrown themselves at Aubrey to make him realize that he isn't such a bad fellow after all. For the thousandth time he wonders whatever possessed him to leave the field clear for Wyatt. Käthe would have honored her promise, she would have married him if he hadn't sent Wyatt off to Victoria to fetch her and Erich, if he hadn't lied outrageously by telling her that he'd misjudged his affections as well as his abilities to be a good father to another man's son. Yet even released from the pangs of conscience, Käthe didn't leap into Wyatt's open arms but instead returned to Germany, taking Erich with her, using the accrued profits from Kingsmith's and the money he took from his own savings as her "salary" and "bonus" from CI-4, as she'd told him she would, to feed, clothe, and medically rehabilitate thirteen orphans at the Garmisch-Partenkirchen chalet, the modest beginnings of the far-flung Children's Foundation. It wasn't until two years after the war that Käthe took his arm to descend the staircase of Porteous's house for her marriage to Wyatt.

On the red cinders contestants are lining up in the electronic starting blocks. A crimson-jacketed judge raises the starting gun. The Kingsmith roar—*Marlys, Marlys, Marlys*—is swallowed by the reverberating thunder around the grandstand.

The finish is close.

The family, like everybody else in the Olympic Stadium, peers expectantly past the Olympic flame to the immense television screen. Kingsmith, M., has not qualified.

Tears show on Käthe's cheeks.

"Don't choke up, love." Wyatt hugs her against his side. "Marlys knew what she was up against, she told me just getting this far as a contestant was her biggest thrill."

Käthe's tears, though, are not for her granddaughter's loss but for another Olympics. For the heartbreakingly young Wyatt with his arms raised in triumph, and for the line of relatives she sees—actually sees—superimposed on the blue-shadowed stands across the coliseum. Sigi in his field-gray uniform, Araminta with her flaming red hair, the foreign uncles and aunts, her parents so proud and dear, Porteous turned in her direction as if he could see her. Of all of them in that row of seats, only that boy who exuberantly waved his straw boater, only Aubrey, is in the land of the living.

Then the past fades, and Käthe is once again surrounded by her family, the descendants of her beloved ghosts. Knuckling away her tears, she rests her head on Wyatt's shoulder.